Forlorn Hope

*For Mr. Mullins,
Hope you enjoy the
book as much as I've
enjoyed our friendship
over the last seventeen
years. Thx!*

Forlorn Hope

Justin Bryant Jones

Northwest Publishing Inc.
Salt Lake City, Utah

Forlorn Hope

For information address: Northwest Publishing, Inc.
5949 South 350 West, Salt Lake City, Utah 84107
SP/LC 12 31 93
PRINTING HISTORY
First Printing 1994

ISBN: 1-56901-158-3

NPI books are published by Northwest Publishing, Incorporated,
5949 South 350 West, Salt Lake City, Utah 84107.
The name "NPI" and the "NPI" logo are trademarks belonging to
Northwest Publishing, Incorporated.

PRINTED IN THE UNITED STATES OF AMERICA.
10 9 8 7 6 5 4 3 2 1

Acknowlegements

My thanks to:
My wife Melissa for always believing in me, from the
beginning until the end;
My parents and grandmother for their constant support;
Craig Bishop for his help, companionship, and above all for
the many late nights he spent rescuing me from myself
("honorificabilitudinatatibus");
Jason Stone for never running out of bizarre things to say,
no matter how serious the situation, and for always helping
out when I need you (say hello to little sister for me);
Brandon, Christopher, Mr. Mullins, Elizabeth and Daria for
their friendship and for keeping me confused almost
constantly—whether you know it or not, you inspire me;
My favorite fungus-maker, Mrs. Mac for her patience and
fostering (keep shoveling);
The English and Writing Departments of Oglethorpe
University for all I have and will learn from you;
And especially Joy Huddlestun, if it were not for you, I
don't think I would have ever started this book.

Table of contents

Entropy

The morning was cool and crisp with the faintest tinge of frost upon the ground, yet it appeared gloomy as the sun attempted to shine down upon the almost barren earth, illuminating the ugly bleakness of the Great Expanse. The moors, impotent and moribund, stretched onward for as far as the eye could see in all directions, destroying any hope of deliverance from anxiety. A few brief, colorless outcroppings were the only bastion of life amid the dying land, forming a huge depiction of deathful isolation that seemed to be everywhere, surrounding everything. An occasional bosque containing willows and ash trees presented an illusion of escape, but upon closer examination, undergrowth of extreme thickness clogged them, entwining them in smothering death, making them actual havens for evil, for foulness. Isolated hills cast deep shadows into shallow gorges of derelict night, creating an eerie image, a threatening disjuncture of morning and night.

Lying atop one of these hillocks, surrounded by the autumnal chill, was a sleeping assemblage of people. Three men, three women, and a dwarf were huddled closely around

a small fire, seeking as much heat from it as it could impart.
However, the small blaze could not fight back the chill mist or
the galvanizing hatred of the Great Expanse. The only balm
for such utter, uninterrupted discomfort was sleep, but among
the group, one man was waking, leaving behind the comfort
of dreams.

David was aroused by the misty sunlight creeping across
his face like a spider in its web. At first he attempted to brush
it away with a futile hand, but he soon realized that morning
had come and, with it, consciousness. He roused himself,
climbing to his feet and stretching his stiff muscles, working
the sleep out of them. David was a towering figure, standing
nearly seven feet with tremendous arms and an immense chest
supported by heavily muscled legs garbed in dirty, tight-
fitting brown breaches. He picked up his weapons belt and
strapped it across his back, loosening the blade, a five-foot
long sword, in its metal-tipped leather scabbard. He bent over
and gently shook the beautiful woman who lay asleep at his
feet.

Jessica gazed sleepily into David's piercing ice-blue eyes
enshrouded by his long, coarse brown hair that hung loosely
about a deeply tanned face. The sun cut shadows across his
high forehead and long, pointed nose as well as outlining the
zig-zagging scar under his left eye. The beginnings of a beard
lined his firmly set jaw and bull-neck.

"Wake up, sleepy head," said David gently, his deep
baritone creeping from between smiling lips.

"What time is it?" whined Jessica .

"How would I know?" he asked with a smile. "I left my
watch at home."

She smiled reluctantly. "Some help you are!"

As David helped her to her feet, Jessica dusted off her
once-white clerical robes, straightening them on her slender

form. Her tanned face was very attractive with eyes like onyx and curly sable hair that lay lightly upon her slender shoulders and streamed down her back. She stood barely as tall as David's chest, but her size by no means made her seem weak. She seemed to glow with potency, authority and an inner might, yet her aura also radiated kindness and serenity, naming her a source of sanctity. She kissed David lightly upon the cheek as he strapped on his armor and went to awaken the others.

As the party prepared to continue their sojourn in Sidan, Amy spoke. "How much longer will we be in this godforsaken land?"asked the cleric. She wore travel-worn white robes like Jessica's. Her black hair was shoulder-length, straight, fine, and thick. She glowed with a less intense corona of power and kindness than Jessica, and hers seemed tainted with emotion and ambiguity, betraying her doubt and guilt as easily as a scarlet engraving upon her breast.

"About another week," answered Christopher, not taking his eyes off the large brown mare he was hitching to the covered wagon. Christopher, a wizard, was an agile man of slender build, standing about six feet. His nimbleness was apparent even in the menial task that he was then undertaking; the way his fingers danced from strap to strap, the way his balance shifted with every movement to compensate for any unexpected action of the horse, the way his coal black eyes danced from blinder to harness and back illustrated his dexterity, belying his somewhat gangly form. Raven hair and a full pointed black beard outlined his pallid face like an outcry of mystical power, a warning to thieves and brigands. He wore long black robes that held a tinge of blue in them like liquid energy, making him appear eldritch, almost ominous. Resilient mischief was wrapped around him like a robe, churning animosity.

"Oh," said Amy, downcast, "so long."

"We've already been in Sidan for fifteen days," said Brandon, as if their estrangement was unimportant. "What difference will another seven make?" The dwarf stood almost five feet tall and had extremely broad shoulders complementing his massive chest. His stout body was supported by a pair of tree trunks that passed for legs. His face was pitted and scarred in numerous places around his large, round nose and was adorned with a brownish red beard that extended down to his belt. The dwarf's coarse hair was the same color as his beard and lay in tufts on his shoulders and neck. There was a tremendous double-bladed axe strapped to his broad back that glittered in the early morning light with a promise of celerity.

"I guess it won't," said Amy, a little startled by Brandon's bluntness. "Does the Great Expanse lead all the way to Mount Apocrys?"

"No," answered Christopher. "After about two more days, we'll enter a greensward. It'll be a lot more pleasant than this stretch of hell."

They packed their baggage, donned their traveling cloaks, and finished preparing the horses for the next leg of their journey. Some were harnessed to the covered wagon while others were simply saddled and decked out for riding. The wagon itself was quite large with room for three in the front, including the driver, and was piled high with cooking equipment, extra clothing and supplies—food and other necessary accouterments of a journey. Its exterior consisted of the seat, large spoked wheels, a setup for three to five horses, and the bowed cover, now stained from its original white by the elements.

They soon got situated and began their day's journey with as much enthusiasm as they could muster—which was no great amount. The terrain they traveled through was as dismal as could be imagined: soggy, devoid of life, and interminably humid. But as they traveled westward, trees became more and more frequent while the ground dried up noticeably. Dells and glens passed by more often, and the hills appeared in bunches instead of simply the occasional mesa or hillock.

As morning grew on, they plunged headlong into an unseen mire that nearly swallowed the lead horse and Sean, the party's thief, who rode on its back. With great difficulty, they rescued the two and bypassed the bog, furtively cutting along its circumference. Even in this unlikely position, it was easy to see how strong Sean was, and he moved with such agility, secretiveness radiating from him in waves of promised mischief. He wore a leather jerkin and breaches with high, soft-soled boots and large, hoop earrings to fit the swashbuckling picture. He moved with such surreptitious sureness and impeccability that one could recognize him for a thief even if he did not wear the assorted tools of the trade—knives, picks, and files.

Not long after they left that hazard behind, they found themselves passing through a patch of rocky tors like the jagged memories of a once great mountain chain. They slowly wound through the hills, ascending as little as possible, stumbling over the detritus that blocked the less than clear path. They peered about them expectantly, as if something important were about to occur, as if Fate were looming over them, foretelling their future with dire consequences. The impression of foreboding hovered over them, weighing them down as if the concerns of the world were placed on their less than adequate shoulders, withering their hopes, compressing their senses to hopeless bounds. They progressed slowly like thick, flowing ichor through the small range of hills, always staying at berth from the tors as if their distance would keep them distended from Fate, but as they rounded a particularly large hill, they found themselves in a large, nearly circular flat, inhabited by short grey humanoid figures.

At first they mistook the beings for statues since they were motionless, but the wizard quickly relieved them of this idea. "The Etolea," he breathed quietly, gazing at the barren figures that littered the flat, a mixture of curiosity and amazement echoing in his voice.

At the mention of their name, the Etolea came alive, their little bodies slowly becoming animated and their faces turning toward the group. They stared up at the party with eyeless sockets that seemed to peer farther into them than any eyes should, probing their souls with meticulous precision. After a moment of this silent regard, the Etolea turned inward, staring at each other with as much intensity as they had given the confused and frightened party, but they almost immediately turned back, as if their mental conference had affirmed the group's right to continue. Their grey, featureless faces soundlessly grinned at the party as if they knew more about them and their purpose than they possibly could. Finally, one Etolea at the front raised a very large, six-fingered hand and beckoned them onward through the circle, calling to them with irresistible intensity, ordering them to continue their journey with haste.

David stared at the figures for only a moment before he was compelled to lead the party slowly through the Etolea. By instinct alone, he managed to draw his sword as he led his tall white horse by hand through the flat, followed silently by the others. The Etolea watched their progress, grinning and gesturing, wordlessly calling them through the flat, always backing away from the party so not to impede their progress. Some stood apart, arms akimbo, watching obscurely as the humans passed within their midst while others imitated their leader and beckoned to the party, smiling with toothless mouths, always offering them safe passage. It was as if the Etolea, through that brief probing sightless stare, knew who they were and what they were doing…and approved.

As David reached the far side, a little more control eked

into him, and he waited for the others to continue through as he guarded their rear, sword raised protectively. After all had passed, David stood motionless, watching the grey men with curious, untrusting eyes, sword recumbent in his arms. Finally, as he turned to leave, one raised a hand above its head and waved a farewell, nodding ever so slightly as if to say "until we meet again."

As David joined the others, Christopher was breathlessly explaining what the Etolea were. "They're an obscure race who like to isolate themselves, shunning the violence that is so common in others. But they're not really as different as it may seem. They're just one stage in the evolutionary chain of humans on Sidan."

"Darwin would've really loved these guys," commented Sean. Everybody eyed the wiry six foot man momentarily, not really sure how to react to his sarcasm. His ebony eyes and short black hair glinted with a glossy blue-black luster, and his hand rested on the short sword that he wore on his left in perfect position for a cross-body draw, and a dagger hung at his other side.

"You can't mean that man evolved from those things!" protested Amy, looking at Sean and Christopher, aghast, her cornflower blue eyes radiating intense emotions, disgust and skepticism. "They're nothing like us!"

"No, Amy. Man did not evolve from them," answered Christopher somberly. "He evolves into them." Shocked silence surrounded the group for a moment like an ambiguous grin as the import of Christopher's words sunk in. "They're what man becomes after many millennia of evolution. They're rumored to be peaceful vegetarians. Most people say they're harmless but some say that their power is so great that they don't dare use it against anyone. I don't know whether either of these theories is right, but I do know that, before now, nobody has ever seen an Etolean up close. We're the first."

"I always did vind genetics vascinating," said Sean, mocking an Austrian accent. "Maybe ve should leave Brandon vith the Etolea. It might be a pleasant change for him to be able to look someone in the vace instead of the navel."

Brandon attempted to slug Sean but missed and fell off the wagon with a thud. The thief began to laugh uproariously.

"Stop joking around," commented Jodi reprovingly. "This is a serious situation." Jodi was the company illusionist. She was tall for a woman and wore long deep-blue robes that matched her eyes almost precisely. These orbs leapt about intelligently, and her auburn hair flowed majestically down to the small of her back, a trace of fire flitting in the wind. Her powers were obvious at first glance as clouds of illusion, glittering variations of light seemed to billow from her...but only if you saw her out of the corner of your eye. A serious investigation only showed a very attractive redhead.

"Will they follow us?" asked David, watching behind the party cautiously.

"I don't think so," answered Christopher, stroking his beard. "They've probably never left these hills."

"Then let's get away from here," suggested Brandon, struggling to climb onto the wagon again and scowling at Sean spitefully. "I'll be more comfortable when we've left them far behind."

So they continued forward as fast as the rugged ground permitted, struggling through the detritus with as much speed as possible. Not as quickly as they might have liked, they left the tors behind, entering the Great Expanse's empty moor again. They traveled in silence, encapsulated in their own worlds, surrounded by ever-present malevolence. Around noon a rain shower struck without warning, drenching them to the core and destroying any optimistic feelings that might have been hidden within their dejected hearts. They traveled for a short time amid the frigid rain that left them waterlogged, drowning in discomfort, but finally they could stand it no longer.

They stopped for lunch in a bosque that would protect them from the rain, praying that the shelter offered would spread into their unprotected hearts and awaken their sleeping hopes. The trees that surrounded them were predominantly scrawny, sick-looking pines, but there were several twisted dogwoods that seemed to intertwine about each other and the larger trees in a cold, unholy orgy of contempt for those they sheltered. The trees did, however, form a fairly tight roof over the depressed party's heads, giving them a chance to dry. The shadow that the copse cast was nearly complete; the trees obscured the sun as well as the rain, permitting almost no light to shine upon their downcast heads, making the shelter cold. This seemed to state as clearly as any dirge that there was no escape from the Great Expanse.

The sparse grass that lined the ground was mostly brown and dead. Mold and slime grew on the trees, and the vines that hung loosely about their distorted, gnarled limbs cast ugly, serpentine shadows through the dead heath. The rain only barely dripped through the trammel of limbs and tangled brush that covered their vulnerable heads, and where it did manage to break through, muddy puddles pulsed like putrid boils.

In this patch of trees, they dined on dried meat, which they were growing terribly weary of, having lived on it for several days. They drank water from flasks and took a few sips of wine to warm their stomachs even if their hearts were to be cold as a glacier.

"I'm getting really sick of all this gloom," commented Jodi uncomfortably. "I would really love to see some color other than brown or sickly green." She gestured at the rotting, moldy trees and pulled her legs up close to her chest as if they could protect her from the chill sarcasm that surrounded her.

Though the others agreed with her, they did not feel inclined to comment on it. Instead, they concentrated on the food, hoping that the nourishment of their bodies would also give sustenance to their wearying hearts.

Half an hour later the rain stopped, and they continued their journey, as downcast and dejected as ever. They had decided, however, that it would be best to travel as far on that day as they could; so they slogged on in the wet, passing through terrain of brown and grey, reluctantly swallowing the monotony like a foul-tasting medicine. More hills crowded around them like unfeeling yet oppressive onlookers, and they saw another chain of tors to the south which they purposefully avoided, preferring the less populated moor. They saw trees more often, and amid some of the larger bosques, they glimpsed brief chances of hope—an occasional mimosa or convolvulus flourishing in the dying land like a promise of salvation. Soon they became unaware of their surroundings, except these brief snatches of life, and went on in silence, all thoughts removed from their numbed minds.

They soon found that the sun was beginning to grow low on the horizon and started looking for somewhere safe to stay. As night began to enclose them, they saw a large group of trees creeping up on them in the distance. As they grew closer, they noted that it was almost like a small twisted forest set amid an even more twisted moor. They made for the cover, however, seeing it as protection from danger during the night. Soon they were able to make out a large path in the wood, large enough to admit the wagon. They immediately aimed for it and quickly reached the arch that swallowed them like a gate to hell. Their hopes raised a little by this stroke of luck, they rushed on, looking for a clearing or other place large enough to stay in, reveling in nature's triumph over the Great Expanse.

They noticed with something akin to joy that the blooming trees and flowers were more prevalent in the midst of this forest, and the twisted vines and thick underbrush were all but gone. A large patch of clintonia glistened in the twilight off to the right, the golden flowers flashing like hopeful eyes. Jessica hopped out of the wagon and picked one of the beautiful flowers, stopping long enough to sniff a few more. She then hopped back onto the wagon, placing the golden flower behind her ear like a prize for her survival.

As they traveled farther into the forest, they noticed the moss that was flourishing on the ground, trees, rocks, and everywhere else it could find hold. With completely undisguised jubilation, the party watched as squirrels, rabbits, and other small mammals raced spasmodically about in the treetops, through the brush, and over the path as if winter's breath were on their very heels. The group felt their juices start flowing as they realized that tomorrow they would reach the end of the Great Expanse, and they smiled at each other, a little happiness finally breaking through the sickly silence that had filled them for too long.

They were ecstatic to see the dry ground that would be perfect to sleep on and the wood that would be perfect for building a fire. They reveled in their new-found luck, not believing that anything could work out so well on such a miserable day. It seemed so good…too good.

Then disaster struck. One fell, unmedicable blow that left them violated with surprise. Suddenly there was a large group of men around them, ten maybe fifteen, all with swords drawn and looks of bloodlust on their jeering faces. Then the party noticed, standing at the forefront of the group, a very large, scarred man and a smaller dark one. Peccare and Tohzahi, their most hated enemies, had been waiting for them!

What a perfect place for an ambush, thought Sean to himself, feeling like slapping his forehead in disgust. Why had he not noticed the setup? Why had he not expected an ambush in this place? His next thought was to turn and run, but there were a dozen or so more men behind them, sealing the trap. With disgust, they realized that their only choice was to fight a battle that was stacked heavily against them, though it was not hopeless.

David drew his sword with a ferocity that he had never before felt as he looked at the laughing faces gathered about him. His companions reacted with the same vehemence, preparing for battle though they were badly outnumbered. Then David became aware of the air of anticipation that hung about the forest as if some dreadful event were about to occur. It felt as if a pall had been placed over the clearing, encasing the air in a stagnant bubble that halted movement, even life. Everything was so still, too still. Evil seemed to creep ardently through the clearing, searching for another victim to encase in total desolation.

"What's going on here?" asked David, becoming aware of something he had not previously noticed. There, standing behind Peccare and Tohzahi, was a tall being dressed in black robes, enshrouded in a darkness all his own. The figure raised one hand and, as the robes fell off the front of his arm, black skin was revealed, not the black of the Negroid Chiaroscarians, but blacker than the night that was pressing in, blacker than death, blacker even than the pits of hell. The hand had very long, dark fingers that were tipped with claws instead of fingernails. As the hand dropped again with something akin to audacity, a glowing sphere appeared in its mate, and a pained scream erupted from the wagon behind David; not a scream of fear or a scream of pain, but a scream of total desolation, a scream of unimaginable despair.

The black figure disappeared, leaving only eldritch laughter and the impression of vast, unknown evil.

David went pale. He knew what had happened even before he burst into the wagon where Jessica and Jodi had been riding. He knew the voice of that scream and dreaded seeing what he would see, knowing what he would know. There, lying on the floor, was Jessica, her delicate form draped in Jodi's frail arms like a fractured leaf. She was not moving. "She just fell," said the illusionist helplessly. Rage struck David like a fist! He felt tears of hatred and anger running down his cheeks unrestrained as he burst from the wagon, storming with menace. He was totally out of control! The only thought in his mind was vengeance!

Peccare and his men were already attacking, and the small party was attempting to hold them off as David leapt from the wagon down amongst his enemies, slashing as he let an agonized scream fly from his lips in a bellow of pain, striking with sword and iron fist. He slashed and cut wildly, not knowing what he was doing, only that his love was lying in the wagon hurt, maybe even dead. He slaughtered everyone that came near him, destroying like Plague and Pestilence themselves. Chunks of flesh flew and blood spurted all over him, mixing with the tears and sweat that streamed down his arms and face, twisted by anguish and rage. Death and grievous pain seemed to radiate from him like sublime heat from dry ice, billowing through the clearing in agonized screams and tormented execrations. David fought onward, pursuing the center of his vertiginous rage, fighting for stability, finding only more victims. He killed and killed, wiping out all life that approached him, not even taking time enough to check the being for friend or foe. He could not even hear the screams that radiated from both camps in waves of anger.

He knew nothing, felt nothing until he reached the area for which he had been subconsciously aiming. He looked up and saw the face of Tohzahi gloating in front of him. Past visions of this evil man raced through David's conscious, searing anger through his psyche like a comet. He saw Tohzahi threatening Jessica lasciviously; he saw a letter, promising them all death; he saw Tohzahi facing him in the coliseum in

Tyrol; he saw death and destruction as tangible beings, all with the features of Tohzahi—black hair, slightly slanted eyes, olive skin, hoop earrings, curved longsword, high boots, and always that eternally jeering face. He vaguely recollected Sean warning him that Tohzahi was a Dauthi, an assassin trained in the seaport of Dartmoor with as much ability with a sword as the best warriors as well as the ruthless agility of the best thieves.

It was all David could do to keep from leaping on Tohzahi with his bare hands, but he managed to face the Dauthi sword raised as if to protect him from the evil laughs that the assassin hurled at him. David attacked with such ferocity as he had never felt, pain and anger pushing him through his limits, past feeling, past consciousness, and into unfeeling darkness. Tohzahi blocked David's first few blows easily enough, but he quickly realized that the warrior's continuous enraged on-slaught was too much for him. He began looking for an escape, any way to flee, but it was too late. He was trapped, as much a prisoner to David's rage as the warrior himself.

David's sword finally connected with Tohzahi's gut, and blood spurted as the madman ripped his sword free, raising it again like the executioner's axe. He brought it down as hard as he could on Tohzahi's head which split like an overripe melon, spilling its contents on the ground at David's feet.

As David realized that he had killed Tohzahi, a bit of control eked into him, and he looked around, taking in the gory scene. Brandon was nearby, wreaking havoc with his great axe, but his own blood stained his forehead like a fleeting trail of compassion. Sean was flailing about near the wagon, a sword in each hand as he tried to protect Amy and Christopher from their assailants. He was holding his own but was rapidly growing weary, sweat streaming down his face. Amy levitated men into the air and dropped them, sending them crashing onto the heads of their companions like falling boulders. As

David watched, Christopher raised his hand, palm outward and lightning erupted from it like an electric cry, incinerating a large group of men and sending others flying from the explosion.

There was someone missing though; where was Jodi? Then David saw her, or he assumed it was her. She had taken the form of a large ogre and was busily smashing Peccare's men who fled from her in horror. The beast stood over eight feet tall, with mottled pink skin and sparse, tufted hair. Its arms were much too long for its body and were tipped with huge claws like dirks. The face was bulbous, eyes bulging from their sockets, nose rounded with a large ball on its end, mouth circular and constantly open, revealing a mouth full of frighteningly long, sharp teeth. David recognized it as a magnificently structured illusion, but the beast was really hurting Peccare's men, smashing them into bloody pulps and cracking their heads with deadly accuracy. How was she accomplishing this feat? Illusions can't hurt people, can they?

Suddenly a mace struck David on the back, only a glancing blow thanks to his heavy chain armor, but enough to return his attention to the peril at hand. He whirled and dispatched his foe, constantly searching for the other man whose life he needed to consume. Memories of Peccare swam through his consciousness with the intensity of an eel, leaving the evil man's mien like an afterimage in his mind. He saw Peccare dangling an old man off the ground by his feet; he saw his own arrow protruding from the evil warrior's arm; he saw himself bound to a tree as Peccare knelt in front of him, torturing him maliciously with a curved dagger; he then saw Peccare threatening to rape Amy, then Jodi, and finally Jessica.

As David remembered Jessica, his anger redoubled, and he found himself searching harder for the evil warrior who had caused her to be hurt. Peccare was his only exodus from this explosive rage.

Due to the sheer ferocity of the party's attack, the ambushers were beginning to retreat, fearing the party's deadly vengeance; they knew they had the advantage of numbers, but no one wanted to risk being one of the casualties. As David saw them begin their retreat and heard the shout for full withdrawal from somewhere in the forest, he started to pursue the troops, hoping to destroy them all, rape their little minds. It was the only way he knew to avenge Jessica's pain, but he was stopped by Sean's gently restraining hand upon his shoulder.

"Let them go," said Sean. "We have more important things to take care of." He glanced toward the wagon.

Even before David's mind built up enough courage to follow Sean's gaze, he looked around him, trying to rationalize everything that had just happened, trying to find a meaning, a purpose. There was death all-round him, and the stench of spilt blood and scattered innards poisoned the air. Bodies littered the ground everywhere his gaze fell—beside him, behind him, in front of him, all-round him. Everywhere he looked, death stalked him. He saw Sean beside him, a glitter of sanity amid the ludicrous, unnecessary destruction that surrounded him. He saw Amy climbing back into the wagon as his gaze did finally return there, but he also peripherally saw Brandon's prone form lying atop a mound of worthlessly destroyed life. Then—amid all the death, all the destruction, all the macabre and gory bodies, amid the darkened trees—he heard a sound. A cardinal that sat on a limb to his right surveying the scene whistled and trilled, his song drifting on the stale wind like a regenerative cloud, repelling its putrefaction. The happiness of the red bird's call denied the death, denied the slaughter, denied even the existence of lifelessness. This thrilling sound awoke David from his paralysis and for a moment he felt victory's morbid thrill, though he still recognized the immense malevolence of Death's ever-present form hovering over his shoulder like a vulture, searching for more victims. But this relief was enough to awaken his senses, and his gaze rested on the wagon once more as feeling surged into his lifeless arms and impetus returned to his stiff legs. Then thought returned and with it pain.

No! screamed David silently, memories of the past flashing before his eyes; in his consciousness, visions of Jessica spun in a maelstrom. He remembered the past—that glorious time—and moments with Jessica, moments of solitude, quiet and comfortable in each others arms, but the present returned to him, striking him with all the precision of a blacksmith's hammer, shaping his emotions as easily as an anvil. This can't be happening, he rationalized to himself, hurt coursing through his veins. Jessica? Then hope came to his heart. Maybe she's not hurt badly! he insisted. She's strong. Maybe she just seemed hurt! But in his heart he did not believe it.

David, with Sean directly behind him, raced into the wagon and found Amy sitting on the floor with Jessica's head propped in her lap. Amy looked up at David with tears in her eyes. Her face was creased with sorrow and pain as she returned her gaze to Jessica's limp body, hoping that some movement would shake the other cleric's form but none came. Amy bowed further and she shook her head a single time, tears streaming down her face, unheeded. "She's not breathing…and there's no pulse."

David peered down at Jessica for an eternal moment, tears rolling down his cheeks like raining blood as the realization of Amy's words struck home. But Jessica was so beautiful—her hair encasing that immaculate face with a patina of sorrow, her eyes closed in an all too deep slumber—how could she be dead? Yet her body lay still, limp in Amy's fragile arms, the single golden clintonia still resting behind her left ear like a vestige of happiness but more like a reminder of paradise lost.

David felt Sean's hand on his shoulder, but he shook it off, denying the comfort, denying stability, denying even death.

He looked at Sean deeply for a moment, anger flaring again in his icy eyes. "She's not dead!" he roared, shoving Sean away from him as if that denial would bring her back. "She can't be! She's too powerful!"

David took Jessica's form in his arms, eyeing Amy savagely as if her pronouncement had destroyed Jessica's chances for survival. He held the beautiful cleric's limp body tenderly and sank to his knees. "Wake up, Jessica," he moaned. "It's David. It's not time to sleep yet." Tears rushed from his eyes like a streaming river, roiling with pain when she did not answer. He rocked her tenderly, caressing her face with loving fingertips, brushing her lips with his, praying all the while that she would wake up, knowing she would not. "It's time to wake up, sweetheart," he sobbed. "You're safe now—"

He broke off as a tremendous sob racked his body as if he had been stabbed. He bent over Jessica's limp form, clenched in sorrow, sobs wracking his body as denial fled and extreme sorrow flowed through him. Each of David's tears struck the wagon's floor like a knell, sounding death, tolling Jessica's passing even more clearly than Amy's pronouncement. He cried only shortly; soon even that release was not possible.

Sean stood in silence, looking down at David's crushed figure, saying nothing for nothing was appropriate. Tears streamed down his face, sorrow racked his body, and distress for David curdled his knotted stomach. It took all his strength to fight down the sobs that attempted to wrench his lips open, but he knew that he had to stay calm—he had to comfort David as best he could.

As he watched the mighty warrior adorned in silver chain armor overwhelmed with sorrow, he could not help but see the David he knew so well and not the fighting machine that had accompanied him these past few weeks. He saw a blonde-headed young man, roaming the halls of their high school, playing on the soccer field, and riding in his car the summer after their graduation, just before the transformation. He did not see the cavalier who knelt on the floor. Memories of the joy that the boy and his fiancee had shared flooded through Sean like an ebullition of total, flagrant loss. He bit his lip till the blood flowed, forcing himself not to cry out as he saw them together, holding each other, smiling like there was no unhappiness in the world. He saw them laughing together, gingerly kissing as they teased each other, their closeness enough to chase away all fear, all anger, even the horror of death, but to see David holding Jessica's lifeless form so tenderly was simply too much. He saw Jessica as she truly was, a petite lovely thing with thick curly black hair and glittering dark eyes, a charming smile twisting her lips upward. But Sean's attention returned to the present and he watched his friend, promising himself that he would see the deaths of those men, all of them, even if he had to go after them one at a time and rip their cold hearts out with his bare hands. He would make them pay for this—all of them.

Sean sniffed and tried to wipe away his tears enough to talk. He crouched down behind David and hugged the larger man, hoping that he could assuage just a little of the pain, a little of the sorrow. The armor was cold to the touch except where some still slightly warm blood stained it; however, Sean could feel nothing but the warmth of a tender heart. At first David flinched from the touch, but he finally relaxed under the pressure as Amy also embraced him, tears running freely from her wonderful eyes. David accepted their comfort for what it was worth, but nothing could relieve the pain that surged in his veins. Alone, he thought, anguished. I'm alone. What now? It was all he could think about.

At that anguished moment, Christopher entered the wagon, looking very weary. In his arms lay Brandon's unconscious body, blood trickling down his face, his lips wet with crimson life. "You must help him, Amy," said Christopher sadly. "He's dying."

"What about Jessica?" she sobbed.

"You can't help her," said Sean, his voice coarse with sorrow. "We can't lose two today. Do what you can for Brandon."

Amy looked at David once more and watched the glazed eyes stare at Jessica with futile anguish, but he could not see her. He did not even really know what was happening around him. His eyes were for the dead, not the living. Amy then looked at Jessica herself and searched again for any sign of life, anything at all to offer the balm of hope, but she found nothing, only emptiness, an emptiness the likes of which she had never before felt.

She sighed and stood, gesturing for Christopher to lay Brandon on the floor in the center of the wagon. She then approached the body and placed her hands on the dwarf's head, and as his blood oozed between her fingers, she concentrated on healing. She mumbled the arcane words, praying to Galead for soothing, for healing. A rush of power surged through her body, and she felt a tear run down her cheek as the gaping wound closed under her dainty hands. She heard Brandon moan, and at the same time, an amazingly musical voice sounded in her head like the ringing of bells, echoing in the recesses of her consciousness. The voice said, "Do not fear. All will be made whole."

As Amy shuddered and pulled away from Brandon, the dwarf regained consciousness. He sat up and looked at the sorrowful faces that watched him hopefully. His gaze rested on Amy's tearful face, flitted to Christopher's cold countenance, passed on to Sean's worried, anguished visage, and finally rested on David where he held Jessica's limp form with as much care as he would give a baby. As he stared at the two huddled figures that sat on the wagon's floor, comprehension tore through him like a gale, ripping his consciousness to shreds. He bowed his head in remorse, two great tears welling in his dark eyes.

It had happened so quick, so stunningly quick—the enormous adrenaline had left them weak and trembling, unable to focus their thoughts. David thought he was going to be sick, but after what seemed an eternity, they began to regain their senses, each feeling varying degrees of sorrow. None of them knew what action to take next; they were lost amid the wreckage of flesh. Christopher stood, shook himself, and climbed down off the wagon, all the while thinking to himself, We must continue. We must continue. Don't let them stray. The others remained where they were.

"What will we do?" asked Amy somberly.

"What we must," answered Sean. He was now sitting on the floor of the wagon next to Brandon while David stood nearby staring unfixedly. "We'll give her a decent funeral."

"Why her?!" came David's angry voice, annealed by pain, into the conversation. "Why not me?! She was no danger to them. She's no fighter!"

"I don't know, David," answered Sean, looking at his friend. "Maybe they considered somebody who could heal our wounds more dangerous than somebody who fights and kills."

Said Brandon: "But they'd have to be planning another attack for that to be of any use to them."

"Then maybe that's what they intend," offered Sean. "It would explain their too-easy retreat."

"I hope they do come back…" growled Brandon, hatred and bloodlust glistening in his black orbs. "I'll kill every single one of those bastards!"

"I think it'd be wiser to hope for some help first," suggested Amy. "There aren't enough of us. All a fight would accomplish is our own deaths. We'll need help before we can take them."

"But we will," promised Brandon, "and we'll slaughter them all!"

At that moment, Christopher returned to the wagon in a

flurry of black robes, hope flickering in his dark eyes like a crimson flame. "Come outside," he ordered, a transitory smile flitting across his face.

They rose curiously and followed him out of the wagon. David's head was swimming with sorrow, but he felt hope surge into him from Christopher's smile. Could there be something they missed? As David came out of the wagon, he immediately noticed several of Peccare's men tied up in front of some trees at the edge of the wood. They were alive!

As they approached the bound men, Christopher walked purposefully in front of one man. This rather nondescript short fellow had brown hair and blue eyes. His breaches were old and dirty, but they looked expensive as did his red, silken tunic. There was fear in his eyes but a glimmer of hope also flickered within. "I cast a sleep spell during the combat and snared this group," explained Christopher, gesturing at the ten men who sat on the ground. His attention returned to the man at his feet. "Tell them what you told me, and I'll let you live."

The man swallowed and licked his lips, staring with fear in his eyes at the despondent group surrounding him. They looked very grim. "I—" he began but hesitated, glancing up at Christopher fearfully.

"If you want to live, tell them!" insisted the wizard, withdrawing a dagger from his robes and placing it so its tip just pricked the man's jugular vein. A trickle of blood ran down his neck.

"The woman…" started the man, squirming away from the blade and licking his lips nervously. "The cleric is not dead."

"Then what's wrong with her?" asked David, grasping the prisoner's tunic in one great hand and hauling him to his feet as uncertain relief flooded into him.

The man hesitated, struck speechless, so David lifted him off the ground by his collar and repeated his demand, emphasizing each word with a shake, "What is wrong with her?!"

"You know, David, if you relieved some of the pressure on his throat, he might actually answer," suggested Sean.

David released his hold on the man's throat and gripped him by the front of his tunic so that he could speak, but David kept him dangling off the ground where he could not even attempt to run. "What's happened to her?" he asked, trying to stay under control as the silken tunic began to slowly tear.

"She had a Dark Slumbers spell cast on her!" spluttered the young man, gasping for breath.

"What does that mean?!" growled David, throwing the man back against the tree, where he fell, unconscious.

Christopher looked amusedly at the senseless figure for a moment before closing his eyes and muttering a few arcane words. Very soon he reopened his eyes and horror constricted his face. "It means," answered Christopher, "that her soul's been removed from her body. So her body no longer functions but is still living. She'll age very quickly till her soul is returned or she dies."

"Who could do that to her?" asked David, shocked, horrified, and revulsed.

"A malspirare," answered Christopher, fear and hate flickering in his dark eyes.

"What's that?" inquired Sean.

"It's a very powerful and very evil demon. Did you see the thing in black robes that stood behind Peccare before his men attacked? That was a malspirare. They're servants of Ranshar but will aid any person who is intent on some great evil or if they're ordered to by their god. Did you happen to notice the shimmering ball that the demon held in his hand when he disappeared?"

"Yeah," answered David quietly.

"That was Jessica's soul. The malspirare takes the soul and twines it into a ball and then slowly unwinds it. When it is totally unwound, the soul ceases to exist and the body really dies. The worst part of it, however," continued Christopher with a shudder, "is that the soul and its owner no longer exist in any form. If that happens, it would be as if Jessica had never lived."

"What can we do?" asked Sean, horrified.

"The only way to reverse the spell is to get her body to someone who can defeat the demon on his own territory."

"Well, who can do that?" asked Sean.

"Only a very powerful cleric," answered the wizard.

"Could you do it, Amy?" asked David hopefully.

"No. I'm not nearly strong enough."

"Who then?"

"Why, Lady Gahdnawen, of course. She's the strongest cleric on Sidan," answered a voice from behind the gathered party.

They turned, hands reaching for their weapons, as a blue robed figure strode up to them from out of the forest. It was Jodi. The others felt guilty that they had not even noticed her absence; she could have been hurt or dying. They had been so engrossed in their other friends that her absence was simply overlooked. Visions of Jodi, lying dead in the forest flashed through their minds in a premature burial for her, but she met their eyes firmly, curtailing their thoughts.

She looked very strange, very confident; her long red hair was dirty, with twigs and dirt in it. Her face was worn, as if she had been through some great and terrible strain, and her robes were torn and tattered as if they had been ripped by some great beast. Her firm stomach was exposed with a single, shallow cut across it that looked like a dagger wound. Her left arm was stained in blood and her left leg had another great gash in it, but oddly, all the injured places were almost completely healed! Only fading scars remained!

Jodi casually approached them as if nothing had happened and hugged David tightly. "Jessica will be all right," she said with a smile. "I promise. We'll take her to Galead's Temple, and there Lady Gahdnawen will heal her."

None of them understood what had befallen Jodi that day to change her so drastically and completely. They could not even comprehend her ogre illusion; except Christopher who recalled something about illusionists being able to control all senses in an illusion. Maybe she could just make it seem as if she were killing Peccare's men, but that would have used an even more powerful illusion. She could not sustain that much magic for long, could she? The wizard wondered about that; now that he thought about it, she always had seemed to be able to perform "illusions" beyond her ability. However, something in Jodi's walk and stance stated that she would tell them nothing about it. So out of respect for her, they did not ask what had happened to her, or where the ogre had come from. Instead, they made plans to travel to the Temple of Galead and take care of Jessica. No one questioned whether this was right or whether she would live; they only promised to try, to give every ounce of energy in their meager bodies, to continue for her. They owed it to Jessica; she would have gone on forever in defense of any of them, no matter what the odds were. So they would continue, fighting onward until Jessica was safe by their sides again.

Inside the wagon, David sat alone, with Jessica's head in his lap. They had decided to continue before first light in the morning because they all needed some rest after the battle. So David sat very quietly, unbelievably weary. The exhaustion that he felt within him was not only that of the body, but also that of the mind and heart. As he looked down at Jessica's majestic countenance, he noticed the golden clintonia that still lay behind her left ear like a feeble ensign for life. He removed it and brushed it against her cheek before inhaling its exquisite scent. He twirled it between his thumb and forefinger as he bent to kiss Jessica's stagnant lips again. He noticed tenderly that they were still warm; her flame burned on, a living ember of compassion.

A wolf's howl in the night brought David back to himself. He looked down at Jessica's limp form, and his thoughts returned to Peccare, the burning hatred returning with them. He clenched his fists, crumpling the innocent clintonia as if it contained all the world's evil, and grit his teeth, but then he saw Jessica's peaceful face before him like the quintessence of sanctity and all the hatred drained from him. But one more thought entertained him. He remembered three faces: a dark bearded one, an old wrinkled one, and a tanned one with slightly slanted eyes. He then remembered a dream of these three men as they became one, melding into the same being...and wondered.

Shortcut

The sun had long since fled the impending pall of night, and the small group was gathered around a cooking fire that, by default, had inherited the duty of keeping them warm. As they stared at the orange-red tongues of flame, their thoughts fled the present for the past, and they mused on the day's events.

Brandon's thoughts were solemn. He had been through a lot today—he had almost died, and he was not sure of what tomorrow would bring his way. He recalled the feeling of oppression that had so heavily weighed him down when his life was bleeding away, but he also recalled that the pressure had not seemed crushing. Rather it had tried to lift him, release him by pushing him through a wall of mortality. He knew that had he been human, he would have died, but since dwarven souls stay in their bodies longer after death, he had survived. He was grateful for this as he thought of his friends and of the great favor he owed Amy. He would repay her…somehow.

Amy sat next to Christopher, thinking about Jessica. She wondered whether she could fill the more experienced cleric's place among the party, but she prayed that she would not have to. She remembered having lived in the Temple of Galead when she was young, and she had met the Lady Gahdnawen then many times. The Priestess was quite an impressive woman, and Amy knew that if anyone could help Jessica, it would be her. Then her thoughts turned to Christopher and the love they shared. She prayed that nothing would ever happen to him as her thoughts recalled a place she had seen only days ago: a decimated homestead, surrounded by carnage. Visions of a little girl lying raped on the ground and a baby denied life. The memory of that evil evisceration infiltrated her, befouled her, ripped her inviolacy into tattered cobwebs. These memories tore through her consciousness like searing fire, burning her, leaving her paralyzed with fear. Feelings of ineptitude bored into her, making her insensate to the present and openly vulnerable to the unforgotten past that hovered over her like an evil vulture, living off her fear. She shuddered and found herself praying to Galead for protection and strength.

Christopher, the most thoughtful of the bunch, sat close to Amy, wondering about what had happened that day. He tried to figure out what had made the malspirare single out Jessica and not him or one of the others. And who had summoned the awesome spirit to begin with. It could not have been Peccare or Tohzahi; they did not have any magical powers. His thoughts then fled to a different, more introspective line. Christopher had freed the young man who had told them about Jessica and had killed the rest of his captives without a second thought. He did not even think about why he had done it; it was purely instinctual. He was surprised by the increasing coldness that was filling his soul, leaving an emotionless shell. But his gaze then fell upon Amy, and he felt a spark of warmth in his heart. He remembered that day not too long ago when he had realized his feelings for her. He remembered her initial embarrassment at his compliments, but her acceptance came

very quickly. His thoughts rushed through the past as visions
of times spent holding Amy or kissing her or simply looking
at her flashed in his eyes, glimpses of protective emotion. In
her arms, he had found sanctuary from the enclosing winter of
his soul as if her sanctity were enough for both of them.

Sean found himself very aware of the figure, shrouded in
blue, that sat next to him. He was curious about Jodi and what
had happened to her today. He could not understand why she
avoided talking about the ambush or why she was so un-
touched by Jessica's dilemma. It seemed as if she knew more
than the rest of them. Did she? And if so, what did she know
and how did she know it? He shook his head in confusion.

Jodi was not really aware of anyone about her. She was
deep in thought, musing on her involvement in the ambush and
on what had happened afterward. She wished that she had not
been forced into revealing her "other" special power but
thought that the others would not force her to explain it.
Although this was an important event, it was not paramount in
her mind—what came afterward encompassed most of her
thoughts. She could not get out of her head the image of the
visitor she had during her excursion into the wood. An image
of the tiny naked woman with flowing green hair and slender
arms like twigs was etched in her mind's eye. The message of
hope she had received was also engraved there. But what
puzzled her most was why the woman had finally chosen to
come to her. Why, mother?

As morning dawned, the party of weary travelers was
already well on its way north. They had backtracked through
the forest into the Great Expanse's deadly moor and were
heading north toward the Temple of Galead, pushing their
mounts as hard as they dared, as hard as they could bring
themselves to. As the sun had risen to their right, erasing the
memories of darkness on the land, the shadows in the small

party were not lessened; they were instead compounded as it dawned on them that they had very little time to save Jessica.

Brandon, Sean, and Jodi rode at the front on their mounts in silence while Christopher drove the wagon with Amy at his side, eyes downcast with corrupted harmony. Inside the canopy, David sat, staring at Jessica in sorrow. The effects of the spell were readily visible on her beautiful face. On the previous eve, she had seemed a young woman of little more than twenty years, but this morning, she appeared much older. Her life was dripping away like the sands of an hourglass, and as time wore on, her tribulations deepened on her once-youthful face, the years quickly ticking away. She was aging very quickly...too quickly. David was still deep in thought as he gazed into Jessica's deterioration, praying that an antivenin would arise and that time would halt long enough for them to relive their lives, but Father Time paid the young woman's plight no attention and the day wore on.

Outside the wagon, the day could only be described as bland. There was almost nothing of real interest about the temperature, the scenery, the weather, or anything else. It was cloudy, though not rainy, and chilly, but not cold. Sean and Jodi led the way through the moors that had encompassed their journey for too long, while Brandon moved to the rear of the wagon. He was annoyed at having to ride but was too upset to truly care. The dwarf felt terribly sorry for David, praying all the while that Jessica would be fine. The beautiful cleric had been his friend for many years, and he felt very close to her. David had been a good friend for almost as long, and he truly hated to see the man so dejected. Brandon shifted uneasily in his saddle, trying to relieve some of the pain from his saddle sores. He wished fervently for things to be normal again, and more than that, he wished he could remember what normalcy was.

Christopher was still pondering the same thoughts that had

occupied him the night before, and he still felt every bit as dry of emotion. He watched Amy as they rode on, wondering what it was about her that brought him out of his stupor. He finally decided that it really did not matter; he loved her and always would. He concentrated on the possibility of a life together.

There was only one place in the caravan where conversation was even attempted: at its head. Sean had begun to feel uncomfortable riding along in silence, so he decided to try and chat with Jodi. "How long do you think it'll be till we get home?" he asked.

"Where?" asked Jodi, startled out of her thoughts.

"Home," repeated the thief, surprised at her. It seemed to him that everyone except him and David had forgotten entirely that they were trying to get back to Earth. Had everyone lost sight of who they really were?

"Oh." There was a brief glimpse of recognition on Jodi's face but it soon faded. "I don't know."

Jodi's response troubled Sean greatly. As a thief, he had a tremendous sense for what happened around him, and he was getting some really bad impressions. It was bad enough to see David and Jessica in their situation, but Jodi's response to his casual question confirmed a suspicion he had been harboring for quite some time. As they spent more time in Sidan, they grew more and more like their characters. They had been suspicious of this at first, but all the trials they had been witness to had taken their minds off that particular problem. It seemed that Jodi, Amy, Christopher, and even Brandon had forgotten about the life they had left behind. David and Jessica had obviously remembered, but there was no telling what change this new obstacle would have on them. I suppose the reason we three haven't forgotten our past lies in the fact that we are so much like our characters anyway. The others created characters very different from themselves, but we stayed true to our personalities. Though I think I've isolated the problem, no solution seems to offer itself. And I don't think now's the time to act anyway.

A short time before noon, the party stopped for lunch. They had not eaten any breakfast that morning, so by noon they were half starved. They sat beside a small mesa, peering out at the deathful scenery. The Great Expanse had seemed to deepen slightly as they traveled northward, and the brief glimpses of life they had grown accustomed to were growing less frequent. And with that change, the little bit of hope their hearts had been harboring had fled.

Now they sat still, picking halfheartedly at less-than-satisfying food, hoping that David was all right. He still sat in the wagon with Jessica's body. He had not spoken all day, and his friends were growing very worried. So Brandon took him a plate of dried meat, some bread, and a wineskin, hoping that he would accept the vague comforting. "Eat, my friend," he said, offering David the food.

"I'm not hungry," answered David distantly as he pushed it back.

"You need to eat," insisted Brandon, looking at his exhausted friend sadly, noticing that the warrior had not even taken the time to oil his sword and armor.

David shook his head. Brandon sighed, looking down at Jessica's wasting form. He thought that he could almost see her aging in front of his eyes. She appeared to be somewhere near forty, though Brandon knew she was only in her twenties. He shook his head with worry as he left the wagon uncertainly.

Once outside, Brandon returned to the rest of his friends. "He won't eat," he mumbled, sitting down.

"He must," said Jodi, walking to the dwarf's side and taking the food. "Let me try."

As she walked off, the others hoped that Jodi could convince David to accept the food. He needed to keep his strength up as best he could. The illusionist soon returned and her hands were empty.

"He'll eat a little," she said. "Enough to keep him going, anyway."

They could come up with nothing else to make the situation easier from that point, so they resumed their journey in utter silence. They trudged on, watching the colorless scenery pass by and then seemingly reappear in front of them. They would travel by a small mire or a tor or even a miniature forest, and before they had gone another league, another would appear in front of them, reasserting the futility of their actions. They seemed to be getting nowhere. The pressure of all that had happened and what they had seen weighed heavily upon them, and they soon began to tire. Night fell amid the dank coldness of the Great Expanse and still they trudged on, stumbling in the darkness, fighting to cover a little more ground. The moon gave them enough light to see each other, but the ground was obscured by a layer of thick mist that captured the moonlight, suppressing their vision like a cerement. They fought onward until around midnight when their weary muscles could no longer stand to grip the horses' sides.

As they stopped, they decided to sleep in the wagon to keep warm and to comfort each other. They ate a little and soon began to talk of necessities. It was apparent that Jessica would not make it another day; she already appeared to be in her early fifties. At the rate she was aging, she would be over eighty by tomorrow evening.

"We don't have time to make it to the Temple like this," said Christopher, stating everyone else's thoughts. "We're going to have to find some way to make her age slower."

Sean nodded, looking intently at David's sorrowful face. "We've got to do something."

"I don't know how to slow down the aging process," said Amy sadly. "I don't think it's possible for a cleric as inexperienced as me. It would mean completely halting her metabolism, and I'm afraid that if I tried, I'd kill her."

"We may not have a choice," asserted Christopher. "She'll die anyway if we don't reach the Temple, and plain death like you're talking about would be better than her fate if the malspirare wins."

"We can't give up!" broke in Jodi, exasperated at her friends' despair. "Jessica'll make it if we give her the chance! She's strong! I mean really strong! She'll fight that demon with every ounce of power in her body, and she might just win even without the Lady's help! But, if we give up on her, she'll certainly die! So we've got to keep fighting! As long as we struggle for her, she'll push onward. She'd never give up on one of us, and we can't give up on her. We've got to give her the chance to show her stuff! We've got to give her the opportunity to succeed!"

Brandon shot to his feet. "You're right, Jodi. We all know how strong she is. All you have to do is look at her, for God's sake. Even now, she radiates power as if even death couldn't conquer her. We can't give up hope. If we do, we may as well kill her ourselves."

"But how?" asked Amy. "What can we do to help her? If we could get to Lady Gahdnawen now, I'm sure she could save Jessica, but—" she broke off. A light flared behind her eyes like the fire of hope, and everyone's attention shot to her, expectation and excitement spreading like wildfire. An idea flared in her mind, and the more she thought about it, the more her excitement grew. She turned to the wizard, hope brazenly blaring from her. "Christopher! Do you know a spell to let people talk telepathically?"

"Yeah, why?" he asked uncertainly.

"I might could convince the High Priestess to help us get to the Temple faster!"

"How?" asked Brandon hopefully. "What could she do?"

"The Priestess has the power to teleport," she answered. "She could teleport us all to the Temple!"

"We've got to try!" said David hopefully. For the first time since he had learned of Jessica's plight, he felt hope welling in him, real hope, inflating him with life again. Maybe she would make it; maybe the fight was not over.

Amy smiled excitedly, stroking David's cheek affectionately, and gestured for Christopher to begin. It was really a very simple spell, a cantrip needing only concentration and not memorization. Christopher closed his eyes and projected Amy's thoughts toward the Temple of Galead, hoping that the Lady would receive them. "Priestess," called Amy. "Lady Gahdnawen, answer me, please."

There was a glimmer of recognition, and the Priestess' awareness leapt into Amy's mind. "Yes, child," came the musical voice that Amy remembered from her youth. "I'm here."

"Lady Gahdnawen!" She almost screamed the name, relief surging through her veins. "We need you!"

"I know. Be welcome."

There was a surge of power that flowed from the air into Amy's body, and an eruption of light jerked her eyes open. She found herself sitting in the floor of a great marble room, her friends gathered confusedly around her. The white stone seemed to glow with a preternatural light that made it seem as daylight inside though it was the middle of the night. There were three archways exiting the room, to the right, left, and rear. The furnishings were magnificent, made of the finest wood, granite, and even marble. There were several chairs to one side and a table piled high with food of the most appetizing sorts. There was a great woven rug, intricately emblazoned with many holy symbols and cherubs, lying on the floor, thick enough to cover a man's ankle.

At the end of the rug farthest from the amazed group sat a great white marble throne that seemed to glow with the same magical ambiance as the magnificent room. It stood a little

over six feet in height and had many marvelous statues
sculpted into it like insignias of power, icons of strength. To
each side of the great throne, a tall, lovely woman stood, each
with hair like midnight and eyes of grey. Seated on the throne
was a woman the likes of which none of them, save Amy and
Jessica, had ever seen. Her white hair, hanging in loose braids,
reached down to her waist and her eyes were black. These
esoteric orbs seemed to peer through each person as the
woman turned her gaze on them, studying them with eldritch
understanding. Her magnificent white robes had gold trim,
and her face, though very old, was beautiful, as if a sculptor
had cut it away from living rock. She raised her hand, which
was unadorned of any rings or other jewelry, in a gesture for
them to stand.

"Welcome, children," she said in a voice that resounded
off the walls so that every facet of it was noticed. It was deep
for a woman yet resounded like a carillon, echoing in their
minds with pinpoint precision. "You are welcome…and expected."

They all stood in startled silence, David holding Jessica's
limp form in his arms as if she gave him the strength to stand.

She continued: "I am the Lady Gahdnawen, High Priestess of the Temple of Galead." She gestured to the girl on her
right who walked up to David and took Jessica from his
reluctant arms. She then departed through the archway to the
left. "Feed yourselves. You must regain your strength."

David started to protest, impatient to gain aid for Jessica,
but he was cut off by the Lady's marvelous voice. "All will be
taken care of later, but now you must eat." She stood and left
through the left archway, leaving David and the others standing in awed silence.

The woman who stood on the other side of the throne
approached them and introduced herself as Inoce. She was tall
with long black hair that was pulled back in a solitary, tight

braid that dangled below her shoulder-blades. Her grey eyes were deeply set in a nearly perfect, oval face. She had a small nose and thin lips that were spread in an infectious smile, issuing total confidence in her mistress. Her high cheekbones were smooth, as was her entire face, but a small, diamond-shaped birthmark blemished her slender neck like an avowal of imperfection. "Now you must eat," she said, "because that is what the Lady has ordered."

"But what about Jessica?" asked David, gesturing to the archway through which she had been taken, noticing how brazen his voice sounded in the aftermath of Gahdnawen's wondrous musicality.

"My sister, Purus, has put her to bed. The Lady will take care of her, but you must take care of yourselves." She ushered them to the table. "Now, eat."

Not knowing anything else to do, the group sat and ate. The food was truly marvelous, taking their minds off their problems and turning their attention to satisfied stomachs. There was veal and venison, fresh vegetables, and ripe fruit the like of which none of them had ever seen. But the most marvelous part of it all was the freshly baked yeast rolls that they drowned in freshly whipped butter flavored with honey. All this they washed down with a wonderful white wine.

As they finished their meal, Lady Gahdnawen returned to her throne, Purus following, and observed the destitute group with an eye filled with caring. "My children," she began, "it's late and you all will feel greatly refreshed once you've slept. It's past the time for counseling and well into the time for resting. Now, sleep."

"But Lady Gahdnawen," protested David, still feeling uncomfortable and worried. "What of Jessica? Can you help her? Is she all right?"

"I don't know yet," she answered. "We'll see in the morning."

"But she's aging so quickly," broke in Brandon, worried. "Will she live that long?"

"Yes," said the Priestess with a smile. "I've stopped the aging process, but it won't last forever. We must act quickly, but the morning will offer the best beginning. So until then, sleep well." Her words were a statement of fact and not a suggestion. She gestured for Inoce and Purus to escort them to their rooms.

They left through the right archway, all protest laid aside by the Lady's words, and wound their way through hallways of white marble. They passed a garden that was absolutely marvelous, filled to brimming with blooming flowers and flourishing trees as if the seasons held no sway over their livelihood. They noticed the beautiful jonquils and columbine, irises and forsythia, sycamores and willows with undisguised admiration, wondering at the clerics' ability to conquer the cold adversity of the seasons.

However, they quickly passed the garden and found themselves in the guests' rooms. David was placed in a room with Brandon while Christopher and Sean shared the one next to it. These two rooms were connected by an inner door in the north wall of David's room. Jodi was placed in the room directly opposite David's while Amy was taken to sleep with the rest of the clerics.

As soon as David entered the room, he walked to the bed against the opposite wall. He noticed only in passing the beauty of the lavish room and its furnishings. The bed was large with two mattresses and a canopy top; there was a large dresser with a mirror topping it against the south wall, and a few chests lined the east wall, flanking a closet.

David simply approached the lavish bed and fell into it as the exhaustion and anxiety that he had pent up over the last day overwhelmed him. Almost as quickly as he hit the soft mattress and felt the cool pillows beneath his head, he fell into a restful, dreamless sleep, the first he had in two nights. "Sleep well, my friend," murmured Brandon as David drifted off. The dwarf removed David's boots and covered him in the surplus of sheets that enshrouded the bed.

Brandon then undressed himself and crawled into the bed, but he did not fall asleep as easily as David. Instead, he lay there and thought of his friends and his home back in the mountains to the far west for a while. He then slowly lapsed into unconscious ruins and slept amongst the remains of great underground cities that he explored in his dreams. There were huge rooms filled with the hammering of dwarven picks against the Earth's heartrock, digging for jewels and precious metals. There were other rooms with dwarven smiths molding metal into weapons and armor of such fine quality that the gods themselves would be content to use. He wandered halls that were buried deep underground and sang songs in the dwarven tongue of old, thrumming the notes deep in his chest like the strings of a great bass. He swam in rivers of gold and bathed in pools of platinum, wallowing in the extravagance that was his heritage. As Brandon ascended and descended within the depths of dwarven memory, no worry pierced his thoughts, and he slept deeply, more comfortably than he had in many days.

David awoke the next morning, the brilliant sun shining in through a window over his bed. He lay there for a while in what could only be described as a wakeful slumber, too tired to crawl out of bed but too alert to sleep. He soon heard a faint tapping at the door. As Brandon stirred beside him, David raised himself out of the bed and walked to answer the call, noticing that he was still fully armored except for his boots. He stretched grandly and opened the door, admitting Amy and Jodi to the room. They were both dressed in fresh white robes and were noticeably scented with exotic perfume.

"The Lady Gahdnawen wants to see us," began Amy as Christopher and Sean entered the room from the northern door, "but first you should bathe." She pinched her nose, scrunching her eyebrows.

David looked down at himself, noticing the caked-on earth that layered his clothes and deeply-tanned skin like an ineffective ointment. It had been days since he had bathed…or shaved, he thought as he stroked his bearded jaw.

"The bath's right down the hall," supplied Jodi. "It's already prepared for you, and there should be fresh clothes there, too. We'll be waiting for you in my room." They turned and left.

Sean pranced up to David's side from the room's inner door and placed an arm about his friend's shoulders. "We'd best do what they say," he commented, a wry grin twisting his lips. "If we don't, they're liable to come after us with sponge and soap themselves."

"What's so bad about that?" asked Brandon, rubbing the sleep from his eyes.

"A sponge and soap wouldn't be so bad," conceded Christopher, "but the scouring soap and wire brush they'd come after us with would be murder."

David had to grin as he visualized Amy and Jodi chasing after them like overzealous mothers, soap in hand and words of chastisement blaring from their lips. But he felt much more like curling up in the corner and weeping like a distraught child; thoughts of Jessica were once again swimming through his mind. After walking down the hall away from the throne room, they entered a curtained archway and found themselves in a white marble room filled with a tremendous, steaming pool of crystal clear water that filled the room with a white haze like a cloud of remedies. A stoic elderly cleric was awaiting them there. "I'm here to supply you with anything you need," she said in a voice like cracked parchment.

Christopher leaned over and quietly whispered in Brandon's ear: "If penis envy hits you my shrunken friend, just remember that you're a dwarf, and it's natural for you. Your size is nothing to be ashamed of."

Brandon blushed mightily and threw Christopher, clothes and all, headlong into the pool where he spluttered with continued mirth. The cleric cocked an eyebrow before turning her head so they could undress. The water felt marvelous on their parched skin as it lifted the dirt off and removed the dust of many miles of weary wandering. The cleric brought them all sponges and an abrasive soap that cut through the grit and grime marvelously. She then brought knives and mirrors for them to shave with.

As they frolicked in the pool, enjoying the emotional and physical convalescence, they talked of renewed hope for Jessica and for their wearied consciences. The perfect, warm water seemed to cleanse them, wash away their sins in a complete confession of sorrow, replacing their distress with a respite of unbridled relief. They shaved with all the conviction of men certain of and content with their futures, ignoring the possibility of cutting themselves, reveling in the warm comfort that the pool issued into them, contradicting the charged distress that the Great Expanse had embedded in their souls. They relaxed and floated in the billowing clouds of steam that wafted around them in a cotillion of joy, lifting them through their emotional ceilings and into new realms of hope and life.

After a second power struggle between Brandon and Christopher that incidentally was won by the former, they climbed out of the pool, lingering as they dried off, reluctant to leave such luxury. The cleric ushered them, hair still dripping, out of the room making promises of a breakfast the likes of which they had never tasted.

They returned to the hall outside Jodi's room and knocked on the door; it was quickly answered by two smiling faces.

"Much better," commented Jodi, taking in their new white robes and no-longer-grimy hair. She walked to David's side and placed her arm in his. He felt a pang as he remembered the feel of Jessica's hand in his, but he forced the hurt out of him by concentrating on the comforting hope that had been his in the bath. He knew that if anyone could help Jessica, save her from that malevolent fate of nonexistence, it would be Lady Gahdnawen. He centered all his thoughts on her power and felt the old confidence well within him as the remembrance of her wonderful voice echoed in his mind.

They followed the cleric down the hall until she ushered them into a room they had not previously noticed. It turned out to be the official dining hall for the Temple. It was a large room, probably one hundred feet square and marvelously decorated with tapestries and rugs, but the room was mostly filled by the tremendous rectangular oak table that sat in its center. There were many chairs around the table, and Lady Gahdnawen was seated at its head, Inoce and Purus flanking her. She was resplendent in silver robes with gold trim that marvelously accentuated her fine hair and flashing eyes.

"Sit," she said in that voice that still resounded in their ears from the previous night. "We'll eat before we talk."

The guests seated themselves and several clerics began bringing out large trays, laden with food. There was pheasant and mutton with star fruit, kiwi fruit, kumquats, and samara. More trays were brought, topped with sweet breads and honey, and their crystal goblets were filled with an aromatic tea that smelled slightly of thyme and cinnamon. They feasted on the royal food and thanked their hostess repeatedly for her hospitality.

Some time later, Sean leaned back in his chair and grunted happily, totally satisfied, patting his bulging stomach. "I don't think I've ever eaten so well," he said with an earnest grin. He considered burping loudly but decided that in this culture it might not be complimentary. So he satisfied himself with a quiet belch behind his closed fist.

"Sweet," whispered Jodi sarcastically.

"Thanks." So much for politeness.

Amy leaned toward Sean, smiling to herself. "Now don't forget, Sean, they probably count the silverware after every meal, so don't steal anything."

With a blatant show of indignation, the thief straightened in his chair and placed a hand over his heart, obviously cut to the quick by the cleric's jibe. "How could you think such a thing of me?" he asked, a mischievous sparkle in his eye.

"Easily," answered Amy seriously. "After all, it is your profession to steal. Why shouldn't we suspect you?"

Sean shrugged, grinning broadly.

"Well then," said Lady Gahdnawen, standing, "it's time for us to talk. Let's retire to more comfortable quarters." She stood and led them back through the throne room and from there through the left archway. They walked down the main hallway until it terminated at a door that the Priestess opened, quickly following her guests into the room. She quickly shut the door behind her. The chamber was comfortable, but not overly lavish, with some cushioned chairs placed around the fireplace, which held a roaring fire. There was a single window in the room that overlooked the magnificent plain that encircled the temple. If you looked out the window, which faced westward, it would seem that you could see forever since the plain continued for as far as the eye could see without interruption. There was a door in the right wall through which a luxurious bed could be seen, and a door to the left led to a bathroom.

There was a large couch in the northwest corner of the room, which contained the sleeping form of Jessica. She had not aged since the night before, and as David approached her limp body, he noticed that she had been bathed and clothed in fresh robes. He was beyond tears now as he grasped her hand and stared sorrowfully into her stagnant, closed eyes. He sighed and joined his friends in front of the fire.

"There's much to be said and little time in which to say it," began the Lady, gesturing for David to sit in the wing-backed chair at her side. "First, I think you should tell me your story." She peered at David intensely. "From the beginning, before your arrival in Sidan."

David was a little startled by the Lady's bluntness but realized that she had to know where they came from if she called them by name, and she did have every right to be blunt. After all, it was her help that they were seeking. So, as he sighed and began, he did not notice the strange looks that passed over his companions' faces, one of faint surprise and dawning recognition—such a strange reaction. It was as if they did not know what he was talking about. "I guess that would be when we went to the Doc's house for our usual session of gaming. Everything started off so normally. Who'd have thought it would develop into this? Anyway, we went to his house at 4:00. The summer was about halfway over, and we had been at his house almost every Saturday since we graduated…"

Doctor John Richards was a college professor who taught honors chemistry and, oddly, philosophy. He was thirty-seven years old and still unmarried, but that was about all David knew about him. They had met at a role-playing convention that David and a few friends had attended. They were in the same group of gamers, and to the surprise of all, they discovered that the Doc lived within ten minutes of the small town in north Georgia in which they lived. He seemed nice and when they discovered that he refereed some games, they decided to join him in one on the following weekend. After the first session in which he showed an unnatural talent for making the game realistic, they were hooked. They had been playing with him on every Saturday over the summer for the last three years, with very few exceptions.

As David and Jessica entered the room in which they traditionally gamed, they saw that everybody else had already arrived. Brandon, Sean, Christopher, Jodi, and Amy were all gathered around the table, chatting idly.

Jodi was a tall, slender girl with short brown hair and big blue eyes. A quick glance at her as she talked made it obvious that she was basically quiet but enjoyed talking with her close friends and, at times, seemed addicted to that very pastime— in other words she could talk the ears off a cornstalk. But generally she was shy with a sweet, undisturbed quality about her.

Amy, a more outspoken girl, was barely taller than Jessica, almost on a level with David, with light blue eyes and strawberry blond hair that reached down to her hips. She was talkative, always open and eager to chat.

Glancing up at Brandon as they passed by, Jessica and David took their seats at the table and assessed the familiar surroundings. The room they inhabited was scarcely decorated for the Doc did not seem to believe in extravagance in the home—actually he did not seem to believe in extravagance at all. The only really comfortable place in the house was the living room that was unmistakably pampered as his favorite. It was plush and decorated lavishly with paintings and oriental rugs and many other expensive furnishings. However, the gaming room could be described as bare and uncomfortable if it were not for the great mahogany table around which they sat. Its legs were carved into the legs of a lion, each ending in a large clawed paw that grasped an iron ball that held the weight of the magnificent table. Everyone had a wooden chair with a flat pillow, which offered little comfort, but the Doc would sit in a high-backed black chair at the head of the table that looked like it could make Scrooge grin with pleasure. The Doc provided a glass of tea at the beginning of each session, and there were also three full pitchers for refills so they would not be interrupted by refreshment breaks.

David turned to Christopher who was seated on the other side of Jessica and spoke. "We're supposed to start a new campaign today, aren't we?"

"Yeah," answered Christopher, smiling broadly as he brushed his blonde, almost white hair out of his face, bright blue eyes glittering. "I hope this one's as good as the last."

"The Doc did do an excellent job of it," replied David, remembering the excitement of their last adventure. "I felt like he was the director of some epic movie I was acting in."

"More like a puppet-show where he was the puppet master and we his puppets," put in Sean, his red hair pulled back into a pony tail.

"Eerie metaphor," said David, grasping his hand in greeting.

"Simile," corrected Jessica.

"Whatever. It's eerie anyway. I don't like the idea of being someone's puppet."

Christopher nodded and leaned back just as the Doc entered and sat. He reclined in his black chair and fixed each of them with a cold, emotionless stare as they joined him at the table. He was an ominous figure, tall and dark, with black hair and a shaggy black beard that enshrouded his face and intensified the bright blue eyes that peered out of it. He rarely smiled, unless sarcastically, and laughed even more rarely. He would seem rather strange to a newcomer, but these young adults were unperturbed by his overbearing and haughty presence. His complexion was sallow, almost yellow, and made him appear empty, closed. He always appeared tired but, nevertheless, was constantly alert and as quick as a whip. He was dressed, as usual, in a white shirt and black slacks, both of which had been precisely ironed and creased. He arranged his equipment in front of him and inquired flatly, "Shall we begin?

"First of all, I have supplied each of you with your usual refreshments. They should keep you satisfied for the session. Let's have a toast to luck today." Everybody raised their glasses and took a sip of the extremely sweet tea. "Next, we'll choose what characters we'll use for our upcoming campaign. Christopher, we'll start with you."

"All right," he said cheerfully. "I'll use Omnibus. At sixteenth level, he's the party's most experienced wizard."

"Okay. Jessica, you're next," said the Doc, making a few marks on the legal pad that lay in front of him.

"I'll take Sister Anna. She's a seventeenth level cleric so she should be able to heal any wounds we get."

More scribbles. "Okay. David?"

"Graham. He's only fifteenth level, but he's quite a fighter. And you can't have an adventure without fighters."

"Amy?"

"Sister Victoria. It might be a good idea to have a second cleric along in case Sister Anna gets hurt; she can't heal herself. Sister Victoria's fourteenth level and powerful enough to make a difference."

"Brandon?"

"Rork. He's the strongest fighter we have since he's a dwarf even though he's only fourteenth level, and Graham can't handle everything." He winked at David who smiled in return. "Though he'd like to try."

"What's that supposed to mean?!" interjected David, but a quick look from the Doc stopped his protest.

"Jodi?" said the Doc, ignoring Brandon's giggling.

"I'll take Aurora the Illusionist. She's only fourteenth level but can make some pretty lifelike illusions, and you never know when that might come in handy."

"And Sean."

"Martin. He's fifteenth level and quite a thief as well as a trained assassin. He can fight pretty well too, if he has to."

"But he's a lot better at running away," mumbled David. Sean grinned, making his face appear even more rodent-like.

"Then the party's assembled and I'll remind the magic using characters that you can only use spells that you've memorized. However, at any time in the campaign, you can choose to spend some time memorizing different spells. Wizards must study their spell books and clerics must pray to their god or goddess. The illusionist only has to rest to regain her powers. All right, then Omnibus may choose seven spells."

"Okay. Fireball, Invisibility, Lightning Bolt, Sleep, Burning Hands, Summon Elemental, and Impotence."

"Why in hell did you choose Impotence?" questioned Sean.

"It's wonderful for revenge. I make it a point to carry at least one curse with me wherever I go. Sort of like a magical American Express Card."

"Sister Anna has eight," continued the Doc while the others shook their heads.

"Light Cures, Great Cures, Create Food and Water, Light, Charm, Dispel Elemental, Dispel Undead, and Remove Magic."

"I'll remind you that healing spells can be reversed into harm spells without further memorization. Sister Victoria has six."

"Light Cures, Great Cures, Lock Door, Levitation, Protection, and Vision."

"And Aurora, you have five spell points worth of illusions. For each sense that is affected by an illusion, one spell point is removed, and there is a time limit."

Jodi nodded her understanding.

"Then all the mechanics are finished, and we can begin the adventure," completed the Doc.

David, with the others, sat back and prepared to listen to one of the Doc's long, ornate descriptions. They were prepared to bathe in his words and feel the reality of imagination flow through their bodies. However, David found that he was feeling a little groggy and attempted to stifle a yawn, but he failed miserably, managing only to make it more noticeable. He looked about and saw some similar reactions in his friends. He was glad that he was not the only tired one of the bunch.

And the Doc began. "You're floating down the Meandering River in your newly acquired raft, enjoying the luxury of a few moments of rest between adventures. You know your next mission well. The wizard Marrano has offered a great sum of gold in return for an amulet that is to be found in a cavern under Mount Apocrys and guarded by a powerful but insane wizard. This amulet is rumored to have the ability to transfer its user into another world, but you care little for your quest right now as you lazily float down the river past the city of Estrus. The spires of this great city reach far above the surrounding trees, which are many and various; fir trees, fruit trees, oaks, evergreens, and a few scattered dogwoods. Amaryllis and petunias abound amid the beautiful forest, but the most prevalent scent comes from the many patches of clintonia that flourish on the ground along the river. As you float by one particularly large patch of the beautiful golden flowers, the intoxicating scent overwhelms you with a sense of well-being, and you notice in passing that in the center of this bed of glorious affinity, a very large red flower—probably a columbine—spreads out above the others, embracing them in its warm, gregarious grasp…"

The Doc was doing a marvelous job of describing the scene in tremendous detail. David could practically see the trees and city around him, smell the indescribably beautiful scent of the flowers as they passed by, and hear the quiet murmuring made by the Meandering River as it pulled him slowly southward. As Richards described the large red flower that rose from amid the golden haven of clintonia like a beacon, a monolith for protectiveness, David felt himself reaching out for the crimson flower, trying vainly to bring himself within its wondrous grasp. As he stretched for the beauteous surroundings, a feeling of strange universality engulfed him, and he found that he just wanted to close his eyes and bask in the wonders surrounding him, bathe himself in the river and then let the sun dry him as he lay in the flower's comforting grip. He felt the land of dreams encapsulating him in euphoria, and he consciously gave in to temptation. As he totally relaxed and yearned to dream of the land the Doc was offering him, he was occluded from the vision by his closing eyelids, but instead of seeing less, even more details washed over him, and he found himself strangely comforted by the Doc's droning voice as it wandered into infinity, dragging David's consciousness with it into the void, into darkness, into sleep...

An identity crisis

David awoke and rubbed his eyes. He felt like he had been asleep for hours but knew it could only have been a minute or two. He stretched hugely, leaning back in the chair with a tremendous yawn, and found himself immersed in water. He flailed about wildly, trying to get reoriented and reached up, feeling for the side of the pool in which he was certain his friends had dumped him. Instead, he grasped something wooden, very unlike the side of a swimming pool. Then a gnarled old hand wrapped around his wrist, and with a grip of iron, it hauled him out of the water. He lay on his back for a few moments, coughing the water out of his lungs, and finally forced himself to open his eyes, fearing what it was he would see.

"You okay, David?" asked a short but enormously stout man standing over him.

"Uh, yeah. Who are you and where the hell am I?" he replied after gazing about at the vaguely familiar landscape for a long moment. He was on a raft floating down a river. There was forest all-round him except where a city broke through the trees to his right, and a pleasant scent enfragranced the air with fruition. There was a large patch of columbine on the western bank with a large red flower looming protectively over them.

"It's me! Brandon!" replied the dwarf. "And don't you recognize where you are? It's the scene the Doc was describing to us just a minute ago. That's Estrus poking its head out of the trees, and this is the raft we stole on our last adventure and I'm Rork, the dwarf! We're all here, but the others are still asleep."

David felt momentarily dizzy as he peered about him at the trees, the city, Brandon, but mostly at the bodies of each of his friends who were scattered about him on the raft. They had all been changed into their characters from the game. "No. That can't be right," he said finally in a hushed and confused murmur.

"It is though! For God's sake man, look at yourself!"

At the dwarf's prompting, David raised one of his hands to get a better look at the rough appendage. It was then that he understood why he had so much trouble swimming when he fell in the river. The hand, wrist, and arm were all encased in a silver-tinted mesh of chain armor. His entire body was covered with the stuff except for his head, and he noticed that a chain hood lay on the raft to his right. Even through the armor, he could be certain of the extreme bulk of his body. Its muscularity was obvious, and in response to that realization, he found himself flexing his muscles in sequence, then all together.

"Don't let your head swell too much, David," interrupted the dwarf. "I've still got you beat." David stared in amazement as the dwarf flexed his enormous pecs, which bulged hugely, straining his chain mail to its limits—and nearly beyond. "Go look at your reflection in the water." David stood, preparing to obey the command, and nearly fell to his seat again. He towered over his friend, and not just because Brandon was a dwarf! David must have been seven feet tall! Staggering to the edge of the raft, he knelt and grabbed hold of the side, leaning out over the water to peer at the visage that stared back at him defiantly, undermining what reality should have been. The face that he saw was definitely not the one he was used to seeing every morning in the mirror. It was older, maybe 25, with brown hair that extended down well below his shoulders and cold, ice blue eyes that peered out from his deeply tanned, hawk-like face. He returned his gaze to the dwarf and inquired intelligently, "That's me?"

"Yeah! Welcome to reality, David, or should I say Graham."

David almost fainted; the strain was too much for him, but he caught himself before he tumbled back into the river's calmly flowing depths. He then took a good look at his friend, hoping to see some resemblance between the dwarf and the Brandon he had known for years, but he found none—he definitely remembered Brandon as a tall brunette with deep blue eyes. Instead he found a tremendously stout dwarf warrior clad in chain mail, an axe strapped to his back like danger incarnate, and a long pointed beard was tucked into his belt.

"How'd we get here?" inquired David, finally understanding the portent of their situation, accepting it for the present.

"I haven't the faintest idea really, but, you know, the Doc's tea tasted a little strange to me. As if there were something added to it."

"Now that you mention it, it was awful sweet. And right after I took a drink, I started feeling a little groggy. Do you think we were drugged?"

Brandon nodded. "But we'll never find out just sitting here."

"Agreed, but what can we do? And where can we go?"

"I don't know, but I guess the first thing we should do is

wake the others…that should be fun," added the dwarf with a smirk.

David grimaced, realizing that the others would take it as badly as him, probably worse. And what about Jessica? How could he explain this to her? He pushed himself to his feet and felt something hard knock against his mailed leg. He looked down and saw that it was a sword, very long and very deadly, that hung in its scabbard at his side. At the sight of this weapon, David realized the dreadful acts that this body he inhabited had committed. He had visions of himself swinging the sword mightily and sheering through people's limbs, leaving them lifeless husks that dripped the remnants of humanity. A wave of nausea overcame David, and he turned to retch noisily into the river, trying to cleanse himself, trying to efface the visions from his mind.

He turned back to Brandon, embarrassed, expecting to be laughed at, but he saw only sympathy in the dark eyes that regarded him. He realized that the same thought had probably crossed Brandon's mind. He shuddered at the idea of having to kill again while realizing that it might be necessary, but he quickly regained his composure, realizing that he should worry about that when the time comes. The two friends, man and dwarf, turned and approached the others, dreading the task ahead of them, hoping beyond hope that they would wake up and find themselves at the Doc's table again. They each felt as if they were ascending to Golgatha, Fate pushing and prodding them from behind, forcing them forward in time.

Everyone was awakened and comforted as best they could be—which was not very much, not nearly enough. Initially, they started peering about them at the scenery, at once repulsed by where they were and attracted by the intoxicating beauty that engulfed them. After a few moments of shocked silent regard, they began asking questions like "why" and "how." In answer, David and Brandon told them about their suspicions of the Doc and his abnormal tea.

"That bastard!" exclaimed Jodi who had taken on the appearance of her character, Aurora. Her anger was apparent in her dancing eyes, which glowed as if the fire in her auburn hair had manifested itself in them, a living inferno of anger. "Why would he do this to us?!"

"Yes, why?! He had no reason," said Amy or rather Sister Victoria.

"Maybe we're just some sort of guinea pig," suggested Christopher-Omnibus.

"Who cares?!" interjected Jessica, now Sister Anna. "All that matters is how we're going to get home! We're stranded in a world we know nothing about, in bodies we're not used to, and in a situation we're not capable of handling! What'll we do?!" She was quite upset and buried her face in David's chest with a sob.

As Jessica's tears dripped through David's armor and streamed coldly down his chest, he unhappily realized that he did not have the answers to their problem, only more questions. He was just as worried as the rest of them, but he knew that disorder would bring their downfall; control was their only hope. He must find a way to keep them together and return them to the world from which they had been torn.

"I think I know what we can do, Jessica," said Sean-Martin, interrupting David's train of thought after a powerless moment of silence. "Our solution's at the end of the quest that Doc Richards set up for us. You know, the amulet that allows its user to travel to other worlds. Why else would he have introduced us to that particular artifact before we were transferred? It's a bit too coincidental for me to stomach."

"We can't trust what he said!" shouted Jodi disdainfully. "He's lied to us about everything else! Why should we believe him about the amulet?!"

"Because we don't have a choice," answered Sean smoothly.

"Sean's right. It's all we know to do," added David thoughtfully. "I don't blame you for not trusting the Doc. I don't trust him either, but if the amulet exists, it's something to bargain with—and if he can transport us here, there must be a way back. I hate it, but we've got to do what the Doc's suggested." No one, not even David himself, caught the irony in this oddly worded remark.

Jodi reluctantly gave in but none of them were particularly pleased with the decision.

"Where do we go from here? We don't even have a map," commented Amy dryly. "We can't just wander around without any idea of where we're going or where we've been or even where we are."

"We're obviously at Estrus right now, so why don't we beach the raft before we float by and go into town to see about that map you mentioned…and get some food while we're at it," commented Brandon. "I'm hungry."

"Good idea, but where do we get the money?" asked David.

"Well, I've got a purse with some coins in it, don't you?"

David searched himself and found at his belt, like everyone else, a small sack that contained some gold and silver coins that were adorned with a crown and a sword, secured with a draw string, at his belt. "Well, that solves that problem, but we'll need to get some supplies for the trip and mounts to ride. And we don't even know how much we should spend on it all," he finalized.

"If it's like the game, we'll have plenty," said Brandon. "I've got about twenty gold coins and twice as many silvers. That should take care of most of what we need in itself. So let's get going."

They beached the raft in a small clearing and disembarked, finding themselves feeling much steadier on the dry land than they were on the drifting raft. They prepared for the short hike to the city, but Sean noted that it was getting dark and hesitated. "It wouldn't be a good idea for this large a group to hike through the forest in the dark. Why don't we send a small party to get the equipment and return in the morning?"

"It would attract attention for all of us to come traipsing into town after dark, wouldn't it?" agreed David. "Who do you think should go?"

Sean pondered. "Two should be enough. How about me and Brandon. You and Christopher stay with the ladies. The two of us should be able to get everything we need easily enough, and we can put the supplies in backpacks or onto the horses for transport. A larger party would be senseless."

"Okay, you two be careful...and try not to get hurt or into any fights. We'll see you tomorrow morning...about nine, so don't oversleep."

"If we're not back by then, send out a posse. Let's get going, Brandon." And the two, thief and dwarf warrior, slid off into the forest.

"Good luck!" came Jodi's voice from behind David, as they disappeared into the trees.

David stood watching his friends leave, wondering what was happening at home and what their parents would do when they did not return from the Doc's. He noticed that Christopher, Jodi, and Amy had begun talking quietly a short distance away, trying to comfort each other as best they could with idle chatter. He looked down at Jessica who he was still holding gently and noticed that she had finally stopped crying but was still appreciative of his comforting, staring silently into the forest. "You okay, hon?" he asked.

"Yes, David. I'm sorry I lost control, but I'm just so scared...and it's getting dark. What'll happen if we're attacked by something out here all alone?" she asked, her voice shaking slightly.

"Don't worry about that," answered David, his voice full

of confidence he did not feel. "In our new forms we can take care of ourselves." With these words, he realized that if Jessica were in danger, he really would be able to use the weapon that hung at his waist. Releasing her, he drew the sword for the first time and gazed at it, wondering at its morbid beauty, its unnatural power. It was a five-foot, double-edged bastard sword with an ornately carved pommel of black steel wrapped in fine tanned leather. The cross bar curved up slightly at the ends, rounding the handle of the sword enough to make it look sleek and swift. In that instance, David realized that in his real body, he would barely be able to swing the ominous blade, but as Graham, he could wield it freely and with much adroitness. As he swung the blade in a shallow arc, he felt a surge like electricity flow through him. This told him better than any words that his suspicions were right; while in this body, he could fight as well as Graham. As confidence welled in him, he started swinging it more vigorously and began leaping about, testing his balance and strength, experiencing his power. He stared at the blade in his hands as it swished through the air with a flare as if the sword itself was a sentient being, crying to be set free, screaming for blood. He wondered, could this be another Excalibur or a Gram or Laevateina, but smiling grimly, he decided that it was not. He knew that it held no magic; his bare hand was the only force controlling it—and he was not King Arthur.

He returned his gaze to Jessica, emotions soaring as his adrenaline rushed, and saw with a pang that she was standing still, looking into the darkening woods forebodingly, as if Fear himself were floating at its edge. She rubbed her arm, searching for a little comfort that she could not find.

David had an inspiration! He approached her, sword still in hand, and as she turned to look at him, he knelt, offering her the pommel of his great sword.

"Will you accept me, milady, as your protector and eternal

confidant?" he asked grandly. "I will swear to protect you with my life and to do everything within my power to return you safely home."

She blushed and looked down demurely, not knowing quite what to say, but it was apparent in her eyes that she was flattered, amused, and maybe even a little comforted by the teasing offer.

"Will you have me milady?" he repeated.

After a moment, she smiled and answered. "I will." She giggled, looking happier already. "You're such a ham! But a more splendid role you've never played—I love you," she said, realizing that, in his new form, David would be quite capable of fighting off just about anything in these woods. As David returned to his feet, Jessica embraced him strongly, feeling much more sure of their safety and eventual return home.

"Hey, this ain't half bad, milady!" exclaimed David, grinning as he squeezed her stronger and planted a big kiss square on her cute little nose.

Jessica pushed away from him and stepped back, giggling. "Milord, I'm flattered to have you as my Cheval Blanc," she said with a curtsy, bowing her head under the compliment.

"Oh, Tish. That's French," teased David, kissing her hand gently.

"Sorry to interrupt this tender moment guys, but how about helping us get a fire started," suggested Christopher from a few paces away. Jodi and Amy were giggling at them.

"Okay," said David, all seriousness. "Ladies, we would be much obliged if you would start cleaning an area for the fire pit while myself and Christopher make an excursion into the deep, dark forest for some wood," said David, teasing them, while he realized that it was getting chilly and visibility was poor. He just hoped that nothing would come across the clearing until they got the fire started.

Christopher and David wandered off into the woods while the ladies began raking away sticks and leaves from the ground and made a circle of stones in its center. It was odd how quickly and easily they set at their task, as if they knew exactly what to do and had done it a hundred times before. Soon David and Christopher heard a few giggles as the ladies found something amusing. The wizard looked at David and smiled. "I'm glad to see they can still laugh, find humor in what's going on. I was worried that we'd all get too down."

"Yeah. The same thought crossed my mind," agreed David. "It's a relief." He paused. "I didn't want to bring it up in front of the girls, but I was just wondering: what do you think our parents will do when we don't come home tonight?"

Christopher fidgeted slightly. "I don't know what yours will do, but I doubt my dad'll even notice."

David shook his head. He had forgotten for a moment how bad Christopher's relationship was with his father. Ever since his mom left, it seemed that the two of them could not exchange even the slightest civility without it decaying into a shouting match. "Come on, Chris. You know he'll have a shit-fit if you're not in by eleven."

"Serve the bastard right, too," returned the wizard. Maybe this'll take some of the starch out of his britches."

David met his friend's gaze seriously for a moment, but somehow, the wizard's grim visage, portraying one of Christopher's most rebellious glances struck David as funny and he laughed.

"You look like a character out of a really bad horror movie," he said, trying to imitate Christopher's look.

The wizard looked offended for a moment, but his friend's own comic appearance defeated his seriousness. So he laughed back, picking up a small piece of bark and tossing it at David.

"You insult me," said Christopher, his lips moving after his words stopped in a bad imitation of a worse martial-arts flick. "Now you must die."

A short, laughter filled battle ensued—which incidentally Christopher won since David was such a big target—and then they continued gathering wood for the fire, really looking forward to the roaring fire, company, and laughter that the night promised. They pranced through the wood that glowed with beauty even in the twilight, gathering kindling and larger branches, admiring the various flowers and trees that flourished within the pristine wood. David sighed, falling prey to nostalgia momentarily, as thoughts of knights and dragons loomed in his consciousness like icons of a more wonderful realm, memories of Tolkien's wondrous works playing on his mind.

The two men returned to the clearing and began assembling the wood in the fire pit amid the twilight's meager illumination. David used a flint and tender set that Christopher had pulled out of his robes to start the wood ablaze, and after a few moments, the fire was roaring in the pit. They quickly gathered around it, warming themselves as best they could. It was now full dark and the only source of light was the glowing fire and its inverted reflection in the river.

David was sitting next to Jessica, thinking about what must be done to return them all to safety when in a flash, he realized that he had overlooked one minor detail. "Damn!" he exclaimed politely, peering at the faces around him, annoyed with himself.

"What's the matter, David?" asked Jessica, startled and concerned.

"I just realized an oversight we made by letting Sean and Brandon go into Estrus without us. We don't have any food for tonight."

They all realized, after a few giggles, that it was definitely a problem, no matter how minute. David pondered on it and, after a short time, it came to him. "The answer's been right in front of us all the time!" he said, slapping his forehead with an open palm. "Jessica, you've got a Create Food and Water spell, don't you? Why don't you just conjure us up something for dinner?"

"That's a great solution except for one thing," she replied. "I don't know how."

"Sure you do," asserted Christopher. "Your body knows how to do it. All you have to do is concentrate and let it do the work. Give it a try."

So Jessica closed her eyes and concentrated on fresh fish, bread, and water. The more she thought about it, the more she wished she had some. She thought about how each substance tasted, how they felt, and how they looked; very soon her mouth began to water. Then, she suddenly felt a quick surge in the back of her mind and a tingling in her extremities. She heard herself quickly mumbling arcane words that she did not recognize, and the hair on the nape of her neck stood on end as if static were pouring through her body. A chill ran up her spine and she shuddered as the lyrics came to a climactic crescendo. She gasped and opened her eyes with a start. There, on the ground in front of her, were a couple of live trout, some bread that was still steaming, and a full waterskin. She felt strangely warm inside and very proud of herself. She had done it.

"There you go," she commented gaily with a big smile for each of her amazed friends.

"What was it you said?" asked Amy, staring.

"To tell you the truth, I haven't the slightest idea. The words—or whatever they were—just came out of my mouth. I didn't try to say anything at all. I don't even remember what I said," she answered.

"It was the reflexes of Sister Anna taking over in your body," said Christopher. "It's second nature for you to cast spells, so your body just reacted like it has countless times before, without consulting your mind."

Jodi picked up a wet, limp fish and frowned. "Hey,

waitress," she called. "I ordered mine well done. Take this back and get it right this time."

Said David, "What's the matter? Don't like sushi?"

"Actually I've never tried it and I don't intend to now."

"You people are so ungrateful!" said Jessica, feigning disgusted incense. "What do you want? Perfection?"

"It would be nice," answered Christopher and Jodi as one.

"Ungrateful louts," mumbled Jessica, punching Christopher in the gut.

"All right, all right. Enough teasing already," said David, grabbing a trout and unsheathing his dagger. "Let's cook the fish; I'm hungry." He began cleaning the fish and then roasted them on spits over the fire, sectioning them equally, and promptly distributing them. They all thanked Jessica for her contribution—though they still teased her about bringing uncooked food—and found themselves feeling much happier after the refreshingly satisfying meal. Surety among the five was building, overcoming the fear they had initially felt, leaving them confident in themselves and their companions.

"Do you really think we'll get home?" asked Amy somberly as the fivesome gathered closer around the fire to talk.

"Of course we will, won't we, Chris?" prodded David, nodding to the dark figure who sat cross-legged on the far side of the fire.

"You bet," he answered. "If you remember, in the game, our characters are more than capable of taking care of themselves, and we're definitely able to use their powers as Jessica has shown us—we'll get back." He placed an arm around Amy's shoulder in a comforting gesture. "If anyone in this world is capable of retrieving that amulet and using it to get home, it's us. As a group, we can handle just about anything."

"Do you really think so?" she asked, still not quite sure.

"Yes! All we need to hold our own in this world is our bodies and our supplies, which we'll soon have."

Amy smiled at Christopher. She believed what he said and knew that their characters were good…very good.

"Not to mention," added Jodi, "we come from a world of technology and thinking. We're much smarter than the average person in this world. If we can't out-fight them, we can certainly out-think them." Jodi had taken their transformation better than the rest of the girls and realized the need to stay under control, though she was having to fight pretty hard to stay calm, anger and fear encroaching upon her sanity's respite.

"Why, is what I want to know," said Jessica. "Why?! Why did the Doc send us here? He's always been nice to us before. It just doesn't make sense." She still looked a little upset, but no longer because of the transformation. Instead, she was bothered by the Doc's betrayal.

"It seems to me that the only plausible answer would be what I said before: we must be guinea pigs," said Christopher while searching the faces of his friends for some support of his theory. "He doesn't have any reason to hate us, as Jessica has pointed out, so that rules out malice. We do know that he's a chemist and a philosopher, and he's constantly experimenting. We could be taking part in one of his strange experiments. It's the only plausible answer I can see."

"I agree," said David and Christopher looked grateful. "It's the only thing that makes sense. When we get back, we'll find the truth, but until then, we need to concentrate on returning. I really look forward to seeing Richards again!" The hatred and anger in David's eyes sparkled as their pale blue color took on an even icier complexion of spite. He longed for the day he would see the Doc again and repay him for his "kindness."

"Where're we to go from here?" asked Jessica after a few moments of silence.

"We won't know that until Brandon and Sean get back

with the map, but I suppose we'll head in the general direction of Mount Apocrys," answered David.

"Do you have any idea how far that might be?"

"No, we can't be sure yet. All we know is that we've got to get home, and we've got to do something about Richards," he replied.

"What should we do with him?" asked Jodi.

"We've got to teach him a lesson and keep him from doing the same thing to another group of people," said Christopher, rationalizing more for himself than for the others.

"We might have to kill him," said David, anger welling in him, but he was unsure of whether to feel glad or sad. Actually, he was a little appalled that the suggestion had come from his mouth.

"It's illegal, David. We'd go to jail. There must be another way," said the wizard. "I think we'll have to give it some thought. Who knows, maybe something'll come during the journey."

"I think we should kill him!" said Jodi furiously, contemplating what she would do to him—and his genitals. "I can't believe you're even considering something else! This is dangerous! We might be killed! We've got to repay him for his treachery and keep him from causing any more!"

"Apparently, he doesn't expect us to get killed. Otherwise, sending us would be totally useless except for revenge, which he has no reason to want. And we can't select an action until we've all cooled down a bit," replied Christopher, peering hard at Jodi. "I suggest we get some sleep and talk about it again later."

"Christopher's right," put in David. "Let's go to sleep. I'll take the first watch and wake Christopher around two. We'll let you ladies rest tonight. It's been a big day."

Christopher nodded his agreement. David stood and walked a short distance away and sat cross-legged while the others curled up around the fire for warmth.

As night wore on and he found himself tiring, David's mind began to wander. This is all my fault, he said to himself. If I had just listened to Jessica and stopped gaming, none of this would have happened. He sat brooding for a few moments until he realized that he was being too hard on himself. After all, if they had stopped gaming, the Doc probably would have found another group to send to Sidan. It really could not be his fault, and he was sure that Jessica saw it the same way. Anyway, is this so bad? I used to always dream of being a great warrior, adventuring in some magical realm. Well, here I am. I'm a warrior in a huge and muscular body, and I can definitely fight. Whenever I touch my sword, I can feel how good I am with it. It's like a sort of surge, then a flow from my mind into my body and finally into the sword, but it's not only the fighting skills. I feel Graham within me. I may have entered his body, but he has definitely not left it. I can feel that my intelligence and reason are stronger than his, but his instincts for survival and common sense are overwhelmingly greater than mine. This connection of my mind in his body is disturbing to me, but I find myself liking Graham, though I've never really met him. I could get used to his body and his presence, as long as I was master, of course. No, I don't dislike my position, but what about Jessica and the others? I know they don't feel the same way, and I have to do my best to get them home. Union ethics and all. I've got to return with them because I can't leave Jessica in this world that she's not compatible with. The others, I'm sure, want to return too. I'll stay with Jessica. I couldn't leave her even if I wanted to. We'll return to our own world and be happy there. It's safe and comfortable, with all we need, including each other—still, comfort isn't everything. God! I'd kill for a Coke and a cheeseburger! Both worlds definitely have their advantages. But it amazes me that this world could really exist! Could this mean that everything we imagine really does exist some-where? Maybe that's why we can imagine it.

As his thoughts wandered, David was joined by a sweet, musical voice. "Hi David. Mind if I join you?"

Startled, he replied, "Hm? Oh, no. Glad for the company, but what are you doing up, Jessica? It's almost midnight." He felt guilty as he realized he was on watch and had not been paying attention to his surroundings. Then he took a deep long look at Jessica as she had become. She was still attractive, but now her beauty was accentuated by that powerful aura that seemed to surround her, magnify her, push her into the surreal. Looking at her was like staring into the face of a god. Her dark eyes seemed to bore into his personality, into his being, leaving him open to any suggestion she might have. He was awakened from his musings by her answer.

"I had a nightmare and woke up, so I decided to check on you. Anything happened?"

"No," he said, thinking about how strange it was for someone as powerful as her to suffer from nightmares. "I was just sitting here thinking."

"About what?"

"How much I'd like a kiss."

She giggled and bent close to caress his lips with hers. As they met, David's arms intertwined about Jessica's slender waist, and her arms glided around his neck. The embrace excited David immeasurably, as if electric current was flow-ing through Jessica, enlivening her and spreading into him. Then they kissed. Their love for one another surged through their bodies, spiritually uniting them and renewing their faith in one another. Floating through time with relaxed bodies, they allowed their worries and tension to flee.

"Jessica, I love you."

"I love you too, David," she said, gingerly touching his lips with her fingertip.

"You'd better get some rest. I've the feeling that tomorrow's going to be a long day."

"All right." And she rose to leave.

"Good night," David said as he watched Jessica return to the fire. He thought, She's so different now. She's still just as caring and kind; that's more than apparent. But she seems so clear, more real than before. I guess it's the power that Sister Anna holds enlivening her, making her qualities seem more intense. Seeing her like this only makes me realize more that I could never leave her.

The next two hours crept by slowly, and David awoke Christopher before laying down next to Jessica to sleep. None of them knew of the troubles that would come upon them in this new and strange world. They did not know what the people or the terrain was like. All they had to go on was a fading memory of a game a long way from there. Was that enough? Could they trust that waning remembrance? And was the Doctor really to blame or was he simply a scapegoat for their anger? They did not know. All they did know was that night had come and that the morning must follow the night, even here.

Estrus and after

"Fortunately, nothing else happened to us that night, but as for Sean and Brandon…" trailed off David, smiling at the dwarf affectionately.

"Hey, don't look at me. I'm the one who got us out of that mess," said Brandon, elbowing Sean in the ribs a little harder than was necessary.

"All right, all right. I'll admit it; things got a little outta hand," shrugged Sean.

"A little out of hand!" exclaimed Brandon. "I'll show you out of hand!"

Lady Gahdnawen smoothly interrupted the dwarf before he could show Sean his fist, forestalling the violence. "Brandon, tell me what happened to you in Estrus."

Brandon glanced at Sean angrily before starting his story. "Well, Sean and I made our way through the woods toward the city, expecting no problems what so ever. Or at least I didn't expect any. I think he planned to cause trouble, but anyway, we crept through the forest in the dark toward Estrus, and what a city it was…"

The city of Estrus: decadent and nefarious. In this evil pit of so-called civilization, violence and murder are commonplace. During the day, the gates are open and the city spires appear grand and majestic, beacons of beauty to travelers. Viewed from a distance, no one would ever suspect the lawlessness that permeates from its inhabitants like a mephitic vapor. The reek of the city, originating from the manifold dung heaps that fill the cracked and littered streets and alleys, was like a pernicious mist that clung to those unlucky enough to enter its presence. The buildings; smithies, taverns, inns, and general stores; were in a state of disreputable and disgraceful abandonment. This was the appearance of the city under the bright and flattering sunlight, but when it is night…

A distant scream filled the air and was quickly stifled by an unseen force. It was full dark and the only light eked from the waning crescent of a moon, which lay half-hidden by a thin layer of smog as it hung motionless in the thick air above the city. The closed gate, once beautiful, was rotten and black, like a warning of putrid malevolence. The forest surrounding the city was still and silent except for the crepitation of insects, rustling of small rodents, and the occasional flutter of a bird as it fled from the deplorable city. There was a slight movement in a bush outside Estrus' walls followed by an odd gurgling noise.

"Can't you be quiet for just a little bit!?" came an irritated whisper.

"Sorry," apologized a huskier voice adjacent the first. "I'm hungry."

"All right, Brandon. We'd better get started then, before it begins complaining again."

"Hold on, Sean. Why are we breaking into the city?"

Sean sighed. "Because the gates are locked after nightfall and they don't let anyone in."

"Why don't we wait until morning?"

"Because David and the others are expecting us back early tomorrow and we need to find the stores we need. Besides, I'm hungry too."

"Oh."

There was another gurgling noise followed by a sigh before the two shadowy figures—one man, one less than man—inched their way up to the city's wall twenty yards from the gate. The stone was old, and many small niches and crevices eagerly offered themselves for hand and foot holds. Sean rose and placed himself flat against the wall like a shallow bump on the less than flat surface. He stood motionless for a moment, collecting his thoughts, before he began scaling the twenty-foot barrier with the dwarf following directly behind, armor clinking lightly against the stone. As Sean quickly reached the top, he turned and waited on his struggling friend who was not quite half way up the wall.

"What took you so long?" whispered Sean with a smile.

Brandon, sweating profusely and breathing hard, returned the jibe with a steely look. The two then descended the other side of the wall a little slower, entering the city with much caution. They rested momentarily and set off in search of the stables and a general store so that they would not have to search in the morning. After searching under the light of the moon and its shallow corona for approximately fifteen minutes, they found both as well as an inn in which they could stay the night. They paid a silver piece for a room and entered the inn's crowded common in order to eat.

This room was small, with a bar at one end and a few tables scattered throughout it. Both the bar and the tables had chairs filled with loud men and a few less than wholesome looking women scattered inordinately between them. Sean and Brandon seated themselves amid the ruckus at a table in the corner and sat back to listen to the trivial talk around the room. It was merely the ravings, mostly lies, of drunken men about their many wenchings and other unwholesome exploits. Soon the bartender came and took their order, promptly leaving to fill it. He returned with a tray of steaming roast and potatoes as well as two mugs of ale filled to brimming, spume rolling down the sides. It was a pleasant dinner filled with more exaggerated stories and roughhousing, jests and joking. The only serious disturbance was a drunken fight over a woman for which the two men were promptly ejected by a very large, bald man covered in tattoos.

After his fourth mug of ale, Sean was feeling pretty happy and was getting a little rowdy himself. He soon found himself joking with a short, suspicious-looking character named Slear who, according to himself, was quite an accomplished thief in those parts. Slear was busily telling Sean an unamusing story about how he and a few friends broke into a traveling merchant's harem and stole his three favorite wives. Sean, being less than sober and much more than tipsy, found the story terribly funny and tumbled out of his chair, laughing with drunken glee. As he landed, his purse split and all his money scattered on the floor with a loud jingle. Brandon, who remained sober, retrieved the coins but not before many eyes—including Slear's—had seen the large quantity of money that the two carried. There were a few disdainful mumbles and more than a few malicious glares amid the customers as Brandon helped his still giggling friend to his feet. The dwarf drug Sean up the stairs to their room, furtive greedy eyes following them each step of the way like vultures lusting over their prey.

"You asshole!" shouted Brandon as they reached their room. "What the hell's got into you!?" Sean answered with a bubbly giggle before he finally passed out. "Whatever happened to thieves being careful and stealthy? For God's sake, I thought the dwarves were supposed to be the drunkards!"

Brandon roughly—actually brutally—put Sean in bed and stomped around the room, cursing in every language he could think of and a few he made up on the spot. The room was dark with a single window looking out over an uninviting alley. A very uncomfortable-looking bed, containing Sean's limp body, was the only furnishings, which was probably a blessing. If the other furniture looked anything like the bed, it was better that the room lay bare. Brandon cursed Sean's stupidity once more along with his own inattentiveness. He thought that he should be very careful that night and sleep very lightly if at all. Unstrapping his axe and laying it beside him, he curled up in a shadowy corner. He had a feeling that Sean's accident would cost them in more ways than one.

Brandon awoke in the early morning to a shuffling sound and a light whisper only slightly more than a breath. He looked up slowly, careful to make no sound, and saw three black figures crouched in front of the window eyeing Sean greedily. Brandon grasped his axe as he heard one whisper in the thick accent of a seaman, "Where's the dwarf?"

You'll know soon enough, thought Brandon as his reflexes took over.

Leaping to his feet, he swung his axe at the startled form of the seaman. Brandon felt very little resistance as the huge weapon passed through flesh and bone and a head thudded onto the floor next to its body, which twitched with muscle spasms as blood spurted from its fragmented neck. He swung at the second intruder who futilely attempted to block the blow with his short sword. The sword shattered and its owner found the dwarf's axe embedded deep in his side like a steel organ. He collapsed, clutching the wound as his life flowed between desperate fingertips, stained crimson. The third figure was prepared. There was a flash from his hand, and Brandon stumbled backward with a sharp, excruciating pain in his left shoulder. The intruder took his advantage and hurriedly climbed out the window to safety, leaving behind the bodies of his dead friends.

Brandon grabbed at the knife that protruded from his left shoulder and angrily jerked it out, tearing his fury from him with the blade. The pain dizzied him but Brandon stirred himself to rip the tunic of one of the intruders and wrapped it about his bloody shoulder, trying to stop the bleeding. As the flow of adrenaline faded, he saw the effects of his actions and shuddered at the corpses. He comforted himself by repeating over and over that it was Rork that killed those men, not me. He soon forced himself to throw the two mutilated bodies out the window, but he kept the head of the first man to teach Sean a lesson—one that he would never forget.

Sean awoke the next morning with a tremendous hangover and attempted to divine where he was. He saw Brandon glaring at him spitefully and reluctantly raised up. He then found himself staring at the decapitated head of a man, which returned his gaze emptily with upturned, lifeless eyes. There were flies and ants on it, carrying tiny trundles down its face, and blood soaked the foot of the bed where it sat, crusted to the sheets. "Holy shit!" swore Sean as he rolled off the bed and stumbled to the window, retching noisily. In the predawn light, he looked at the ground under the window just to see a decapitated body and another, eviscerated one with its innards lying beside it, both spattered with bile. He retched again, dirtying them even further.

Brandon took the head and threw it over Sean out the window where it landed with a sickening thud near its body. He then peered coldly at the thief who returned to the edge of the bed, still looking more than a little green.

"Feeling better, Sean?" asked Brandon acidly.

"What the hell happened? And what was the purpose of that little prank?!" Sean's face was livid with emotion: anger, disgust, pain, fear, revulsion, but mostly confusion at Brandon's angry leer.

"Your overindulgence in liquor last night damned near got us both killed! How's that for starters?"

Sean then noticed his friend's blood-caked shoulder and his stomach did another flip-flop, though this time he controlled the overflow. "Jesus, man! What happened?" He stood, head spinning, to examine Brandon's wound more closely.

Sean listened intently to Brandon's explanation, though still feeling sick, as he tried to extract some of the fragments of chain mail that were embedded in the dwarf's flesh and redressed the wound. "I'm sorry!" he said after Brandon had finished. "I didn't plan to get drunk."

"I know, Sean, but if you intend to do it again, be more careful and make damn sure that I'm not around," sighed Brandon. "We'd better get going. We've only got about three hours." Sean nodded, hands pressed against his temples like poultices, hoping that the pain would be squeezed out.

The two exited the inn while the bartender stared at them amazedly, obviously surprised to see them still alive. They nonchalantly tossed an extra silver to him for the mess in their room, hoping that nothing else would come of it.

As they walked the streets toward their places of business, the sun attempted to shed some meager light upon the dismal streets of Estrus. These cluttered roadways were practically empty of people except some beggars and a worried-looking merchant who was being greedily eyed by a group of very unwholesome appearing persons, probably petty thieves.

Sean and Brandon soon arrived at the general store they had chosen to do business with on the previous night. It was a small, one story hovel with small holes in the walls. It was very run-down but was in better shape than any other they had seen. They entered and approached a plump little man who was standing behind a desk at the far side of the store. "May I help you, sirs?" he inquired with a broad smile.

They gathered all the food they could get into the four saddlebags they found hanging on the wall: bread, cheese, flasks of water and wine, dried fruit, flour, and other non-perishables. They acquired a few pots for cooking, blankets, a flint and tender set, and some extra cloaks, placing them in seven backpacks, one for each member of the party, and finally inquired "Do you have any maps?"

"Aye, sir. I'll fetch one for you," said the owner who quickly went into a back room. He soon returned carrying a rolled up, cracked parchment. "My finest one!" he exclaimed proudly, offering it to them with a flourish.

Brandon took the parchment, unfolded it, and began studying it intently, searching for their probable destination. He remained motionless for quite some time before looking up at the store owner again. "Our destination is not on this map. We're headed for a mountain known as Apocrys. Do you know where it is?"

"Nay, master dwarf. I know not, but you're not the first to ask me this question today. Another man was in just a few minutes before you arrived; he was looking for the same place." Sean and Brandon gazed at each other, shocked, wondering who would be searching for Mount Apocrys besides themselves.

Finally Sean broke the silence. "Do you know where we might find a map with this mountain on it?"

"I'll tell you as I told my previous visitor. Follow the river north from the city for about three hours and you'll find a little shack in the woods. This belongs to a hermit. He is old and more than a little crazy, but he's the best map-maker in these parts. If anyone has a map with your destination on it, it's him."

They thanked the man and paid him for the supplies, promising to return for them shortly and left. They entered the rundown old building that served as the stables and were met by a tall, muscular older man with a thick salt-and-pepper beard. "May I help you?" he inquired in a deep, resounding bass.

"Yes. We need some horses. And I think a pony for my

friend here," answered Sean.

"Yes sir," nodded the large man, smiling down at the disgruntled dwarf. "Come with me and I'll show you what I have." They inspected many animals and finally chose a fine, strong white mare and an equally large black one, a smaller black horse, and three average brown ones. Brandon gained himself a shaggy, sturdy mountain pony since it would be difficult for him to ride a full-sized horse. Their last purchase was a sturdy brown mare to carry their baggage. They were preparing to leave when Sean noticed a covered wagon to one side of the stable. He inquired of Brandon about its worth, and they decided to purchase it as well.

"How much will all this be?" asked Brandon.

"With the wagon, the total will be fifteen gold and seven silver, but I couldn't help noticing the way you're favoring your shoulder, sir," he stated almost apologetically to Brandon. "It's obvious from the hole in your armor that you've recently been hurt. I am also an armorer, and I wonder if you would like to purchase some extra weapons. I gather that there will be danger on the quest that lies ahead of you."

"That might not be a bad idea. What do you think, Rork?" asked Sean, using his character's name so as not to attract attention with a name so unbecoming of a dwarf.

"Let's take a look at what he's got," answered the dwarf, gently rubbing his shoulder.

They entered a door at the end of the stable and found themselves in a room enshrouded by weapons: rapiers, long swords, axes, bows, shields, and armor of different sorts and sizes. After a lot of shopping, they purchased a large dagger for each of the girls and for Christopher, a long bow with a quiver for David, and a few extra throwing knives for Sean. The armorer also patched the hole in Brandon's hauberk. They packed everything in the wagon and hooked up the horses.

After a little haggling, they settled on a price and Brandon counted the money out into the shopkeeper's hand.

They then returned to the general store for their supplies, which they loaded into the wagon and onto the pack horse. They climbed into the wagon's seat and casually rode out of the city without stopping. They did not notice the steely grey eyes that were peering at them greedily from the upper story of a building along the edge of the gate. These eyes, followed by a small, ugly man, crept stealthily along in the woods behind them, just out of the wagon's view.

It was a warm and clear morning. The sun was still low on the horizon but shone brightly down on the grateful plants and animals that drank its brilliance like a healing elixir. The evergreen trees were a deep and healthy hue of green, but hardwoods were showing the tell-tale signs of mid autumn; the leaves had changed colors and many had fallen to the ground, leaving barren remnants of beauty. The few flowers that were still blooming were brilliant where their splashes of color were sprinkled about the trees and grasses. The Meandering River flowed lazily southward while the light of the early morning sun coruscated in it, almost blinding any who gazed at it. Birds chirped in the trees or fluttered southward on light cheerful wings while small animals rummaged in the bushes for food or climbed trees to eat that which they offered.

David noticed this sarcastically, feeling little of the same emotion. He was anxious about Sean and Brandon; it was nearing the hour of their expected return and there was no sign of them. He frowned, turning his gaze toward Estrus' spires, wondering where they were and what they were doing.

"Cheer up, David," said Jessica from behind him, placing her hand on his shoulder comfortingly. "They'll be here. They've still got another half hour or so, and you know good and well that they're quite capable of taking care of themselves."

David relaxed a little—a very little. "Maybe, but none of us know anything about this world...I just wish they'd hurry."

"Well standing here and worrying won't make them get here any faster. Come over and sit with the rest of us. It'll make you feel better. It's like watching the clock: the longer you watch, the slower time passes."

David smiled weakly and turned to join them. He was thinking about how Jessica could always cheer him up, no matter how down he was, when suddenly there was a crash in the woods directly behind him. He whirled with lightning reflexes and his sword was in his hand before he knew it. Lumbering out of the woods, came a short figure dressed in chain armor, carrying an assortment of paraphernalia in his arms and in the backpack that crowned his wide shoulders. He dropped his packages with a crash and grunted in relief, looking wearily up at the two startled figures who were staring down at him.

"Not a very nice welcome for someone bringing gifts," commented Brandon dryly. "I didn't expect a twenty-one gun salute or anything, but if I'd known I was going to be attacked, I would've stayed away longer."

"You stupid dwarf! You should know better than to sneak up behind me like that," David laughingly commented as he sheathed his sword and clapped Brandon's right shoulder strongly. "Where have you been?"

"Wake up, David. I've been in Estrus. Remember? I'm on time aren't I?"

"Don't pay any attention to him, Brandon. He's just been moping around, worrying needlessly all morning," commented Jessica with a punch in the side for David and a hug for Brandon who flinched as his left shoulder was knocked. "What's wrong with your shoulder, Brandon? And where's Sean?" she asked, peering behind him as Christopher, Jodi, and Amy joined them.

"Now that's gonna take a little time to explain, and I think I'm gonna need a little help first," Brandon said as he wincingly removed his hauberk and revealed his wounded shoulder.

Silence reigned amidst the group for a moment until David caustically questioned, "What's happened?"

"Nothing much really. There's no problem, but I'd appreciate it if you'd doctor my little booboo while I explain," he said to Jessica, hoping that his nonchalance would rub off on the others.

However, there was concern in everyone's face as Jessica approached the now-sitting dwarf and removed the bloody bandages from his shoulder, inspecting the crusted wound. He slowly began to explain what had happened while she tore a small strip of her robe off, wet it in the river, and cleaned the wound thoroughly. It was small but deep and cut through the top of his left pectoral muscle. The worst thing, however, was that little fragments of Brandon's armor were scattered within the wound. Jessica placed her hands on it and concentrated hard. In her mind's eye, she pictured the fragments being pulled out and the wound closing. She mentally watched the scar slowly fade into a pale streak across Brandon's otherwise dark skin. She felt that familiar surge as arcane words deluged her lungs and fled quivering lips. She felt movement under her hands and a tightening of muscles in Brandon's shoulder. She shuddered and opened her eyes to see Brandon staring at her, obviously impressed by her abilities. "Thanks," he finally said, feeling the now healed shoulder.

"Sure," she smiled, opening her hand and letting the metallic shards fall between her fingers. "But be easy on it. The knife penetrated muscle, and your shoulder'll be sore for a couple of hours."

"No problem." He stared at the scattered shards of his armor as he flexed the shoulder, feeling a small twinge of pain, a very small one. "Anyway, we left the city and realized that we couldn't bring the horses or wagon through the woods to you guys. So we hid them a short distance from the road west of Estrus, and Sean stayed with them while I came to tell you. I told him that we'd go ahead and see the hermit for a map and return for him sometime tomorrow."

"Are you sure Sean'll be all right by himself?" asked David.

"I wouldn't worry," assured Brandon. "The wagon's well hidden and he doesn't have any more ale. It'd be pure chance if anyone found him. I'm more worried about how this hermit's gonna react to our request for a map."

David laughed. "Well, from what you said, I think he's just a harmless old man. He's probably a little crazy, but he doesn't sound dangerous."

Brandon nodded. "Oh. I almost forgot. I've got a few little presents for everyone." Brandon distributed the daggers and gave David his bow and quiver of white-feathered arrows.

"I don't suppose you brought anything for us to eat, did you?" questioned Christopher, secreting his dagger somewhere in the many folds of his robe.

"In my backpack," said Brandon with a smile. "What did you do for dinner last night, anyway?"

"We ate very well, thank you. We simply had Jessica conjure up some trout."

"Oh. That's too bad," said Brandon sarcastically.

"Hadn't we better get going?" asked Christopher.

"Yeah, I guess we'd better," said David. "But let's eat some breakfast first."

They ate some bread and finished off the trout from dinner, washing it all down with cool, fresh water from the flowing river. Soon afterward they shouldered their burdens and began their trek northward through the trees on the river's bank.

"I wouldn't have forgiven Sean so easily," said Jessica after listening to Brandon's story again since she had missed part of it while at the river, wetting the bandage.

"Well, I was pretty mad, myself, but I don't think he'll do it again. Anyway, we have to stick together till we get home. Maybe I'll roll his house or something when we get back." They all laughed.

"How much longer do you think it'll take us to get to the hermit's house?" asked Amy. "I'm getting a little tired."

"Probably about another hour," answered Brandon. "Maybe we should stop for a rest."

They rested in a small vale of birches and drank deeply from the river, quenching their thirst as best they could. The first two hours of their trip had passed fairly quickly; it was a beautiful day for a walk. The sun was shining brightly in the clear blue sky while nature frolicked under her magnificence, enjoying the autumn sun.

"Something's been nagging me about what you told us," said David seriously to Brandon after a few minutes of relaxation. "The man at the store told you that somebody else was looking for Mount Apocrys. Who do you think that was? And why was he looking for it?"

"I don't know, David," he answered also worriedly. "It's been bothering me, too."

"Well, according to Richards, that wizard Marrano made his plea for help to anyone who wanted the reward," stated Christopher who had just joined them. "This fellow probably heard about it and wanted to cash in on it."

"Yeah, and that means we're in a race with this guy, and we've just gained ourselves an enemy," said David. "I don't like that a bit." He paused. "Also, Brandon, I've been meaning to ask you how you took it when you had to kill those intruders. The rest of us might have to do the same before we get home." He said this slowly and reluctantly, watching Brandon intently, hoping that his probing would not upset the dwarf too much.

Brandon took a deep breath. "I just told myself that it was Rork that had done it and not me. I really didn't feel like I was in control. The fighting was pure reflex."

David nodded as the ladies returned from the river where they had been refreshing themselves, wetting their face with the cold water. They sat and rested for a few more minutes before Amy suggested they continue.

The last hour of their journey seemed to last longer than the first two combined; the farther they went, the more densely forested the ground became and the more difficult it was to continue. Brandon took the lead, his axe swinging like a scythe, to clear a path for them.

"Wait," David whispered, motioning for them to listen. They heard a high pitched voice nearby along with deep-throated laughter. They slowly continued in the direction of the sounds.

"I told you! I don't have it! Just leave me alone!" squealed the frightened, higher voice.

"That's not what we were told," said a rough, scratch baritone. "Now tell us where it is or we're gonna have to get unpleasant."

"May your mothers drown in camel spit for this you devil driven bastards!" shouted the high voice defiantly.

"My mother's already dead, so curse her all you want, but I still want to know where you've hidden it," said the deeper voice unconcernedly.

David and the others peered from the bushes into a small clearing with a wrecked and ransacked shack in it. There were a number of rough-looking individuals, maybe twenty, crowded around a larger, uglier man. His face was pitted with several crisscrossing scars and twisted into an evil grimace. He was well over six feet tall and heavily muscled, though still smaller than David...barely. He had a short, rather disgruntled-looking old man by his feet, dangling him off the ground. The poor old man was valiantly, albeit unsuccessfully, attempting to hit the other but his long, white beard was dangling over his eyes, obscuring his vision and blunting his agility.

"Leave me alone!" he shouted, flailing wildly.

David ushered Brandon around to the far side of the clearing and sent Christopher off a short distance to the left. The ladies retreated into the forest while the warrior strung his bow. He nocked an arrow and let it fly; it struck the leader in the arm. The man screamed and dropped the hermit, who landed on his head with a grunt and scurried away on all fours. Brandon came roaring out of the bushes with his axe raised. Some men turned to meet his charge but at the same moment a burst of flame erupted amidst them. The fetid stench of charred flesh filled the air as men, some burning, scattered in a confused ruckus. Another arrow sung from David's bow and struck a man solidly in his left eye. Brandon was engaged with three men as David leapt into the turmoil, sword sweeping from its scabbard like a manifestation of vengeance. He dispatched one man quickly through his lower abdomen and turned to meet another when a deep-throated yell rang through the trees, and the remaining men fled toward the shout, desperately evading the fighters' blades.

David gazed about him, sword dripping blood. Brandon was standing perhaps ten yards from him with his axe still raised and two bodies on the ground at his feet. One's head lay a few feet to his side while the other was cleanly shaven in two at the waist. Brandon's beard and arms were drenched in blood. There was a man lying in the middle of the clearing with a shaft protruding from his face. Christopher entered, looking at the remains of three men, charred beyond recognition, and frowned. "Only three," he murmured and his frown deepened.

David and Brandon looked at him silently for a moment before turning their gazes on each other and bursting into laughter. "Don't feel bad, Christopher," said Brandon at length, wiping away his tears. "Each of us only got two."

"Yeah, but I was aiming for a much larger target," he returned in a slightly regretful voice. "I should have got at least five."

"So, do better next time," said David, still grinning with inappropriate mirth. "Well, guys, I believe we've reached our destination."

"I think you're right, David. What there is of it," commented Christopher with a smirk, viewing the "house" at the center of the clearing. It amazed them all that the effigy was still standing; large sections of the walls were missing, and the ceiling leaned dangerously toward the river. The wizard sighed as he looked at the fruit of the first stage of their journey.

At that moment, the women returned. Jessica took one look about her at the carnage and wrinkled her nose in disgust. "Can we clean this place up a bit? It doesn't exactly pique my appetite," she commented with a vestige of a smile.

"Sure, sorry. Come on guys," said David, turning to meet the task. He wondered at Jessica's reaction. He would have thought that she would have fainted at that sight, and why was he laughing at murder? He had just killed two men and felt no remorse for the deed. He decided that he would have to think more about it later, but now they disposed of the bodies in the woods and returned to the clearing.

"Where's the hermit?" asked Amy, looking uncertainly at the clearing's unstable centerpiece.

There was a yelp and the sound of someone scrabbling along inside the termite-infested hut, and they caught a glimpse of a hunched figure fleeing away from the doorway.

"Does that answer your question?" asked David with a smile. He then turned to the shack and took a deep breath. "Come on out!" he yelled. "We won't hurt you!"

No answer.

"We just want to talk!" he continued. "The men who were here before are gone. You're safe!"

"Who are you?" came a small and muffled, yet defiant, voice from inside the shack.

"We're simple travelers in need of your service. My name is Graham," replied David.

"What do you want?"

"We're looking for a map."

A pause. "There are maps in Estrus. Go there and leave me alone."

"We already tried the city. Our destination isn't on any of their maps. They told us of your great skills, and we came in search of you."

"I'm just an old man! How could I help you?!" shouted a small, angry figure, appearing in the doorway.

"Indeed no, sir. You're much more than an 'old man'," replied David cajolingly. "You're an expert mapmaker."

The small figure smiled. He was perhaps five feet tall, very old and very dirty, with a scent that was overpowering even from a distance. His white beard hung down to below his knees, its tip caked in mud and other, less easily recognized, substances. The dirty gray rags that he used for clothing were ripped and plastered to his body by years of scum and dirt. "I am Rocnar Da'arputni. Come in and we'll talk." He turned and entered his house as the group followed, smiling at the old man and wrinkling their noses at the scent.

The shack looked, if possible, worse from the inside than it did from the outside. The sickeningly musty smell that enshrouded it was caused by the combination of years old dirt and mold that covered the wooden floor and the table. Aside from the table, a small wooden one with one leg shorter than the others, the hut's only furnishings were a chair and a pile of straw, apparently a bed. There were cobwebs all over the place and small rodents and reptiles were scurrying about on the floor and walls anxiously. A particularly large snake had taken up residence on the table and struck at anything that challenged its authority. It hissed at the hermit as he walked by. The little man murmured something but obviously shied away from the reptile.

David introduced the rest of the group by their characters' names as Rocnar stared at them suspiciously.

"All right then," he said. "I know who you are, but what do you want?"

"As I said before, we're travelers in need of a map to guide us," answered David. "Our problem is that none of the maps we've seen have had our destination marked on them. In Estrus, a man told my companion Rork," he indicated the dwarf, "that you were a skilled mapmaker and that we should see you for one."

The little man frowned. "Where do you want to go?"

"A mountain called Apocrys."

Rocnar stared at David suspiciously. "Why do you want to go there?"

"We're on a quest," answered David carefully.

"For what?"

David looked hard at the hermit. "A man," he lied.

Rocnar frowned, saying nothing. "The men you chased off were also after a map to Mount Apocrys. I wonder if there's a connection." It was now their turn to stare. "What'll you give me in return for the map?" he asked, smirking.

"We're willing to pay. How much do you want?" answered David.

Rocnar smiled. "Ten pieces of gold."

"I'll give you five," said David.

"I said ten and I meant ten! That's how much I want!" shouted Rocnar stubbornly, balling his hands into fists and banging on his chest as he hopped up and down.

David stared at Da'arputni momentarily and sighed. "Very

well. Ten it is." He removed his purse, counted out ten of the shiny coins and handed them to the little man who snatched them up greedily and ran out the door.

"Where's he going?" asked Brandon, half intent on following the crazy old man and beating the map out of him, but Christopher grabbed his shoulder.

"Let him go," he said. "He'll come back."

"How can you be so sure?"

"Trust me."

Brandon looked up at Christopher quizzically and shrugged. "Your call," he said, displaying his hands helplessly.

"Who is he anyway?" asked Jodi momentarily. "You act as if you know him."

"I'm not quite sure who he is," answered Christopher with a frown. "But there's something familiar about him. I can't quite place it, but I feel like I know him." They all stared at him silently.

"I wonder what he'll do with that money," mused Amy.

"I haven't the slightest idea," answered Christopher. "But I bet he won't spend it on a new bath tub." They laughed as Rocnar returned with a rolled-up parchment.

"Here," he said and handed the scroll to David, collapsing onto his straw bed, belching loudly. There he lay while all attention turned to the map.

David unrolled the parchment and stretched it out on the unsteady table after brushing the defiant snake off with his sword. As David and the others studied the map, he realized that it was, indeed, magnificent; very smooth and very precise in both appearance and feel. David's eyes scanned it thoroughly until they came to rest on a name written across a mountain peak on the west side of the continent. It read, in great red letters, "Apocrys." It was far away from the city of Estrus, near the western coast, and the road seemed fraught with everything from mountains to swampland.

"How far is that?" asked Jessica from David's right.

"A little over a fortnight's fast riding but longer for you— much longer," answered Rocnar, now sitting in the chair near them. A sigh emanated from the figures around the table almost as a single breath.

"Well, at least we know where we're headed now," commented Amy, feigning happiness in an attempt to cheer up the company—and herself. They were now seated about a small campfire outside Rocnar's decrepit hut. They had been forced out by the little man because of their "civilized stench" after being fed something that only remotely resembled food— actually more similar to thick glue but black.

"Two weeks! What'll be happening at home while we're gone for so long?" asked Jodi, worried and outraged at the magnitude of their loss.

"I don't know," said David. "All I do know is that we've got to get to Apocrys and home. We can't worry about how long we're gone or what's happening there. Not now, at least. That's secondary. We've got to concentrate on what we're doing." He was trying to keep some semblance of order to their position in spite of the distress that everybody—including himself—felt as the realization of the length of their journey crashed into them, numbing their senses. He knew that they had to keep everything focused on the dilemma at hand if they were to survive. That meant not worrying about what was happening at home or how long they had been gone. Any distraction at a crucial time could be fatal for one or all of them.

"David's right," said Brandon. "Let's not worry about home till we get there. Personally, I'm a little tired, so I'm gonna turn in. Wake me for the second watch." The dwarf curled up next to the fire and promptly slept. He was reluctantly joined by the rest of his companions except David who took the first watch, leaving the dog watch for Christopher.

As he sat, David thought about the events of the day. He had killed two men and wounded another, but he felt no remorse for his actions and, even more amazingly, no fear of revenge. None of the others had seemed to feel at all badly either. This seemed very odd to him. And what about Jessica and the other women? None of them had even flinched at the sight of the dead, mutilated corpses on the ground. It was all very confusing. Maybe it had something to do with the fact that none of them had really been in control of their actions. He knew that he had not thought to swing his sword or to shoot his bow; his body's reflexes had taken over. It really was not him, or the others, that had killed the bandits, that had committed those repulsive crimes, but that still did not explain the ladies' reactions. He would have to ask Jessica about that—what she felt and why she reacted so callously.

David thought about this for the rest of his watch but never came up with any satisfying answers except a vague theory about temporary takeover by their characters' minds. After he woke up Brandon and lay down to sleep, his last thought was of Sean. Was he all right? And had he had any trouble in their absence? But exhaustion finally won out and he slept undisturbed.

"And while these guys were sleeping easily, I was watching over our wagon," complained Sean to Lady Gahdnawen.

"That doesn't sound too hard," said the Lady assuasively.

"Well, it wouldn't have been if things had gone as smoothly as I expected, but things became a little more complicated due to forces beyond my control."

"Beyond your control, my ass!" broke in Brandon. "You know as well as I that it was as much a direct result of your drunken escapade as the three cut-throats who broke into our room in the inn!"

"Honestly!" complained Sean, grinning slyly. "I'm completely innocent."

Brandon rolled his eyes and shrugged, overwhelmed by the thief's audacity.

"Please continue, Sean," prompted Gahdnawen, and the thief began his narrative.

It was dark, and Sean sat cross-legged between the horse-accompanied wagon and the road, perhaps fifty yards away. He had lit no fire for fear the light might attract animals or thieves. He sat on a blanket he had acquired from the wagon so that the chilling earth would not sap his warmth. He knew that it would be a long night since he could not sleep, but he comforted himself with the reassurance that he would sleep the whole night tomorrow. Tonight, however, I've got to watch over our possessions. He yawned sleepily.

Crack!!

Even as he heard the sound from behind the wagon, he silently scampered away into the woods surrounding the clearing and climbed a tall oak. High in the branches, he had a good vantage point from which to view the dark clearing in the meager moonlight that infiltrated the trees.

From there, he could see the improvised surreptitious movement around the wagon, and he knew that he had not imagined the sound. His sharp eyes saw figures creeping around the clearing. One, two, three, four, five... He sat motionless, watching the figures systematically search the premises, seeing their furtive actions—actually, they were pretty clumsy, but they were trying awfully hard to be stealthy.

Then his quick thieves' ears picked up words in the night. "Where's the owner?" asked a high-pitched nasal whisper.

"I don't know," answered a deeper one. "He must've heard us coming. That little man should've been easy prey."

Damn! thought Sean to himself. I was watched. They

know there's only one of me…but I still have the advantage.

"He's got to be around here somewhere," said a third voice.

"Maybe he's run," came a fourth as it and a fifth shadowy figure joined the group forming in front of the wagon like a shadowy black mass.

"I doubt it, Lacrec. He's probably nearby," returned the deep-voiced one. "He didn't look like the type to run so easily."

"Graft, go and look around the woods. We'll continue searching the wagon," said the third figure, and the one with the high voice disappeared into the trees to the right of Sean, moving actually quite sneakily. The thief chuckled to himself as he followed the fool.

Graft, a lean man of thirty-two years, had followed Sean and Brandon out of Estrus that morning and knew how clumsily they had trod. Therefore, he was not afraid of the little man sneaking up on him. Besides, he had always prided himself on his stalking ability. He was mean and ruthless, with no living relatives and few friends. He had killed often before and smiled to himself as he premeditated killing this little man. He could almost taste his prey's blood as he felt the man's presence nearby and knew that their encounter would be soon. His acuity was alerted as he felt something close behind him, and he whirled…

Rhiza, Lacrec, Tam, and Fala stood about the fire they had carelessly built while awaiting Graft's return. "Where is that fool?" Rhiza was asking when a figure stumbled out of the trees. "Well, did you get him?"

The figure took another step and fell on his face in front of them. "Damn!" shouted Rhiza as he drew his sword and advanced on Graft's limp body. He turned the body over and studied it. Its stomach had been sliced open, and Graft seemed to be fighting to hold his innards in even after death. Then

Rhiza noticed that a message had been carved into the man's chest. It read: Bugs One : Fudd Nothing. Rhiza kicked the body and cursed it as his three comrades stared in horror.

"What the hell does that mean?!" he shouted, half expecting to see giant roaches crawling out of the trees.

"Oh, God!" wined Fala. "What's happened to him?!"

"What's a Fudd?" asked Lacrec, eyes looking worriedly about him.

"Forget it, dammit! Split up! Tam, you come with me! Lacrec, you and Fala search eastward! If you don't find anything within ten minutes, get your asses back here!" They left.

Lacrec and Fala crept stealthily through the woods. Ten minutes passed slowly so they turned and headed back toward the camp. Quickly, Fala who was leading fell flat on his face with a grunt, bloodying his nose on a root.

"You clumsy fool!" said Lacrec laughingly. "Can't you manage to stay on your feet?"

"Shut up!" snapped Fala, angry and scared. "I tripped over something." He reached down and felt a large, taught vine over his feet. "What the—" he began but halted when he saw a movement in the woods.

A shadow crept out of the trees and stood behind Lacrec. "I'm hunting hunters, heh, heh, heh," it said as it drove a shimmering dagger deep into Lacrec's ribs. "No more meek little wabbit for me." The shadow then passed back into the trees like a fuzzy memory of horror as the whimpering Fala jumped to his feet and started running, screaming in panic. He ran away from the camp.

Rhiza and Tam had found nothing and had returned to the camp quickly. A scream echoed in the night to the east as they stood, impatiently waiting. Tam looked at Rhiza uncertainly. "Fools," he retaliated.

A few minutes passed, silence enshrouding the trees, but

then an object flew from the woods and landed in the fire, which sputtered and cracked in return. The two stared at it and, looking lifelessly back at them were the eyes of Fala in his decapitated head, rictus gaping in a silent scream as the fire melted his skin, hair curling in seared strands. The sickeningly sweet smell of charred flesh filled the air as Rhiza rushed for the trees with his sword at the ready. Tam heard the clang of metal a single time, followed by a grunt and a thud as his leader collapsed at the tree-line, spurting blood from the gash in his throat.

Silence returned. A few minutes passed; Tam stood motionless, paralyzed with fear, awaiting his doom. A thump behind him and the reaper had come. Sean jerked the man's head back. His throat was slit within a split second, and the crimson fluid did not even have time to stain his tunic before Tam's body hit the ground. Sean cleaned his dagger and sword on Rhiza's shirt and searched the bodies for anything useful. "Damn. No carrots," he murmured to himself as he searched and disposed of the bodies mechanically, unfeelingly. He extinguished the fire and threw the still-smoldering head into the woods.

"The bunny from hell," he laughed as he sat back down, smiling quietly.

In the morning at Rocnar's hermitage, Christopher awakened them all and they breakfasted on the old man's gruel which he grudgingly passed out in minute shares. They thanked him for his "generosity" and started back toward Estrus, looking forward to their reunion with Sean.

In their wake, ululating laughter, unheard by them, crackled from the hermit's shack like electrified animosity. Not the high-pitched cackle of the crazed little man, but a deeper more cruel laugh like the barking howl of a rabid wolf. If someone had looked back and was very perceptive, they might have seen more than they had bargained for. They might have perceived, very far away, in the back of their mind, a man dressed in black with a shaggy black beard sitting in a high-backed chair laughing at the party as they walked away. The master of puppets was very pleased with himself today.

Slough of Despond

It was a dreary morning, dew on the grass, as the company trudged through the forest in total silence except for a few scattered words that squeezed from gloomy lips like murmured resignation. Very little noise was heard in all of nature's abode. The animals were hushed and quiet as if in anticipation of a great and tumultuous storm. Indeed, there were dark, angry-looking clouds on the eastern horizon, and a chill breeze originating from the same direction whisked by, bringing the clouds closer and closer with great alacrity. A solitary seabird was flying inland, flapping its wings at a leisurely pace as if he were unaware or unafraid of the storm that was breathing Death's cold breath down his neck.

"Looks like we're in for some foul weather," commented Christopher gloomily, gesturing over his left shoulder at the impending storm.

"Will we have enough time to make it back to the wagon before it hits?" asked Amy, looking at the storm balefully.

"There's no telling. It depends on how fast it's coming at us," answered Brandon. "But I don't think we're gonna make it."

The remainder of the trek back to their point of arrival was

wearying, for no one was much in the mood to discuss anything—
except for scattered complaints about the angry clouds. The events
of the prior day, especially the realization of the distance they must
travel, lay heavily on their shoulders, weighing them down more
than any armor or baggage could. It dampened their spirits even
more than the slight mist which soon began to sprinkle down on
their heads.

As they reached the clearing in which they had spent their first
night, the storm hit in full force. Its fury was magnificent! Trees
bowed under the force of the wind and the rain pelted them like
hail. Soon their clothes were soaked and their hair was plastered
to their faces, but they trudged on, denying the howling wind and
violent rain that roiled around them.

David's long brown hair was drenched and fell in front of his
eyes, obscuring his vision. It ignored his futile attempts to brush
it back and continued annoying him. His armor felt interminably
heavy and slick as it slid on his chest and arms, chaffing the skin
badly. "If I don't get out of this rain soon, I'm gonna rust in place."

"Like the tin man?" inquired Jessica, a faint smile teasing the
corners of her mouth.

"Follow the yellow brick road!" added Brandon.

David grunted, glaring at Brandon and attempting to scowl at
Jessica.

"How much farther?" inquired Christopher, a convulsion of
thunder making his words barely audible.

"We're almost there," answered Brandon. "See, there's Estrus just ahead of us."

Estrus was, if possible, even worse in the rain, as a musty odor
was added to the fetor of defecation that pervaded on the road. This
worsened the effect of nausea on them and made their stomachs
churn uncomfortably. They traveled along the road, their impetus
barely lasting, until Brandon stopped, ushering them into the
woods.

As they entered the foliage, the smell of greenery stifled

the reek of putrefaction, making it possible for them to breath comfortably again. This they accepted most gratefully, taking their breaths in great mouthfuls as if they were drowning. They followed the small trail that materialized in front of them and soon came across a clearing that contained a wagon, a number of horses huddled closely in front of it. The remains of a campfire lay in front of the wagon along with a small vigilant figure who was huddled up next to it, a blanket almost completely covering him.

"Sean!" shouted Brandon as they entered the clearing. "Don't you have enough sense to go in out of the rain?!"

The hunched figure grinned up at him and leapt to his feet, pumping Brandon's outstretched hand. "You know I've always been a bit of a puddle-hopper," said Sean jokingly to his friends. "You look as wet as I feel. Let's get inside." He bowed and ushered the others in, shivering and shaking with the cold wetness.

"Much better," said David, removing his corselet and drying it as best he could with a blanket he found within. The other pieces quickly followed.

It was a little crowded in the wagon with all of them crammed into it, but it was still much more comfortable than standing out in the rain. The closeness was not a total detriment, however, for the body heat that was created warmed them and helped dry their dripping bodies. They removed their cloaks and donned the new ones that Brandon and Sean had purchased in Estrus.

"Did you have any problems, Sean?" asked David after they had dried off.

"Not many," he answered with a malicious grin. "What about you? What'd you find out?"

"Mount Apocrys is about two weeks ride west of us," David replied, looking curiously at Sean, wondering what "not many" meant. "And we're not the only ones headed that way. We had a run-in with some mercenaries and had to kill a few men. Surprisingly, they were also looking for a map with Mount Apocrys on it."

"Probably the same guys we were told about in Estrus."

"You said you didn't have 'many' problems," truncated Jodi. "What exactly does that mean?"

Sean told them his story as best he could; in other words, he exaggerated a little about how many thieves there were and how great he was, but he did pretty much cover everything that happened—and more.

"You've got to make a joke out of everything, don't you?" brandished Jessica.

"Only when the opportunity arises," corrected Sean. "And in this case, it arose greatly."

"Personally, I'm glad to see that Bugs finally got smart and snuffed ol' Elmer," commented Jodi. "Hurrah for Social Darwinism! Survival of the fittest!"

"Well, I still think it was a bit melodramatic," asserted Jessica.

"What does that matter?" asked Christopher. "I'm certain they wouldn't recognize it if it were."

"All right, all right," gave in Jessica. "I can see I'm outnumbered. Put up the thumb screws and let me go."

"If we have to," whined Sean. "But only if you tell me more about what happened to you. All I've gotten so far is the end of your trip; tell me more about your encounter with the mercenaries."

"Well, I don't know the whole story because I was sent away during part of it," she said with a frosty look for the smiling David. "So I'll let David tell you about it."

Sean turned to David—no small accomplishment in the cramped quarters—and cocked an eyebrow curiously, wondering how in the world the warrior had managed to send Jessica away from anything. When David had finished telling about their encounter with the vagabonds, Sean halted him with an upraised hand and turned to Christopher. "Only three?" he asked, shocked at first, but a grin suffused his face and he began to laugh.

Christopher looked back at him frowning, then smiling, and finally laughing, himself. After Sean had gained control again, he said, "Sorry to interrupt, David, but that was just too much. 'Only three?!'" he laughed, wiping the tears from his eyes and fighting furiously to stay his laughter. "Poor baby!"

David finished the story but not before he had added a few rude comments about his armor and the weather.

"Looks like we all got our metaphorical feet wet yester-day, doesn't it?" asked Sean as he looked at the others.

"And our literal ones today," said Brandon, eyeing his wet armor and tunic as well as the glistening axe that leaned against the wagon next to him, realizing that he and his friends had all managed to kill several people within the last twenty-four hours.

"Speaking of which," said David. "I've been meaning to talk to all of you about that. We just killed several men and none of us seem to feel the least bit sorry about it, at least as far as I can tell. Back home, if you even saw a dead man, Jessica, you'd have nightmares for a week. And I dare say that the same goes for each of you, too." He gestured to the other women. "What's happening to us? How is it that we killed eleven men yesterday and are sitting here joking about it? What's gotten into us?"

"I don't know," answered Jessica. "It just didn't bother me, except the stench, that is. I don't know why, but it just didn't."

"Me neither," reiterated Amy. "It was as if I had been desensitized to those emotions." Jodi nodded her agreement.

"It felt to me like I was out having fun," said Sean. "I just didn't think of it as being murder, if that's what it was. It came naturally...like I'd done it countless times before." Nods from the other men. "I did it and didn't think about it. Even on reflection, I don't regret it."

"I wonder if it might have something to do with spending so much time in the bodies of people who killed as a way of life," said Christopher pensively. "You know, the more time I spend here, the more desensitized I am from my own emotions. We become our counterparts in this realm...sort of a self-defense mechanism since none of us could survive here as we were."

"That makes a strange sort of sense," commented Brandon. "When I killed those guys in Estrus, I was bothered a little, but yesterday I didn't even think about it. Like the second time was easier than the first or the longer I'm here, the more automatic it is."

"Does that mean that eventually we'd be completely taken over by our characters?" asked Amy, alarmed as the idea sparked in her mind.

"That's a definite possibility, but I think it would take much longer than we're going to be here. Besides, if we're conscious of the fact, it'd be very hard for us to lose control. All they do is take over during times of stress and danger," said Christopher uncertainly. "But we'd better make sure we don't get too carried away in those situations."

"I'm starting to feel uncomfortably like Bill Bixby," commented Sean humorously. "If my skin turns green, I'm gonna have a nervous breakdown."

"You must be right," said David, ignoring Sean entirely. "I can feel that Graham is still inside my body, but I can also feel that my mind is a lot stronger than his. I don't think he can regain control while I'm aware of him...and yet—we did kill, without thinking. It's like when you're a kid playing soldier, shooting people with your plastic pistols."

"Some game," commented Amy.

Christopher looked at David thoughtfully. "Yes, I can feel Omnibus too, but for now I'm stronger than him. However, I'm growing more like him by being in his body. I'm sure of it."

There was uneasy agreement among them, and they were glad for the warmth and closeness of each other as they watched the deluge outside. A stranger seeing this group might think, "How sad and lost they look." Their words became fewer as their thoughts flew home on halcyon wings until, around noon, the rain slackened off and finally quit. Their roving minds centered more on the present, leaving the past for the future as they roused themselves once more.

"What say we eat some lunch and begin our journey?" suggested Jessica. "The quicker we get started, the quicker we'll get through."

"Good idea," commented Brandon, rubbing his belly hungrily.

They lunched on cheese and bread that had stayed pretty much dry in the packs that were stacked in one corner of the crowded wagon. It was definitely not a filling meal and aided very little in raising their downcast spirits, but it did give them enough strength to continue. They spent the better part of an hour hitching the horses up to the wagon, and when the large white mare refused to be so imprisoned, David finally decided to ride it. Brandon also kept his shaggy little pony free, and Sean kept the sleek black mare loose in order to run reconnaissance for the company as they rode through the countryside. They hooked the pack horse to the back of the wagon so that it would be pulled along behind where it was out of the way but could not escape.

As they regained the road and struck out northwesterly, David, Brandon, and Sean rode ahead of the wagon while the women stayed in it and Christopher drove. The muddy road was completely deserted as they began their trek, but as the clouds passed overhead, the sun began to peek out from behind its shroud, and the temperature started to slowly rise along with their hopes. A few peasants and merchants passed them on the road, but they ignored these travelers and concentrated their thoughts and words on each other.

"It certainly is a nice day to have started so miserably," David heard himself saying through smiling lips.

"Yeah," agreed Sean with his customary grin. "How far should we travel today?"

"I'm not sure. I don't think we know how to judge that, but I guess we should make it a pretty good distance onto the plains."

No truly important thought interrupted the riders as they rode on at a comfortable pace, and after a few hours, they reached the edge of the forest and entered onto a broad expanse of grassland. The grass was not even wet from the storm that had passed a short time earlier, and the flowers blossomed grandly about them; daisies staring up at them with smiling faces and dragon-lilies snarling at them as they passed, attempting to ford their progress with blazes of crimson.

"Mind if I join you?" asked Amy of Christopher as she peeked out of the wagon with excited blue eyes that leapt from one flower to the next, then to the sky and the brilliant sun that shone in it.

"No, not at all," answered Christopher with a broad smile for the young woman who had barely been a high school graduate days before.

"It really is beautiful out here, isn't it?"

Christopher looked at Amy for a long moment, smiling at her with his eyes as his lips perked at the corners before he straightened them once more. "Yes, it most certainly is," he answered, though he was paying little attention to the day about him and more to the night that encircled Amy's head in a billowing cloud of short curly hair. "Much more now that you've joined me."

As Amy realized what Christopher meant, she looked a little startled, but she soon regained her composure. "I've never seen grassland like this before. Have you, Christopher?" she asked with a deep probing look into his eyes as he looked away at the beautiful countryside. She was very curious why Christopher had suddenly noticed her.

"No. I can't say that I have," he answered before returning his gaze to her face. "It reminds me of photographs I've seen of Ireland, but there were hills there…and those pictures weren't as beautiful as this. After all, they never had you in them."

Amy blushed outright at Christopher's undisguised admiration. She was not quite sure how to react. For an answer she simply looked at Christopher with a number of different emotions in her liquid eyes. She pursed her lips and began to speak. "I—" But she was cut off as Jessica and Jodi's heads poked out of the fold of curtains that hung in the doorway of the wagon.

"Hi there," said Jodi as she seated herself between the two robed figures. "We thought we'd come out and enjoy the view, too."

"Sure," said Amy, attempting to hide the blush that was still rosying her cheeks. "I'm going back inside anyway." She returned to the protective canopy of the wagon, Jessica taking her place.

After returning to the solitude of the wagon's interior, Amy tried to contain her emotions—or at least understand them. Her heart was pounding and her breath was coming in gasps. She did not know what was happening to her. Christopher had never acted that way before, and she had never felt anything like the emotions that were churning inside her, making her so weak. She had always found Christopher attractive, but she did not think he even really noticed her. She slowly regained control and sat down to try and discern what had just happened. To her own surprise, she found herself smiling broadly.

As the day began to draw to a close, they decided to halt and drove off the road. They built a fire and unhooked the horses from the tack, letting them graze for a short time before tying them again to the wagon's side.

"I don't know about you guys, but I'd like some fresh meat for dinner," suggested David.

"Oh, that would be sooooo nice," answered Jodi whose stomach chose that exact moment to grumble loudly. The others giggled at her but quickly found that her stomach was not the only one growling—and Brandon's was roaring like a lion.

"How about some fried chicken," suggested Sean, rubbing his hands together.

"Yeah, with mashed potatoes, green beans, French fries, and how 'bout some yeast rolls," added Amy with a smile.

"Good idea. Why don't you go pay a quick visit to the Colonel? I'm sure he'd appreciate your business." They all laughed merrily at Brandon's snide remark. "While you guys are cracking jokes, I'm sitting here starving to death."

"I think I'll go for a hunt and save our shrunken friend from certain death," said David, stringing his bow and starting off into the closing darkness. He soon returned with two fine conies.

"Hey! I ordered chicken!" complained Sean with a grin. "And rabbits aren't chickens! I'm sure of it!"

"If you can find a chicken, I'll be happy to cook it for you," answered David as he stuck the rabbits on a spit and placed it over the fire that had been prepared in his absence. "But I haven't seen any recently."

As the rabbits roasted, the party inhaled the exciting aroma. "I don't know if I like the idea of eating rabbit after my little encounter with Fudd and his companions. I feel like a cannibal," said Sean humorously. "Besides, it brings back memories of the last time I had rabbit."

"Oh, really?" asked Jodi. "And when was that?"

"Why, Easter, of course," answered Sean with another grin. Disgusted groans and a few scattered laughs leapt from his fellows' mouths.

By the time the rabbits were done, the company was starving for the food as well as for silence from Sean's jibes. They dined on the steaming meat with bread and some wine from the flasks. It was all very refreshing—especially the wine—and put them in the mood for a deep sleep.

"I'll take first watch tonight," offered Christopher after he had finished his meal. "But I think I'll take a short walk first, to wake me up before the rest of you retire for the evening."

"I'll go with you," said Amy, rising to her feet hurriedly to join the wizard, eyes downcast demurely to hide her excitement.

Christopher stared at her for a long moment in silence before they left the camp, and Amy felt the blood rush to her face again.

"What was that about?" asked Jessica of David after the couple had left.

"I may be wrong, but it looks to me like we have a romance budding in our midst," he answered with a smile.

"Well, I don't know about them, but there's another romance blossoming inside the firelight."

David smiled at her and then drew her into a warm embrace. He guided her over to the fire where the others already lay. "Let's lie down and wait for our 'young lovers' to return."

Christopher and Amy did not return for a long while, and when they did, they stayed awake together for the first watch. Their proximity and their exchanged looks said that their walk had turned out to be much more than a simple stroll in the countryside. It seemed that a more powerful magic than any wielded by man was alive and well in this world of dreams.

"Perhaps this is a good place to stop for now," interrupted Lady Gahdnawen. "The clerics of the Temple will undoubtedly wish to hear the rest of your story later. They love to hear about what's happened to travelers in our world."

"Then tell us," asserted David, pleadingly. "How's Jessica?"

"She's fine for the time being," answered Gahdnawen, "but we must act quickly. The spell I've cast on her will last perhaps a week but no longer. We must decide what to do and soon."

"A malspirare has taken her soul," began Christopher, squirming. He looked more than a little uncomfortable in the white clerical robe that he was wearing.

"I know what's happened to her," interrupted the Lady coldly. "Under normal circumstances, I could defeat the malspirare and retrieve Jessica's soul easily, but there are some circumstances here that will make this case much more difficult."

"What 'circumstances'?" asked Jodi from David's left.

"For one, Jessica's soul is not the soul that rightly belongs in this body. Also, the malspirare that took her soul is a very powerful one that I have met on more than one occasion: Menovence. There is great enmity between us." This last she said with a little flicker of emotion in her eyes, the first she had shown. "But the most difficult part of it is that she's been under the spell for longer than it's wise for her to be. It'll be most trying and will take more time than you have since you cannot stay here for more than a few days."

"Excuse me for interrupting," broke in Sean, "but why's that?"

She looked at him sharply and spoke reprovingly. "There is a little matter of a quest, is there not, thief?" she said with more interest than it seemed she should have in the matter, but nonetheless, Sean felt rebuked.

"But why is there such a hurry?" asked Brandon. "The amulet'll still be there when this is taken care of, won't it?"

Lady Gahdnawen peered at Brandon for a long moment before answering. "No. No, it won't. Your acquaintance, Peccare, is still intending to take it, Brandon. You must beat him to it!" She stressed this last remark sharply. "There's more at stake than you know."

Confusion clouded their minds momentarily. What did she mean?

"If the amulet falls into his hands, there'll be hell to pay," she continued. "The fact is that you may stay for two days only. At dawn, two days hence, I'll set you on your way, and you must finish the task that's been appointed to you. I'll do all I can for Jessica," she said, staring at David intensely. "You must trust me. But that's enough of this talk for the morning." She stood. "You should spend the day recuperating from your travels, which have been long and trying. You may do as you like, but I recommend spending some of the day in our gardens. It's most restful there and your spirit, as well as your body, will heal amongst its medicinal odors. I'll spend the rest of the day learning as much as I can about Jessica and will call you back again this evening to tell you how I've fared. Until then, my children, I will say farewell."

At her last words, Purus and Inoce entered and led them out of the room. There were many longing looks cast back at Jessica as she lay, unmoving on her large couch. There was much they wanted to ask of Lady Gahdnawen; they had only voiced a little of it. But perhaps they could learn more later, after they had rested.

They all followed the two sisters back to the guest rooms

once more. Standing outside the doors, Inoce spoke to them. "You are permitted to go anywhere in the Temple. If you find yourselves lost or confused, simply ask one of the clerics that should be around. They will direct you."

Purus added, "Everybody here is aware of your presence and of who you are though they don't know where you are truly from. They'll help you in any way they can. We'll be in our Lady's quarters, helping her, if you need either of us." She and her sister turned and left.

"Well, what'll we do?" asked Christopher, looking a little more morose than usual.

"I think I'll do a little exploring," answered Sean. "I'd like to see what the rest of this place looks like."

"I don't feel like exploring," said David somberly. "I think I'll go to the gardens to rest. Maybe they can heal some of my wounds," he said without sincerity, stroking the argentic streak on his face as if it were a recalcitrant emblem of his pain.

"I believe I'll join you," said Jodi cheerily from his side. "I can use the rest, too."

"I suppose I'll try to find the library," said Christopher with a mote of spite. "If this accursed place has one. Maybe I'll be able to learn a new spell." He marched off, Amy following in gloomy silence.

"Don't steal anything, Sean," said Jodi as she and David walked off towards the gardens. Sean smiled back at her as he passed.

The thief wandered around the palace, simply exploring in order to learn the ways of these strange people. The clerics inhabiting the Temple of Galead were not like Jessica and Amy; they were less outspoken and more introspective, almost shy. At one point in his travels, Sean found himself in a large room cluttered with great machines. These mechanisms, although definitely crude, were indisputably used for sewing. Upon closer examination, the thief noticed that they really were not machines but only an extremely complicated loom.

As he wandered in the room, Sean was brought to his senses by a sound behind him. He turned and found himself facing the most beautiful woman he had ever seen. She gasped as she met his eyes. She was almost as tall as him, with long black hair that hung in curly spirals down her back. Her eyes were intensely intelligent, looking as though they understood everything that Sean had ever thought, although they did not hold the same omniscient twinkle that Lady Gahdnawen's had. Her slender body was clad in the same white robes as all of the clerics, but there was a turquoise arm band wrapped about her left biceps. "May I help you, sir?" she asked haltingly with a very shy smile that seemed to brighten the room even more than the luminescent stones that it was made of.

"I—" faltered Sean. For the first time in his life, Sean was utterly and totally at a loss for words. She looked back at him and blinked her ice blue eyes. Mouth slightly open, she took in his sleek form: the ruggedly handsome face; the black, flashing eyes; the sharp, jutting chin; the blue-black hair; the well-muscled body; the unnatural charisma.

As the two stood there, gawking at each other like two twinkle-eyed adolescents, another person entered the room, interrupting their quietus. "I see that you've located our sewing gallery," said Purus as she approached them. "This is where we sew all our garments and tapestries."

"Remarkable," said Sean, quickly regaining his composure.

"And I see you've met Bellus," continued Purus smiling at the beautiful cleric who returned the smile, a little shaken. "I only came to tell you," she continued, speaking to Sean, "that the noon meal will be served in the dining hall in another thirty minutes. You are, of course, invited to share it." She bowed. "I must tell the rest of your friends, however, so I'll leave you in Bellus' very capable hands. She's one of our most promising young clerics." Purus left.

The thief and cleric stood there for a moment, staring at one another silently, before Sean broke the silence once more. "Bellus," he finally said. The young cleric almost blushed when she heard her name. "Would you mind showing me how one of these machines works?"

Bellus bowed and quickly began explaining the mechanism, still blushing slightly. It was really fascinating and would have kept Sean's attention, except that he could not concentrate on anything except the cleric's face. For some reason, he was completely drawn to her and could not think of anything else. She was beautiful, but it was something more than that. Something about her overall demeanor drew him to her like a moth to a flame.

After a quick demonstration, Bellus attempted to leave, but Sean held her back. "I'm afraid that I don't know where the dining hall is from here," he lied. "Would you kindly walk me there?"

Bellus looked more uncomfortable than ever, but she seemed pleased by the prospect. Her knowledgeable eyes now held fascination, but Sean did not notice this. He was too busy trying to figure out why he felt so nervous all of a sudden.

As they walked down the hall, Sean asked Bellus about herself. "I'm a simple student," she answered with a smile. "I'm learning the art of the cleric, now."

"Purus spoke highly of you," offered Sean. "Do you excel at your learning or simply hold an innate talent for healing." He paused for a moment only. "I'm fairly sure it must be the latter."

"Why do you say that, sir?" she asked, curiosity overcoming her shyness.

Sean smiled. "Because, I know that if I were sick or dying, a simple glance at your lovely face would be enough to give me the strength to carry on."

Bellus blushed magnificently and shifted uneasily, unsure of what to say. She did not know whether to be pleased or embarrassed, so she settled for a combination of the two, blushing and smiling. "Thank you," she breathed dizzily.

"Bellus," continued Sean, feeling confidence welling inside him, "Would you do me a favor?" She looked at him with pure and innocent apathy, nodding ever so slightly. "Would you please meet me in the sewing room after we've eaten? I'd like to speak more with you about the Temple."

"I'd love to!" was the excited reply that rushed from her lips before she could stifle it. She blushed again at her forwardness. "Anything to serve you," she added hastily, trying to cover up the excitement that her smile exuded by bowing her head meekly, gazing at him from under thin eyebrows. However, Sean was no fool. He recognized her excitement and was thrilled by it.

As they reached the dining hall, he thanked her for her company and bade her farewell, saying that he looked forward to seeing her after lunch...and he really did.

Visions of mortality

Sean entered the dining hall and sat next to Amy; everyone had already arrived. As he looked about, the thief noticed that there were a number of high-ranking clerics, male and female, seated with them at the table. They were garbed in silver robes like Lady Gahdnawen's, only without the gold trim. He looked at each of them intently, summing them up with that singular glance, before returning his gaze to his friends. David looked sad but seemed to find much comfort in Jodi's smiling presence. She was telling them about the gardens she and David had relaxed in.

According to her, these had to be the most beautiful gardens in the entire world, with everything blooming and flourishing even though it was now past time for them to flourish. She was very emphatic about the beauty and intoxicating scents, describing in detail the joy she had felt while basking in their loveliness, bathing in their effervescent aroma.

When he was asked about his morning, Sean only said that he had been exploring the premises. He did not tell them about Bellus. He was not sure why, but he felt that he should keep quiet about that meeting and their impending rendezvous for now.

It was as he finished his description of the palace that the clerics began asking about their trip. With a sigh, David dove into the narrative with a rapidity brought on by his over-whelming desire to escape the tale—or at least its telling. "Our first day along the plains that lead up to the Desert of Suspi was quite bland and needs no description. However after we had spent our first night there, I had an interesting encounter that I would have rather avoided. However, with the aid of our illustrious dwarf, I was forced into it. Anyway…"

"Get up, David. We've got company," came Brandon's voice out of a haze into the sleeping warriors drowsy mind.

However, David forced himself to swim out of that se-verely shadowed sleep and leapt to his feet, sword in hand, peering about him for the intruders and finding…nothing. "Where?" he whispered to Brandon, whom he noticed had not even removed his axe from its back-strap.

Brandon laughed at his friend wholeheartedly. This con-fused David even more, and he found himself growing angry with the dwarf. "Right behind you."

David whirled, sword at the ready, and felt something cold against his leg. Startled, he jumped and looked down into the gaping maw of a strange animal, but upon further examina-tion, he realized that it was just a dog. Not even a pretty one. Just a mutt of some sort with long brown hair caked in mud and brown eyes peering out from behind a mouth predominantly occupied by a tremendous slavering tongue.

"I think you can put up your sword, David," Brandon commented with a wry grin. "I don't think we're in any danger."

"You scared me you bastard! Where the hell did this mongrel come from?" he asked, attempting to shake the dog off his leg where it was busy licking and sniffing.

"From the west," answered Brandon.

"Why'd you wake me over a dog?"

"Well, I thought you liked 'em, and it's about time to get up anyway."

"Well, I don't. I'm partial to cats; so next time let me sleep."

"Okay, compadre."

"I thought we were under attack again," continued David, beginning to see a little humor in it all. "I damned near wet my pants, too."

"It looks to me like someone beat you to it," said Brandon, looking at David's right leg, a smile spreading across his face.

David then felt something warm and wet trickle down his shin and looked, fearing what it was he knew he would see. The dog had apparently mistaken David for a fire hydrant and was properly using him as one.

Brandon started laughing tremendously as David tried to kick the dog away with little success. "I think it likes you, David." Brandon laughed harder.

The uproar finally awakened the rest of the party, and before David knew what was happening, Jessica was on her knees at the dog's side, caressing and stroking it lovingly. It soaked up the attention like an ecstatic sponge and immediately took a liking to this kind, warm lady. "How adorable," Jessica commented as the others joined her. "Where'd he come from?"

"He just walked up," answered Brandon with a smile that utterly disgusted David.

"Oh, David. He's so cute," said Jessica, still smiling. She received a scowl in return and paused at this unfitting reaction. "What's wrong with him?" she asked of Brandon, gesturing at the disgruntled man.

"He's just a little upset because the dog wet on him,"

Brandon answered, barely getting the words out before he relapsed into a state of hysteria.

"You're kidding." She looked at David and began to giggle herself.

He did not take that at all well. "What's so funny?" he asked almost angrily, glaring down at her.

"I didn't know you were so good with animals, David," said Christopher, scratching behind the dog's ears as it wagged its tail happily. He glanced over at Amy who blushed quietly.

"Where's Sean?" asked David, attempting to change the subject.

"He decided to run on ahead a short distance. He'll be back soon," answered Brandon, wiping tears from his eyes. "He woke up when the dog wandered up."

"What'll we name him?" asked Amy.

"How about Puddles," offered Jodi with a laugh, still petting the canine's flank.

"We're not naming it anything," said David firmly. "We're not keeping it. It'd only get in the way, and besides, it probably belongs to someone."

"Now, David, you're just mad because it took you for your average, everyday, John," spluttered Jodi. "We know better, and it's really very sweet. It might even be helpful."

"How?"

"Well, maybe it can hunt or track or something," suggested Jessica, stressing the final word.

David guffawed. "Yeah, right, and maybe it can fly, too! Not likely!"

"Spare us, David. You're being unreasonable."

"I am not."

"Yes you are," said Jessica, a flinty look sparking in her eyes as her aura deepened with emotion.

"We're not keeping it and that's final."

"Damn dog's gonna bring anybody around straight to us," said David, watching Puddles prance about the wagon as they traveled on through the greensward.

"Relax, David. There's nothing any of us can do about it," said Sean from atop his black mare at David's side. "You know if Jessica gets her mind set on something, she gets what she wants."

David sighed. "I know, but it really is foolishness. We don't need anything else to take care of. It's difficult enough taking care of ourselves."

"Well, just suck up and go on. All we can do is accept it, and who knows, a pet may really help everyone relax," commented Sean.

"Yeah, maybe," acceded David.

"By the way, did he really piss on you?"

"Yeah, he really did," answered David snidely, and Sean stifled a laugh.

At David's angry stare, Sean wiped away his grin and said, "Maybe I should run ahead for a short distance before I piss you off."

"Good idea," said David, ignoring the obvious connotations of that particular statement.

Sean kicked his horse into a gallop and rode off. David slowed his pace until he was riding parallel with the wagon where Christopher and Jessica rode up front.

"Isn't he cute?" asked Jessica again, watching Puddles as he continued playing.

David grunted. "Sean's decided to run a quick recon of the area up ahead, so I thought I'd come back here. Brandon seems to be preoccupied," David commented while looking behind the wagon where Brandon was bringing up the rear. The poor dwarf was having trouble with his pony. It wanted to go south, and Brandon was furiously fighting to keep it aright. Cursing, he yanked on the reins to straighten the pony out and nearly unsaddled himself.

"Yeah, I noticed that," said Christopher. "Dwarves aren't very good horsemen, are they?"

David shook his head and smiled.

At that moment, the dog barked loudly and took off at breakneck speed in the same direction Sean had gone: northwest.

"What's wrong with him?" asked Christopher of Jessica.

"I don't know," she answered, her voice echoing the worry in her eyes. "I...follow him...as quickly as you can. Something's terribly wrong here. I can feel it."

They did as she said unquerryingly for Jessica had an uncanny ability to sense wrongness, but as they started to follow her instructions, Sean came galloping back towards them. Out of breath, he stopped beside the wagon, motioning for them to stop. As they did so, he breathed, "We've got to cut north for a while."

"Why, Sean? What is it?" asked Jessica. "What's up ahead?"

"You don't want to see it, trust me," he said, looking back over his shoulder at the trickle of smoke that rose out of a dip in the road some distance ahead. He shuddered. "Just do as I say. It's terrible!"

"What is it Sean?" pressed David. "What's so terrible?"

Sean hesitated for a moment and then took a deep, shuddering breath. "There's a homestead ahead and..." He hesitated again.

"Yes? And what?" prompted Christopher as the other girls poked their heads through the curtain and Brandon pulled up beside them, still cursing his pony.

"Well, it's been ransacked. Believe me, if you can possibly avoid it, you don't want to see it," finished Sean looking disgusted. David knew that if it revolted Sean so badly, something worse than just a burned home was up ahead. He also knew that the ladies would not want to see it...and neither would he.

"Did Puddles go there?" asked Jessica.

"The dog? Yeah, he passed me on the way back. I have a feeling that we've found his masters."

"Well let's go get him back," said Jessica as she took the reins from Christopher and began moving the wagon forward.

"Wait, Jessica," pleaded Sean. "You won't like what's up there, and it's not necessary that we pass through. I'm asking you, please don't go."

"Sean, if we hide from our fears or shun what disturbs us, sooner or later it'll creep up on us, and personally, I'd prefer to surprise the horrors in my heart rather than be surprised by them. So, let's go ahead and get it over with." She continued onward.

Sean sighed and followed the wary procession towards the trickle of black smoke that was steadily rising up ahead.

After a distance, they reached the terrible scene and it was, indeed, monstrous. The stench was enough to gag a coroner! A house and barn were both burnt nearly to the ground and were still smoldering along with all the other structures in the area; wells, fences, even a doghouse. All the animals; cows, sheep, pigs, and goats; had been slaughtered and their remains were strewn about or spitted and left hanging in the air obscenely.

There was an extremely large pole stuck in the ground directly in front of the remains of the house. On it was the head of a man with eyes rolled back. The mouth was left open where its swollen tongue protruded grotesquely. Bugs crawled all about it and into the mouth where they carried little bits of flesh out, but compared to what else the scene held, this was pretty.

The party dismounted and climbed down off the wagon so they could better examine the gruesome site. They walked past the pole and found the naked body of a young girl, maybe thirteen, tied to the earth in a spread eagle fashion. She had obviously been raped repeatedly and brutally. There was so much dried blood on her body that the teeth marks and bruises that covered it could hardly be seen, making an obscene spectacle out of innocence and purity.

Brandon draped a blanket over her so the vultures that circled overhead could not defile the body any further. A whimper was heard from inside the remains of the house. Jessica walked towards the sound, followed by the rest of the party, but Sean stepped in front of her. "Jessica, haven't you seen enough?" he pleaded futilely.

Jessica smiled at him. She did appreciate his concern, but she needed to see the rest of the carnage. For some reason she felt compelled to do so and continued, patting Sean's shoulder as she passed.

As she entered the house, David at her side, she understood why Sean had been concerned. Silent screams echoed off the nearly non-existent walls, obscenely evanescing in her mind like writhing masses of childhood defiled, left crippled and distraught by horror. Tied upright in a chair near the center of the house was the decapitated form of a man. The aged tunic that he wore was soaked in blood and ripped in many places where he had been brutally beaten and tortured. Laying in front of the chair was the bloated body of a woman in her mid-thirties that exhibited the tell-tale signs of a recent pregnancy. She was stripped not only of her clothes but also of her unborn child. She was bruised and dirty as was the fetus that lay a short distance to her side. The positioning of the three figures suggested that the man had been forced to watch while his unborn child was prematurely ripped from its mother who was then raped repeatedly. They probably did not even decapitate him until they had finished with his wife. Puddles was crouched at his feet, whimpering pitifully, sniffing at the blood-soaked floor as if he hoped to find some remaining sliver of his master's life in the congealing pool.

They stood there for a very short time, taking in the

disgusting scene that surrounded them. Then Amy fainted into Christopher's arms, disrupting the placid room with move- ment. The wizard lifted her easily from the ground. "I'll take her back to the wagon and try to revive her." He walked away.

Jessica felt rage burning inside her. The hatred spread like wildfire into the deepest reaches of her mind, enraging her and searing this picture into her memory like a brand on a calf. With eyes burning, she turned on Sean. "Who did this?" she demanded with as much control as she could muster.

Sean took a deep breath. "I warned you, Jessica. I knew you wouldn't take it well." And he had. For some reason, he had expected this reaction from her.

"I asked you a question, Sean. Who did this?"

The thief looked at Jessica, robe rustling in the foul wind that blew through the "house." A mixture of emotions clouded his thinking: sympathy, sadness, anger, and even fear. "I'm not sure, Jessica, but I did find another body on the other side of the house and…" He paused for a moment, swallowing. "I think he was one of the people who did this."

They followed Sean to the other side of the house where they found the body of a man who had his throat slit by some sort of small knife. The body had the habiliments of a merce- nary and that much was certain. His skin was deeply tanned, and he was heavily armed.

"He's one of the men from the hermit's house!" asserted David. "I remember the face distinctly! I had turned to meet him when their leader called the retreat!"

"Fools!" shouted Jessica as more rage flared within her. She had to literally fight to stay in control as a vision flared through her mind. The emotions in the area were too strong. Jessica found herself standing outside the house before it had been burned as the family worked and their murderers ap- proached. She saw the rapes, the evisceration, the cold- blooded slaughter of innocent lives and she felt the need to scream. As she returned to the present, her emanations blared in a shriek of power, blinding her friends, searing emotion into the heavens like a ladder. "Insipid, arrogant fools!" she screamed, vowing to have revenge on the animals that could destroy life so uselessly. "How dare they defile this place and these people in such a way! They will pay!"

"You should have killed him, David," said Jodi with an angry, disgusted look in her eyes as she kicked the dead mercenary's carcass.

"I really wish I had, but it wouldn't have helped that little girl or her parents."

Christopher had returned to the wagon with Amy's unconscious form in his arms. He retrieved a small vial of smelling salts from a backpack and unscrewed the top, waving it lightly under Amy's nose. She regained consciousness almost immediately and looked up at Christopher, eyes filled with horror.

"So terrible...so brutal," she breathed.

The wizard bent close and embraced her, holding her and rocking slowly until she calmed. "I know. I've never seen anything like it either, but that sort of thing happens all too frequently."

"But it scared me so terribly. What if we're attacked like that?"

Christopher held her firmly, stroking her hair, planting kisses over her face and hands. "Don't worry about that. I won't ever let anything happen to you, sweetheart. You're safe as long as I'm around."

She began to softly weep—not because of the fear that infested her soul but for the poor child who had been deprived of life by such wanton brutality.

Christopher lifted her chin and kissed her gently. "You have my word that as long as I live, no harm will ever come to you. I promise you that on my life," said the wizard, mistaking her tears.

She looked at him, her beautiful blue eyes glittering with

sorrow as tears streamed down her cheeks. She bent forward and kissed him again. "Thank you, Christopher. I believe you." They sat there, in each others' arms for a short while, seeking and receiving the comfort that only lovers may grant.

Brandon, David, and Sean buried the three mutilated bodies of the homesteaders, leaving the intruder to rot in the sun. They raised a cairn over their bodies, and Jessica blessed each grave. After several minutes, she had managed to regain control and had organized them to this end. However, the image of Jessica, standing like an incarnation of vengeance over the dead mercenary, was still pulsating in their consciousness, awakening them to her power and engraving her eruption into their psyches. They tried to block the image out, but as the sorrowfully angry group left the scene, it was all they could see.

Puddles sat on his haunches by the young girl's grave, as always her protector. He would sit there and keep her safe from anyone or anything that tried to do her harm, be it another brutal man or a hound from hell, it mattered nothing to him.

They rode on for a few hours in silence until Brandon finally suggested that they stop for the night, and as they did so, built their customary fire by which they all soon gathered. They retrieved some dried meat, fruit, and wine, that had been purchased in Estrus, from their packs. Very little food was eaten that evening, but more than enough wine was drunk.

Soon they all dozed off into a fitful sleep that was frequently interrupted by nightmares. There was a common denominator between all of the dreams, however: the horrified look on the face of that poor little girl who had done nothing to deserve the treatment she had received. They all realized in that sleep, whether they understood what they dreamed or not, that this vision of mortality could only be a presage to the dawning of a new life for them. A life filled with many horrors but just as many joys. A trip into the pandemonium of life that so matures a person that he will never again be unthankful for his happiness, nor take the precious gift of life for granted.

As they awoke the following morning, they found themselves remembering little of what they had witnessed on the previous day. It was as if a block had been placed in their minds, relieving the pressure of disquietude and numbing them to the past. David stood, stretching hugely as he gave a great yawn. He peered at his friends who had begun gathering all their belongings again. Jessica was collecting the left-over meat and wine flask; Christopher, with Sean's help, was attempting to refasten the horses to the wagon. Jodi was putting out the fire that was still smoldering slightly from the previous eve; and Brandon was trying to saddle his pony once again while quietly cursing to himself as the shaggy beast fought him every step of the way. The only person, aside from David himself, who was doing nothing was Amy. She was sitting up front in the wagon, watching Christopher attentively with shining blue eyes as he reattached the horses. David soon found himself doing precisely the same thing only he was staring at Jessica. She was standing slightly uphill from him, a silhouette against the sun. He watched as she stretched, her arms spread wide and it seemed to him that she was limned by the sun, deifying her magnificence in the orange-red splendor that was rising beyond her.

Then a second vision seemed to polarize Jessica. David saw her standing in a similar fashion, only anger crackled from her in tongues of flaming emotion, and she raged, the angel of death exacting her toll on all that would cause harm to the world. Her extreme, just power was terrible and kind, loving and mendacious as her energy crackled through her body. Then an echo of magical light brought David back to the present, and the disturbance was wiped from his memory. He saw Jessica as she was again, darkness against the light of a rising sun. Her face was surrounded by a sheer, silky black film that settled about her shapely shoulders like a fine, clinging mist. As David watched her, he felt his pulse quicken, and he ascended the distance to stand behind her, placing his arms lightly around her waist. He held her tightly against him.

"Mmm. What's this wonderful bit of attention for?" she asked playfully as her long black hair swept about in the wind, temporarily blinding David in its sable richness. He buried his face in her hair and breathed in its scent.

"How could I resist such a vision? Am I still dreaming?" he asked teasingly as he nipped at her neck playfully.

"Now stop that!" she cried, turning around in his arms. He held her happily, feeling her cheek pressed against his thickly muscled shoulder. He bent and kissed her. "Now that's more like it," she said as she returned his kiss, lovingly.

"Uh, hum," interrupted a voice from behind them. They turned and were met by Jodi's smiling face. "Sorry to inter-rupt, but I believe we're ready to go."

"Yeah, okay. I suppose we've gotta get going again," David returned as he surreptitiously swept Jessica off of her feet, a surprised yelp fleeting from her lips, and carried her easily to the wagon.

The sun had fully risen now and they rode in merriment, marveling at the beauty surrounding them. The grass was a rich emerald green as it swayed in the strong, autumnal wind like servants surrounding them and bowing at their passage. The bright blue sky was only interrupted by a few fluffy white clouds that smiled down on them as they rode in wonderment. The sun, majestic in its radiance, looked down on them from over his cloudy servants' shoulders and joined in on their great laughter. All was well! All was very well! How good to be alive on this outstanding morning! The woods rejoiced around them. The earth released its verdant smells; life surrounded them and their no-longer-restive spirits were high as they soared through the brilliant sky.

Returning to the earthly plane, the wagon rolled on with the horses treading lambently on the road that they traveled. In front of it traveled a pair of tall horses, one black and one white, each baring a rider. The two men, smiling at some witticism, frequently laughed jubilantly. Christopher and the women rode in the wagon's front, amazed at the pure and unspoiled beauty that surrounded them. Occasionally one of them would leap off the wagon to pick a flower or retrieve a colorful leaf or simply to frolic for a few moments amid the wonders of Mother Nature as she illustrated her divine benevolent tendencies. Following the joyous party was a more angry and completely befuddled character.

"Damn strumpet," muttered the dwarf to himself as he valiantly attempted to stay astride his wandering and rebellious mount. The pony was just as interested in the beautiful day as the people were. "I'd rather walk than have to put up with you, you ungrateful nag! Out of all the ponies in this world, why did I get stuck with a complete ass?!"

Utterly disgusted with his mount, Brandon kicked her hard in the side and she took off. Running wildly past the wagon, the pony definitely did not intend to stop. "Help!" yelled Brandon as he flew by the two lead horses, jerking frantically on the reins. Sean and David looked at each other for an amused moment, not sure whether to sit back and laugh or to give chase. Finally, they kicked their horses into a gallop and raced after their laboring friend.

Very quickly Sean and David caught up with the dwarf and succeeded in calming down the excited pony after Brandon had rather ungracefully dismounted—in other words, he fell on his head.

"Let's stop for a bit," suggested David, amused but sympathetic as the wagon caught up with the horses. "We've got to find some way to keep Brandon out of trouble," he teased, and the dwarf scowled.

"I'm sorry for being such a bother!" spat Brandon as he stalked off the road and sat himself down with a thump.

The rest of the company climbed down off the wagon and joined the disgruntled little man. "This body is the most useless one I could have possibly ended up in! Damned thing can barely go faster than a walk let alone run or ride a stupid horse worth a shit!" fumed Brandon to the amusement of his friends. "Can you imagine what it's like to be four and a half feet tall?" asked the dwarf who was now beyond anger; he was verging on the point of giving up. "That's damned short! If my arms drug the ground, I could lope around like a monkey!"

"Yes, Brandon. We know. If you think real hard you'll remember that back in our own world you were taller than the rest of us, and now you're getting a taste of what it's like to be short," commented David with a smile for Brandon. The dwarf started to retort but could not bring himself to say it. With a sigh, he lapsed into an exasperated silence.

"Well, if you can't ride your pony, then the solution's very simple," said Jodi. "Why don't you just ride in the wagon?"

"Because there's not enough room for five people to fit comfortably, that's why," he answered.

"I'll be happy to ride a horse," offered Jodi. "Then there'll be room." Brandon looked at her for a moment and then nodded without a word.

So, thus they continued. Sean and Jodi rode in the front while David brought up the rear. The rest of the company lounged in the wagon, either napping in the back or enjoying the scenery up front. Occasionally Sean would disappear to make a scan of the upcoming landscape, but he would quickly return with news of more open territory.

In the front of the wagon, Christopher and Amy found

themselves alone while the others slept. "Can I ask you a question, Christopher?" began Amy solemnly.

"Yeah, sure," answered Christopher, turning to look at her. "Shoot."

"What's got into you?" she asked. "I mean, you've never seemed attracted to me before... Why now?"

"I'm not really sure," he answered, wrinkling his forehead in thought. "I just remember looking up and seeing you standing there, so beautiful and majestic. It just sprung up out of me from some place I didn't know existed."

"But...I mean...You never acted like that when we were back at home." She hesitated, then sighed, giving up. "I guess what I really want to know is: when we get back, are you still gonna care for me?"

Christopher turned to look fully at her, stricken. "Of course I will. I don't know why I never said anything before; I just didn't. But you can be sure that now that I've spoken up and realized my feelings, I won't renege on them."

"Are you sure?" she asked demurely.

"I am," he asserted with a strong, reassuring look deep into her eyes. He then reached over and hugged her strongly with a robed arm before continuing. "I love you, Amy, and I won't leave you."

She sighed and leaned against his shoulder happily. She thought to herself, It doesn't matter—now is what matters and he's wonderful.

The company rode on for the rest of the day happily, except for Brandon who spent the majority of the time asleep or sitting in silence in the rear of the wagon. Around noon, they stopped and ate a quick lunch of dried meat and chatted idly. They were all in good humor, laughing merrily at each other but mostly at Brandon who still sat in brooding silence, angrily ignoring their jokes. Only an occasional grumble came to his lips or a full sentence on the uselessness and futility of dwarven bodies. After eating, however, he seemed to feel a lot better and began talking more freely as they remounted and left.

Continuing through the plains, they soon began to notice a subtle change in the landscape. The first tell-tale sign of this was that the road on which they had been traveling since they left Estrus disappeared entirely and abruptly. Water-holes and streams became less and less frequent the farther they traveled, and the green grass soon faded into yellow finally giving way entirely to sand.

"Well, it looks like we've reached the edge of the Desert of Suspi," said David as he trotted up beside the wagon, peering into the barren distance, watching the sand writhe with heat.

"Yeah," agreed Brandon. "We'd better decide which way we're going to go since we no longer have a road to guide us."

"It looks to me," said Jodi, staring at the map that had been unrolled, "that we need to travel northwest, straight at that mountain chain. It's probably the closest source of water."

Jessica agreed. "After that we should continue until we reach to the edge of the Teuton Swamp and the city of Tyrol. From there we can just travel straight across to Mount Apocrys. If we continue at the rate we've been going, it looks like we should be there in another week or so. I think Rocnar miscalculated a bit, don't you?"

"Yeah, but that's only if everything continues so smoothly," said Christopher. "This area of the world is a lot wilder so we're gonna have to be more careful."

Brandon nodded, a pensive, uncertain look on his face attracting everyone's attention. "Christopher's right. I feel like there's something I should remember about that chain of mountains. I can't think what it is, but there's definitely something about it that I should know. We'd better be very careful."

Silence hung in the air for a moment before Amy rudely interrupted it. "Whether there's something to be wary of or not, I think we'd better get started. I'd really like to reach the mountains before dark."

"Well, why don't we stay in the desert tonight and begin our trek over the mountains in the morning?" asked Brandon, still trying to remember whatever-it-was. "I really don't want to be there at night."

"The Desert of Suspi is populated by lawless nomads who'd as soon cut your throat as talk to you. I know that there's something in the desert to be scared of, so I think I'd rather take my chances in the mountains," commented Christopher. "Besides, at night the desert gets very cold and there are no animals to hunt...unless you consider lizard a delicacy."

Since this appealed to no one except Sean, the company began their journey through the desert. It was a desolate place, haunted by legends of the people who inhabited it. It was said that the nomadic people of Suspi had once been a great and prospering nation and that the area they lived in had once been a great greensward, actually an extension of the one they had just left behind. According to legend, the King Suspi died without naming his heir and his two sons, Prince Zuyder and Prince Nysa, went to war to decide who would be king. Each knew that their armies were equal and that if they fought only with these armies, the war would perhaps never end or would end with no one left to rule or serve.

To solve the problem, Prince Zuyder called upon a wizard to aid him in the war. The wizard opened a portal to another dimension and summoned forth an army of demons led by one of the Devils himself: Grenla. After Prince Zuyder's minions crushed Prince Nysa, he proclaimed himself king. As payment for his services, however, Grenla claimed the land for his own and razed it to the ground, turning the fertile earth into sand and the trees into infrequent cacti. After Zuyder saw what

Grenla had wrought, he demanded that the land be returned to its earlier state. The Devil laughed, cursing Zuyder and all of his people for eternity.

"Ever since, they've been a race of dirty and deformed people who kill anything that enters the desert, but they're also terrible cowards. They'll run from anything that looks too dangerous," finished Christopher, relating the story to the others. He did not know where he had heard the legend but told it as though he had heard it a hundred times. As they rode through the desert at as fast a pace as the horses could stand, they found themselves looking from side to side in search of leprous attackers. "If we come across a few of the nomads, we could easily take care of them, but they do move quietly in the desert and could sneak up on us at night. That's why I think it'd be wise to get out of the desert before nightfall."

"Is that story true?" asked Amy curiously.

"Who knows, but the nomads are dangerous and horribly deformed. That's all that matters." A nod from Amy illustrated her agreement as they continued on with less talk and more watchful eyes.

As the sun was growing low on the horizon, they began to see a mountain range in the distance, and they picked up their pace in a hurry to reach them. As they trundled over a large sand dune, they were brought to a halt by a group of disfigured humanoids. There were about twenty-five of them, all dirty and dressed in shredded grey or black rags that barely covered their twisted bodies. Their chancrous skin was covered in boils, and their hair grew only in dirty patches on their sun-darkened mottled bodies. A howl erupted from the lepers as they shuffled closer, raising bent and rusted weapons threateningly.

There was a second of indecision while David joined Sean at the front of the wagon, each with sword in hand before they plunged into the group of gangrenous rogues. Jodi retreated to beside the wagon as Brandon leapt into the foray, axe raised high above his head, a battle cry roaring from his throat like thunderous rage.

The two mounted men were flailing about furiously, hurling forms from them, ripped to shreds. As their blades met flesh, there was almost no resistance. The nomads' flesh was simply so rotten that it almost ached for cleaving. Arms and heads flew amid a steady flow of gore as Brandon swung his axe savagely, slicing through their social courage like a hot knife through butter. However, the three defenders were being overwhelmed by the sheer numbers and ferocity of their bestial attackers.

As it began to look hopeless, another figure, tall in a black cowl, leapt into the tumult. He had no weapon, but his hands were alight with a blue-white flame that burnt into any he touched. The nomads were taken aback by Christopher's sudden appearance as he busily threw burning bodies about, and his friends continued their savage hacking. Soon, as the numbers began to dwindle, the nomads broke and fled into the desert, and the four bloody figures returned to the wagon, wiping off their weapons and hands as best they could, trying to clean them of the unclean stench of fouled flesh and blood.

Jessica and Amy were already on the desert floor, ready to aid their valiant friends who waved them off. "Let's wait till we've reached the mountains to take care of our wounds. Just in case there are any more of them about," suggested Christopher, shaking off Amy's help. "Is anyone hurt too badly to continue?"

No one was, so they continued riding in silence as they watched the shapes on the horizon grow ever nearer. The mountains were tall and heavily forested, although rocky outcroppings were numerous where their jagged shards pierced the green covering. As they grew closer to the mountains, some shrubs and minimal amounts of brown grass appeared in the earth which grew less sandy and more loamy. They reached the edge of the mountains as the sun came to rest on the tallest peak.

"Where do we find a path through these mountains?" asked David worriedly. "We can't just cut straight over them. That'd take days."

"Well, I believe that's for our esteemed colleague the thief to tell us," answered Christopher, smiling at Sean who returned the grin with a slight bow.

"Any idea where I should start looking?" asked Sean.

"This place looks familiar to me," murmured Brandon. He stood silently for a moment, holding everyone's attention. He then looked up and held certainty in his dark eyes as he gestured to the north. "Try that way."

Sean looked curiously at Brandon for a moment but jogged off to the north with a shrug. During the thief's absence, Brandon spoke. "If I remember correctly, there's not a path big enough for the wagon. The one I remember should barely be large enough for the horses, so we'd better prepare ourselves to ride horseback for a while." He made this last remark with a hateful glare for his little pony who snorted in return, raising her nose defiantly. "I think I'll walk," he mumbled, eyes downcast.

They were still laughing when Sean returned. "There's a path leading up into the mountains just a short distance to the north." He turned to Brandon. "How'd you know it was there?"

"Like I said, Sean, I feel like I've been here before. I'm also sure that whatever happened to me when I was here, wasn't pleasant."

"Well, in any case, there is a path, but I don't think we'll get the wagon through," continued Sean. "The horses should be able to make it okay, but it's too small for anything else. We'll have to move all our supplies onto the horses and into our backpacks."

They followed Sean's instructions and moved all the supplies they had the heart to give onto the packhorse. The rest was distributed between the other horses and the backpacks. As they began to leave, Sean set the wagon afire.

"Why'd you do that?" asked Jodi.

"If someone's following us, they won't be able to learn anything from what we left behind."

After a very short walk in the impending darkness, they came across the path which ascended up into the mountains, winding around the first escarpment so that its destination was obscured.

"This is it," mumbled Brandon as he began to lead his pony forward and upward. "I'll lead the way, Sean. I've been here before."

None of them questioned him any further and followed him quietly up into the mountains. The path lead them a short distance up the first peak and then turned off, leading around to the other side without ascending to the summit.

As they rounded the first peak, they were impressed by the magnitude of the mountains. They were much larger than the party had seen before, their snow-tipped caps visible high up among the clouds.

As the shadows lengthened and the sun disappeared fully behind the peaks, they saw that the path led up into another mountain lined in trees of various types. It wound tortuously up to the snow-capped summit and down the other side. They made it perhaps a quarter of the way up that mountain before they found a small, level portion that was clear of trees.

"This'll be good for the night," commented Brandon as he lead the party into the clearing. "Let's set up camp."

Brandon and the women built a fire while Sean, Christopher, and David trekked off into the closing darkness in search of food. They soon felled a buck and quickly returned to the clearing, bearing its gutted form.

The fire was roaring and warm against the chill mist that settled on the grass about them. David cut the meat into sections while Amy began cooking. She prepared the entire beast but packed most of it for later use before sitting down to a happy meal. All but Brandon joined in on the chatter that encircled the clearing; he was restless and worried for some reason he could not quite define.

When the rest of the party decided to go to sleep, Brandon took the first watch. He sat next to the fire, his axe in his lap, wondering what it was that had him so on edge. He never saw the eyes that stared at him out of the trees behind his back and then quickly eased off into the forest. All he saw was confusion.

Ancestral homes

"Wake up! We're under attack!"

The shout awakened David with a start. In a fraction of a second, he was on his feet, sword at the ready, Sean right behind him. Both were half-expecting to see a rather dirty dog defecating on their supplies, but unfortunately, that was not the case. Standing on the opposite side of the fire was a small, bent figure holding a great double-bladed axe in a pair of gnarled old hands. Sean and David, quickly followed by the rest of the waking party, joined Brandon in front of the fire.

"What is it?" asked Sean hurriedly, his dagger and short sword both raised protectively in front of him as if they could protect him from fear.

"Look there," answered Brandon, pointing out into the trees that surrounded them.

At first they saw nothing, but after their eyes adjusted to the dim moonlight amid the close-knit trees, they were able to discern what had so disquieted their friend. There were eyes. Many, many eyes, all focused on them and their fire. These bulging bulbous eyes were glowing faintly with their own secret form of fluorescence.

"What are they?" asked Jodi after a moment of silence.

"I remember why I didn't want to enter these mountains," said Brandon in way of answering. "They're infested with orcs."

"Then we're all right. They're afraid of light!" offered Christopher, relieved as he gazed intently at the fire behind him.

"Not firelight," answered the dwarf, shattering Christopher's hopes. "Only sunlight."

"Why aren't they attacking, then?" asked David uncertainly.

"They're building their numbers. Every minute we sit here talking, more and more of them arrive."

"How many are there now?" asked Jessica.

"Probably fifty."

"Fifty! Can we handle that many?" asked Sean, alarmed by the overwhelming numbers.

"I don't know, but I think we're about to find out," answered Brandon, gesturing towards the trees once more.

They peered after him and saw a face looking back at them. It was a disgusting mixture of man and swine. The body was about five feet in height, with gray-brown skin and charcoal hair. The feet were cloven hooves, and the hands were human, complete to the thumbs. It held a wicked-looking scimitar. The face was the same ugly color as the rest of the creature with a huge gaping mouth, containing tremendous stained teeth, more like tusks than anything else, that extended well out of its mouth, almost touching its flat snout. Saliva dripped from its mouth and hunger shone in its bulging, yellow eyes. Black hair capped its head, resembling a mane that only covered the center of its pate and extended down its broad, muscular back.

The party knew then that they had to act. Like a finely tuned machine, David, Brandon, Sean, and Christopher encircled the fire, encasing the others in the middle. Almost immediately after they formed the cordon, the Orcs came howling into the clearing, blood in their bestial eyes.

There were hordes of them, each appearing uglier than the previous one. Some had the pig-like look of the first one, but others looked much more human, as if they were men that had been twisted by some foul evil. The four men overcame their fear and fought valiantly, slaughtering the beasts one after the other, and a score of them lay dead after only a few minutes.

David stood, towering over the beasts, swinging his sword with broad two-handed strokes that killed two or more of them with each sweep. He had just slain his tenth when he saw a figure fall to his left. He hazarded a glance and saw that Sean had been overrun by five Orcs at once, and David moved to aid his friend immediately. Grabbing two Orcs, one in each hand, he hoisted them off his fallen ally by the tuft of their necks. They dangled in the air for a moment, snapping and clawing at David's arms until he threw them with as much force as he could into another advancing troop. He smiled as he heard the rewarding crack that signaled the breaking of bones and saw all seven of the creatures lying in a heap near the trees' edge.

In the mean time, Sean had freed himself from the other three which now lay dead at his feet as he, covered in their blood as well as his own from a nasty bite in his right shoulder, shouted his thanks to David before he continued fighting. Brandon was holding his own well, a pile of broken bodies lying at his feet, but the beasts just kept coming. Christopher was also faring well. He was amazingly quick with his dagger and none of the Orcs had even touched him, but he, like the others, was slowly being worn down. "Something must be done!" he shouted, sweat beading on his brow. "We can't hold out much longer!"

There was an answering movement from behind the wizard, and as the four continued fighting, an explosion ripped through the air, a discharge of anxiety. All movement stopped as everyone, man and Orc alike, turned to face the blast.

Standing in the middle of the flames of their once-small campfire was a huge figure. It must have stood twenty feet as it towered over them menacingly. The entire being was not even visible for, at ground level, the creature's stomach began, not its legs. It was made of flame, red and burning all over. It's face was flat but with the same gaping maw that belonged to the Orcs, only ten times larger. The eyes glowed red and flame shot from them when its gaze shifted. It's long crimson hair hung down into the flames and seemed to burn just as the rest of its tremendous, muscular body did.

A tremendous, deep voice boomed from the creature's mouth. "YOU HAVE ANGERED ME!" it shouted, its flaming, reptilian tongue slipping out at the Orcs. "YOU HAVE ATTACKED MY SERVANTS AND YOU MUST PAY FOR YOUR IMPUDENCE!" As the thing's voice echoed in the night, it raised a single clawed hand and pointed at one small group of Orcs at the clearing's edge. A bolt of fire shot from its fingertips and exploded in the center of the group, sending Orcs flying through the air, some on fire, others in pieces. As they landed amongst their fellows, those left living bolted and ran into the trees, not even stopping to look back.

The tiny figures of the party continued to stand gazing up at the gigantic figure that towered over them, wondering how to react. Then Christopher began to laugh, mirth reflecting in his eyes. When he approached Jodi and clapped her on the shoulder, his friends gazed at him as if he had lost his mind. "Very nice, my dear," he commented. "Very nice."

"Thank you," she answered as the gigantic monster faded into black and their fire subsided to its original size. "I thought you might like it."

"I sure did," he answered. "Very, very well done and precisely timed."

"Hold on a second," commented Sean, raising his hand. "I think I missed something."

"Yeah, me too," included David as the rest of the group nodded their baffled agreement. "What the hell was that?"

"That, my dear David," answered Jodi, smiling broadly, "was what you call a fire elemental."

David stared. "How'd you manage that?! You can't summon elementals let alone control 'em."

"No David, she can't," offered Christopher, "but she can make great illusions, can't she?"

"Wait a minute! That was an illusion?!"

"Good, you're starting to catch on now."

"That's incredible!" said Amy staring at Jodi, awed. "I mean, I know you're a good illusionist, but that completely fooled me! I'm amazed! You saved us all!"

Jodi smiled at her. "No. I just did my part. Well, there's another close call we managed to scrape through. Is everyone okay?"

"Yeah," said Sean rubbing his wounded shoulder lightly. "How about giving us a little warning next time, huh?"

"There wasn't time. I had to surprise them as much as possible."

"Wait a minute," interrupted Brandon, looking as if he had found a flaw in the fabric of reality. "If the elemental was an illusion, how did it manage to blow those Orcs away with a fireball?"

"Well that startled me, too. You see, that started as an illusion as well, but I think I got some help from our esteemed wizard for that little trick."

"Yes, I threw a sneak fireball into the Orcs at the same time Jodi made the illusion. I thought it would magnify the effect."

"Well, that it did," said Brandon. "As well as scaring the rest of us out of our skins. Anyway, we've been lucky. We'd better be very careful for the rest of the night, set a double watch or something."

"Why?" asked Sean. "Those Orcs won't stop running till

tomorrow, and I don't blame 'em. We're safe until next sundown."

"Not quite, Sean. There're worse things in these mountains than Orcs, and I'll feel better knowing that we'll have plenty of warning if anything else shows up."

"I'll stay with you the rest of your watch, Brandon," offered Jodi, setting sights on the double-watch theorem.

The dwarf agreed, so the others returned to their restless sleep with two persons on watch at all times. Luckily, nothing else happened across their camp during the night and their sleep went undisturbed until morning when David and Jessica awakened everyone. They broke their fast with some of the deer they had saved from the previous evening and packed everything they could fit into their saddlebags. The rest went onto their backs, and they continued their journey through the mountains with much exuberance, eager to escape the danger as quickly as they possibly could.

The day remained nice, clear and cool, for their trip through the mountains, but soon the path wound its way up the mountainside until it came to a dead end. There was no way to climb the sheer face of rock that now blocked their way; it was completely flat, no hand or footholds marred its smooth surface.

"What now, dwarf?! I thought you said this path leads out of the mountains," said Sean, made irritable by the wound in his shoulder. On the previous night, they had decided not to heal this wound, for it would take one of their Great Cures spells due to the number of scratches, and it was not really all that bad, bleeding little and scabbing quickly.

"It does, thief! You of all people should know about secret entrances!" blurted Brandon, and Sean lapsed into silence.

Everyone stood quietly as Brandon removed his axe and leaned it up against the wall on his left, out of his way. He then approached the rock face and put his hands against it, the rest of his body slowly following them.

As his muscles flexed and strained against the unmoving surface, a deep thrumming sound vibrated up out of his chest like the voice of an earthquake, and the sounds shaped themselves into words of some language unknown to the others. As the words rebounded off the wall, the rock face gradually turned blue and soon began to glow, pulsating in sequence with the cadence of Brandon's song. As the dwarf continued to sing, sweat now beading his brow like tears of strain, he pushed harder and harder, and the rock began to become a paler and paler shade of blue, passing through the midnight blue of the sky during a bright night, through the blue of blueberries on a blossoming vine, through the blue of a bright cerulean sky, and finally into the color of a raindrop hanging on a spider's web as the early morning sky reflected in it. The stone continued getting lighter and lighter until it seemed almost transparent.

As the party watched in astonishment, the rock faded and they could see straight through it into a passage of stone, finely carved out of the heart of the mountain. The path continued down into it. Then, slowly, the dwarf pushed his way through the "rock" until he was on the other side, all the time singing in that deep thrumming dwarven voice. Suddenly, Brandon altered his singing and the vibrations faded into a single monotone, and with his voice, the slab solidified, sealing Brandon within the mountain.

"Brandon!" shouted David as he crashed into the stone wall, all his strength and weight behind him. He pushed with all his might, aided by the rest of the party, attempting to open the passage again, but their attempts were futile. The rock would not budge.

As they began to give up hope for Brandon and despaired, a grating sound built in their ears, and ever so slowly, the mountain's wall swung open like a revolving door, revealing the passage once more as it led deep into the mountain, curving off to the left. There, standing against the wall, hand on a stone lever carved into the form of a warhammer, was Brandon, grinning proudly at his friends.

"Third floor. Silverware and women's lingerie. All aboard."

"You damned dwarf! Why didn't you warn us?!" shouted David, all the while grinning at the small, stalwart figure.

"Would you have believed me?"

"No, but…"

"Okay, then forget it and let's get going. I'm afraid we're gonna have to leave the horses here, though. They wouldn't make it through." They accepted the dwarf's word and transferred everything to their backs that they could carry and slowly traipsed into the cave.

"Wait a minute, Brandon. Don't you think we need a light?" asked Sean.

"Yeah, I forgot. You can't see in the dark, can you? Well, in case you didn't know, I can." He smiled, eyes coruscating quietly in the darkness.

"I guess that body does have a few advantages, doesn't it Brandon?" asked Jodi, smiling.

"Maybe, just a few." Brandon returned her grin. "But we don't have any torches for you."

"We've got something better," said Jessica, glowing quietly in the darkness. She closed her eyes and raised her hands, a slow cadence eking from her lips. Momentarily there was a flash of light and a small floating pellucid ball appeared over her head, glowing brightly blue. "There you are." She grinned again, this time ear to ear.

"Light spell," mumbled Christopher.

Jessica nodded as Brandon returned the lever to the upright position, sealing them in. He then jogged down to the front of the single-file line they had formed, taking the lead.

This cave was unlike any that had ever existed in their other world. It was obviously not natural, smooth with manifold and various decorations molded from the rock as well as many passages branching off as tangents. There were miniature towers, elaborately carved from stalagmites, with windows and doors as well as tiny gargoyles to scare off any minuscule attackers. There were forests carved from clusters of tiny stalagmites with tiny animals amongst them, and above these Lilliputian forests were diminutive clouds as well as a dwarf rock sun that actually glowed, suffusing the miniature scene with unnatural light.

As they wound their way through the tiny world, Brandon halted them so he could speak. "We've got to continue quietly through the rest of the cave," he whispered. "I let you stumble around so far because we were far enough out of their hearing. Now we're too close for carelessness; so, be quiet."

"Whose hearing?" began David before Brandon silenced him and cocked his head, listening. The others did likewise, wondering at his actions. The silence of the cave grew until it began to feel oppressive, swallowing them in imagined sound. Then they managed to pick up the sounds that were being carried to them through the passageway, faint reverberations in the dark.

Somewhere in the distance, the sound of low guttural voices chanting in some long-forgotten tongue was heard. The cadence rose and fell threateningly, thrumming danger and evil into their hearts with unbelievable density. It soon became apparent that the sounds were growing closer, and Brandon gestured for them to follow him as he started to move quickly back up the passage from which they had come.

They jogged up the passage for roughly thirty yards before Brandon made a quick right into a small side passage. They followed it for a short distance before it made another sharp turn, this time to the left. Brandon stopped them just on the other side of the curve and peered back around it, gesturing for Jessica to cover her light.

The quietly radiating cleric called the radiant ball down to her palm and placed it within her robes, and they found themselves drowned in total blackness unlike any they had ever experienced. Then the voices were heard again, even closer, growing in magnitude. Brandon continued to peer out from around the corner and, with his infravision, saw a company of cowled figures moving slowly up the main passage. Though they were only blurry red forms, radiating heat to his sight, he knew exactly what they were.

As they passed, he turned and whispered for Jessica to release her light spell once again, and they began to creep through the cave once more. After a very few moments, Jodi quietly asked, "What were you looking at, Brandon? Who were they?"

"They're called Fifaaks. They're a tribe of ogre with nearly human intelligence. Those particular ones were Fifaak priests, holding some kind of ritual in worship of their dark god, Ranshar. They live in total darkness, though they can survive in firelight and do sometimes use fire in ceremonies. These caves are their homes."

"Great," commented Sean sardonically. "So you brought us into ogres' caves. That really took some incredible smarts, shorty."

"There's no other way out of these mountains!" said Brandon urgently, angered by the thief's remark. "This is it!"

Sean grunted, and they continued down the side passage until it merged with what they assumed was the main passageway again. They walked on for quite some distance until Brandon once again motioned for Jessica to cover her light.

After she did so, they were soon able to distinguish a pale iridescent light ahead, and they continued towards it. Very quickly they entered a great hundred foot square room that was probably every bit as tall as it was wide. They were looking down onto the main part of the room from a balcony that encircled it at about twenty-five feet from the floor. Brandon pointed across the balcony to another passageway that was directly on the other side of the room, apparently their exit. He then shifted his gaze to the contents of the room itself.

Gathered within were many great figures well over seven feet tall and of an even heavier build than Brandon. Their entire naked bodies were covered with brown hair, and their flat faces were mostly mouth, each filled to brimming with large, pointed teeth. Their faces were completely bestial, extremely hairy, with great eye ridges that jutted out over black sockets, and huge round noses that unerringly dripped. Each figure carried some sort of huge weapon in its clawed hands, either a great cudgel or a huge sword or axe. At one end of the room, there was a gigantic rock throne, with another Fifaak seated in it. This great beast was larger than the rest, almost reaching eight feet in height, with the same tremendous build as the rest but with much more muscle and a bit less fat. His great hand, larger than a man's head, rested on a huge axe that leaned against the throne.

The most gruesome sight of the room, however, was the altar in its center. It was a black marble slab with two great midnight posts arranged at each end. These posts were also black with a wooden beam connecting them and tremendous bat wings stretching out on each side. Beside the grotesque symbol lay an argentic fire alight with ethereal flame that issued smoke into the cloying air. There were a few robed Fifaaks stationed around the blood-spattered altar, chanting in deep, ominous voices and holding the form of a naked emaciated man who struggled futilely against their tremendous strength. Soon another robed Fifaak, apparently the high priest, walking with a slow, swaying gait approached the altar, chanting in his deep, guttural voice. He then produced a wickedly carved black knife from his robes and slowly, with much care, carved a small, many-pointed star in the struggling man's chest as he screamed in agony. Then, almost systematically, he carved another, smaller one on his sacrifice's forehead as the poor man jerked spasmodically. The priest stopped chanting, and as the reverberations faded, he plunged the dagger into the helpless man's solar plexus and drove it up under his rib cage. The man exhaled a single sharp breath before giving himself up to kind death. The Fifaak removed the knife and reached his hand into the gash. The skin folded under like a rubber change holder, and the priest fondled about for a moment before extracting his blood-soaked hand, holding the sacrifice's heart. The Fifaak lifted it high in the air and plunged it down into the fire like a purging of sins. The fire sputtered momentarily before roaring in grateful glee and flaring crimson as if the blood had been transformed into profane flames.

As the shocked party watched the sacrifice in silent disbelieving disgust, a number of forms slowly sneaked up behind them out of the darkness. A huge, hairy arm snaked out and wrapped itself around Sean's neck, grasping him by his wounded shoulder. The thief let out a single startled yelp of pain and surprise, but that was enough. The attention of all the Fifaaks on the floor was then directed at him. A deep-throated bark erupted from the great mouth of the ruling ogre, and the beasts rushed for the crude stairs that ascended to the balcony on which the intruders stood.

As the trapped party turned to meet the Fifaaks that had crept up on them, Sean braced himself and, with a great surge of strength, flipped the savage that held him over his back and off the balcony to its death. The thief then turned to meet the group of five ogres that stomped out of the passageway as Christopher made a few quick motions with his hands and mumbled some unfamiliar arcane words. He vanished. At the same time, Brandon and David rushed out to meet the barrage of Fifaaks that had swamped the balcony.

Sean whirled and met the five figures with a combination of lightning-fast reflexes and deadly accuracy, stabbing then parrying a thrust and ripping the beast's front open. A third Fifaak rushed at Sean, who lambently dodged aside and met another beast with a dagger in the ribcage. The monster that had missed Sean then brought his club to bare on Jessica who stepped back, mumbling a few words. The beast's eyes burst into brilliant light, blinding it. It stumbled, screaming in pain, scratching at its eyes until they bled. Jodi pushed the Fifaak hard, and it tumbled off the balcony, landing with a sickening thud.

As Sean finished off his last monster and ran to aid the others, Brandon and David met their first group of Fifaaks with a clash. Brandon, swinging his axe, cut through the legs of one beast, severing them at the kneecaps, and it tumbled from the balcony. Meanwhile David flailed about him with his great sword, meeting the beasts muscle for muscle and slaying them with efficiency and accuracy. Within a matter of minutes, a number of beasts lay dead at the two warriors' feet, but even with Sean's help they were forced back as more joined the onslaught.

Then to the surprise of all, a shout was heard from the Fifaak king and the monsters stopped fighting as if they had been paralyzed. Standing behind the throne with a knife to the king's throat was Christopher, now visible and smiling evilly with triumph.

"Amy!" he shouted. "Levitate yourself and the others down!"

Amy concentrated, chanting quietly, and brought the rest of the group to rest gently on the floor of the cave. Once there, they ran to Christopher's side.

"Thanks," breathed Brandon to the grinning wizard.

"Later," broke in Sean, holding his wounded shoulder. It was bleeding again. "Let's get outta here."

Christopher nodded, and Brandon led the group to a passageway on the lower level, a little to the side of the one they wished to enter. The wizard then said something quietly to the great beast in the throne and promptly drove his dagger deep into its throat. The beast let out a single scream before it died, blood spurting from its jugular vein in unison with its fading heartbeats. Christopher then ran to the passageway amid screams of rage from the surviving ogres who had begun trying to get down from the ledge. He stopped in the entrance of the cave and raised his hand, pointing at the altar. A bolt of lightning erupted from his fingertip and struck the marble base, exploding on impact, showering the chamber with dust and chunks of rock. He then aimed another lightning bolt at the staircase and let it fly, killing any Fifaaks on it and stranding the rest on the upper level.

Amid all the confusion, the party made their escape through a passage that took them on a bee-line straight to the rear entrance, a door identical to the one through which they had entered. They poured out of the exit, grateful for the confusion that the murder of the Fifaak king and the destruction of their black altar had caused.

Brandon pulled the lever to shut the door again and then came to the front of the group where they had paused at the door. Jessica canceled her light spell as they looked about to get themselves oriented before they continued. By the position of the sun, they deduced that they had been underground for about three or four hours; it was nearing mid-day. It was also obvious that they had come a great distance. They could see the desert just over a few more mountains extending as far as the eye could see to the west.

They renewed their trek, continuing down the path and began to talk. "Brandon, how come you know so much about these mountains?" asked Jodi, curiosity in her eyes.

Brandon paused before he answered. "They used to be

called the Jhirean Mountains, named after a dwarf king many ages ago, and the caves were made by dwarves. No ogres, no matter how smart, could ever carve or work stone anywhere near as well as the dwarves. The magic that was needed to gain entry to the caves is dwarven magic." He paused, looking upset. "The Fifaaks came after the Desert of Suspi had been created and stole the mountains from my ancestors, driving them into the lower part of the Azure Mountains. Knowledge of the Jhirean Mountains is still kept by the dwarves, however, and is passed down, generation after generation through maps and oral tradition."

"Aren't we headed toward the Azure Mountains?" asked David after a moment.

"Yes," answered Brandon. "But we'll be too far north to come across any of my kindred. Show me the map, and I'll show you where they live."

At this suggestion, they stopped their walk, expecting David to pull out the map so they could look. Instead, he said, "Shit! I must have lost it in the caves!"

"We can't go back after it," complained Jessica, frowning.

"No, the Fifaaks would capture us in a minute," said Brandon. "It looks like we're gonna have to rely on our memory."

"Do you think it'll be enough?" asked Amy.

"Yeah, Apocrys is due west of Tyrol," answered Brandon. "I also get the impression that it'll stick out like a sore thumb amongst the other mountains. It shouldn't be any problem."

They continued for a short while before stumbling upon a stream. There they stopped to rest for a moment. They found themselves in a small valley between two mountains. On the other side of the mountain to the west, the desert sprawled before them like quintessential loss, total emptiness. It actually seemed a shame to think of leaving these gorgeous mountains and entering the bleakness of the Desert of Suspi again even though the mountains were so dangerous. They were tall and majestic with snow-capped peaks and rings of color that reached down to the valley's floor: first white, then beige, then blue, followed by red, brown, and finishing with green. The overall effect was breathtaking, leaving them speechless as they drank from the babbling brook that wound its way out of the mountains and fed a small lake that was seen a little farther north of them.

After they had drunk their fill, they continued on the trail that wound around the border mountain and sat them once again on the verge of entering the desert.

"Are we gonna have enough water to last us?" asked Amy after a moment of silent regard for the sandy wasteland.

"I've got one full waterskin in my backpack," said Brandon. He had kept it, along with some of the deer from the night before. "I filled it at the stream. That should keep us alive for a while. How long will we be in the desert?"

"Most of a full day," answered David. "After what we've put up with in these mountains, though, I look forward to it. We can post a double watch again if we have to. Besides, I'd rather face those nomads any day than fight more Fifaaks. They'd be coming after us with blood in their eyes, and I don't blame 'em. After all, the wiz over there killed their ruler and desecrated, excuse me, annihilated their altar." David winked at Christopher. "Why'd you do that anyway?"

"I found myself really disliking those beasties," answered the wizard. "So I asked myself what I could do to really piss them off, and the answer was to destroy their religion. I don't think they'll be doing any more sacrifices for a while. It'll take some time to build another altar and get a new ruler."

"Also," added Jodi. "How did you get off the ledge without breaking your neck?"

"It was quite simple, actually. With a little help from Amy, I levitated down to the floor" he said, putting an arm around the furiously blushing cleric.

They started their trek into the desert then with perhaps an hour and a half of daylight left. They walked in silence, very weary, for it had been a very trying day. As night began to settle about them on the desert floor, Sean, who had been bringing up the rear, collapsed in a heap.

Jessica, followed by the others, raced to his limp body, wondering what evil had befallen him. It was then that they noticed the thief's tunic; it was soaked with blood. His right shoulder, where the Orc had bitten him, had a terrible suppurating wound on it that stank of infection, venom wafting out of it.

"Start setting up camp, David," ordered Jessica. "Sean needs help, and only Amy and I can give it to him. She'll stay with me; you get the rest of them to make camp and build a fire. I'm going to have to cauterize this wound at the least."

David and the others built a fire out of some dead shrubs and twigs that they found nearby while Jessica and Amy got to work.

"Sean?" asked Jessica. "Can you hear me?"

He nodded vaguely, fever racking his body like searing pain. He looked terrible, his face and body covered in sweat where it was not covered in blood. The wound consisted of about ten small holes, apparently teeth marks, with four scratches along the center. These last four marks were deep and pus oozed forth from a bloated boil that had formed over them.

"When did you start having trouble with this shoulder?" Jessica continued. "Was it when the Orc bit you?"

Sean shook his head. Something must have happened later to have infected this wound so badly.

"Was it when you were fighting with the Fifaaks?"

A nod.

Jessica sent Amy after Brandon while she continued to comfort Sean, stroking his feverish forehead as it rested limply in her lap. Amy and the dwarf soon returned.

"Can I help?" asked Brandon seriously.

"I hope so. Tell me, do the Fifaaks carry any sort of poison in their claws?"

"Yeah, sometimes they dip them in poison, why?"

"Look at Sean's shoulder." She pulled the tunic back and revealed the bubbling wound. Brandon winced. "Look at those scratches and how infected they are. Could that be from poisonous claws?"

Brandon swallowed. "Yeah."

"Do you know the poison's name?"

"Yeah, sure, but what's with twenty questions? Just heal him; he looks like he's in a lot of pain."

"I've got to know what I'm healing before I can do it, and if I try to heal the wrong thing, I might do more harm than good. So what's the poison called?" she insisted angrily, glaring at him corrosively for wasting time.

"It's called Koijio. Know anything about it?"

"Yes. It's a nerve poison. We've got to neutralize it before it reaches his brain."

"Can you do that?"

She sighed. "Yes, but it'll take a while, and Sean'll be weak for a few days. His shoulder and chest'll hurt for a week at least, and tomorrow, he won't be able to walk."

Brandon nodded and grew quiet.

"Sean, I'm afraid this is going to hurt quite a bit, so brace yourself," said Jessica to her friend as she drew her knife and cut off Sean's tunic. She then handed the knife to Brandon to put in the fire. "Amy, let me have your dagger."

As Amy gave it to her, she took Sean's hand and held it tightly. Jessica then cut the boil off Sean's skin while he writhed and found not enough strength to scream. She buried the sore in the sand down wind a fair distance, wiping the blade on her white robe. She then began enlarging the scratches by cutting them open; Sean squirmed a little before kind lady darkness relieved him of consciousness.

When Brandon returned with the red-hot knife, Sean's chest had been opened enough to clean the area completely of dirt. Brandon could see the muscle itself, surrounded by tissue, some living but mostly dead, and felt his stomach do a spiral depression as he stood still. The dwarf remained silent, watching as Jessica placed her hands like a poultice on the gaping wound, blood oozing up between her fingers to cover her hands. She spread her delicate fingers wide to cover the entire wound and began chanting mystically, magic pervading within the sound of her voice.

She pictured the poison as an evil black liquid that was invading Sean's bloodstream. She then envisioned it leaving his system and concentrated on sucking it out of his body entirely. She felt the magic racing through her like an iridescence beam of light, and her body felt like a giant vacuum, sucking the poison from Sean. There was a short struggle where she pitted her strength against that of the poison, but she finally conquered, a spasm making her rigid, hands closing into fists as all her muscles flexed with the fit. There was an explosion in the sand where she had buried the boil, showering sand into the air.

She opened her eyes and sighed, peering down into her open palms. What she saw there was a pool of dark liquid settling in her hand, a miasma rising like fog from it. She turned her hands over and the venom poured into the sand where it hissed and steamed until Amy buried it. Jessica wiped her hands in the sand and brushed them together, knocking the dirt off.

Brandon was thoroughly nauseated, and bile climbed to the top of his throat as he watched the steaming poison. He forced himself to swallow, but the sickness in his stomach remained.

"Give me the knife, Brandon," ordered Jessica. "The one you put in the fire." He handed it to her as if it were something harmful and helpful all at once.

She ripped a portion of her robe and placed the strip over the wound in Sean's chest. She took the glowing knife and burned the cloth into the gash where it seemed to magically fit like skin, molding itself to his shoulder. She gave the knife back to Brandon to clean and replaced her hands on Sean's chest, chanting softly. She traced the outline of the cloth, and it slowly faded into sallow skin. After a very short time, Sean's chest looked as if nothing had happened to it except for the alabaster patch of skin that predominated his right shoulder.

Sean lay rigidly in that same spot for the rest of the night. The others ate and drank a little around the fire except for Brandon who could not bring himself to touch anything. He was still too nauseated.

Problems with Peccare

"Has your shoulder healed properly, master thief?" asked one of the clerics, concerned. This somewhat short, plump man had introduced himself as Bacceron, one of Lady Gahdnawen's top priests.

"Yes, it's healed nicely, thank you," answered Sean, rubbing his shoulder thoughtfully. "Although, that's not one of the events in my life I'd like to repeat."

"I should think not," said Amy. "But you'd probably be just as hard-headed and keep it to yourself again if it did. Someday that'll probably get you killed."

Sean looked abashed and David continued the story. "The next morning we woke up feeling much more refreshed than we had previously. Sean was still very weak but had enough energy to eat a little breakfast. His wound was almost unnoticeable except for the patch of pale white skin on his shoulder..."

"How're you feeling today?" asked Jessica of the thief.

"I'm weak, but I don't feel sick anymore," answered Sean. "I just don't have any energy...never been so weak."

Jessica nodded and returned to the others. "He's doing just fine, but he won't be able to walk today, and we don't have the supplies to make a stretcher. Somebody's gonna have to carry him."

"I'll carry him for as far as I can, but Sean's no featherweight," said David with a great yawning stretch. "I'm not sure I can hold him all day long."

"I'll help," offered Brandon.

"I don't think that'd be a good idea. Frankly, my friend, you're a little too short to carry him in your arms, and it wouldn't be a good idea to put him over your shoulder. His wound might reopen. Of course, he wouldn't have far to fall should you drop him," David chortled.

Brandon grunted. He was happy to let someone else do the work, but he was also annoyed at being left out due to his height. "Well, then let's get going."

David approached Sean, lifting him with ease, and they began their trek through the last stretch of desert.

"Sorry for the inconvenience, David," said Sean after a few moments. "I hate to put you on the spot like this."

"Don't worry about it old friend—could've been any one of us. Just next time you get poisoned, share it with us before you collapse, okay?"

"I'll keep it in mind."

They trudged on in silence, the blistering sun beating down on their heads like a gigantic war drum, and their bodies were quickly drenched in sweat. They stopped infrequently to get a drink from Brandon's solitary waterskin and rest, recovering minimally from their exertion.

They watched the sun's movement all day long, hoping that it would soon disappear and give them some relief from the blistering heat. They watched it climb high in the sky until it reached its zenith and then slowly descend, groping for the horizon with ethereal fingertips.

Late that afternoon, the party saw another metamorphosis in the scenery. Around five o'clock, they happened to stumble across a waterhole where they refilled Brandon's skin and wet their faces, terminating the effects of the baking sun. The refreshing water renewed their very lives, and they began to talk once more.

"Looks like we're nearing the edge of the desert. The Teuton Swamp must be getting close," commented David, resting his weary arms. He'd been carrying Sean for nearly ten hours with few breaks.

"I'll be happy when we get out of this horrid heat," added Jessica, standing beside David, sweat streaking her face.

"Yeah, tell me about it," said Sean, sitting up. His strength was growing but even this minimal exercise was difficult. "Watching you guys walking on and on is making me very tired." He stretched.

"You bum!" accused Jodi, staring at him incredulously. "You've not done a single thing this entire day!"

He smiled. "I know."

"Son-of-a-bitch. I'm getting the feeling he got hurt on purpose, just so he wouldn't have to walk the rest of the way." Jodi pretended anger and disgust.

"That's right," he sighed dramatically. "You hit the nail on the head. I went through all that hell—getting poisoned and Jessica carving on me like a roast—just so I could bum around all day. I admit it. You've figured me out."

"Good con," commented David, bending down to pick Sean up once more. "Fooled me completely."

They walked for another hour before the swamp came into view, but even before they saw it, they knew it was there. They smelled it. The vile odor of decay was wafted down into their midst by a strong easterly wind, sweeping the reek through their ranks.

"Ugh!" commented Jodi humorously. "What a stench!

Almost as bad as Brandon's breath!"

"Hey, my breath's never been that bad," said the dwarf, hurt.

"Wanna bet?" supported Sean.

The thief grinned at his friend's wilting gaze as they continued to march towards the repugnant odor. The swamp was a dark, disgusting place that looked none too inviting, with twisted trees that were dark with slime. As they grew closer to it, the ground began to get soggy from the dingy water that seeped into the loamy turf from the morass, suffusing the earth with nauseating spilth.

Before they were within a hundred yards of the swamp, insects began to antagonize them with glee, reveling in their rapacious appetites. These bugs resembled mosquitoes for the most part, but their size varied greatly. Some were as small as gnats, but others were as big as small birds, biting and stinging them, leaving huge whelps where they landed. By the time the party actually entered the Teuton Swamp, they felt as if they had been eaten alive.

"These damned bugs are terrible," swore David as Sean slapped at a large one that had settled on his chest. "If we ever get to the other side of this swamp, there won't be enough left of us to continue."

"Isn't there anything we can do about them?" asked Jodi, disgustedly flailing at the mosquitoes around her head.

"We could enlist the help of some sort of giant frog," suggested Sean, brushing at his face. "What are they, anyway?"

"They're called tershumquids," answered Christopher. "They're not dangerous, just damned annoying," he commented, slapping.

"I'd kill for some bug repellent about now," mumbled David.

Christopher looked thoughtfully at David before wander-

ing into the slough for a moment. When he returned, he was
carrying a large white root like a radish with lumps. "Wipe the
juice on your exposed parts and the bugs'll leave you alone,"
he said, breaking a piece off and wiping the clear, thick liquid
on his arms, legs, and face, covering them thoroughly.

David sat Sean down in the muck, amid some rather rude
complaints and suggestions, and took the root, doing as
Christopher had instructed, the others quickly imitating him.
Amy wrinkled her nose at the offensive smell as she wiped the
stuff on. "If I came across somebody that smelled like this, I'd
leave 'em alone too."

After all had treated themselves, they began to slosh
through the marsh again. To the relief of all, the tershumquids
did leave them alone, looking instead, for sweeter prey with
less disagreeable odors.

They traveled on through the mire for another hour before
they came across a place suitable to stay the night. It was a
small clearing with dry ground and a large willow tree provid-
ing cover. There was a section of deep water directly south of
the trees and a small creek, surprisingly clear, flowing parallel
to the lake but to the north of the tree. They built a fire with
wood they had to search and search for, but after they got it
going, it was more than happy to stay lit, slowly swallowing
the slightly damp lumber, hissing and popping as its blue
tougues reached water and wood respecitvely.

David stalked off into the mire westward, searching for
some form of edible animal. He soon returned with a mamma-
lian creature that remotely resembled a large black squirrel
though it had no fur. As they roasted it, a deep, forbidding
darkness closed in about them, engulfing them in its effacing
coldness.

They ate the squirrel, which had very little taste but did fill
an empty stomach, in silence except for the frogs and lizards
that kept them company for most of the night, croaking and

crepitating, rustling and splashing. They drank the last of the water from Brandon's water skin and soon drifted off to sleep except for David who took the first watch.

He sat in silence, watching the area about him intently, attempting to strip away the darkness like old, black paint. He felt odd; a sort of foreboding was building within him...he felt worried, terribly worried. What's wrong with me? he asked himself. Why am I so on edge all of a sudden? There's nothing around me. I don't see anything threatening. Everything appears as it should.

He continued his rationalization, trying to convince himself that nothing was wrong, but he never totally relaxed, nervousness keeping him rigid. He sat in silence, wondering what it was that was unnerving him so badly. Maybe it was just the strain. The last few days had been terribly stressful for him. He yawned and stretched grandly, flexing his muscles, trying to fight the stiffness that was setting in his arms from carrying Sean so far. He should have let someone help.

As his thoughts wandered, he caught some movement out of the corner of his eyes. Foreboding creeping down his spine, he turned to see what had moved and was amazed. There was a large green tentacle, looking almost like a root, snaking out of the water to the south, grasping for firm holds. It was slowly making its way towards his sleeping companions.

"What the—" he began, but another large tentacle wrapped itself around his waist and, in one great whoosh, squeezed all the air out of him. It was joined by the first tentacle, which stuck itself in David's mouth so that he could not scream—not that he could have anyway; he could not even breath. Slowly, relentlessly David was dragged into the lake, fighting all the way.

Brandon awoke. He thought he had heard a splash somewhere in the darkness. He looked around but saw nothing unusual, so he started to turn back over. But suddenly he realized that not only had he seen nothing unusual, he also had not seen what should have been there. Where was David?

The dwarf stood, loosening his axe in its straps across his back in case there was trouble. "David?" he whispered, attempting to locate his friend, wondering if he had simply stepped into the darkness to relieve himself. "David?"

A tremendous splash in the lake next to the clearing shattered the silence with resounding volume, and Brandon whirled, whipping his axe out protectively. In the middle of the lake, a tremendous, tentacled beast reared up, holding David tightly in a grip of iron. It had one great eye centered in its spherical head over a clacking beaked mouth. David was struggling with the thing, but it was simply too strong for him; he was growing weaker every second.

"David!" shouted Brandon, rushing into the water to aid his friend. He had to swim out to where the struggle was taking place, and that was tremendously difficult because a dwarf's flesh is much more dense than a human's. By pure strength of will, he finally reached David, and standing on the monster, he began hacking at the bonds that held David.

Brandon's axe severed one tentacle, freeing David's left hand which reached for his dagger. Brandon continued to hack at the beast which seemed to be made out of something much harder than wood, doing very little damage to it. Gaining his dagger, David twisted and stabbed the knife deep into the monster's great, solitary eye.

A pained scream erupted from its beaked mouth while a thick green liquid rushed from its wound. It threw David powerfully away, hoping to crush him with the force. The flying giant slammed into the willow tree with a thud and slid to the ground where he lay, not moving.

Brandon continued struggling with the beast, until one great tentacle slapped him, sending him flying back to the shore. He landed with a grunt and slowly regained his feet as the monster sank back into the murk, nursing its wound. Brandon then heard a high, inhuman giggle from behind him and turned quickly to see a number of small, blue humanoids disappearing into the darkness. He ignored them for the moment and moved to where David lay in a heap with Jessica bent over him, examining him.

"David! Are you all right?" he asked, breathless and dizzy.

The giant groaned, attempting to sit up, and Brandon leaned him against the tree for support. His nose was bleeding and one of his eyes was already swelling from the impact. There were a number of splinters embedded in his skin.

"I'll be okay...I'm just a little dizzy," answered David quietly as Jessica tilted his head back and peered into his eyes, probing him for serious injury. "What the hell was that?"

"A kraken," answered Christopher from behind Brandon.

David looked up at the wizard. "I thought they lived in salt water."

"Apparently not exclusively. I've heard legends of them in lakes and killing animals as they went by, but I've never heard of such a small one attacking a man from a pond like that."

"Small, huh?!"

Christopher nodded.

"David, do you know how lucky you are?" asked Jessica after she had thoroughly inspected him for breaks.

"That's not the word I'd of used," he returned with a wry grin as he rubbed his neck. "I feel like shit."

Jessica looked at him wiltingly for a moment. "You've just been thrown thirty feet into a tree by a kraken, and you don't even have a concussion. You're very lucky! If you didn't have such a hard head, you'd have been killed by that!"

David nodded uncertainly, and Jessica cleaned up his bruised face, helping him move to the fire so she could remove the splinters from his face and chest. She removed his hauberk and lay it by the fire.

"I'll take over your watch from here," offered Christopher after David had been thoroughly fussed over—and at.

David accepted and was preparing to settle down to sleep when he noticed that something was missing from his belt. His purse was gone. "Damn!" he swore, sitting back up slowly. "I must've lost my money pouch in the struggle!"

It was then that they noticed that everybody but Brandon had lost their purses.

"What happened?" fumed Jodi. "We couldn't all have just dropped them!"

"I think I know," said Brandon angrily. "When we were all trying to help David, I noticed some little blue men running into the swamp. Anybody know what kind of men are blue?" he asked.

"Little blue people?" asked Sean. "Did you get hit on the head, too?"

"Shut up!" retorted Brandon. "No and unlike you, I don't get drunk and make an ass of myself either!"

"Gremlins!" exclaimed Christopher after a second.

"Damn!" commented David again.

"I bet they magically forced the kraken to attack us, and when we were distracted, they stole our money," said Christopher, snapping his fingers.

"What're we gonna use to get more supplies with once we reach Tyrol?" asked Jodi.

"Or to find somewhere to sleep while we're there?" added Jessica unhappily. "Brandon doesn't have enough for all that."

"We'll just have to figure that out when we get there," answered Christopher. "Something's bound to turn up."

"Wow!" commented Sean sarcastically, gesturing at Christopher. "Look what we have here! A real live optimist! I've never seen one of them before! Maybe we should have it stuffed!"

Christopher frowned at the thief. "If worse comes to worst, we can always get our esteemed thief to steal something for us—if he can."

"There's no sense in standing here bickering about it," interrupted Jessica. "Let's just get to sleep and worry about it when we have to." She looked at each of them with steely eyes, and they lapsed into silence.

The rest of the night was spent in uneventful sleep, worrying whether or not they would find some way to replenish their supplies for the rest of their journey. Somewhere deep within the recesses of their minds, they also wondered if this occurrence was strictly incidental, or if someone had planned it. The answer was found, of course, a long distance from there, in a black chair that they all knew quite well. Doctor John Richards laughed harder, enjoying their plight.

They awoke the next morning to the sound of rain falling in the marsh. Since their camp was made below the great willow tree containing the markings of David's head, very little of the rain had reached them.

"This is gonna be a really great day," complained Sean. He was, however, feeling much better after his night's rest, now standing and strolling about, testing the stability of his legs. "How ya feeling today, big fella?" he asked David, patting him on the back a little too hard.

The warrior looked up at Sean and scowled. His arms hurt from carrying Sean so far, not to mention the throbbing headache that he still had from his confrontation with the old willow tree. He looked rather gruesome, the way he just sat there and grimaced. His left eye was swollen shut and the white scar below it only made him look more disfigured, as if he had lost a fight with a bear—a Kodiak. His brown beard had grown full and was thick with dirt, like his hair.

"I'll take that for a 'not so good'." Sean answered himself and turned to leave his silent friend, hoping David would not hurt anyone today—especially him. He walked over and joined Jessica. "What's bothering Mister Happy over there?" he asked.

She looked back at him and smiled wanly. "He's tired, sore, and angry with himself. He thinks he should've seen that attack coming last night."

"Oh? How come you know so much?"

"Trust me," she smiled. "I think I know David well enough to determine that."

"You're probably right."

They began their journey that morning with downcast eyes and frowning faces as Sean led the way through the swamp, his sure feet picking out the safest paths. There was much activity in the bog that day, frogs were singing in chorus with the stridulating insects while the snakes roamed, searching for food. All different kinds of reptiles were seen slithering through the murk or climbing trees with clawed feet while a few small mammals, like the one they had eaten, skittered out on limbs wet with rain. But perhaps the most noticeable animals were the fish. The rain had brought them to the surface, hunting for insects that crawled across the water. Some of these fish the company recognized, but others were more exotic, the likes of which they had never seen. Some were long with rainbow colored skin in place of scales, like the rainbow trout, but were fatter and had no visible eyes. Instead they snaked their long tongues out of their mouths as thermal detection, like the serpents that swam with them. There were strange amphibious creatures basically like frogs but with definitely mannish qualities. All together, the animals in the Teuton Swamp were more various than in any other part of the world.

The trees they traveled under were thick above their heads;

so they only caught brief glimpses of the cloudy sky above. These same trees, mostly live oaks, were covered in slime and had many vines swinging about in the almost imperceptible wind. At one point, Sean began to push through a cluster of the vines when a hand snaked out from behind him and grasped his wrist.

"Don't bother the vines," ordered Christopher. "Some of them are dangerous. They're like giant leaches that'll attach themselves to you and drain you dry. It's better to avoid 'em."

Sean continued more carefully than before, looking about at everything, especially the vines, searching for danger at every step. The others followed him through the slough. At some points their feet would be sucked under by deep mud, and at others they would almost fall on unsteady patches of ground that sneaked up on them without warning. The deeper they got into the marsh, the soggier the ground became until it finally was practically nonexistent. They had to wade through the murky water, going as closely northwest as they possibly could.

"Are we ever gonna get out of here?!" fumed David after a half day's march.

"Another few hours, David, as far as I can tell," answered Christopher stoically. "Be patient."

"It could be worse," comforted Amy. "We could still have insects swarming about us."

David grunted.

"Lighten up David!" reprimanded Jessica, running out of patience. "Feeling sorry for yourself isn't going to help matters." She probed him with an intense stare.

David returned her gaze and grunted again, lapsing into silence.

They marched on for another hour or so before stopping for lunch. They finished the deer that Brandon had managed to save and sipped a little water out of a clear stream they stopped by. It was the only water they had seen all day that looked drinkable, so Brandon refilled his waterskin before they continued their march, watching the scenery change about them once more but this time in a favorable light. Slowly the ground grew less soggy and the undergrowth grew less dense, making it much easier to travel. After about another half hour of walking, they found themselves on a path that was slowly meandering its way out of the marsh. They followed it for perhaps a mile until it opened onto a clearing, the first real opening in the swamp they had seen. Excluding David, the party flooded into the clearing, happy to see the sky again as the rain poured down on them, bathing them, cleansing them.

David somberly watched his friends rush into the clearing, still feeling guilty, and as they bathed in the rain, he got a terrible feeling deep in his soul, as if a demon had grasped his heart with icy fingers. "Something's wrong here," he murmured. He froze for a moment when he saw figures drop out of the trees behind his friends. As a club struck Brandon in the back, David ripped his sword from its scabbard and pounced into the clearing. He skewered a man who was about to grab Jodi, and another chill ran up his spine, an ill omen. He began to turn, bringing his sword to bear on the figure that landed behind him, but he was not quick enough. A club contacted with his skull, and pain poured into him, blinding him with bright light. Another blow and he fell limply to the ground, unconscious.

"Wake up, you useless piece of garbage!" shouted a man, kicking David hard in the side.

As the air gushed from his lungs, David regained consciousness, pain forcing him to open his eyes. He looked up at the figure that had kicked him, gasping for breath. With his solitary working eye, David peered at the figure, pain and fear making his blood boil. He had seen this man before; it was the same fellow he had shot in the arm outside Rocnar Da'arputni's hovel.

David's mind reeled, but he forced himself to think, suppressing his anger as best he could. How long had he been unconscious? Minutes or hours? He looked about him, trying to get his bearings, hoping that something would click. He was tied, hands behind his back to a tree. To his left, Sean sat in the same predicament with Christopher on his other side, bound and gagged. The wizard's eyes glinted with promised anguish for his captors. Sean peered at David with worried, but alert, eyes. David turned his head to the other side and saw Brandon's unconscious form tied to another tree. The dwarf's head lay on his chest, his eyes closed; a nasty knot was forming on the back of his skull.

David took this all in before returning his gaze to the clearing in front of him. There were a score of men standing close by, staring casually at him and his compatriots. In front of the throng, a tall, burly man, nearly as large as David himself, stood staring down at his prisoner with a smile. "Nice to see you again," he commented in a deep, intelligent voice.

David returned the man's gaze steadily though his head screamed from where it had been hit, and the world was slightly blurred by his infringed sight.

"Do you remember me?" asked the figure, coming to stand in front of David. There he knelt, peering directly into David's steely blue eyes, grinning maliciously. His scarred face was mere inches from David's when he reached out and grabbed the captive warrior's chin. "Answer me," he demanded, slapping David hard with a callused hand.

David's head spun as he struggled to answer the man. "Yeah, I remember you," he said, staring at his tormentor in disgust.

"Good, because I remember you, too. You put an arrow through my wrist," he said, gazing at the scar in his right arm.

"You also took a map from the hermit that I wanted. If you tell me where it is, I'll kill you first. That way you won't have to watch your friends die." He gestured at Sean, Christopher, and Brandon. "They refused to tell me and will pay for it with very slow deaths."

David stared up at him, raising his chin with as much dignity as he could, and spat in the man's face. "Go to hell!" he shouted, regretting the tone of his voice. It made his head spin again.

The man stood up and gave David a solid kick in the jaw. David felt himself beginning to fall into unconscious ruin again and fought it, using his anger to keep him awake. "Who are you?" he asked more for the comfort of his own voice than out of curiosity.

"Oh, excuse me. I forgot to introduce myself. I'm called Peccare. I'm a mercenary. I already know who you are, Graham. You see, I returned for the hermit later, and he told me who you all are...except for this man at your left." He turned to look at Sean questioningly.

The thief pointedly returned Peccare's gaze for a moment before answering. "I'm Martin of Sukhur, thief and assassin," he said with as much dignity as he could muster, given his position.

"Never heard of you," Peccare said, returning his attention to David, ignoring the enraged thief. "Tell me where the map is."

David looked up at Peccare again and sneered. "I don't know."

Peccare sighed. "Very well then. We'll do it the hard way." He turned and looked at the laughing men gathered around him. "Tie his feet."

Two men came forward with rope and began tying his feet to spikes, but David managed to kick one in the jaw for which he received a brutal slap. Sean turned to David. "Stand fast, my friend. We'll make it," he said with a quiet smile. "We always do."

"Shut up!" shouted one man, backhanding Sean viciously. The thief grunted and grinned at his assaulter.

Peccare approached David, his feet now tied, and drew a curved dagger out of its sheath at his side. "Are you sure you won't tell me?" he asked, casually stroking David's chin with the knife. David took a good long look at the dagger, hoping that he would have the opportunity to use it on its master. It had a polished foot-long blade, decorated with spiraling black roses. Its curved handle was fashioned into the head and neck of a hunting bird, probably a hawk. This visage was flanked by two smaller eagles' heads, rictuses open in vicious, silent squawks.

David looked at the man and answered, "I told you. I don't know."

"Very well." Peccare ran the dagger down David's bare chest, leaving an angry streak of crimson where it passed.

David grunted and then smiled at Peccare maliciously. "It'll take more than that," said David, hoping to frustrate his tormentor.

"Don't worry, Graham. I have much more." Peccare continued the torture unmercifully, cutting deep gashes in his chest, arms, and legs and then beating him savagely with a whip and a club. After what seemed to David an eternity of fighting his want to cry out, Peccare stopped for a moment and looked into his captive's eyes. "Bring me the salt."

David sat stoically, frowning deeply but saying nothing, as one of Peccare's men brought a bag full of salt. Peccare reached his hand into the bag and pulled out a handful, letting a little drizzle between his fingers onto the ground. "Where's the map?"

"Go to hell," was David's only answer as Peccare dumped the handful of crystallized pain onto David's bleeding chest, rubbing it into the wounds with enough force to embed the particles into his flesh. He fought harder than he had ever fought before, refusing to give Peccare the satisfaction of hearing him scream. He went rigid, flexed against the agony, hoping that the locking of his muscles would paralyze his nerves enough.

Finally the pain abated, and Peccare stepped back to get a better look at David's mutilated body. "Well, it looks like this form of torture won't make you talk, but I never thought it would. It was mostly for my amusement, anyway. I know another way that surely will."

"No chance," answered David defiantly, weak with pain but strong with anger.

"Don't be so sure of yourself, man," said Peccare with a grin. "You have absolutely no idea what I'm going to do. I believe I might enjoy this even more than beating your wretched face in. Please, Graham, watch closely."

David did watch, curious and worried as Peccare paced slowly over to the right side of the clearing, strutting his power. It was then that David saw, with horror, Jodi, Amy, and Jessica, each tied to a tree in a standing position. The three women looked scared and disgusted as Peccare approached them.

"Graham!" shouted Peccare as he reached the three women. "Which one is yours?"

David saw in a flash what the man intended to do. Anger, topped by frustration, began to build within him, burning him, searing his attention on Peccare in a white-hot flare. Pain no longer mattered, only hatred and wrath.

"Is it this little brunette?" he asked, approaching Amy, stroking her buttocks lovingly as she squirmed away from his touch as if it burned her. Christopher flinched, straining against his bonds, the veins standing out in his neck and in his face. "Oh, I see," said Peccare. "This one's the wizard's. Then we'll come back to her later, but first a little taste of what's to come." He took his dagger and slowly cut a shallow wound in her bound left wrist. She whimpered from the pain.

David's anger was building, growing stronger and stronger with every step Peccare took. As the mercenary approached Jodi, David's adrenaline started flowing and, out of pure anger, he started straining against the bonds that held him, pitting his will against their solid might, no longer able to stay static.

"How about this one?" Peccare asked as he drew close to Jodi, caressing her leg where it showed out from under her robes. "Is this fine redhead yours, Graham?"

David's muscles were flexing throughout his body, pushing his tendons farther than they were meant to go. As he grew taut, blood coursed from the new wounds that had been formed by Peccare's dagger. His wrists started bleeding very freely, wetting the cords that held him.

"Not a strong enough reaction with that one," said the mercenary, cutting a small gash in Jodi's left thigh. He started forward again, grinning to himself. "I guess that leaves this pretty little cleric over here." He walked closer to Jessica who gazed at him haughtily, as if she were above fear of him. Her aura seemed to swell and then turn in on itself, intensifying her power.

David's vision was beginning to get blurred with pain and rage as he struggled with the bonds that held him, pitting all of his strength and some that he did not know he had against the puny ropes that contained him.

"I must compliment you, Graham. You have excellent taste in women. She does seem a little too arrogant, but that'll soon end. I'm sure I can knock her off her pedestal," commented Peccare as he finally reached Jessica and, pulling her to him, kissed her savagely, running his hands over her hips. He pricked her throat with his dagger and blood stained her robes.

David no longer felt anything; indeed the only sensation he had was of pure, focused rage. The only thought in his mind was that he must break the bonds that held him, release the terrible flood that coursed through his venous body. He must! No matter what happened to him, he must succeed!

Jessica struggled against Peccare, but he was much the stronger. Finally, she kicked out with her leg as hard as she could and smiled as she felt her knee make satisfying contact with Peccare's groin.

David was still struggling with his restraints, but he could feel them starting to give. He sensed their weakness and pushed toward it.

Peccare doubled over, and his men began to laugh. He then stood straight and slapped Jessica across the face with a powerful backhand. Her body went limp for a moment before she regained her senses. "Shut up!" shouted Peccare at his men who quickly grew silent.

David glanced up in time to see the blow that Peccare landed on Jessica, and also to see him begin to remove his clothes angrily as he approached her. The mercenary turned and shouted at the bound giant, "Watch this, Graham! Maybe you'll feel more like talking after you've had a good show! I've pricked her with one dagger; but this one cuts much deeper!" He grabbed his crotch.

Jessica had her eyes closed, afraid yet certain of what she was doing. She prayed. She prayed harder than she ever had before. She prayed for the help she needed to defend herself from Peccare's lust. She reached out to Galead for protection, all the while confident that something would happen. She felt the almost imperceptible tingle of contact and knew that her goddess had heard her prayers. She smiled silently to herself as she opened her eyes, waiting for Galead's intervention.

As Peccare returned his lusty gaze to Jessica and raised her robes up over her hips, something snapped within David's psyche; he seemed to go mad. He strained and struggled harder, calling on the strength that was hidden within his soul. He felt the adrenaline coursing through his veins as real as the tree behind his back and the ropes around his wrists and ankles. Then, in one split second, he felt every nerve within his body burst with rage, sending fire into his extremities. He pulled and pulled, jerking as he screamed, releasing every ounce of power within his body and channeling it into his massive arms. Just when he knew that his body lacked the strength to break free, more energy surged into him from somewhere he could not ascertain. He enveloped the strength, intertwined it with his own and released everything into one mighty jerk. With a satisfying rip, the ropes that bound him burst, leaving him free and unchained!

As David realized that he was free, his purpose leapt into frame, focusing him yet leaving him chaotic with the savage glee of power. David leapt to his feet, a raging menace! His eyes flared with such anger that all he could physically see were the two forms at his right: Jessica staring at him, loving yet unsurprised and Peccare cursing as he shouted to his men and pulled up his pants. As David began racing towards them, he became aware that a figure had risen from the ground to his left. He paid it no mind, however, knowing that whoever it was could take care of himself.

A great shout arose from Peccare's men as they rushed to meet the giant, sure of his easy defeat. David barely took notice of them. As they came within reach, he broke them like twigs, leaving their forms wrecked and useless. Their puny weapons did not matter to him; all he could think about was Jessica, and then, a memory flared at the back of his mind. He saw a little girl lying in the dirt, raped, and her mother lying, cut open, with her unborn baby torn from her! He saw four lives ripped from their familial solace and left, bleeding their horror to ears that could not hear. As the vision faded, more anger than David had ever felt rushed into his mind, giving him strength and power that he had never before had!

He broke into splinters the tiny men that rushed forward to meet him! The wounds that he suffered from their swords and daggers were little more than simple pin pricks beside the pain he felt in his soul! He needed to reach Jessica and make Peccare pay, end his riot of violence! He felt a sharp pain in his hand as he grabbed a sword from one attacker's grip! He threw the sword away but felt it slick through one of his fingers before it was wrenched from its wielder! It fell to the ground somewhere as David's mind screamed at him: "Peccare! Peccare! Kill Peccare!" and then he heard "Jessica! You must save her!"

This was all he could hear, see, or feel. He lived and breathed this solitary thought as he raced for Peccare and Jessica. He saw again that young girl who never had a chance to live her life, and then he saw that unborn fetus that never had the chance to feel the sun on its face, or to smell a flower, or to hug its loving mother...

And then he was there, at his goal! Peccare turned to meet him, dagger in hand, prepared to kill his attacker. "You're dead, Graham!" he shouted as he charged at the enraged man.

David screamed, all his fury being vented by his yells, as the two giants collided with a thud! They wrestled about for what seemed an eternity until David felt a pain lancing in his side! He knew that Peccare had stabbed him, but it did not matter! He continued fighting! Finally gaining a good hold, David picked Peccare off the ground and flung him down! He was on top of Peccare before the mercenary had a chance to react, pounding his fists into the man's face!

He pounded and pounded until he felt a tremendous blow knock him off Peccare! He attempted to turn over, but the weight on him was too great. He was being crushed! He could not breathe! Then he felt some of the weight being lifted off him and a few screams with the clash of metal! He threw the rest of the bodies off him with a final surge of adrenaline! Regaining his feet, he looked around and saw two valiant figures fighting off many.

Then a yell resounded from somewhere near David and all the figures broke, running for the trees! At their head ran Peccare, beaten, bruised, and bloody, but still alive. The figures disappeared into the marsh, and David stood motionless for a moment, shocked beyond reaction. Finally, he stirred himself to approach Jessica where she was still tied. He walked up to her, feeling dizziness envelope him as pain flooded into his body. He fell against her and hugged her close, tears of release streaming from his eyes. "Are you all right?" he managed, feeling the energy pour out of his body with the blood that poured out his side.

"Yes, David," Jessica answered. She looked tired and very angry, glittering with ire. "Are you?"

David paused, his head swimming. "I—" he began but no longer had the strength to remain conscious. He fell to the ground in a heap at Jessica's feet. The last sound he heard was the scream that erupted from Jessica's throat; then blackness enshrouded him.

Anodyne

David heard sounds from out of a shroud of black. Swimming through the darkness, he searched for the source of that wondrous voice. He broke through the surface of unconsciousness and, as if from a long ways, saw a kind, beautiful face peering down at him, speaking his name. "David? David? Can you hear me?" it asked.

He tried to answer but could not muster the strength. He felt himself sinking back down into unconsciousness, but he did not have the will to fight the maelstrom that sucked him into oblivion.

David heard the sound again, a kind voice calling his name. He made for it, swimming with all his strength for that sweet, musical sound. He broke through the tremulous surface again, and there, staring down at him with a smile on her face, was Jessica.

She was gripping his hand, squeezing it, hoping that her touch would awaken him, return him to the conscious realm. "David, can you hear me?" she asked urgently, praying for a response, any response—a squeeze, a twitch, anything to reassure her of his alertness.

David peered back at her, struggling to speak, but no sound would arise from the haze that surrounded him. He fought with the invisible bonds that held him like ropes, struggled to break them, pulled the little energy he had left into his mind and asserted it against the weakness of his body.

"David?!" Jessica almost shouted the name. "Speak to me!"

He struggled harder against his negation, his denial of life, and Jessica's assertion of authority was the catalyst that finally released him, gave voice to his thoughts. "I hear you," he managed though his voice cracked with the strain. He tried to speak again, thoughts flooding his mind, questions that must be answered, words that must be offered. "Where am I?" he rasped, the spume in his throat almost stifling his words.

"You're in a room in an inn. We're all here," she answered. "We came to Tyrol last night, carrying you. We had to find somewhere out of the weather where you could rest, regain your senses."

"What's wrong with me? What happened?" asked David, fighting his fatigue. He could barely stir himself enough to think.

"You overextended yourself," she answered. "Your body only has so much strength, you know. But you need more time to recover, to conserve your strength."

"But—" he began to protest, but she cut him short.

"No buts about it. The only reason I awakened you now was to make sure you were recovering well. Now, you've got to rest or you won't be able to move at all until tomorrow. Sleep and I'll answer all your questions when you awake." She bent and gently kissed his forehead.

David did not want to sleep, but he knew he must. In fact, he did not have the strength to stay awake. So as insensibility spread throughout his body and unconsciousness took him, he found himself giving in and promptly slept.

This sleep was haunted by dreams of a man, tall and scarred, heavily built like David himself. He saw this man holding Jessica's unconscious form in his arms as he laughed at David, gloating over his prize. David raced after him and found that he could no longer see either of them. He felt a sharp pain in his back and whirled to see Peccare standing with a bloody dagger in his hand. He felt himself falling, deeper and deeper into the nightmare's death; then he woke.

Jessica and Sean were standing over him, reading the nightmare in his face. David looked around for the first time, realizing that he was in a well-furnished room. The bed in which he lay was soft, with posts of brass or bronze, he was not sure which. The windows had lace curtains and there was a large, oval mirror on the wall. There was also a chest against one wall, apparently for storing clothes, and two doors exited the room, one beside the chest, the other beside the mirror.

"Well, hello there," said Sean, grinning as usual. "Nice to see you've returned. No more dreaming with the dead?"

David smiled at him and attempted to sit up. The effort dizzied him, but nevertheless, he managed it. "I hope not, and it's nice to be back. But I'm afraid I don't know how I got here. I can't remember anything after…" he trailed off. Everything past his battle with Peccare's men was shrouded in a roiling haze. He thought he remembered being touched by something…something inhuman, perhaps divine.

"Well, as for how you got here, I'll tell you. Brandon and I carried you the whole damned way." Sean smiled down at him, rubbing his arms. "I think that makes us even, but let me tell you, my friend, you're heavy as hell. Have you ever considered going on a diet? I didn't think we'd ever get here. Next time you get hurt like that, make sure there's an ambulance around, okay? The stretcher we built helped, but not much."

David laughed, but quickly stifled it, holding his head as if his feeble hands could keep it from splitting. "Oh..." he moaned. "Don't make me laugh."

"That'll teach you," said Jessica, smiling vaguely.

David nodded, still holding his head. "Now, would somebody please tell me what the hell happened?"

"I'll let Jessica do that, David," said Sean. "I've gotta go. See ya later." The thief turned and left through the door next to the chest. David saw that it lead to a hallway before Sean shut it behind him.

"So," said David, looking at Jessica. "Tell me."

The cleric, dressed in clean white robes, came and sat next to David on the bed. "Okay," she said, grasping David's hand in hers, emotion glistening in her deep eyes, a caress of stars. It was then that David noticed the stub where the left index finger on his right hand should have been. He vaguely remember the blade that tore it from him.

Jessica stroked his sore quietly before beginning. "Apparently, you expended all the strength in your body trying to rescue Jodi, Amy, and me from Peccare. With all the wounds and beatings you received, you completely exhausted yourself. You almost died, and would have too, if Amy hadn't cast a Light Cures spells on you. Anyway, you just didn't have enough strength left in your body to keep your heart beating. That and the great amount of blood you lost are the reasons you're so weak."

David watched her closely as she talked. She looked really beautiful...her eyes deep with concern and her hair framing her face like a sable habit.

"Lucky for you," she continued, "that Sean was able to free his hands. I still don't know how he did it though; I saw the knots they tied him with. I guess it's just that thieves' training of his. Anyway, he got himself untied about the same time you broke loose, and while you were tossing people about, he untied Christopher. Those two fought off the rest of Peccare's men and freed us. You were the only casualty.

"After Peccare ran off, Amy cast her spell on you, expecting you to revive. None of your wounds were really all that serious except the one in your side and it was easy to heal. When you didn't wake up, the two of us looked you over and discovered how drained you were. We then marched into Tyrol, which is where we are, and got a room in the finest inn we could find, The Blue Dragon. Of course we didn't have enough money to stay, so I charmed the owner, a short fat man named Eligere, and he's letting us stay for free. So here we are, and we're still alive." She bent and embraced David strongly. Though her tone was light, what she said and the way she held him so tightly touched David deeply. He recognized exactly how scared she was, and then the fear washed over him too, reminding him of all that had happened in that clearing in the Teuton Swamp, and even more, what could have happened.

They sat there for quite some time before Jessica forced herself to release him and raised up. Her cheeks were damp and her eyes were brimming with tears. "I was so afraid," she said quietly. "For a while, I thought I'd lost you." As she bent to kiss David again, he noticed that she was trembling.

"Jessica," he said softly, not sure of how to console her, "you know that I wouldn't leave you. I couldn't." He let her dark hair slide through his fingers like ebony tears. "I gave you my word that I'd get you home, and I will...I will! If I had to come back from the dead, I'd find you and carry you back to our world. Nothing can separate us."

She raised her head and stared at him. The tears and trembling had subsided but sadness and fear still echoed in her gaze. "David...I was paralyzed with fear. All I could do was pray and that helped. But you were the only one who could save us. You strained until your heart nearly burst!" She paused, struggling to keep her voice steady, placing a hand gently on his chest. "Thank you for saving us. Peccare would have raped me then turned us all over to his men, but you stopped him!" she breathed timorously. "When no one else could help, you pulled through for us. Thank you."

He looked at her and smiled. "You know I wouldn't let anybody touch you that way." He could not even bring himself to say the word. "Especially some vagabond like him. Now, how 'bout some food? I'm starving."

She smiled down at him and wiped her eyes, glad for a chance to dwell on something more normal for a while. "I'll get you something." She left through the same door Sean had.

David did not tell her that their encounter with Peccare had scared him too. When he awakened, tied to that tree, he thought they were all going to die. It scared him more than he had ever been scared before, but he fought…for her. She gave him the strength.

When Jessica returned, she bore a tray with her. It contained a bowl with some pasty substance and a mug of water. "Gruel!" protested David in disgust. He had really hoped for something more solid. "I hate gruel!"

"Yes, but you'll eat it because it's good for you," said Jessica with a smile. "Anything more substantial would probably come right back up." She sat down on the bed and began feeding him the tasteless stuff.

"I can feed myself, ya know," he complained as a second spoonful was thrust into his mouth.

"I doubt that," she said, preparing another bite. "You probably couldn't raise your arms that high."

David, being the rebellious patient he was, tried and discovered that it was true. He could barely move at all; so he sat there and suffered through being fed, not really all that bothered by it. He sort of liked having Jessica make such a fuss over him…as long as nobody else was around. With each bite he took, he felt his strength resurge in him.

Before he had finished, the rest of the group entered the room, grinning and making cracks about "spoon-feeding." His only response was a scowl.

Christopher approached him. "You look…" He paused, suppressing a chuckle, searching for some way to be truthful and complementary at once. "Better."

David glowered at him. "Thanks."

"Any luck?" asked Jessica, turning to look at Sean who was just now entering.

The thief opened his mouth to reply but was truncated by David. "Any luck with what?" he asked, still frowning. "And where has everyone been?"

"Oh, it's nothing to worry about, dear," answered Jessica as she wiped his mouth with the spoon. "Just looking for a way to earn some money. We don't have enough to buy supplies."

"Oh…yeah," answered David, remembering as a wave of culpability swept over him.

Seeing David's reaction, Jessica reprimanded him. "Now stop that. It wasn't your fault."

"Then whose was it?" returned David defiantly. "If I'd been paying as much attention as I should have, I would've seen the whole thing coming and we'd still have our money."

"It wasn't your fault, David, but even if it were, it's neither here nor there. It's over and we can't do anything about it. So just forget about it."

David lapsed into silence.

"Do you want me to answer your question or not?" asked Sean after a moment.

"Oh, yes," said Jessica. "Please."

"I think I found a way."

"Really? How?" they all asked almost at once, turning to look at Sean.

"You see," he began, "there's a brothel just up the street, and they're looking for a few good girls…" He broke off as

Jodi kicked him hard in the shin. "Ow!" he protested, taking his weight off that leg and hopping on the other exaggeratedly. "I was just kidding."

"Did you really find a way?" asked Christopher skeptically. "Or do you just enjoy getting our hopes up and dropping us off a cliff?"

"I did find a way," answered Sean, moving away from Jodi. "In three days, a tournament's going to be held in Tyrol's coliseum. It's like gladiator fighting, but the weapons aren't real or aren't dangerous or something like that. I didn't get the specifics. Anyway, the person that wins, gets two hundred gold pieces and that's what counts. I figure we've got three contestants: myself, Brandon, and David."

"You'd better make that two, Sean," said Jessica, looking at him reprovingly. "David shouldn't…"

"I've got to Jessica," broke in David. "We need the money. I've got three days to rest up. Don't you think I'll be okay by then?"

Jessica watched David for a moment and then sighed, realizing that this was the only remedy he would find. If he was ever going to stop blaming himself, this would be the way. "Yes, I suppose you'll be all right, but you won't be at your best. You're a fast healer but not that fast."

"I'll be all right. What do we have to do to get in on the action, Sean?" he asked, now smiling.

"It costs a gold piece per person to enter, Godfather," grinned the thief.

"Then get the money and make the arrangements," suggested David, feeling much better now. Sean and Brandon left.

Christopher came to David's side. "If you need me, I'll be in the library. I'm trying to learn some new spells. Take care of yourself." He took David's hand and gave it a firm balmy squeeze before leaving.

Amy then approached. "I've gotta go, too. I'll be in Galead's temple within the city. I need to spend some time in prayer." She turned to Jessica. "I think you need to come, too."

"Yes, but I need to stay with David more," stated Jessica.

"I'll stay with him," offered Jodi. "All I need to regain my abilities is rest. I can do that right here."

"I don't know…" Jessica began but Jodi interrupted her.

"Just go. I can take care of him, and you won't be any help in the future if your goddess won't answer your prayers."

"Well, okay," she finally conceded. "But if he gives you any trouble, don't refrain from letting him have it." She winked at David who was smiling broadly. "What're you grinning about?"

"Oh, I don't know. I just really love having beautiful women fight over me. It's a real ego booster."

All three of them bent over and, as one, gave him a great big kiss. "That's good," said Jessica, "but you'd better soak it up now because it'll never happen again. Your ego doesn't need boosting." She turned to leave.

Amy kissed him on the forehead. "Thanks," she whispered. At his smile, she turned and the two clerics left the room.

"How are you, David?" asked Jodi, pulling up a chair from the corner.

"I'm all right," he answered. "Just tired…and sore," he added, trying to stretch but halting as the pain spread through his limbs.

"Do you really think you'll be able to fight in the tournament?"

"Yeah," he answered, not feeling very confident. "I'll be fine by then. Like Jessica said, I'm a fast healer."

There was a short silence before Jodi continued. "I want to thank you for saving us from Peccare. I thought we were all gonna be raped and killed. I was getting really scared."

"I know," he said, reaching for her dainty, pale hand. "I

was scared too, but more than scared, I was angry. I was so damned angry! I don't know where all that fury came from, but that's what gave me the strength to break free."

"In any case, David. Thank you." She bent and hugged him.

"Hey, maybe I should take up rescuing beautiful maidens as a full-time profession," he said with a grin. "I've never been hugged and kissed so much in my life."

She smiled at him. "Let's not let it happen again, though, okay?"

He nodded. "I don't suppose this inn has a toilet, does it?"

Jodi grinned at him. "As a matter of fact, it does. It actually has indoor plumbing."

David was amazed. Indoor plumbing? In this world? Well, I may as well take advantage of it, he thought to himself. "Then would you mind helping me to the bathroom?"

At her nod, he threw back the covers, intent on climbing out of bed, but he then became uniquely aware of the fact that he was not wearing anything; he was totally and indisputably naked. He blushed tremendously, quickly pulling the covers back over his bare lower half. "I don't suppose you know where my clothes are, do you?"

Jodi was blushing too, but she stirred herself to go to the chest and search through it. "Your clothes aren't here," she finally announced. "But there're some others. I don't know how well they'll fit, but they're better than nothing." She brought out a beige balmacaan spattered with cheap gems and a pair of purple tights which she carried to the bedside.

"I'll look very ridiculous in those," he said.

"Yeah, but they're all I can find."

He sighed. "All right, then. I suppose they'll do."

"I'll turn around while you put the trousers on," suggested the illusionist.

"Uh, Jodi?" he said, after some struggle. "I'm afraid I'm not strong enough to get these tight pants all the way up."

She blushed. After much struggling and much more embarrassment, they got the mauve tights on David. They were not long enough and were much too tight, but they were clothing and covered him. He then pulled the coat over his broad shoulders and felt it tear up the back from the strain.

"Looks like you'll have to do without a top for now," suggested Jodi, removing the torn vestment. "Probably best anyway. Let your wounds breathe."

They finally struggled David out of bed and hobbled him towards the bathroom. On the way, he noticed his face in the mirror. It was pale and streaked with that same white reminder of pain under his left eye. His eye was swollen, distended with pain, and a second, red scar fleeted across his jaw. He reached to stroke the new wound and noticed once more the stump that was his right index finger. He shook his head slowly, painfully as he passed through the door into the bathroom.

The toilet did not have water in it and did not flush, but it was indoors and had a chute leading down to some unknown area of the inn and from there probably into a sewer. There was also a bathtub with a rope to pull for servants to bring hot water. There was a drain that would be pulled after you finished your bath to let the water run out, with a tube probably leading to the same place the toilet drained to.

Jodi left and soon returned to help David back into his room. He crawled into the soft bed and promptly returned to sleep as if he had taken a sleeping pill. As he dosed off, he knew he would feel better when he woke.

The next three days were spent recovering from the ordeals they had survived and preparing for the upcoming tournament. The magic-using members of the party spent their days trying to learn new spells and their nights resting up for the journey they would undertake come the fourth day of their stay. On the other hand, Sean and Brandon spent their time training for their fight, and when David woke on the morning of the second day and Jessica deemed him strong enough to train, he joined them.

The first thing they did was try to learn more about the tournament. Upon in-depth questioning of some inhabitants of the city, they discovered that the Games, as they were called, were very similar to the games played by the gladiators in ancient Rome. However, the weapons, when used in combat, were made safe so the danger of death would be lessened.

Early on the morning of the tournament, all that had paid their participation fee were to report to the stadium located at the city's center. The stadium would be divided into different areas for the different weapons that the participants used. The most competitive area was, of course, the sword. The winner of each event, who was determined by process of elimination, received two hundred pieces of gold. When a person was knocked unconscious or five minutes had elapsed in a round, a winner would be chosen by a judge. That person would continue to the next round. Each person would fight until eliminated, and the person left at the end was the champion of that section. Sean had chosen the thrown dagger for his weapon, Brandon had the axe, and David, the sword.

After learning the general rules of the game, the three men retired to a secluded part of the grounds of the inn, actually the garden, to practice. They found a cleared out area with soft ground and spent the entire day sparring with each other and then practicing technique by themselves. David was having a little trouble adjusting to the stump that replaced his finger, but he was doing quite well all things considered. During their session on the first day of David's return, five rough-looking men saw them practicing and approached.

"What can we do for you?" asked David breathlessly of them as they grew closer.

One man, apparently the leader, smiled at David and

spoke. "We were just watching you practice." He was a husky man in a plain black tunic and breaches. His boots were nearly knee-high, like balmorals. His brown hair was pulled straight back into a neat pony-tail and his slightly slanted brown eyes glittered with knowledge. His dark skin covered a well-built frame that was undoubtedly quick and ruthlessly agile. He wore a single black glove on his right hand, apparently for a better grip on the fine saber that hung on his left hip in a perfect position for a cross-body draw. A dagger with an ivory pommel adorned his other hip.

"Now that you've watched, why don't you just turn around and let us get back to work," suggested Brandon, holding his axe closely but not threateningly.

"Oh, don't worry, friend dwarf. We will when we're done," returned the same man.

"We're not going to bother you, little man," added another. "We won't hurt you."

"How comforting," answered Brandon angrily as the intruders laughed merrily.

"Well, I now suggest that your business is finished, friend," said David bitingly, growling the last word. "So you may leave us to our own." He began to turn.

"I was just wondering," continued the first man. "Are you planning on fighting in the Games?"

"I don't think that's any of your business—" began Brandon before David interrupted him.

"We are," he answered. "Why?"

"I just thought you might like some friendly advice. If you intend to win, you're going to have to be much better than what your practicing shows."

"Thank you for the advice," said David, turning again. "We'll hold our own."

The men began to laugh again, and at that same instant, Jessica entered the garden from the inn. "You'd better come in guys," she said, approaching them and eyeing the newcomers suspiciously. "It's about time to eat."

"Whoa," said the leader. "Take a look at that bitch! I bet she'd go for a good price on the market!" The man began to approach Jessica.

David moved quickly in front of her, shielding her from the ruffian. "Back off," he warned.

"Relax, big guy. I just want a quick taste to see if my suspicions are justified." He began to go around David who raised his arm to stop him. The intruder took this for an attempt at violence. The man, a full head shorter than David and not nearly as massive, slugged David hard in the kidneys.

David stood, unmoving, and looked down at the smaller man. "I'll give you one more chance to leave," he said easily though his stomach was on fire from the blow. Normally it would not have fazed him, but he was still weak from his encounter with Peccare.

"I told you, fella!" said the intruder. "I'm not leaving until I'm damned ready!" He attempted to go around the larger man. David was furious now and reached out with lightning reflexes, gripping the smaller man's throat. The intruder gasped as he was lifted off the ground by David's tremendous arm.

"I asked you to leave, asshole, now I'm making you." David hefted the man and threw him into his comrades, creating a writhing mass of arms and legs on the ground.

After they regained their feet, the ruffians drew their weapons and started to go after David as he was joined by Brandon and Sean, but they were stopped by a gesture from their prone leader.

"Not yet," he said. "We'll come back for the cleric when the Games are over. She'll be begging for us after we humiliate her protector in front of the entire city." He then stood and faced David once more. "I am called Tohzahi, and you will face me in the Games if you make it far enough. I haven't lost in the swords competition in five years. We'll meet again, however, even if it isn't there. You see, Graham, a friend of mine named Peccare asked me to have a word with you. I intend to kill you," he said, grinning, as the group of friends looked at each other with unsure glances. "Until then, friend, farewell." He turned and left with his four companions directly behind, shooting black looks back.

The group stood in shocked silence for a moment before Jessica regained her senses and ushered them into the inn for lunch. Eligere had supplied them with a whole roasted pig with boiled potatoes, bread, and fresh vegetables as well as some very tasty ale. The innkeeper was about five and a half feet tall with dusty blonde hair and blue eyes in a pudgy, almost pig-like, face. He was obsequiously polite, offering to help in any way he could. David asked him if Tohzahi was really the swords champion for the last five years. Eligere simply looked at David seriously and nodded.

That evening, they all met in David's room for a talk. David told the others what had happened during their practice and about Tohzahi's relation to Peccare.

"What'd he look like?" asked Christopher, an odd look on his face.

"He was about Sean's height and of a husky build," answered David. "He wore a plain black tunic with breaches to match it, and his boots were almost knee-high. He had dark skin, brown hair, and his brown eyes were slightly slanted."

"Did he wear a black glove on his right hand?" asked Christopher.

"Yeah!" said David, surprised. "Do you know who he is?"

"No," answered the wizard. "But he followed me and Jodi into the library earlier today." Jodi nodded.

"I've seen him, too," added Amy quietly. "When I went to the temple by myself yesterday, while Jessica was taking care of David, I saw him standing outside, watching me."

"It's obvious," stated Sean, "that this man is an assassin of some sort. He means to kill us and get the map for Peccare. I didn't mention it before, but the way he moved reminded me of some of the assassins I trained with in Dartmoor called Dauthi. Their master, Tupeti, puts as much emphasis on their swordsmanship as on their stalking ability, so if he is a Dauthi, then he's dangerous."

"What do the people from this city look like?" asked Brandon, a little worried.

"Dark skin and slanted eyes, just as our friend Tohzahi," answered Sean.

"Well, sitting here worrying about it won't help matters any," stated David.

"No, it won't," agreed the thief as he looked at David anxiously. "But you'd better be very careful during the Games if you face him. Watch for tricks and subterfuge; it's a Dauthi's specialty."

"Don't worry about me, Sean," said the warrior. "Just concentrate on your own success."

"I think we'd better talk a little about where we're gonna sleep tonight," suggested Brandon. "It probably wouldn't be safe to sleep in singles like we've been."

"What would you suggest?" asked David.

"Let's put each of the women in a room with a man," answered the dwarf, thoughtful. "Tohzahi might break in and try to take one of us. Jessica can stay with David, Amy and Christopher, and me or Sean with Jodi. Let her choose."

"I've been waiting for this opportunity for years," said Sean, creeping over to Jodi's side and placing an arm about her firm waist.

"You can't mean to put me in a room with this lunatic," she complained, looking up at Sean's grinning mien. "I'd feel safer with Tohzahi." She twisted away from him with a smile.

"Hey baby, don't leave me," said Sean following her, still grinning. "I know you didn't mean it."

"Seriously guys," broke in Brandon. "This way'll be much safer."

They finally agreed and went to their own rooms in pairs, and Jodi was to stay in a room with both Sean and Brandon. After the others had left, David took Jessica in his arms and kissed her. "We'd better be getting to bed, honey," he teased.

It was then that he noticed that something was bothering her. "What's wrong, Jessica?"

"I can't share your bed, David," she responded quietly.

"Why not?" he asked, perplexed.

"You know that chastity is one of the vows I took when I became a cleric."

"Jessica," he said. "I'll behave myself." His voice had an edge to it. "Even if you weren't a cleric, I wouldn't do anything against your will. I'm a little hurt that you bring it up."

"David," she said, taking his face in her hands. "I don't want to put any pressure on you."

"You won't, and even if you did, I don't think I'm up to wrestling with you," he said, realizing that he had misunderstood her and trying to cover up with jokes. "If it means that much to you, I'll sleep in the chair."

"No, David. You've been hurt and need your sleep. I'll sleep in the chair."

"Now, Jess, you know I won't have that. Shall we spend the night arguing about who gets the chair? Besides," he said with a twinkle in his eye, "you know that Amy's sleeping with Christopher."

"Hmmm…" She chewed on her lip pensively for a moment. "Very well, I'll sleep in the bed with you, but we can't touch. I'm human too, ya know…well, maybe a 'good night snuggle' or something, but that's it." She giggled softly, a charming smile twisting her lips.

"Okay, good," he said, holding her gently in his arms as he kissed her forehead. "If I role over in my sleep though, mark it up to a wet dream...and don't zap with that damnable chair bit."

She laughed at him, squeezing strongly. "I do love you, dear," she said. "Even if you are a pervert."

Amid peals of laughter from jokes and gentle tickling, they crawled into bed, separate but still together. David lay awake for a short time after Jessica had fallen asleep on his chest. He stared at his hand, turning it over and over again, staring at the empty space where his finger should have been. He was worried about the upcoming tournament and the rest of their journey. Even if he beat Tohzahi in the Games, the Dauthi would probably chase them all the way to Mount Apocrys. He sighed greatly with much sorrow and worry as he dozed into a fitful sleep, flexing and unflexing his hand to fight the phantom-pain.

The next morning, they arose early and bathed, a purgation of the soul for all of them. Jessica returned to her room after cleaning up. She had been gone for only a moment before a startled yelp erupted from her room, and David, with the others close behind, ran swiftly to the cry.

As they entered, they saw Jessica standing in the shambles that was her room. The bed had been ripped apart and all of the furniture broken; the window had been forced open to allow the intruder's passage. Jessica looked at David, her eyes glimmering with worry. "I found this," she said, handing him a piece of parchment.

He opened it and read:

Graham,
Very clever of you, my friend. I do wonder how you figured out that I would come for your little cleric, though.

Maybe some day, before I kill you, you would be kind enough to tell me what made you hide her. But it really doesn't matter. I'll take care of all of you anyway. It'll just be later.

I really can't stay any longer, someone might come in and find me here, and then I'd be disqualified from the Games. We can't have that, now, can we? So, I will say that I believe you'll make it to the finals tomorrow and you'll fight me. If you live through that, then I'll have to kill you while you're traveling towards Mount Apocrys. Yes, I know where you're going, and I even know where it is. I will kill you, Graham. If you're smart, you'll sleep with an eye open for as long as both of us live and probably longer. If you're not smart, you'll die soon…very soon. So, until we meet again, goodbye.

Tohzahi

P.S. Give Sister Anna a kiss for me.

David passed the letter to the others.

"This guy's becoming a real pain in the ass," commented Brandon.

"Yeah," agreed Sean. "We're gonna have to do something about him. He's too dangerous to have him following us around, but he's also too smart to put himself in a position where we could get at him easily. We're gonna have to work at this one."

They left the ransacked room to eat breakfast in the inn's dining room. "Thank you for your foresight," said Jessica to Brandon on the way to the table.

The dwarf blushed a little and smiled at Jessica. "What are friends for?"

"Whatever they're for, I'm glad I have friends like you," she answered, kneeling to hug the still blushing dwarf.

"I'm gonna get jealous in a minute," interrupted David.

Jessica stood and embraced David. "I love you," she whispered.

"And I love you." And he did—more than he ever had before.

The rest of the day was spent in preparation for the tournament. The fighters trained and fought more, building their reflexes to the max while the others searched for somewhere to purchase all the goods they would need for the last leg of their journey. Both groups felt successful in what they accomplished during the day and longed for tomorrow to be over.

By the time night fell once more, David was feeling as good as new, and he knew that he was as ready as he would ever be to face Tohzahi. He slept soundly with Jessica at his side, wondering why Peccare had not already left to retrieve the amulet if he had a friend who knew where it was. It did not make sense to David and neither did any of Tohzahi's actions. Why did he hate David and the company so much? And why did he look so familiar, all dressed in black?

When in Rome...

Once David had reached this point in the story, everyone had finished their meal, so he decided to discontinue the telling for a while. He did promise, however, to finish at dinner, so the priests and priestesses reluctantly let them leave.

After exiting the dinner hall, Christopher decided to return to the temple's library. The wizard, Amy still at his side, followed the passage down to a vestibule. A hallway opened to the left which they followed until it emptied into a tremendous room. This magnificent chamber, if it could be called that, was the library. As much as he hated to admit that the Temple's library was impressive, Christopher was overwhelmed by the sheer quantity of books located in it, the tremendous amount of knowledge stored within the thousands of tomes.

Christopher walked meaningfully down the center aisle, looking from side to side, until he found the section he had been searching for. In the shelves that stretched well up over the tall wizard's head, black bound books were stacked, emanating coldness, murmuring malevolent intentions. He quickly started shuffling through them, intent on finding some specific volume.

Amy spoke, interrupting Christopher's train of thought. "Christopher...I need to talk to you."

Annoyed by the interruption, Christopher turned, intent on scolding her but then became uniquely aware of the tearstreaks on her cheeks. "What is it?" he asked.

"I'm not wanted here," she said with some difficulty, trying to hold back the tears which stung her eyes.

"What do you mean?" he asked, confused.

"The clerics I share a room with... They welcomed me cheerfully enough, but I couldn't help but feel the looks they gave me when my back was turned." She paused, swallowing hard. "They're contemptuous of me."

"Why?" asked Christopher, not sure what to say. Though he really did not care what the clerics thought, he knew that Amy did.

"They know I've broken my vow."

"What vow?" asked the wizard, knowing already what the answer must be. He had hoped nothing like this would happen, but of course, his luck was less than enough to keep it at bay.

"My vow of celibacy," she answered with a sob. Christopher gently took her in his arms and held her until she could speak once more. "I'm surprised Lady Gahdnawen hasn't asked to speak to me about it yet."

"What would she want to say to you?" asked Christopher, knowing again what the answer would be.

"She'll take away my powers," she answered sorrowfully. "I don't know what to do."

"She'll be kind," he answered. "After all, there are extenuating circumstances."

"Like what?"

"Like, we're in love."

"Do you think she'll consider that?"

"Of course she will," he answered, taking her to him and holding her, hoping that everything would be fine, knowing that nothing would ever be "fine" again. After Amy relaxed, she helped Christopher find what he was searching for, though she was still unsure. Here they spent the rest of the afternoon learning of new things in the arcane arts of sorcery.

After exiting the dining hall, David and Jodi watched their friends walk off into the depths of the temple and returned to their restful place in the still gardens. Perch probably described their seat better for whenever they entered the garden, they felt as if they were sitting in a cloud looking down on everything, giving them a feeling of complete and utter safety. It made them apathetic to everything surrounding them, somber yet content.

They sat on a marble bench in the midst of the wonderful sights and scents, imbibing everything around them. There were flowers and trees of many different sorts, from violets to orchids and elms to oaks, as well as plants that neither of them could identify. Exotically flowering shrubs flourished under the sky, the sun warming them and emancipating their wonderful scent. As they sat there, wondering at the magnificence around them, they slowly began to talk, something they had not done in a while. "It's beautiful here," murmured Jodi, nostalgia in her voice.

"That it is," answered David, a smile that had not been cracked in many days creasing his care-worn face. "I forget the blackness of the world when I'm amid such beauty. It casts its spell over me, and I can't help but feel cheered."

"I know what you mean, David. I could just stay here forever," she said, stretching her arms. She found herself breathing deeply, greedily, as if she were trying to inhale all the odor, holding it selfishly in her lungs.

"But if we did that," said David, "we'd never get home." Jodi gave David only the slightest of nods, as if she did not understand what he meant, but due to his emotional state, was unwilling to pursue the point.

"You know that Jessica'll be all right, don't you?" she asked, gazing lovingly at a patch of clintonia.

David took a deep breath, all his memories of an immutable past flooding back into his brain. "I hope so," he answered without strength.

"She will, David," said Jodi, looking directly at him. Her deep blue eyes peered deep into him, unearthing his old confidence. "I know it!" she said with conviction.

He looked back at her and they sat there for a long moment just looking at each other. David put his arm around Jodi and hugged her, feeling reassured by her stolid will. She rested her head on his shoulder, and they sat there in silence for a while, simply being happy with each other's company.

Jodi and Jessica had always been good friends, and as David had come to know Jessica better, he had learned more and more about her meek friend. Jodi had always been quiet; not quiet with shyness, simply quiet like a person not wanting to disturb the sounds around her. David loved her in a unique way, as a person whom he could truly respect and call "friend," and even in her altered state, so much now Aurora, he could see the reflections of her own character.

Time wore on and they drowsed in the sunlight, enjoying the rest and recovering from their wearisome tribulations. As these two old friends enjoyed each other's company, two new friends were learning to be close also.

Sean was sitting in a room that a modern worker would call a lounge. It was small, probably only twenty feet square, with a single door in the eastern wall. Lounging chairs were placed strategically about the room and around a pair of versatile, round tables.

Sean sat in a chair opposite Bellus. They spent their time learning more about each other, and Sean told her about his counterpart's meager life, being raised by his mother alone in a dirty room off an alley in Sukhur and of the quest they were currently on. She seemed quite interested in his story and listened attentively, but somehow Sean knew that she saw beyond that story into his very soul. So, giving in to his desire to share who he was with her, he told her the truth about where he was from, the real purpose in their quest for the amulet, and even about his belief that everyone except him and David had become more their characters and less themselves. Through the whole story, Bellus sat listening with attentive seriousness. She did not question him at all about the transformation or comment on its veracity. Somehow she knew that he was telling her the truth and would not, indeed could not, offer her any more of the story than he did. Having purged himself of so much anxiety through telling the true story, Sean felt that something was happening between them, that by offering up his burden to her and accepting the sense of approval or peace she returned, he was connecting with her.

Bellus felt very much the same way, and wishing to add something more to the moment, to seal the connection, she started telling Sean about her own experience.

"I'm afraid there's not that much to tell about my life," she said with a unique grin that exuded intelligent camaraderie. "I was born and raised in the temple. My mother is a cleric as was her mother before her. I've only been raised to learn and study this art. It takes all of my time, and I must admit that you're the first outsider, if you'll pardon the label, I've ever spoken with. I've never left the temple grounds before. It's all I know." She made a broad, open-handed gesture as Sean listened attentively. "My life has been quite bland so far. The most exciting thing that's happened to me in the last twenty years is meeting you."

This last remark she made with an embarrassed look at Sean who, in another situation, would have laughed. The two studied each other's face. After a moment, Sean bent close to her, intending to gently brush her cheek with his lips, an offer of friendship and thanks, but that was not how it was taken. She offered her lips instead and they kissed, a long deep passionate caress.

After slowly separating, they sat in silence once more, looking deep into each other's eyes. A strong new relationship had been kindled in the afternoon of a mournful day.

"Tell me about the world, Sean," pleaded Bellus momentarily, nostalgia hazing her eyes. "Tell me about the cities."

Sean was quietly surprised, but fondness made the words flow. "The last city I was in was Tyrol on the edge of the Teuton Swamp and the Hills of Glockenshire. It's huge. Probably a half-million people live there and in its suburbs." Sean saw excitement and awe flickering in Bellus' innocent eyes and he smiled, warming up to the story. "When we arrived there, David had been grievously wounded and we put him up in an inn to heal. We were growing a little low on funds and needed some gold, so I went searching for a way to make money. For some strange reason, Jessica wouldn't let me steal the gold for us."

"That's illegal, Sean," interrupted Bellus, "and immoral."

"I know. That's what's so great about it."

Bellus smiled in spite of herself and asked, "Is this Jessica a great cleric?"

"Oh yes," asserted Sean. "She's the greatest one I've ever known." Sean watched Bellus' smile fade in jealousy and felt sudden satisfaction and pride welling within him. "That was until I met you, however. You surpass her."

Bellus blushed gratefully and squirmed with joy. "You're flattering me! I'm only a novice."

"It's no lie," affirmed Sean, thinking what an ironic

remark that was coming from him. "There's something about you… Anyway, while we were in Tyrol, we competed in the Games to get the money for the rest of our journey."

"You competed in the Tyrollean Games?!" broke in Bellus excitedly.

"Yeah," stated Sean, surprised. "You've heard of them?"

"Heard of them?!" she exclaimed. "Of course I've heard of them! They're the biggest gathering of warriors in this part of the world!"

"Oh."

"Please tell me about it!" she begged. "And don't leave anything out!"

Sean shrugged and began.

The sun pushed its way out of the cover of darkness and shone brilliantly down upon the thrilled town. The population was running about in a flurry of expectation, preparing for the Games that they knew would be seen this day. The warriors, walking with great deliberation toward the arena, were greeted with shouts of praise and good luck by the citizens of Tyrol.

Inside the inn that held the group of expatriated travelers, there was also excitement as they sharpened their weapons and donned their gear, preparing for competition. Sean sat, leaning casually back in his chair, flipping one of his many daggers in the air. "Looks to be an exciting day," he commented, balancing another knife on his index finger, as he peered out the window at the excited town. He was dressed in a red tunic and tanned trousers that David had decided he did not just find sitting around somewhere—they fit too well, and there was a belt wrapped around his waist with a scabbard containing Sean's short sword along with his assortment of knives and other paraphernalia. There was also a full purse of money that had definitely not been there the day before.

"Yeah, but let's not get too excited, okay?" prompted

David with a meaningful leer at Sean and his newly acquired raiment. David was dressed in a tight tanned tunic and matching breaches. He had opted to fight without armor since the Games were supposed to be safe. His sword belt had been put over his shoulder so it was out of the way but still easily reached, but now, his sword was in his hand where it was being exuberantly cleaned and sharpened.

Brandon was standing next to the door, wearing his chain armor, when he said, "The others're returning." Jessica, Jodi, Amy, and Christopher poured into the entrance hall of the inn. They had been to the arena to see what was going on.

"Big news," said Jodi, looking somewhere between surprised and tickled. "Did you know that they're betting on the winners over there?"

"No," answered Sean, a little surprised. "They never mentioned that when we registered."

"Well, they are," she continued. "So we put some money down on each of you, and your odds are terrible. Sean's at thirty to one, Brandon's fifty to one, and David's one hundred to one."

"Well, they don't know us very well, do they?" commented Brandon with a grunt.

"Apparently not," said Christopher with a grin. "All you have to do is look at them Brandon, and they'll die of fright."

"Not funny," said Brandon with a glare.

"Now don't tease the dwarf so much," interrupted Amy, approaching him. "I think he's cute." She bent and kissed his forehead.

As she raised up, Brandon blushed furiously and tried to avert his face. He did not appreciate all the laughter that ensued upon his response.

"Damned worthless body," he mumbled as he tried to regain his composure minimally.

"Seriously guys," said David after a moment. "I think

we're gonna have to be very careful today. I'm sure that
Tohzahi's going to try something, so be on guard. If anything
happens, meet back here. By the way, where'd you get the
money to bet with?"

"From Sean," answered Jessica, nonchalantly approaching the big man. "And I think you'd better be very careful
yourself, David. You're the one who's going to be fighting
him in single combat. Don't expect him to fight fair—be on
guard." She checked David's wounds once more, making sure
they were all closed and healing well.

"I can take care of myself," answered David, hugging
Jessica. "But remember what I said. If anything happens,
everybody meets back here." He clenched his right fist, trying
to ignore the stump on his hand. He sighed and continued
sharpening his blade.

After a few moments, David and the other contestants set
out for the arena. They were supposed to be there early in order
to prepare. As they walked down the streets, people of all
sorts, but mostly children, approached them and inquired as to
their names. Some even promised to put a few silvers on them.

Very quickly, they found themselves nearing the towering
structure that filled a clearing near the center of Tyrol. The
building itself was made of granite and marble and built in the
Gothic style with columns, lions, and everything else to fit the
picture. The entrances, one to the east and one to the west,
were archways with statues of lions being ridden by warriors
flanking them on each side. Scores of contestants flooded
through each archway in a rush to make the last minute
preparations that would have them ready for their battles.

As the three warriors entered the archway, they were awed
by the size of the arena. It was arranged circularly with a great
sandy battleground taking up the mass of the interior. Surrounding the floor of the coliseum was a tremendous amount
of seating, probably enough to seat the entire city and half of

the persons in its suburbs. Directly over the great arch through which they entered was a large area that had been set apart from the rest of the seating. This was apparently where the hierarchy of the Games sat.

As David, Sean, and Brandon began to enter the battleground, they were stopped by a guard in a corselet, holding a pike. His blue cape was clasped around his neck by a golden brooch in the shape of an eagle. "Name?" he demanded brusquely.

"What?" asked David, startled.

"Your name," replied the guard impatiently, patronizingly. "What's your name?"

"Graham," answered David with a smile.

The guard scowled at him and shuffled through some papers which sat in front of him on a sort of podium. He found David's name on the list and spoke, "Enter and follow the wall to the right. That is, if you know right from left. Anyway, you'll come to another archway. Enter it and ready your weapon."

David, quickly followed by his friends, followed the guard's instructions. They walked around the right wall, crowded with people of all different types. Men like themselves; more men like Tohzahi; black men from the Chiaroscarian Islands; men from Shapitia, remotely resembling Orientals; dwarves from the southern Azure Mountains; elves from the Shan Forest; minotaurs from the northern Cymra Mountains; Orcs; trolls; and other, less easily recognized people crowded the floor.

About fifty yards up the north wall, they found the archway the guard had spoken of. It was also filled with people, but they were all crowded around a few booths that were against the wall. Finding one that was not as crowded as the rest, the three men approached it. Behind it was a halfling from the Hills of Glockenshire who smiled up at them gleefully. "You want me to prepare your weapons for you?" he inquired happily.

"Uh, yeah," answered David, unsure, drawing his sword and handing it to the little man. The halfling accepted it easily, though it was a good foot and a half longer than him, and quickly put some sort of black substance all around the edges except the tip. Handing it back, he accepted Brandon's axe and did the same. When Sean attempted to hand the little man his knives, the halfling laughed. "What good would throwing knives be, sir, if they wouldn't stick in the target?"

David examined his weapon and discovered that the black substance was some type of rubber. "Sean," he said, "it's rubber, so we don't kill each other fighting. You're throwing knives at a target, not at people, so you don't need the stuff."

Sean nodded and returned his knives to his belt.

"You're new here, aren't you?" asked the halfling, still grinning. At David's nod, he continued. "Well, it's really very simple. It's done by process of elimination. If you get knocked unconscious, killed, or are hit by a blow that would hurt you badly without the rubber, you're out. If neither person's hurt in the five minutes allotted to 'em, then the judge chooses the winner. When it finally comes down to two people, they fight for fifteen minutes. The winner of that battle wins the two hundred gold coins. In the knives contest, you just throw your knives at the target, one against another, and the closer shot wins. Very simple, huh?" he grinned.

"Yeah," answered Brandon looking at the halfling with a smile. As they turned and walked away, he added, "That's the first person I've seen since we've been here that's shorter than me. Poor guy."

"I'm sure he'd appreciate your sympathy," commented Sean.

Brandon glared at him. "When do we get started?"

"By the look of things, pretty quickly," answered David, noticing all the people who had begun to pour into the seating arena.

They passed the time practicing and looking for their friends.

Soon they found them seated in the front row near the eastern archway. They walked up the stairs to their seats and greeted them. "Looks like you've got some interesting competition," commented Christopher, eyeing the broad assortment of characters.

They talked for a few more minutes until they noticed a group of about fifty richly dressed men entering the seating box above the archway.

"Looks like they're about to start," said Jodi. "You'd better get back down there."

They did and found that all the people were crowding around the box, ready to begin. As the men took their seats, one of them approached the edge of the box. He was a small man of about five and a half feet, with a foot-long grey beard. His haggard countenance stated that he was the head of the Games as well as an influential member of the city. His brown robes were in no way plain, with gold and silver trim that made him look powerful. He spoke. "The time has arrived, my friends, for the Games to begin. For those among you"—he pointed to the crowd of warriors— "who are good enough, this is a chance to win honor as well as gold, but for those of you who are less than great, it's time for humiliation and even death. Your choice to be in this great tournament illustrates your bravery, but bravery alone is not nearly enough to succeed here. You must be good. If there's anyone here who wishes to resign, he may do so now." The man paused as silence overcame the coliseum. "Since no one speaks out, we'll begin the Games. The first competition will be thrown daggers." He turned and sat amid the roar of praise that thundered from the throats of the spectators.

"Who was that?" asked Brandon of another dwarf who stood to his left.

"That was Idein, the mayor," answered the dwarf, startled. "This your first time?"

"Yeah," answered Brandon.

Then another man rose and approached the edge.

The dwarf spoke again to Brandon. "That's Eidos, the mayor's brother."

This man wore robes exactly like his brother's except they were grey. He was somewhat younger, with no beard, and was much more burly. He spoke in a deep baritone. "The first round consists of Arios of Shapitia versus Tardif of Glockenshire, Seldcuth of Arran versus Furca of Cythera, Martin of Sukhur versus Kanops of Pindus..."

As Sean's name was mentioned, he turned to his friends. "Wish me luck," he said and slipped away in the direction of the targets.

The man who he was to compete against was tall and slender with black hair and eyes of essonite. Sean defeated him easily. He waited through a few more rounds of ten competitors each until his name was called again, and he competed against an elf named Andor who gave him quite a run for his money.

After approximately ten more rounds of competition, he found himself in the semi-finals. The man he was up against this time was a large native Tyrollean with long stringy blonde hair and dark brown eyes. The man, Ekleikton was his name, threw first. His first throw hit in the second section, not a bad throw. His second was very close to it, and his third hit only a couple of inches from the center.

Sean felt more than a little nervous as he prepared to throw his first dagger. He drew back and let it fly. It stuck, shuddering, in the third section like a blatant sign of the thief's stupidity. Sean could have kicked himself. He had just wasted one shot.

Ekleikton laughed. "How'd you make it to the semi-finals throwing like that. You may as well give up."

Sean leered at him and threw his second knife which landed even with the Tyrollean's last shot. The thief took a deep breath and threw his last dagger in a single smooth motion. It struck just inside his second, winning him the round and allowing him to continue to the finals.

For his last competition, Sean was up against another elf, named Myrr. He was short for his race, barely over six feet, but was heavily built. He threw his three daggers quickly and with accuracy, each landing within an inch of the center. About this time, Sean was feeling really unsure and nervous. He drew his first dagger and threw it. It landed right outside the triangle formed by the elf's knives. His second shot landed just almost even with Myrr's but was still too far from the center and victory.

Sean felt the pressure settling on his shoulders as he looked about, trying to locate his friends again. He soon found them, watching him intently as all in the stadium were. He swallowed hard at this realization. Sean tried to relax, forced himself to blot out the audience as he drew his final knife. He aimed carefully and threw. It landed soundly in the center of the target, shuddering with its own surety. He almost leapt into the air with exuberance but managed to control himself for reasons of appearance. "Damn, that was close!" he whispered under his breath.

The mayor stood to speak. "The winner of the thrown daggers competition is Martin of Sukhur. You may come to claim your prize from the guard at the gate. The next competition is the bows."

After finishing his decision, the mayor seated himself again and his brother stood, listing the first competitors.

Sean returned to David and Brandon, grinning broadly. "Well, you guys really don't have to go on with this any longer, ya know. I've got enough money for us all."

"True," commented David. "But who could pass up odds like we have. Besides, I'm not about to let Tohzahi think he frightened me away."

As the competitors for the bow competition took their

places, Sean went to claim his prize and then joined Christopher and the ladies who greeted him emphatically. The people around him also congratulated him and looked longingly at the sack he carried. Sean was constantly fingering his short sword, made nervous by all the attention on his money.

"You won the event?!" broke in Bellus jubilantly.

"Uh, yeah," answered Sean uncertainly. "Why?"

"That's amazing!" she breathed, staring at him with astonishment glimmering in her eyes.

He felt unusually proud and forced himself not to blush. "Anyway, the bow competition passed quickly. The winner turned out to be the same elf, Myrr, that had lost to me…"

After congratulating the winner, the mayor announced the next competition. "Our two missile events are over and we now enter the violent and more dangerous competitions. The first among these is the large weapons category. This includes axes, maces, clubs, and other such deadly weapons. There's a good chance that, sometime in the next two events, blood will be shed, so everybody be prepared. Now, let's begin."

The names were announced and Brandon did not compete in the first round, but in the second, he found himself fighting a man from Dartmoor who had defeated another dwarf in round one. The Dartmoor had the same slightly slanted eyes and dark skin that Tohzahi had, but he was of a much larger build. He wielded a great deadly flail, the shaft reaching out for about two feet. Two chains sprung forth from the tip, one tipped with a great steel ball with many blunted spikes and the other with what appeared to be a razor-sharp four-pointed star. To Brandon's relief the star was coated in rubber. As the two sparred off, Brandon realized that the man did not have the strength or agility to wield the weapon he held. The Dartmoor raised his weapon to swing it down on Brandon but the dwarf dodged aside and hit him hard with a gauntleted fist in the side. Brandon heard the air gush from his opponent's lungs. Before the man was able to regain his footing, Brandon smashed his axe down on the back of his neck and the man fell, unconscious. Applause and yells of joy bombarded Brandon for his victory.

In Brandon's next round, he was up against a minotaur who wielded a great mace. The bull-headed man towered over Brandon and was undoubtedly stronger. Muscles bulged in his chest and along the legs that held his tremendous weight, and the arms that supported that great steel weapon were huge. Brandon noticed with relief that the beast's horns had the same rubber-like material on them as the weapons; he did not feel like getting gored. The dwarf beat the minotaur with a quick dodge and a strong slice that shattered both of the thing's kneecaps.

In the next five rounds of his competition, Brandon faced two Orcs, a goblin, a Chiaroscarian man, and another dwarf. He beat each of them easily, except the dwarf who got a quick jab into Brandon's stomach with his warhammer, but Brandon still managed to dispose of his foe with a strong, quick blow to the side that left the other in a gasping heap.

In the finals, Brandon found himself facing a foe that he had been watching through the whole tournament, hoping he would not have to fight him, but with his usual bad luck, Brandon found himself standing face to navel with Rogg the ogre. This beast stood over seven feet tall and was monstrously proportioned. His bestial face was perhaps the ugliest Brandon had ever seen, having two deep-set black eyes that peered out from behind a tremendous round nose. Below the nose was a huge mouth filled to brimming with innumerable, razor-sharp teeth. The face was enshrouded by a thick scruff of black hair that hung down to the thing's meager loincloth.

Rogg moved with a speed that was surprising as he circled

Brandon, his huge cudgel at the ready. The beast made a number of attempts at braining the little dwarf, but Brandon dodged each blow. Unfortunately, he was not able to reach Rogg's body with his shorter arms. After dancing around for about ten minutes, Brandon decided that the best strategy for this opponent was to get in close and try to land some quick blows. He rushed into the ogre's body and swung his axe mightily at its legs. As the blade met the creature's flesh, Brandon felt it jar to a stop, and he almost dropped its shuddering handle. The beast was unharmed and aimed a quick kick at Brandon who took it as a glancing blow in the side. It knocked the wind from him, but he was not seriously hurt. Rogg continued the onslaught, still never hitting, but not being hit either.

Then Brandon got an idea, but he was afraid it was already too late. Rogg swung his club down at Brandon who side-stepped, and as the cudgel thudded into the ground, Brandon brought his axe down on it, breaking it in two. He swung again at the startled monster's head, hoping that it would not react in the same way its legs had. The axe met the skull and Brandon felt it shudder with the impact, but it still did its duty. The beast fell to the earth, its skull shattered.

Brandon almost fainted with exhaustion—and relief; he had never fought so mighty an opponent in single combat. He gratefully went and accepted his reward, wishing David luck before going to join the others in their seats.

As Brandon joined his friends amongst startled glances, he realized that Sean was not there. "Where's Sean?" he asked.

"He went to get our supplies," answered Jodi.

"What?!" exclaimed Brandon, horrified. "You let him go off by himself?!" A pause. "Into the city?!"

"Yeah," answered Christopher, confused. "It'll save some time."

Brandon felt sick. "You do realize of course that the entire town is in this stadium, don't you?" Brandon groaned.

"Then, what's he doing?" asked Jessica quietly.

"Oh, he probably is taking care of our supplies," said Brandon unhappily. "He's probably stealing 'em."

"Well, there's nothing we can do about it," said Jessica. "We'll just have to trust him not to get into trouble."

"That's like trusting a wolf not to chase sheep," commented Brandon.

They all unhappily turned their attention to the battlefield. David was preparing to fight an elf who used a sword that was even longer than the bastard sword David wielded.

The company was watching him when there was a startled gasp from Jessica. She pointed down at the battleground. The others followed her finger and noticed a dark figure staring up at them with slightly slanted eyes. Tohzahi whipped out his sword, saluting them, then turned to fight the Orc that was adjacent him.

Ambushes

Sean was wandering around the outer brink of the arena, an odd sensation running its icy fingertips up his spine. He knew that the sixth sense that was presently plaguing his other five never lied. His stomach churned anxiously as his mind whirled, trying to pick up on whatever it was that had caused him to leave his friends. There was definitely something wrong; he could almost taste it but could not quite identify it. After wandering around for a few minutes, he stopped to lean up against a wall, his dark form enshrouded in a deep shadow caused by an overhanging cluster of banners and pennants.

He looked up at the flags, watching them sway in the wind, trying to focus his attention on the curious impression of impending trouble. As he leaned against the wall, three burly men entered the archway in which Sean stood, looking about suspiciously and talking in hushed voices. Sean watched them pass almost peripherally, but just after they stepped by him, he heard one say, "Tohzahi'd better pay us well for this." Alarm bells sounded in Sean's head, and he quickly rushed after the trio.

They walked quickly into a large building that was a very short distance from the arena's northern wall. More alarm bells sounded. Sean stealthily followed them into the building and watched them ascend three flights of stairs. Here they left the stairwell but soon returned baring great ash bows, each with a quiver of black-tipped arrows. They continued up the stairs into a room on the fourth floor. As Sean followed, remaining outside the door, he grew more and more certain that this group was the source of the odd sensation that was pestering him.

David had beaten the tall elf with a few quick slashes—the fellow relied too much on his tremendous reach, over-extending himself terribly. His second opponent, in the fifth round, had been an Orc that charged directly into David, hoping to get a chance to use its powerful claws, but David hit it with one tremendous blow, reducing it to an unmoving heap.

David was presently fighting a large, older man who was probably David's equal in girth but lacked the speed that made the younger man so deadly an opponent. The two men combated, slicing, parrying, and slicing again. David jabbed quickly at his opponent's legs, but it was parried. He feinted a slice to the right but checked it, swinging a quick blow at his face. The older man ducked under the blow, unsurprised, and brought his blade up quickly, slicing the front of David's tunic open, leaving a small cut in his chest. David was surprised that his opponent's weapon could cut, but he soon noticed that the binding around their blades did not cover the very tip of the sword. David recovered quickly and took advantage of his opponent's swelling confidence, acting more discouraged than he actually was. The man started attacking more vigorously, seeing that his opponent was weakened, and paid less attention to his own defensive openings. He rushed David, drawing back to swing a mighty blow at his head, but David dropped to the ground and rolled at his startled opponent's feet. Off balance, the man tripped over David's body and fell heavily to the ground, dropping his sword. David leapt to his feet and put the point of his sword to his opponent's throat, asserting his victory.

Meanwhile, Tohzahi had already dispatched his foe, a Shapitian who fought two-blades style with a broadsword and a dagger. Tohzahi stood and watched David's skirmish, a smirk twisting the corners of his mouth. He knew that David was good but also felt confident that he could beat the larger man. In any case, he had taken a few precautionary measures to assure his victory. That was one of the first rules a Dauthi learned in his training: never leave your back unprotected, it makes too attractive a target.

The next six rounds of competition in which both men participated passed quickly. Both David and Tohzahi had little trouble defeating their respective opponents, and by the end of the second round, David had noticed Tohzahi's mocking figure standing only a short distance from him, battling or watching.

As he reached the semi-finals, David was beginning to tire—the heat was getting to him. He still had not regained all his strength and knew that he was not in the best condition to be fighting. He was up against a tremendous black man who wielded a black, two-handed falchion. A little taller than David, though less thickly muscled, he was clothed only in a pair of lightly tanned breaches that bulged where his tremendous thighs flexed with the shifting of his weight.

Tohzahi was facing another man from Dartmoor who looked like a less tried, though equally fierce, imitation of himself. Dressed similarly and wielding similar weapons, black longswords with a small curve towards the tip, they appeared as if they could be brothers.

As the battles began, David quickly learned that the man

he was up against was both strong and agile, although he seemed to limp ever-so-slightly on his left leg. David centered his movement so his opponent would always have most of his weight on that wounded leg. After a short circle, David moved in, thrusting and slicing furiously at his opponent who blocked and parried every blow that David aimed at him. He was good! Soon David saw that a frontal attack of this sort was useless against this warrior, so he began using a number of feints to the left so the Chiaroscarian jerked away and put his full weight on his bad leg. Then David swung a mighty, double-handed blow directly at his sword. As the weapons made contact with a jarring impact, the black man stepped back with his right foot, leaving his left unprotected. David took advantage of this mistake and bashed his foot into the injured knee. David's opponent took the blow without slowing, but his face registered excruciating pain. David continued his merciless onslaught for the remainder of the time, with no other blows landed.

The judge stopped the battle, hands upraised. "Time is up for the semi-final round. The winner of the match between Tohzahi and Reculen is evident." David looked at Tohzahi who stood, grinning, over his opponent who was lying flat on the ground, blood trickling from his mouth. "The match between Graham and Hinsdorin goes to Graham with a score of one strike to none. In the finals, Tohzahi will face the newcomer Graham."

Tohzahi walked to David's side. "Good to see you again, friend, but I'm afraid this'll be our final meeting. When we leave this place, one of us will be dead."

David looked down at Tohzahi and smiled maliciously. "I almost hate that I'll have to kill you," he stated.

"And why is that?"

"Because, I would've liked you to tell Peccare that I'm coming for him. He'll regret what he did to us."

"Well, maybe I'll have a chance to tell him of your promise," said Tohzahi. "In retrospect."

"We will see."

"So we shall."

"Take your places!" roared the judge.

The two men spread out and faced one another, each bent at the knees and waist, with their full attention placed on their opponent's every movement. They circled for only a moment before Tohzahi made a quick lunge at David who easily blocked it, allowing the Dauthi's momentum to carry him within a few inches of the larger warrior's body.

"You'll have to be quicker than that if you intend to take me," spat David. He was attempting to put up a wall of confidence through which Tohzahi would be unable to see, but the Dauthi was not fooled.

"I will, Graham. Don't worry," he said insolently as he stepped back and saluted David. The warrior was a little bothered by Tohzahi's show of unconcern.

David feinted a few quick thrusts at Tohzahi's midsection and sides, checking for weaknesses and finding none, all the while dodging the Dauthi's ripostes. Quickly the tides turned and the Dartmoor returned the scrutiny by beginning his own testing. David blocked each of the intended pricks and quickly returned a strong slash to Tohzahi's face. Although unsurprised by the attack, the Dauthi was unable to get fully out of its way. The tip of David's blade left a thin crimson streak across Tohzahi's left cheek. Tohzahi then took for his own advantage the moment of victory which David felt. He thrust a quick jab at David's front leg, barely nicking the thigh and causing a trickle of blood to flow down his leg. Tohzahi smiled at David as he dabbed at his cheek with a sleeve.

David decided that this was his opportunity to create a facade to trap Tohzahi. He backed away, acting less aggressive and more defensive. Tohzahi, seeing his advantage, moved quickly up on the larger man, attempting to gain a quick, fatal slice. He continued testing David from all sides, slashing and thrusting with much vigor. David pretended like his left side was less protected in hopes of luring Tohzahi into a snare. He took the bait. Tohzahi gave a mighty thrust into what would have been the left side of David's stomach, splitting his spleen, but the warrior sidestepped and brought his sword down on Tohzahi's extended arm. There was an audible slap where the flat of David's sword struck the appendage, and Tohzahi dropped his sword, making a quick and perfectly executed backwards role away from David. He leapt to his feet immediately, turning towards the northern section of seats and raising his arm.

Sean saw the signal in the same instant the three men squatting at the casement a few feet in front of him did. As Tohzahi threw his arm into the air, the three figures raised their bows, each with an arrow nocked, and prepared to fire. Also at that same moment, three knives swished through the air at the figures' exposed backs, each only a fraction of a second behind the previous. The first dagger struck the man on the farthest left before he released the arrow, but the second and third did not reach their destinations until after two arrows were released. The three assassins collapsed onto the floor, spurting blood from their backs, as Sean rushed to the window, hoping that he had not been too late.

David found himself running after Tohzahi's fleeing form, which had taken off towards the eastern entrance to the coliseum. He did not know where the two arrows that had landed in front of him, one skewering a judge, had come from, but he did know that Tohzahi had to be responsible. He was also aware that the entire arena was in a state of panic. All the people were running for the entrances and a lot of them had already reached them; others still were being trampled by their fellow citizens.

David was only a few feet behind Tohzahi when the little man disappeared into the crowd of people that had swarmed to the archway, trying to get out.

David knew he would never find Tohzahi in the throng, so he stopped running. "Another day, Tohzahi," he said to himself. "Another day…"

His next thought was to find his friends, so he ran to the place where they had been seated during the Games, certain that he would not find them there. He found only debris and a few trampled citizens who cringed at his approach, so he ran back to the entrance and easily forced his way through the crowd. He finally burst through into the streets and set out at a mad dash towards The Blue Dragon. His whole body was screaming for him to stop and travel at a more leisurely pace, but he did not listen to it, bent on reaching the inn as quickly as possible.

When he reached it, he burst through the front door, and ascended the stairs to his room. There, reclining on the bed, was Sean who sat up as David entered. "Glad to see you're still breathing, David." He smiled.

David returned the smile with very little jubilance. The only emotions he felt presently were fear and exhaustion. "Me too," he answered. "Where're the others?"

"I don't know," shrugged the thief. "The last time I saw them, they were still in their seats watching you."

"Oh? Where'd you go to?" asked David suspiciously.

"I followed three guys out of the arena. They turned out to be some of Tohzahi's goons," answered Sean. "My guess would be that if Tohzahi got in trouble, they were supposed to create a diversion and, hopefully, kill you."

"So that's where those arrows came from," murmured David to no one in particular.

"Yep," answered Sean.

"Thanks, I owe you one."

"Call it even."

David smiled, remembering the ambush and thinking that it was actually Sean and Christopher who had saved him there, not the other way around.

At that same moment, the rest of the group piled into the room. "What the hell was that?!" asked Brandon, the quintessential irate dwarf.

Sean smiled at his friend. "It seems our buddy Tohzahi wasn't as sure of himself as he pretended."

"What do you mean?" asked Christopher.

"Well, the arrows that started the panic came from three of his henchmen that I followed out of the coliseum."

"So that's where you went," added Jessica. "Brandon had us all convinced you were off stealing the town."

"Moi?" asked Sean innocently.

"You probably intended to, didn't you?" broke in a rather embarrassed Brandon.

"I assure you, my friend, that as in all things my intentions were totally honorable."

Brandon scowled.

"In any case," continued Sean, "I dispatched them and proceeded to return here...directly."

"Well, I didn't get my prize money," said David, sitting down next to Sean wearily.

"You're lucky to've gotten out of there with your life," said Jessica. "And the others have theirs anyway."

"Well, I—" began David, but he was interrupted when the innkeeper burst into the room, a mound of exhausted flesh.

As Eligere stood in the doorway, clothed in his huge, kimono-like robes, he panted with the exertion of running. The poor man looked as if he had not jogged, let alone sprinted any distance for many years.

As quickly as he caught his breath, he spoke. "Splendid, absolutely splendid. Congratulations," he continued, praising them as he approached all of the contestants, pumping each hand vigorously. When he came to David, his mirth redoubled. "Completely marvelous bit of swordsmanship! Tohzahi hasn't been beat in five years…Or was it six…No, five, definitely five. And what a climax! The judges and citizens were completely and utterly stricken." He laughed merrily. "Especially the one who got skewered." He laughed harder. "I haven't had this much fun in years!" He collapsed in a seat, breathlessly laughing.

"Where can I go pick up my money?" asked David of the innkeeper finally.

Eligere sat up and looked at him very seriously all of a sudden. This was very difficult to do with such a pudgy, chipmunk-like face. "I don't believe that would be a very good idea. No, definitely not."

"Why's that?" asked David.

"Because they'd probably kill you on sight," he answered. "You embarrassed the officials and caused a disturbance at a major civic event. Let alone being an accessory to murder in their eyes. That's punishable by death!"

"Great," commented Brandon.

"Then what do we do?" asked Amy.

"My advice," answered the innkeeper, "would be to get out of the city as quickly as possible."

"But we can't leave without any supplies!" interjected Jodi.

"Well then, by all means, you must get your supplies," continued the innkeeper. "Everything should be fine just as long as nobody sees Graham." He said this with an apologetic sidelong glance at David.

"Then we'll get our supplies this evening and plan on leaving tomorrow," suggested Sean.

As, in general, the entire group agreed with this seemingly solitary solution, Sean and Brandon set out to get their supplies while the others rested their weary minds and bodies. Within two hours, the absent company returned to their friends with smiles of delight spread across their faces. This was an interesting foil for the weary look of apprehensive alarm that their compatriots wore.

"What's got you two looking so jolly?" asked Christopher as the two strode into the room.

"We got really good deals on our equipment," answered Brandon as he came in and collapsed in a chair.

"And how'd you manage that?" inquired Amy from the wizard's side, peering at Sean suspiciously.

"Well, I'd like to say it was because of my superb bargaining skills," began Sean, "but the truth of the matter is that the merchants recognized us from the games and practically gave us everything we needed."

"Does that mean that everything's taken care of?" asked Jessica, sitting next to David's waking form.

"Yes, and it'll be waiting for us at the stables at the western city gates at first light," answered Brandon.

"Good," said David, aroused by the talking. "Then let's get to sleep." He promptly turned over and began to snore loudly.

"Appears to me," said Sean in a whisper, "that some of us've got an early start."

"Yes. He's exhausted," answered Jessica, stroking David's long hair. "Everybody go to bed…and watch out for Tohzahi. He or Peccare might return."

They all retired to their rooms, Amy with Christopher, Jodi with Sean and Brandon, and Jessica remained with David. None of them knew that this precaution against ambush was completely unnecessary, for Tohzahi, Peccare, and all of their men, as well as some newly acquired associates, had already begun their journey towards Mount Apocrys. However, there would be times in the near future when the extra warning of a good watch would have been greatly appreciated.

Suddenly, Inoce entered the room and looked at Sean and Bellus with deep, yet unseeing, eyes. She smiled and greeted Bellus cheerily, not noticing the blush that had slowly risen from her neck and was currently rosying her cheeks. She then turned her attention to Sean. "It's time for supper. The priests and priestesses are anxious to hear the rest of your tale."

"Of course," said the thief, rising reluctantly from his seat. "I'll be right there."

Inoce left and Sean returned his gaze to Bellus. "I've gotta go for now," he said, "but I'll return here this evening so we can talk some more." She smiled at him, but there was an odd sadness in her beautiful, ice-blue eyes. "Bellus, I need to tell you something." He paused.

As Sean attempted to order his thoughts into one statement, Bellus nodded her head and smiled. "I know, Sean. Me too. I'll wait for you." She rose and left, leaving Sean feeling wonderfully warm inside. He stood there for a moment before turning to leave the room.

After Sean arrived at the already-packed dining hall, supper was served. It was a wonderful meal of pheasant and rabbit garnished magnificently with spices. There was also freshly baked bread and unbelievably tasty fruits and vegetables.

As they quickly finished their meal, the priests and priestesses begged David to finish his story, so he told them about their adventures during the Tyrollean Games—about which there were many excited murmurs and exclamations of disbelief—quickly moving on to what occurred afterward.

The seven woke each other on the following morning, feeling a sort of tingling in their minds and bodies, foretelling the change to come. They all seemed to look forward to leaving the city and getting out into the open once again. So they rose early and bathed, dressing in some new clothes which were kindly donated by the innkeeper who arose to see them off. Jessica insisted on paying him overly well for all the help he had given them. So they left the inn, concealed in darkness, though the sun was attempting to raise itself from under the pall of night which stifled it. David was heavily cloaked so that no passersby would recognize him as the quiet group soon reached the stable that contained their supplies: eight horses and a wagon as before. Four horses were already saddled and ready to go. Three others were harnessed to the wagon. The packhorse and wagon were laden with supplies.

Christopher, Sean, and Amy each mounted one of the riding horses while Brandon took up the reins of the wagon, Jodi at his side. David quickly entered the covered wagon where he sat quietly with Jessica.

The stable-master saw them off with a quizzical look, for David who peered back at him from under the recesses of his hood. The group then made their way slowly to the western gate under the early morning sun which, in their anxiety, seemed to shine on them like a spotlight, exposing them to everyone. Likewise, it seemed that the entire city was out early this morning, and all were gathering around the gate. Because of the crowding in the area, it took an inordinate amount of time to finally reach the walls, but once they did, nobody impeded them. David relaxed, letting his breath out slowly as they broke the plane separating Tyrol from the outside world.

After spilling out into the hills that were on the western side of Tyrol, the group followed the main road, hearts bursting within them. David mounted a great roan mare and trotted along side Sean who was leading the train on his own proud black stallion. Sean was whistling "Camptown Races" and David added his basso profundo "do-dah." Behind them, the wagon rolled along, pulled by three brown horses and a white mare who had taken charge of the others. Behind the wagon and the packhorse that was tied to its rear rode Christopher on a palomino which pranced proudly, giving the wizard an even greater quality of power.

The party climbed up and down the Hills of Glockenshire, reveling in the beauty about them. It was now nearing autumn's end and the trees that lined the road were shedding their old leaves, and those still grasping to their branches, found color flaring about them. They took a leisurely pace and too soon found that the sun was a little past its zenith. As their stomachs grumbled, for they had not eaten any breakfast that morning, they found a small glen in which they could stop for lunch. They let the horses graze amongst the trees that littered the covert while they chewed on the dried meat and bread they had brought with them and washed it all down with the red wine that had been so plentiful in Tyrol. The meal took much longer than it should have, for the party chatted and laughed merrily, imbibing the sweet scent of oakmoss. It was so perfect—the day, the glen, perfect!

After they had spent the better part of an hour there basking in the beauty, they repacked and resaddled. They continued their passage down the little winding path, up and down small mountains, across streams, through valleys and alongside small lakes.

Some time around four o'clock, they traveled around a rather large hill to find themselves staring out across a great field that could only be described as a moor. It stretched on for as far as the eye could see, a plain of definitely marshy ground and greensand, frequented by sedges, convolvulus, and other small plants. The monotony was broken infrequently by small outcroppings of trees and occasional hills that rolled on for short distances. The ground was mostly barren except for the brownish grass that covered it like a great woolen rug that had been tread on much too often. The Great Expanse, as it was called, was an area of the world that few people cared to cross. It stretched from the city of Arran northeasterly to the south-ernmost stretches of the Hills of Glockenshire. The southern border was marked by the Shan Forest until it reached the Teuton Swamp which, with the Hills of Glockenshire, marked its easternmost boundary. The Great Expanse was a very gloomy place, with few living creatures in it except small rodents and a few larger, omnivorous animals. Legend also spoke of the evil monsters that were set loose by the worshipers at the Temple of Ranshar within the moor's boundaries. All in all, the eldritch place was mostly avoided by persons of less than heroic stature.

Now the group of travelers stood peering out over the gloomy moors, feeling a little foreboding, but they were of such good spirits at that time that very little could possibly have upset their mood. They started down into the marsh without even a word or a change of expression. They trotted along the road that remained only as an outline in the gloom at a leisurely pace, still chatting happily amongst themselves. The seconds passed into minutes and the minutes into hours until they found that gloaming was settling around them. They had made it a fairly good way into the Great Expanse and began looking for a comfortable place to stay the night. They soon came across a dry, level patch that they decided would probably be the best they would find. Here they stopped, unsaddled their horses, and unpacked all they would need for the evening: blankets, food, etc. They laid the blankets on the ground for each person to sleep on and brought out some more dried meat. David and Brandon wandered, bringing back as much dry brush as they could find. They also managed to bring a little wood but only small amounts; the brush would have to do. So they piled the sticks in the center of their circle and built a small fire to chase off the chill that was beginning to settle across the plain. If they had been paying attention to this change in temperature, they might have noticed that it was slightly abnormal, an almost unnatural sort of chill that started in the pit of their stomachs and spread outward, filling every nook and cranny of their existence.

They finished their meal and settled down around the fire as night fell on them rather more quickly than it should have. As they began to drift off to sleep, leaving Christopher to watch, an extremely dense, roily fog gathered about them, blinding them to the outside, but oddly, it did not come into contact with the light of the fire. It seemed to cringe away from the heat, and instead, satisfied itself on intensifying the deep darkness outside the light of the small fire. As time wore on and the fire grew smaller, the fog came closer and closer to the sleeping group, creeping up on them like notorious confusion.

As midnight grew close, Christopher awakened them all. "This fog's beginning to worry me," he said.

"Why?" asked Brandon, wiping the grit from his eyes. "It's just fog, nothing we haven't seen before."

"It just keeps coming closer and closer as the fire dies down." He pointed to the blaze that was now only a small fire.

"Well, then," said Jodi irritably, "stoke it up."

Christopher did so, still feeling oppressed by the fog.

"Is there anything else?" asked David, preparing to return to sleep.

"Well, I…" Christopher trailed off, licking his lips uncertainly.

"Yes? What is it?" asked David, starting to get annoyed.

"Well, I thought I saw something running around in the mist," he answered, receiving Amy's hand gratefully as a howl erupted from the darkness nearby. Silence ensued for a few moments as they watched the haze about them churn.

"What did you see?" asked Brandon apprehensively.

"It looked like it was on two legs, but I'm not sure because it ran all hunched over like an ape. I only caught a glimpse of it," he added as he looked out into the mist again, his gaze followed apprehensively by the rest of the party.

They stood in silence, shuddering, and not only due to the chill air. Then, all of a sudden, there was a definite movement in the mist!

"There! Did you see that?!" asked Christopher excitedly but wary as he pointed to where the movement had been.

The others nodded and continued peering into the mist, hoping that it was only paranoia. The silence was oppressive as they watched, tension pressing them closer together around the fire. David found Jessica's hand in his as he watched the fog, and he squeezed it. Then, there it was again! Something was running in the mist, circling them, watching them, looking for an opening.

"Shit!" breathed Christopher in a loud whisper, fear radiating from his eyes.

"What is it?" asked David looking at his friend's terrified face.

"A lycanthrope," he whispered as if the beast could hear his voice and wrench his soul from him through his words.

"What?" asked Jodi. She did not recognize the word.

"A werewolf," answered Brandon, fingering his axe nervously. How he wished it had a silver blade.

Amy whimpered.

"Why isn't it attacking?" asked Jodi, horror reflecting in her eyes as stories from her childhood raced through her consciousness.

"It's scared of the fire," answered the wizard quietly, regaining his composure.

"But we'll be out of wood soon," said a terrified Amy, shuddering terribly.

They all turned and looked at their meager supply of twigs forlornly. They would, undeniably, be left in the dark soon…very soon.

"Maybe the werewolf doesn't know that," commented Brandon hopefully. "Maybe it'll go away before we run out."

"Don't count on it," said Christopher almost sadly. "If it's hungry, it won't leave till it's eaten."

There was a great explosion as the fire shot to the sky and then disappeared entirely in a cloud of black! They were left in total darkness. In that same instant, there was a growl and Jessica breathed to herself in a horrified whisper, "Dark spell."

By the pale moonlight, they saw the vague outline of a humanoid creature loping into the clearing on two feet. Then Jessica, acting quickly, waved her hands rhythmically and light flared from her fingertips. She had cast a light spell on herself and she glowed with magnificence, the eldritch light reverberating in her aura. The werewolf—a great beast, towering over all in the clearing, with great jaws containing many long and pointed teeth that dripped saliva—loomed up directly in front of Jessica. It raised its paws, tipped with claws long enough to make a tiger shiver, in front of its face to shield it from the light and rushed at the cleric, growling another spell. She gasped as a shout arose from behind her. "Jessica!" yelled Christopher. "Duck!"

Jessica did not hesitate. In fact, she did not have a choice. The second spell the werewolf cast was a Cancel Magic spell which knocked her instantaneously unconscious. She collapsed in a heap. There was another great burst of light and heat filled the air. By the light they saw, still standing over Jessica, the werewolf, its fur smoldering, with a great char mark on its chest where Christopher's fireball had struck it.

As the others stared at the monster, horrified, it seemed to regain its senses and reached for Jessica again! It grasped her robe, but Christopher reacted again and threw a lightning bolt into its face! Its head exploded, but it still gripped Jessica's robe!

David then jumped at the thing, sword in hand, and sheared its arm off at the shoulder!

"David!" shouted Sean to his friend. "Catch!"

A dagger was tossed through the air to David who caught it by reflex, seeing a glint on its shimmering blade in the darkness. He then took the shining blade and stabbed it deep into the werewolf's chest! The beast stumbled backward and fell to the ground in a lifeless heap with David on top of it!

Amid the horrified stares of the group, the beast, or what was left of it, slowly began to change. The fur sank into its skin, its skew haunches lengthened and formed two legs. Its remaining arm stretched out, hair sinking, until it was a normal man's arm. The body stretched out and bulged at the gut, and the arm which David tore from Jessica's robes reformed, leaving fingers in place of claws.

Another howl ascended through the darkness, and a second beast leapt onto the carcass, ripping and tearing its body, chewing on its innards, and lapping up its blood as the shocked party watched. Another silver dagger sung through the air, embedding itself in the new threat's throat. The monster gurgled as blood flowed from its wound, but still ripped the remaining arm off the dead werewolf. It raced into the darkness, a howl asserting its contentment.

Amy had the presence of mind to try and help Jessica. She knelt beside the sleeping cleric and shook her gently. Jessica awoke with a start and clung to Amy for a moment. David came to her side, helped her stand, and told her what had happened as Sean and Christopher disposed of what was left of the former werewolf's carcass. Brandon rekindled the fire with more twigs, and as the fog receded, he went in search of more fuel. He soon returned, piling a tremendous heap of wood beside the blaze.

Sean and Christopher soon returned, the thief wiping his knife, the silver tip shimmering in the flickering firelight. They returned to their seats around the fire, still shuddering. They soon noticed that the fog had fallen back and mostly dissipated into a more normal darkness.

"How'd that thing make the fire go out?" asked Jodi from Jessica's side where she was still helping David reassure her.

"It cast a Darkness Spell," answered Amy from across the fire. "Didn't you feel the power given off by it?"

"I did feel something," admitted Jodi. "Was that the werewolf?"

"Yes," answered Christopher. "I'd forgotten that they can sometimes cast spells. Their power originates from their dark god Ranshar just as Amy and Jessica's originates from Galead."

"Why did it attack me?" asked Jessica, calm but shaky.

"Because it knew that you were its biggest threat," answered Christopher. He looked very tired with the light from the fire outlining his dark face.

"Me?"

"Yes, you. You're the only one here that knows the Light Spell. Casting it so quickly is probably the only thing that saved your life," answered Christopher with a weak smile.

"Oh," she said quickly, realizing the truth, shock dulling her senses. "Thanks Chris," she added after a few moments of silence, "for the timely rescue."

"Don't mention it." The wizard's dark mien grinned out from under his hood.

"Sean?" asked David from Jessica's other side. "When did you start carrying silver daggers? I thought they were rare, after all they have to be blessed by a priest too, don't they?"

Sean grinned back, nodding. "I stole 'em."

"When?" asked David, shaking his head.

"When we were in Tyrol. I saw them hanging on the belt of some rich, fat merchant, so I took 'em," he answered, still smiling. "This time, you'd better be thankful I'm not as honest as I look." He grinned.

David sighed. "Thanks, Sean...this time," he answered.

Sean bowed as best he could from a sitting position.

"I think it's time we went back to sleep," suggested Christopher, lying down. "We've got a long day of traveling ahead of us tomorrow." He closed his eyes and opened them again only after much struggling. "By the way, my watch is over." He closed his eyes again and promptly fell asleep.

"I'll take over," offered Brandon. "I don't feel much like sleeping now anyway."

So they returned to their blankets, save Brandon, and slept with nightmares all night. All of these consisted of huge hairy beasts with great mouths full of bloody teeth. All except David's, that is. His nightmare scared him more than any monster could. He saw a man sitting at a table in a great black chair, all dressed in black. He smiled at David as two more figures materialized beside him. One figure was very short, a crazed old man with a dangling white beard all dressed in rags. The second figure was of medium height, huskily built, dressed in a plain black tunic and matching breaches. This same man had long boots reaching up to his knees and brown hair and black eyes. Hanging at his side was a slightly curved, black longsword. The three men laughed maliciously at David, and as he watched, they slowly moved together until they were one man, the features of each in his face. This figure stood and spoke one single sentence to David that echoed in his mind for the rest of the night: "We are one."

Starting over

David told the priests the rest of their story in somber displacement, emotionlessly describing what had happened to Jessica, how they had reacted, and how he had finally managed to kill Tohzahi. He told them how Lady Gahdnawen had answered their call and transported them to the Temple and how she had taken Jessica under her protective wing.

After David had finished and the priests and priestesses had started asking questions, Purus entered. "The Lady requests your presence in her chambers," she said.

So they followed her back to Gahdnawen's rooms, hoping they would learn something more. As they entered the elaborate room, David noticed the weighty silence that hung in the air like a chill in the heart of Cybele. He shuddered and slowly sat in a chair next to the crackling fire, rubbing his hands together as if it would warm his soul. Then he noticed that Jessica was no longer lying on the couch in the corner, that, indeed, the couch was no longer there. Visions of kidnappers and demons secreting Jessica away from him flashed through his mind like lucid nightmares, but Lady Gahdnawen entered from her bedroom, allowing David a quick glimpse of Jessica lying on the same couch next to the Priestess' bed.

"Ah, you're all here." She greeted them with that perpetual, reassuring smile. "That's good for there's much to be said. I'll tell you straight out, before we even begin to discuss, that you must leave early tomorrow morning."

There was a general fulmination of dispute, but they were all overshadowed by David's booming voice. "What about Jessica?!"

"That's one of the things we must talk about."

More fear and alarm flashed into David's consciousness, leaving afterimages of life without Jessica. He feared that the Lady meant that it was beyond her power to heal Jessica.

Gahdnawen caught the twisting of David's features and walked over to sit down opposite him. As she sat there, the fire wrapping its pellucid patina around her, she met the worried warrior's eyes. "I have done a great deal of research into Jessica's problem, and I believe my knowledge of her condition is adequate for me to heal her."

There was a tremendous release of breath that thinly covered an even deeper release of pent up anxiety. "What have you learned?" asked Jodi, smiling luminously.

"The malspirare has secreted himself in a castle in a dimension named Absu," she began. "There he sits brooding over Jessica's soul like a hawk over a rabbit. He's slowly draining her until he can swallow her entirely. He doesn't think he's in any danger and therefore I have a great advantage over him, for a predator unprepared can be defeated by the most helpless doe."

"That's good news," said Brandon, almost laughing. "If we've got to leave tomorrow, then you'll confront the malspirare tonight." He grinned in anticipation of having that evil being destroyed.

"No," she said, no longer smiling, but urgent. "It'll take

longer than that. I don't know how long, but it will take more time than we have."

They were greatly puzzled, but Christopher finally voiced their thoughts. "Then how can we leave tomorrow?"

"You're going to have to begin your journey without her, but be assured that before you've finished, Jessica will be at your side. Peccare is already nearing Mount Apocrys. If you intend to reach the mountain before him, you must leave tomorrow." She stared at all of them for a moment before continuing. "I'll teleport you to within two days' walk of the mountains however. That's the only way you'll be able to beat him there. This I will gladly do, but I must tell you now that your quest won't end the way you hope. The events that will occur will be no less satisfactory to you, but they'll be different than you expect."

"What do you mean? What's going to happen?" asked Jodi.

"I can't tell you that. Telling such secrets could possibly ford their happening and change the future. That would be a most grave mistake and one that I cannot allow to happen, but I thought it necessary to offer you some form of comfort." She took a deep breath and continued on another tangent. "Galead requires that there be payment for the services I am rendering to you."

"What sort of payment?" spat Sean.

"I assure you, master thief, not the kind you suspect. I'll simply require each of you to do me a favor in return for Jessica's life and everything else I have given and will give you. But we'll speak more about that later. Now it's time for you to rest and relax in anticipation of your journey's second beginning."

"What're these favors you've mentioned?" questioned Christopher suspiciously as the Lady met his gaze.

"You'll learn that later when I speak with each of you in

private. There are things that you must know." This she stated
with another knowing smile. "But now's not the time for it."

They left, not having learned very much but with hope that
they would know more soon. They felt relieved that Lady
Gahdnawen could help Jessica but were curious as to how.

Soon after leaving, Amy found herself wandering in the
area of the Temple where the clergy were housed. She slowly
approached and entered the room she had used the night
before. It was empty, so she sat on the corner of her cot. She
placed her head in her hands and sighed wearily with fatigue.

As she sat in this position a voice wrenched her from her
self-beration. It asked, "Why so sad, child?"

Amy started and looked up to see Lady Gahdnawen
standing over her with a gentle smile illuminating her face. "I
grieve for what I've done," she answered, knowing that this
was the reason the Lady had come to speak with her.

"And what have you done?" asked the Priestess, her face
still gentle.

Amy was certain that the Lady knew what she was talking
about, but she apparently wanted to hear the words from
Amy's own lips. "I broke my vow," she stated, her voice
shaking with pain. "I'm no longer chaste!"

Gahdnawen was silent for only a moment. "I know,
Sister," she said, sitting beside Amy. "It's that subject I've
come to speak with you about."

"Please, Lady," begged Amy, "I know my sins and I
repent! Please forgive me!" She grasped the Priestess' robe,
tears welling in her eyes and streaming down her cheeks.

"It's not I who must forgive you, child," she stated matter-
of-factly. "It's Galead you must convince of your repen-
tance."

Amy bowed her head, not knowing what else to say. She
had sinned and knew it, but she was sorry, though she could
not really understand how what she and Christopher had done

could be wrong.

"I have consulted Galead on your behalf," said Lady Gahdnawen, standing once more. "And she told me that if you confessed your sins to me, you would be forgiven." Amy almost fainted from relief. She had not expected such benevolence! Not even dreamed of it! "But only to an extent."

"What do you mean, Lady?" asked Amy, overwhelmed with joy but uncertain of the answer she would receive.

The Priestess was no longer smiling when she answered Amy. "First, you must not stray in this way again." This Amy expected but what else? "And I'm afraid that you'll be powerless for several days, but your powers will eventually be returned to you. However, they'll be in a much different form. You will no longer be a cleric, though Galead will hear your prayers just as before. You will instead be the first sorceress under the protection of our goddess. In this form, your match to Christopher will be much more complete and you will be allowed to wed when the time comes, but beware, Amy, for evil will be constantly attempting to convert you to its own purpose. Stand by your convictions and let Galead lead you."

"I will, Lady Gahdnawen," answered Amy, terribly unsure of her ability to do Galead justice from this new vantage. "Thank you," she breathed, mind wandering, uncertain of whether to be happy or disappointed.

"Don't thank me, child," said the Lady. "Thank Galead. I'm terribly sorry for you, Amy. Great harm and pain will be yours because of this decision, but it's a necessary suffering that you must bare for us all. However, now you should bow down and pray to Galead, for she shall hear you and answer your prayers. Also, since you won't have your clerical powers anymore and Jessica will not be along for the rest of the journey, I'll be sending another cleric with you." The Lady left Amy kneeling next to the room's altar. She prayed with all the strength and conviction she had in her heart, hoping for some answer that would console her to her new fate. When she heard the answer, she was greatly relieved by the reassuring presence within her mind. She stood once more, smiling with relief, and left the room in a flutter.

After leaving the Lady's room, Christopher returned to the library in which he had spent almost his entire day. He returned to the section containing the books on wizardry, knowing that he did not have the time to learn another spell but committing himself to the attempt anyway.

"Yearning for knowledge, wizard?" came the voice of Lady Gahdnawen from behind him.

Christopher was not startled by her appearance; he had been expecting her to come soon. Smiling, he turned. There was a trace of malevolence in that smile which the Lady did not miss, but there was only respect and healthy curiosity in his manner. "Knowledge, I have, Lady. I yearn only for more." She frowned deeply at his reply, and he was greatly satisfied. "I was wondering when you'd come to see me."

"Indeed, wizard?" she inquired. "Is there another time which would be more fitting? Did you not know it would be now?"

Christopher looked pensive for a moment before nodding. "Yes, I suppose I did." He took the Lady's arm and escorted her to a nearby seat. "What is it you want to speak to me about?" he asked.

She looked quizzically at him again. "I believe you know that also."

He nodded again, all solemnity now, no humor in his pointed mind.

"You've committed a sin that, had you been a lesser man, you would have already been killed for." There was no trace of emotion in her words; they were simply a statement of fact. "You have caused one of our sisterhood to break an oath. This is a crime beyond all crimes. Do you realize this?"

"I do," he answered, wondering what it was she was getting at.

"You also know that you've been forgiven because you have a purpose in this world that has not yet been fulfilled."

"I know." He paused, but only for a moment. "Can you tell me what that is, Lady?"

"You know I cannot," she answered. "Truly, I don't know, but I do know that it's a great thing you'll do, for good or for evil."

Christopher smiled sardonically at her remark.

"I have noted your interest in that great black book," she said, gesturing at the book of magic he still held in his left hand. He had not even noticed that he was carrying it. Printed on it in fiery letters was the word "Grenla."

"Yes," Christopher answered. "There're several spells in it that I haven't mastered yet. Some of them I greatly desire to understand."

"I've been told that you should be allowed to take the book with you," said the Lady with foreboding in her eyes. "It's yours."

Christopher did not know what to say. He was baffled but he accepted the gift with great enthusiasm. "Thank you," he said as Lady Gahdnawen stood in silence. She approached the shelf and after a time of searching pulled a nondescript white book off the shelf. The only marking on it was an odd arcane symbol that even Christopher did not recognize. "You should also take this book with you, wizard. It's to be Amy's spellbook. You'll know when to give it to her."

Christopher was now very confused. Only wizards need spellbooks. Why would Amy need one? He started to question, but the Lady interrupted him. "Wizard," she began, "you must listen to your heart. The mind is a powerful tool and its mastery is of great use, but the greatest knowledge in the universe is in the realization of the power of emotion. Listen to your emotions and capture the power they give you for it's far greater than any you'll find in a book." She turned and left, leaving Christopher squatting in the library, completely at a loss.

Brandon was walking through the halls of the Temple, wondering at the fine structure. He had spent his entire day, wandering and marveling at the stonework in the great marble building. As he walked, feeling the walls, knowing the power that flowed through them, he sensed a person standing near. He looked up slowly to see Lady Gahdnawen standing at his side. "Good evening, Lady," he greeted.

"Good evening," she answered. "I see that you're interested in stonework."

"As a dwarf, I am, Lady, and I must say that I've rarely seen anything as magnificent as this Temple. It seems as if it were carved out of a tremendous mountain of marble." He was awed by the unbroken, confluent surfaces. "How was it done?"

"By magic," she answered, "and the strength of your own kindred. Perhaps five thousand years ago, the first Priestess of Galead was led to this place by the goddess herself. Then, as the Priestess watched, Galead caused a mountain of white marble to be raised from the ground into the air. This mountain was carved into what is now our Temple by the strength of your ancestors."

"Amazing," said Brandon, wondering why his people did not remember such a feat.

"I agree. I've always thought it to be one of the great miracles worked in our world."

Brandon's thoughts returned to the discussion they had after dinner, and he vaguely remembered that the Lady had spoken of favors. "What favor would you ask of me, Lady?"

he prompted, abruptly changing the subject.

"None, child of the hills," she answered, a fond smile on her face. "Anything you could possibly owe us was repaid by your ancestors when they built this place."

"Then what would you like to say to me?" he asked, knowing that there was some reason that the Lady had sought him out.

"I just want to give you some advice." She smiled at him and placed her hand on his bulky shoulder. "I would advise you to remember your heritage. There'll be use for your powers as a dwarf in the future. There is great strength in your race and all of it is not in the body. Above all, believe in yourself." With these words, she released her grip and walked off while Brandon watched, wondering. What did she mean?

Sean sat in the room where he was to meet Bellus, waiting for her. Instead, to his wonder, he was joined by Lady Gahdnawen. She walked proudly in and sat at his side, in the same seat Bellus had been in earlier that day.

She greeted him happily and with a great smile. "I'm glad I found you," she said. "We need to talk."

Sean knew that she had come for that reason, but was rather surprised that she had come to him and not simply requested his presence in her chamber. "What can I do for you?" he asked curiously.

"You know, Sean, that here in the Temple of Galead we usually deal harshly with thieves, but we've accepted your presence happily and are even aiding you as best we can."

Sean had wondered why they let him stay here since he stood for very little of the same things the clergy did. He nodded for her to continue

"The reason is that we know you'll do us a great service in the future, but that's not what I've come to talk to you about." Sean wondered what service he would do for them, curious whether he would do it on purpose or accidentally. But he did not ask her about it; he knew she would not tell him.

"Why have you come, Lady?" he asked since she seemed to be waiting for him to say something.

This apparently was not what she wanted to hear, but she answered anyway. "I've been informed that you've come to know a certain cleric here at the Temple. Her name is Bellus." Sean nodded, confusion and foreboding clouding his mind. "She's a very promising student, Sean, and we believe she needs to learn more about the outside world. We ask that you do a favor for us and take her with you to Mount Apocrys. You may need her clerical powers anyway."

"Why? We'll have Amy with us," he stated confusedly.

"Her powers have been temporarily taken away."

Sean looked at her strangely for a moment, wanting to ask her why, but he decided to take another course. He could always ask Amy about this later, and Gahdnawen had an annoying habit of leaving before all of their questions were answered. "The journey's going to be quite dangerous, Lady," he protested. "Do you think it's wise for Bellus to come on this journey?"

"I do or I wouldn't have suggested it," she answered in a tone that took the sting from her haughty words. "She's quite naive, Sean, and needs to learn about the world outside, but she is a very capable cleric. In return for the help we've given you, we ask that you take Bellus and protect her with your life, but be wary, thief, for if she is violated in any way while she's on this trip, her powers and your life will be forfeit. She is not an outlet for anyone's lustful desires. Do not allow her to be treated in such a way." As she made her avowals, her voice echoed galvanically, threatening to shock Sean into obeisance.

"Why do you trust her to a thief on a dangerous quest like this?" asked Sean, still not sure of her reasoning and further surprised that she had not left before he asked the question. "Surely you could find someone on a less dangerous mission."

"Most assuredly but you and your companions are the most able group for the job." She paused for a moment before continuing. "And she seems to have taken a liking to you."

Sean smiled. "But of course. Who wouldn't like me?"

"I shall decline to answer," said Lady Gahdnawen also smiling slightly. "Are you willing to do this favor for the Temple?"

Sean nodded, wondering whether he could resist Bellus for the trip. He decided that he would have to after accepting the charge. He was actually very glad to know that he would not have to part with her tonight.

"Good," said the Lady. "I believe that she may be of some assistance on the trip. I'll also say that I feel strongly for her and that you must not take advantage of her innocence. This I implore of you, and know that if you do, I will personally seek you out and have my vengeance."

There was silence for a short time before Sean asked, "Why is it we won't be able to return home immediately after we get the amulet?"

The Lady peered at Sean, an odd, grudging respect obvious in her eyes. "Because, Jessica's soul will be too weak to survive the great strain that a transformation of that type would put it under."

Sean peered at her in silence for a moment, certain that she was telling the truth but also sure that she was holding something back. "I suspected an answer like that, Lady, but how about telling me the rest of it. I mean, I believe you, but I'm also sure that you're not telling me everything."

The Priestess sat in silence, staring at Sean's sincere face. "I'm afraid I can't tell you that right now, but please trust me. I promise that you'll know the rest very soon."

Sean nodded and asked, "How long till we return home?"

"I don't know. It could be anything from a month to ten years before Jessica's soul has healed enough."

"That's not what I asked, Lady Gahdnawen," said Sean, the results of a day's contemplation weaved into this one question. "How long will it be before we're all back on Earth?"

Gahdnawen sat silently for a moment, contemplating the thief's words and then consulting Galead for an answer. She was really learning to respect this man who at first she only despised. "Truthfully, Sean, I don't know when or if you'll return, but I have learned that it'll all depend upon one decision you make. You must make a weighty judgment in your future, and more than you can imagine will depend upon your action or inaction. Please, Sean, for the sake of everyone, consider your actions and listen to how you feel. Sometimes sacrifice brings about more pleasure than indulgence."

Sean sighed. He had been getting a horrible feeling that things were going to come to rest on his shoulders. He hated decisions and always had, but somehow, he had always ended up having to make the most difficult ones. I'm cursed, he thought to himself before continuing. "I have one more question for you, Lady. Why do you care so much about Bellus? She's just one cleric."

Gahdnawen smiled at Sean and left. As she passed down the hall, Sean heard an echo reverberate back into the room. "Because she's my daughter."

Jodi was walking in the gardens where she had returned after the evening meal. She felt quite at home here and seemed to be far away from her problems. She was surprised to turn around and find Lady Gahdnawen approaching her. "Good evening."

"Good evening," she returned, smiling.

"I find it quite restful in your gardens," said the illusionist, stretching her arms grandly.

"It is relaxing," answered the Lady, seeming every bit as awed by the beauty around her as Jodi. "I came to tell you, Jodi, that I know all about you," she said without a second's hesitation, as if it were something for her to spit out in order to finish with as quickly as possible.

Jodi started and looked at her intently. "What do you mean?" she asked, attempting to cover her alarm.

The Lady looked at her almost reprovingly. "I know those things about your origins and your abilities that you hide from your friends."

Jodi knew then that Lady Gahdnawen was telling her the truth. She really did know! "How can you?" she asked, embarrassed and trapped.

"Galead has seen fit to tell me," she answered matter-of-factly.

"What do you want?" asked Jodi, anger now welling inside her. She was sure that the Lady was here for no good purpose though she could not imagine what it was.

"Nothing that you wouldn't have done anyway. You must simply stay by David's side for the rest of the trip to Mount Apocrys."

Jodi was startled by the request because, indeed, she had intended to do this anyway. "And what else?" she asked, suspicious.

"That's all. But when I say 'by his side,' I mean within reach of him at all times. You will know what I mean when the time comes, but heed my words and do as I say."

"I'll do it," said Jodi, eyes flashing with refound dignity. "You won't tell the others about me?"

"No, child. I won't."

Jodi was greatly relieved. She would do this small task for the Lady. Indeed, she had already taken it upon herself to take care of David in Jessica's absence. This only gave her more reason. As Jodi mused, she became aware that Lady Gahdnawen was no longer with her.

David was lying on his bed in the room he shared with Brandon, wondering whether Jessica would really be all right when Lady Gahdnawen entered, Sean silent by her side.

"We need to talk," she began, sitting in a chair near the bed where David sat, Sean emulating her action. "Of the people in your party, the two of you have been placed in very awkward and very essential positions. I'm certain that both of you at some point in your travels in Sidan have been plagued with questions about why all of your companions have acted so strangely when you talk about your home." They both nodded.

"Well, I'm afraid that as your companions have spent time in this world, their counterparts here have had time to retake control of their bodies. They've been slowly taken over by their alter-egos until at this point, none of them really remember that they're trying to get back to Earth. Indeed, they all think the two of you have been acting oddly when you mention 'getting home.' They assume that for some reason you're wanting to return to the cities your counterparts grew up in here in Sidan."

"You mean they've been completely taken over?" questioned Sean.

"No, not completely. Only nominally. Enough so that they can't remember anything about wanting to go home. However, the rest of their psyches are intact. Jodi's still Jodi with the urges and fears of Aurora, Christopher is still Christopher but with the urges and fears of Omnibus, and so on. For all practical intent, they're a conglomeration of the friends you knew and the characters they played."

"Why're you telling us this?" asked David.

"Because you're the ones who'll have to furtively remind them of who they are. You can't just tell them that they've forgotten; that would cause an inner struggle that could possibly kill them. You must guide them so that they'll gradually remember. That's one reason you won't be able to return to Earth when you get the amulet. Though a few of them could survive the transference, some of them would surely be killed by it."

"Is that what you wouldn't tell me earlier today?" asked Sean.

"That's only part of it, I'm afraid Sean. The worst is still to come."

"Wonderful," murmured Sean and David together.

"I didn't tell you everything about Jessica's situation. You see, when her soul's returned to her body, which it will be I assure you, she won't remember Jessica at all. Though I will arrange it so that she will answer to the name, the mind will be completely Sister Anna's. I'm afraid, David, that she won't remember your relationship with her. You'll only be as she remembers Graham; a good warrior and friend. Nothing more."

Sean and the Priestess were studying David intently, hoping that he would take this knowledge pretty well. He sat stoically still for a moment then spoke. "Somehow I expected that. Then, am I doomed to lose her?"

"Not necessarily," answered Lady Gahdnawen. She was very pleased with David's control and foresight. "You must coax her into remembrance just as you coax the others; however, you'll have to be doubly careful with her. The transformation is much more complete and, therefore, will be much more difficult to undo. I cannot stress it enough that you be careful with her. Also, all those in your party know that you and Jessica are more than just friends, and in order for you to be subtle enough with her, it's imperative that she not be reminded by others of your relationship. Therefore, when Jessica is returned to you, I'll cast a spell on them so that they'll forget all about it. You two will be the only ones who remember. I'm sorry David."

"Thank you," murmured David. "It makes sense that

Jessica'd be affected in this way, but why have the others forgotten themselves and Sean and I can still remember everything?"

"I'm not completely sure, but from what I know of you two, it seems that you're very similar to your characters in many ways. David, you're very much the chivalrous sort just as Graham was, and Sean you're very like a thief."

"Was that a compliment?" asked Sean, a forced smile quirking his lips. The Lady smiled slightly back at him before continuing.

"So I would imagine, that you have been taken over slightly by your characters, but it makes such a minute difference that you can't even tell. Or perhaps, you subconsciously know how to keep your characters suppressed much better than the others. It must be something along those lines though."

"Thank you, Lady Gahdnawen," said David quietly. "Thank you for explaining and for being up-front with us. We need the help."

She nodded. "Sean, I believe Bellus is waiting for you. She'll be wondering if she's been stood up. You'd better go to her."

Sean nodded and exited, leaving David and the Priestess alone.

"What favor can I do for you, Lady?" asked David sitting up the rest of the way.

"There's much you can do for me, David, but I promise you, the reward will be well worth it. Indeed, it'll be Jessica's life and all the help I can give you with your friends."

David nodded. "Just name it."

David and Lady Gahdnawen spent the better part of an hour discussing what the Priestess had planned. Soon afterwards, Brandon entered and found David already asleep. He joined his friend, more rested than he had felt in a long time. He had been told that they would be awakened before first light and everything would be prepared for them. Brandon did not know whether to be happy or sad about leaving. The best way to find out is to go ahead and sleep. I'll see how I feel in the morning. Nobody knows what the new day will bring, he thought to himself as he undressed and crawled into the soft bed. There he slept in a dreamless slumber that was not truly refreshing. What would happen tomorrow? Or the next day? He did not know, but then again, he probably did not want to.

The next day came much too early for Sean's liking. He forced himself to climb out of bed, Christopher following his example. Before they had even reached the floor, there was a knock on the door. Sean groaned as he stumbled to the door, already knowing who it was that would be on the other side. "Is it time?" he asked, pulling on the door which grudgingly gave.

As it swung open, the smiling form of Bellus, now clad in a plain brown tunic and britches, said, "It is."

"Where're your robes?" asked Sean, his curiosity waking even before his brain.

"The Lady suggested that I go in disguise so no one will know I'm a cleric. I don't really know enough to handle myself," she answered. "Good morning, Christopher." She greeted the tall wizard who stood yawning at Sean's back.

"Good morning, Bellus," he returned, finishing his yawn. He ran an experimental hand across his unshaven chin. "Is everything prepared for the journey?"

"Yes. Do you want to bathe this morning?"

"I think we should get as early a start as possible," he answered. "Are the others awake?"

"Yes. They're waiting at a table piled with enough food to feed us well into next week." She smiled broadly, anticipation coruscating in her eyes. She was really very excited about getting to go on a journey.

"Just a second and we'll join them," said Sean, returning to the interior of the room, Christopher following slowly. They both changed back into their traveling gear as Bellus waited outside.

The feast that awaited them in the dining hall was no less than Bellus had promised. There was pheasant and a rabbit along with roulades and succulent fruits to clean the palate. They ate merrily with Lady Gahdnawen at the table's head, enjoying the luscious food. After finishing the meal, she stood and spoke: "It's time for you to depart, friends, for if you don't leave now, you'll never reach your destination. Please follow me." She left the room, the travelers trailing after her.

She led them back to the room in which they had arrived two nights before. There were backpacks in the room filled with food and clothing, blankets and pots, and all the other necessities for the trip. "I regret that your stay has been so short, but it's necessary. We will meet again, and soon." She smiled down at them from the throne in which she had seated herself and gestured for them to take up the baggage. Each one placed a backpack on his or her back, smaller ones for the ladies and larger ones for the men. "I'll teleport you to within two days of Mount Apocrys, but that's as far as I may. Good luck, my friends, and I look forward to our next meeting." She then turned to Bellus. "Be careful, daughter, and learn. Remember all you have been taught and above all do not reveal yourself to any people you meet. Take care of her," she said with an encompassing wave and a stern look for Sean in particular. "She's still young and may need the guidance you can giver her."

"We'll take good care of her," promised Jodi from Bellus' other side, placing an arm around her.

"I know you will," she said with a penetrating look.

As Jodi's smile faded, Lady Gahdnawen finished: "It's time for you to leave." She stood and began to concentrate, her hands weaving a complicated concatenate in the still air of the silent room. Soon her hands began to shimmer, little flecks of variegated light flickering on her fingertips. A wind came from nowhere and seemed to sweep the group into the air and whisk them away, through the walls and over leagues of open ground in a fraction of a second. As reality bent, the wind whispered to them in a voice that echoed in their minds. It said, "Beware!"

They opened their eyes and found themselves sitting on a hillock in a plain that was barely visible by the light of an orange sun that was just peeking over the horizon. It was an amazing sensation to sit there and realize that only a moment before, they had been somewhere far off, in a much more secure locale. They had been teleported once before—to the Temple—but at that time, they were too weary for the shock to register.

"I feel like I've been dropped off a cliff," commented Sean, feeling his midsection to assure himself that it was still there.

"Me too," agreed Christopher from a short distance, sitting firmly on the ground, wishing fervently that he had not eaten so much breakfast.

"Exactly where are we?" asked Bellus, peering about her in the dim, foggy morning.

"In the far west section of the plain that contains the Temple of Galead," answered Jodi standing beside the young cleric turned adventurer.

It was then that David noticed the belt wrapped around her waist with a short sword and dagger attached to it. "Do you know how to use that?" he asked Bellus, gesturing to the sword.

"A little," smiled Bellus. "We're taught how to defend ourselves in the Temple but that's all. They don't teach us anything offensive."

Said David, "Well, by the time we get you back to the Temple, you may know a little more about it—a little more than you'll like. I'll teach you a little swordplay tonight when we camp. It may be worth it to you."

"Thank you," she answered.

"We'd better get a move on," offered Christopher, walking up to David. "The quicker we get to the mountain, the quicker we'll be done with this whole business."

A general nod and they shouldered their burdens, wishing fervently for a horse or wagon, but knowing that they would be useless as soon as they reached the mountains. They began steadily walking to the southwest, sloshing through the dew-ridden grass and wading through the knee-deep mist that hung low on the ground. They were glad for the long boots that kept them dry. The sun slowly rose at their backs, making their shadows long in front of them and a little to their right. This source of light and heat continued to close in behind them, making the land slowly visible in front of them. With relief, they noticed that this plain was nothing like the insipid moors of the Great Expanse. It was green and lush with grass, tall and waving in the wind, creating ripples in front of them, not unlike a lake.

They talked only sparingly as they trudged on in single file, David leading. Bellus was silent, taking in the beautiful plain for she had never seen any scenery accept the minimal landscape that was visible from the windows of the Temple. She was breathless, loving every minute that she spent under the warm sun. The sky was a brilliant cerulean with sparse fluffy white clouds floating lazily above them, brightening the day with their own comfortable laziness. It was cool, but not cold, the perfect temperature for a walk. They pranced onward, across the rolling plains, frequently coming across small rodents or grazing animals and occasionally a dell with larger animals in it—deer, gazelle, and even some wild horses. Bellus looked wonderingly at all the creatures, having seen only drawings of them in books except for the birds, squirrels, and rabbits which had found a home in the Temple's garden.

It was not long until the sun was at its zenith above their heads, and they could see the mountains of the west in the distance. Soon after the sun had begun its descent, they stopped for the noon meal under what seemed almost a small orchard, for it was full of trees bearing different types of fruit. Some were common apples or oranges, while others were more exotic, pomegranates or passion fruit or other types they had seen only on the Priestess' table. Here they sat in the shade and ate the fruit and sweetmeats the Lady had given them. They drank the wine and longed for the end of their quest…or did they? They were not quite sure.

David was still quiet where he sat with Jodi at his side. He had spent the entire day sunk in thought…sometimes about Jessica and sometimes about the things the Priestess had said after Sean had left; they troubled him greatly. He did not understand why she wanted him to do the things she had said while they were alone in his room, but he would do them, for Jessica's sake. For her, nothing was too much or too strange.

Jodi sat by his side, seeming to nap in the shade but actually thinking some of the same thoughts as David. She was also wondering how the Lady knew so many things about her that she had not even told her friends.

Christopher and Amy were both sullen and quiet, not wishing to speak, uncomfortable because of what had passed in the Temple. However, Sean and Bellus sat listening intently to Brandon as he told them stories of the dwarves that he remembered and the places they inhabited in the far west. He told them of tall mountains and deep caves, all filled with great gems and rivers of gold flowing to lakes of platinum. He spoke of the great underground cities they lived in and of their civilization built on smithing and stoneworking, of their lives and loves, their thoughts and hopes.

After they had eaten and rested for a quarter of an hour, they stood and reshouldered their backpacks, continuing the journey. They walked on, speaking only in fragments and watching the mountains in front of them grow nearer on the horizon.

As evening fell, they were within half a day's walk of the mountain range. Here they stopped, before night had fully set in, and built a fire to chase away the chill which was fast coming on. It was a small fire but enough to keep them warm. David felled a deer on which they feasted, finishing almost the whole beast in that one sitting. After eating, they sat down and began to talk.

"We'll reach Apocrys tomorrow," stated Brandon somberly. The elusive mountain had become an enigma to them. They had wished to reach it, but now that it was within their reach, they found themselves ambivalent, unsure of whether they wanted to arrive or not.

"How far into the mountain chain is Mount Apocrys?" asked Amy. She sat next to Christopher, but they were not as near as they had been on the nights before their reaching the Temple of Galead. There was a polar rejection to their closeness as if they wanted to touch but were too afraid of what it might awaken in them.

"Not far," answered Christopher. "It's a tall red mountain with several passages leading to its depths, but they all lead to one point, a large chamber in the center of the mountain. It's there that the amulet's supposed to be."

"And its guardian," added Brandon who was quietly leaning against a tree, picking his teeth with a rib bone.

"Yeah, its guardian..." Christopher trailed off.

"Exactly what does guard this amulet?" asked Bellus curiously.

"A wizard," answered Christopher. "He's said to be very old and extremely powerful but insane, really more beast than man, as if the magic has taken too large a toll on him. Legend has it that he's somehow linked with the mountain itself, that they're somehow one. We'll know what that means soon enough. We should concentrate on other matters for the moment."

"Yes," agreed David, standing. "It's time to see what our new friend knows about defending herself." He smiled at Bellus who stood up with him. They moved a little ways from the fire as the others turned to watch.

"What do you want me to do?" asked Bellus, smiling in anticipation.

"Defend yourself." David crouched into a fighting stance, slightly bent at the knees and weight balanced on the balls of his feet. He moved quickly up against Bellus, but not as quickly as he could, holding back until he could be sure not to hurt her. She sidestepped and kicked him in the rear as he passed. She's quick, thought David. That's one advantage for her. But is she strong? He rushed her again but too quickly for her to avoid this time. He grabbed her right arm with his left hand and placed his other hand firmly on her shoulder, preparing to bend her backward, but she leaned into it and, with all her strength, threw herself groundward. David flipped over her and landed on his back with a grunt.

There was much applauding and laughing. David stood up again, rubbing his backside, and looked at her with more respect as he feigned great pain. She did seem to know a bit about martial art defense, but he wanted to know if she could handle a sword as well. "Sean," he said, "lend me your short sword." The smaller man complied and tossed David the two foot blade. "Now we'll see if you know how to fight with a weapon. Draw your sword," he ordered.

Bellus did as she was told, jerking the short sword loose from its sheath at her side and holding it nimbly in her left hand. David had not previously noticed that she was left-handed but was glad to know that she had a few small advantages—if she knew how to use them.

They circled and began a short sequence of lunges and parries, thrusts and feints, testing each other's abilities, ripost-ing often. Bellus was quick and strong for her size. She was an able fighter and gave David a run for his money, but the more experienced fighter took one of her thrusts and, with a quick flick of his wrist, sent her sword flying end over end. Bellus was surprised, apparently having never been disarmed before, but David retrieved her sword for her and gave Sean his own.

"You're very good, Bellus," said David. "I'm impressed. I don't think I've ever seen a cleric who could fight as well as you."

"But you still beat me," she said, pursing her lips in frustration. She was feeling a little discouraged by this seemingly easy defeat. She had always thought that she was the equal of any with a sword—apparently not, but she could adjust.

"Yeah, I beat you, but I'm a lot stronger and have the reach on you. I'm also much more experienced and have probably had a great deal more training, but you fight very well. I'd be pleased to have you on my side in a fight."

Bellus smiled at David happily as they returned to their seats. "Thank you. Do you have any advice for a poor, inexperienced person like myself?"

David chuckled, realizing just how his words had sounded. "Just keep practicing. If you don't use your skills, you'll lose them."

She nodded.

"If you're done playing now," interrupted Sean. "I think it's about time for bed."

There was a sigh of general agreement. "Who'll take first

watch?" asked Brandon, yawning explosively.

"I will," offered David, he was not feeling very tired. His adrenaline was coursing from the fight, and he would find it impossible to sleep for a time.

"Good," said the dwarf. "I'll go last." He lay down on the blanket spread on the ground next to the small fire and slept, quickly and deeply.

The others followed slowly except for Jodi who insisted that she was not tired and stayed awake with David.

As they all drifted off into a sleepy haze among the hoots and chirps of murmuring night animals, Jodi and David sat quietly, thinking about what the morning would bring. It was one day closer to seeing Jessica again and that was what David centered on.

"Do you think we'll have much trouble getting the amulet?" asked Jodi in a whisper.

"I don't know," answered David from her side. "The only person who really knows anything about this fellow is Christopher, and all he knows are rumors. The Guardian might not even exist, but if he does, I'm sure he'll fight us."

"Somehow, I get the feeling that he does exist," said Jodi.

"Me too, but you can always hope."

"True."

After a time of complete quiet and not-quite-relaxation, David spoke. "I'd like to thank you, Jodi," he said, tenderness and appreciation in his rough voice.

"For what?" she asked, startled.

"For being here for me while Jessica can't be. I've recognized your support, and I really do appreciate the company." He gingerly placed an arm around her.

"I love her too, David. I've been her friend for a long time. She's more like a sister to me than anything else…And you may as well be my brother. I'd do anything for either of you."

"I know, Jodi. I feel the same way. I haven't known you as

long as Jessica has, but I do know you well enough to be sure that you're a caring person whom I respect." He smiled at her. "But enough of this sentimentality. It's late and time to sleep."

They both fell silent after that and Jodi slowly drifted in and out of sleep, comfortable with David's reassuring arm around her, relaxed by his words and comforting. She dreamed of Jessica and knew again that she would be all right, but there was more danger in their future—she knew it. She sensed it with all that she was. She knew that there were greater and more dangerous things that this party must do before they succeeded in…whatever they did. This feeling was promoted by the things that Lady Gahdnawen had alluded to. There was more to come, and she was happy that it was this group she would see these dangers with. They were reliable, although a little eccentric. Any one of them would sacrifice themselves for the others. She did not know when that might be necessary…probably too soon.

Here she completely faded, giving in to the slumber that coursed in her veins, welcoming the sleep and enjoying its comfort. If she had known what was to come, she would not have slept that night or any other until their ordeals were over.

The effigy

The next day started no differently from any that the small party had endured in the last few weeks. The sun rose, the fire was fully extinguished, and the baggage was repacked; nothing the least bit different, except the presence of Bellus and the ragged scar that was cut out of the western sky by the Azure mountains. Although the morning seemed rather mundane, the rest of the day promised to be much more than the morning foretold.

After everything had been prepared, they continued the last leg of their journey in the early morning light. Even from this distance, it was apparent that the journey through that crag-infested jungle would be long and arduous for the steep and jagged cliffsides thrust themselves forth like gargoyles from otherwise smooth mountainsides.

As the sun, once again, rose from a little behind their left shoulders, the party grew closer and closer to the forbidding obstacle that towered over them. Mount Apocrys was the tallest mountain in the chain, and as they grew closer, they imagined that they could pick it out, a short distance from the true beginning of the chain. The closer they got, the more they became aware of the terrible remnants of orogenesis that lay between them and their destination like a wall of hatred.

As noon approached, they found themselves at the foot of the first mountain, a relatively small tor with deciduous trees growing along its sides. The ground leading up to it had grown steadily more hilly and rough, and they felt themselves growing weary as they approached its incline. They were used to the level ground they had traveled for the last two days. In exhaustion, they decided to stop for lunch before they entered the Azures proper.

"I must admit," began Amy, removing her pack from her weary shoulders with a sigh of relief and stretching her back to relieve its stiffness. "I don't look forward to scaling those peaks. They look like they'd give a mountain goat problems."

"Maybe there'll be a path," suggested Sean, hopefully.

"There isn't," stated Brandon, gazing happily at the mighty structures in front of him, memories echoing in his mind. "The Azure Mountains are totally untamed. It's the only mountain chain in the world that's still wild and unmapped."

"Great," said Christopher sardonically as he sat and began rubbing his feet with calloused hands. He did not understand why they were so sore today; he had not had any problems with them before. He decided that he must have grown lazy resting at the Temple of Galead. "Then how do we travel through them?"

"We make our own path," answered Brandon simply.

"Terrific."

They sat and ate the little bit of deer they had left and more of the sweetmeats from their packs. They drank from a nearby river that flowed out of the mountains by them. There were many stories told about this strange roily river named for the chain of mountains from which it stemmed. It was deep and flowed strongly, steadily winding southeast from the Azure

Mountains down into the eastermost part of the Gulf of Chiaroscaro. What was so odd about this particular river was that it defied one of the major laws that governed nature. All rivers are supposed to flow towards the closest body of water from their origin, but the Azure flowed a long way southward and away from the closest body of water, the Turba Sea, another enigmatic body of water. The thirsty party did not discriminate against the river, however; they simply drank from its cold, refreshing waters and probably would have done so even if the water had been mauve or chartreuse or some other unnatural color.

They sat on its bank a while, dreading scaling the mountains, except Brandon who seemed to relish the thought. After a time, the dwarf finally suggested that they begin their journey. They reluctantly complied and returned their burdens to their shoulders. They then began to slowly make their way towards the great mountain that towered over them.

As they grew nearer the great structure, it became more apparent that what Brandon had said was true; there were no paths leading into the mountains or even a hunting trail on which to walk. As they began their slow ascension of the first mountain, weariness weighed them down.

"There's a little traveler's joke made about this mountain," commented Brandon as he led them up the surface, forcing a path through the underbrush.

"What's that?" asked Sean who was not in a very good mood but was willing to be enlightened, hoping a good laugh would lift his spirits a bit.

"Well, this mountain has a funny name. That's all," answered Brandon, smiling broadly.

After a moment of silence, David prompted: "Don't keep us in suspense, Brandon. Just tell us."

The dwarf smiled down at the man who was bringing up the rear of the close-knit group. "The mountain is called

Octh'oran, dwarven for destiny. So it's said that those who climb it are ascending their destinies."

Bellus giggled and Sean smiled but no one else stirred. They did not find the joke humorous since, after all, it was the case.

The trees that grew thickly about Mount Destiny were almost leafless since fall was thick in the chill air, and the party felt rather unsafe climbing the face for any around to see. This spurred them to travel as quickly as possible around the tall mountain in search of cover, no matter how tired they became. Their paranoia was somewhat relieved when they rounded the side of the mountain, now heading due west. With this change in pace, for now they traveled downhill, their spirits grew a little lighter.

"You know," began Sean, coming up beside Brandon as they traveled through a more open area, meaning six feet between trees, "this reminds me of a little tune I heard once."

"Oh?" asked the dwarf, returning his friend's smile dubiously. "What tune is that?"

"Well, I'll sing a little of it for you," he answered, putting his arm around Brandon. "Hi ho, hi ho, it's off to work we go." He laughed at his own wittiness as Brandon scowled at him, not knowing what the thief was talking about. "The only problem is that we only have one dwarf. Where are the other six?" he continued chiding Brandon who elbowed him hard in the ribs, certain that Sean was making fun of him somehow. "Hey, where's Snow White, Grumpy?"

"What's so hilarious?" asked Bellus from behind them. "I don't get it."

"Why here she is!" said Sean, laughing harder. "I just didn't recognize her out of her traditional blue and white dress. Besides we're six dwarves too short, but then again, one dwarf's too short!" Sean laughed harder, almost falling in his jubilance, only catching himself because he hit a tree.

Brandon kicked him in the butt, hoping to reassemble his brains, but even this jar could not stop Sean from laughing harder. David stood at the back of the group slowly laughing, trying to hide the giggles behind a single hand, but it was to no avail; Brandon saw him anyway and scowled, turning to answer Bellus' question.

"Don't worry about it. He's just making some sort of crack about my size." Sean continued his laughing. He plopped to the ground, trying to get some air in his lungs.

"He seems to think it's funny," prodded Bellus, pointing at Sean's convulsing form.

"Yeah, but he's an idiot. He'd probably think leprosy was funny."

"Hey," said Sean, regaining control—a little. "That's not very nice."

"Glad you noticed," returned the dwarf as he pranced ahead of them once more, if it is possible to prance with such short, stumpy legs.

"You people are really strange," muttered Bellus, helping Sean to his feet and supporting him as they followed Brandon down the slope.

They continued for the next few hours with this same frugal mentality, not caring if someone heard or saw them. Sean's joke had done what it was intended to; it lightened the mood enough to allow the party some confidence, some reassurance that they just might make it through this journey. Though they did not understand it, Sean and David's laughter was enough to make them smile too. The party watched the scenery around them, noticing how the leaves were varied; some were a dead brown and others were brilliantly crimson, with only a few green splotches left. The shrubbery was mostly dead and easy to push through. The higher they climbed, the colder it got, but they always descended to a warmer climate again.

They soon found themselves in a valley between two mountains. It was from this view that they got their first close glimpse of Mount Apocrys. It was a sight that they would remember for the rest of their lives. The mountain, an ugly red brute, stood in front of them, taunting them with self-assured mendacity. They saw it a little less than clearly in the half-light they received deep in this combe, as the sun set on the far side of the mountain. It was tall, taller than any they had seen before, and was very jagged, looking like some great egregious old man who had climbed well past his prime and was now becoming stiff with age. The rough features frowned down on them like a gargoyle as they stood staring upward at the peak. About three-quarters of the way up the mountain, two large caves led into its depths like great all-seeing eyes, sockets that could see into eternity. They seemed to look through the group, into their very soul, draining all feeling from their chilling bodies and leaving them empty husks that bled their thoughts into the effigy's mind.

As they stood staring at the mountain in a reserved quiet, the sun finally disappeared behind the peaks, leaving the face in shadow and them in darkness. It was here, under the stare of that great and seemingly omniscient face, that they stayed the night. They felt uneasy as they unpacked and built the small fire they were accustomed to, warming up to it in the chilly evening. They ate and settled down to talk before they slept, for none of them felt quite like closing their eyes. The feeling of being watched made them uneasy, almost paranoid to the point of insomnia. They found themselves peering about them into the darkness, and sometimes they even searched for the great eyes of Mount Apocrys in the night, knowing that he would be watching them from behind his roughhewn eyebrows.

"Eerie mountain, huh?" commented Sean more as a statement than a question.

"That it is," answered Jodi quietly. "I've never seen anything quite like it before."

"Me either," stated Brandon, "and I've seen many types of mountains. It's, by far, the greatest I've ever laid eyes on."

"It seemed to be looking down at me," said Amy with a slight shudder. "Like it was watching my every move, waiting for a chance to attack."

"I'm glad I'm not the only one that got that impression." David's uneasiness was apparent in his voice. "It seemed to be watching me, taking me in like a man might take notice of an ant that was approaching his feet."

"You're right," said Christopher, speaking quietly, "but not entirely." He paused until he had everyone's attention. "I felt the eyes on me, too, and they seemed to be coming from the face of the mountain, but in fact, the eyes were real. I've heard of it in the legends but didn't believe it. I perceived the eyes like a tangible presence, peering down at us and laughing. There's someone in that mountain who watched us approach." Everyone was quiet, looking at Christopher and then at the mountain as he sent a finger like an accusing lightning bolt up to point at the mountain's dark face. They had long since stopped questioning the wizard's intuition. If he said there were real eyes, then there were. "We'd best watch carefully tonight. Though I doubt he'll make any move against us outside the mountain, I'd feel more comfortable with the reassurance of a double-watch."

"Why don't you think he'll do anything tonight?" asked Brandon, fingering the axe that lay across his lap. He had just finished sharpening it. That action, for some strange reason, relaxed him and made him feel more confident, more certain of himself.

"Whoever was watching us," he answered, "did not seem to want to leave his stronghold for some reason. I sensed his reluctance as I sensed his eyes. I don't think he'll give us any problem tonight, but there are other things in these mountains that we may have more reason to fear."

They took the wizard's advice and set two-man watches for the night to be sure there would always be someone watching, even if one of them fell asleep. As usual, David and Jodi took the first watch and sat together quietly, lost in thought. They were relieved an hour before midnight by Sean and Bellus. After returning to their blankets next to the fire, Jodi fell asleep at once, but David lay awake for a short time, thinking about what the next day would bring them. Tomorrow, they would enter the mountain they had longed to reach ever since they had been stranded in this land, but he was sad because Jessica would not be with him. What would happen tomorrow? And the next day? What would the next year bring? Or the next? Nobody knew. With these thoughts in his mind, these feelings of unimportance and helplessness to fate, he fell into a deep sleep and dreamed. What it was he dreamed, he would not be able to remember when he woke, but perhaps it was better that way.

"Wake up," came the voice of Christopher out of the darkness. David heard it but was reluctant to respond until he remembered where he was, under the shadow of that great, oppressive mountain. "It's after dawn."

He was urgent; there must be some reason for his insistence, so David roused himself to awaken. As he opened his eyes, he saw by the light of the tiny fire that Christopher held the Grenlan Tome cradled in his arms. Brandon was at his side. "What is it?" asked David, sitting up at last.

"It's time to get up," commented Christopher reprovingly.

David looked at the sky. "It's still pitch black!" he complained.

"Yes, but it's dawn," he urged. "There's some darkness hovering over this valley that's not allowing the light to enter.

There's some evil here that's aware of us and wants us at a disadvantage."

David stood and stretched, muscles straining against the idleness that encompassed him. "What should we do?"

"The only thing we can," returned the wizard with something akin to a grin. "Bring him as much trouble as we can muster."

They awakened the others and explained the situation. Amy and Bellus both were bothered by the cumbersome illucid dawn that seemed to rest just out of reach over their heads. With much anxiety, they packed their bags and prepared for the ascent to the great caverns in Apocrys they had seen on the previous day.

"Keep quiet," urged Christopher, taking up the lead. "It'd be to our advantage to surprise him." Christopher knew that the wizard, Crasen was his name, was somewhere in the mountain, waiting, preparing his powers to resist their approach. As Christopher began ascending the cliff, he felt the heavy Grenlan Tome under his robes like a reminder of responsibility. He went over, once more, in his mind the steps to casting the new spells he had learned since he had first seen the book. He knew that he would need them for this last part of their journey. He stumbled over a rock and cursed the lack of light. He wished Jessica were there to cast a light spell for them, but it would reveal their location anyway, so maybe it was better to do without.

After he stumbled a few times on the detritus that littered Apocrys' side, Christopher felt the stout body of Brandon thrust past him into the lead. He cursed himself for forgetting that the dwarf could see in the dark; Brandon would be a better leader than he up this treacherous cliffside.

It took them three hours to scale the mountain to the flattened area like a patio at the height of the caves. From up close, these two crevasses, standing over ten feet in height, did not look like eyes. Christopher noticed with much chagrin that, instead, they looked like two huge rictuses, gaping for them hungrily. As they had climbed, the darkness had dissipated only minimally, but it was enough to see that there was something scrawled on the cliffside between the two openings. The writing was dwarven, so Brandon interpreted.

"'Beware any who enter, for this place is cursed. Housed within is a being who is held only by his own great avarice. Beware the simple and embrace the difficult, stay in the dark and avoid the light, destroy the light and enter yourself.'" Brandon paused. "Scrawled a little below that message is another, shorter one."

"What does it say?" asked Christopher.

"'Beware of pigs.'"

"Well, that helps a whole hell of a lot, doesn't it?" commented Sean.

"Yep," said Brandon placing his fists on his hips, striking a pensive pose.

"I expect we'll learn what it means after we're inside, so let's get started," said David, starting to approach the cave on the right.

"Hold on a second," said Christopher, stopping David with a gnarled arm. "I know what the last line means. 'Beware of pigs.'"

"What, Christopher?" asked Bellus concernedly. "What does it mean?"

"Orcs," he answered, "are pigs. We're in danger. I can smell it."

At the moment he said this, they heard the echoes of hoofed feet pounding in the caves. The party was surprised by how quickly they reacted to this revelation. They each removed their pack, piling them in a heap with Amy, Bellus, and Jodi stationed around them. Then David, Sean, Brandon, and Christopher formed a cordon around them, weapons drawn, preparing for the onslaught that would sweep into them.

Then, with a speed they did not suspect, the orcs, porcine and foul, erupted from the left cavernous opening. Line on line of them flowed out, forming a great semicircle around the party while the protectors formed a wall in front of their friends. The beasts stood, snorting and growling, building up their courage to attack.

The orcs and the defenders were both surprised when Christopher, standing between David and Brandon, withdrew a long dagger from his robes and made several sweeping gestures with it, leaving pellucid streaks of blue in the air. The dagger began to change, growing longer and wider, taking on the shape of a great black eldritch sword, longer even than David's bastard sword! Christopher seemed to struggle with it for a moment before he made some more gestures and spoke a single word that none of them could seem to remember after it had been said. Then he began to change, too. He grew taller until he towered over even David by half a foot, his body growing wider and wider in proportion to his height, and finally, his dark robe changed into ebony plate armor!

Everyone was awestruck! The great black warrior raised his sword high and plunged into the confused and frightened orcs, his startled allies directly behind. The orcs at the front tried to flee, but they were spoiled by their companions who stood directly behind. The altered wizard swept about with his eldritch blade, cleaving through four of the foul beasts with one blow. David, putting aside his confusion till later, fought beside the figure, slicing at anything that offered itself to his sword which sung death like a dirge. Brandon swung his axe mightily, ripping through row upon row of ugly monsters, while Sean stabbed at any orc that came within his reach. The bloody bodies began to form mounds at their feet as they fought their way on, trying to gain ground, but the sheer number of orcs made it impossible. Instead they were slowly being forced backward, towards the women.

Sean looked back to see what was happening behind him and was surprised to see that the females had not even moved. Then with a shock, he saw, creeping out of the other cave like a covert cloud of evil sickness, another small group of orcs. "Look out!" he screamed as he began to rush back to their aid, knowing already that he would not reach them in time.

The ladies turned and saw what had frightened Sean. An orc lunged at Bellus but she stepped backward and made a gesture with her hand. The orc grabbed at her, and Bellus put her hand against its hairy chest, gently pushing backward. The orc flew away from her, head over heels. There was a smoldering hole in its chest the size and shape of a small feminine hand. This startled the other orcs enough to let the ladies draw their weapons, and Sean had enough time to reach them. "What the hell was that?!" asked the thief.

"A Harm spell," answered Bellus, raising her short sword to defend herself as the orcs rushed at them. "Mother made me learn it."

Sean parried a thrust from an orc scimitar and stabbed his short sword into the thing's stomach. Kicking the first beast away, he sliced another's throat with a precise, backhand blow. At his side, Bellus fought with her short sword and dagger simultaneously, parrying with the dagger and stabbing with the sword. Jodi parried with her dagger and seemed to be slashing at the orcs with her other hand. As Sean looked at it closer, he noticed that pain seemed to radiate from it, and the orcs she struck screamed and fell. A sensory illusion, thought Sean as he saw the bloody claw-like marks that she left on the orcs' bodies. She must be making them feel illusory pain.

Amy for the most part tried to avoid the beasts, but she did manage to stab one in the throat. It fell, gurgling, with blood squirting from its neck and rushing from its mouth in time with its fading heartbeats. After a very short time, there were ten orcs lying dead at the feet of three very bloody women, and Sean had returned to aid the others.

The four men continued their battle, slaughtering the orcs as they came near enough, but they were slowly being pushed back. They fought on, despaired by the sheer number of opponents they faced. After they had been fighting for what seemed hours, a loud voice broke loose from the skies overhead. It shouted "STOP!" The orcs and startled fighters looked up to the sky to see that the voice had come from a dark cloud hanging over the battlefield like an evil eclipse. The orcs cowered from it, some of them even dropping their crude weapons and huddling on the ground, covering their ears with dirty paws. The voice continued, "SINCE YOU PIGS ARE INCAPABLE OF KILLING EVEN THIS MEASLY GROUP OF VAGABONDS, I WILL TAKE CARE OF THE IN-TRUDERS!" The orcs cowered even lower. "LEAVE!" They scattered, fleeing down the mountain, up it, around it, and in any other direction away from the voice, leaving the party alone with the dark cloud. "ENTER, FOOLISH ONES!" it shouted. "EMBRACE YOUR DEATHS!" The cloud slowly dissipated and left the party standing in silence, wondering what had happened.

"What the hell was that?" inquired Sean in a small voice after the dark shape had faded.

"I don't suppose it was another grand illusion?" questioned David, glancing at Jodi who shook her head.

"No. But it was just a simple trick," answered Christopher, or the hulking giant that the wizard had become, "used to scare those who aren't experienced in magic."

"Works great," breathed the thief, trying to swallow his heart once more. "Scared the shit out of me!"

Silence reigned for a moment as they regained their composure and caught their breath once more. Jodi spoke: "Well, just standing here isn't going to do us any good."

"True," agreed David. "But what're we going to do next?"

"What say we go into the mountain," suggested Bellus sensibly.

"That's why we're here," mumbled Christopher.

"By the way, Chris, what exactly have you done to yourself?" asked Sean, staring at the ebony figure who towered over him.

"It's a spell I learned from the Grenlan Tome," answered Christopher proudly. "It's called a Paladin spell. It changes the caster into a tremendous fighting machine. The only drawback is that you don't control how long it lasts."

"Oh."

"Shall we go?" asked Amy, dwarfed at Christopher's side.

"Yeah," answered David. "But we won't be able to see a thing. We don't have any light."

"Then I guess I'll have to go first," suggested Brandon. "As long as we stay close, I should be able to lead you."

David nodded. "Then let's get going."

They stared at the cryptic message scrawled on the mountainside once more, committing it to memory before they slowly approached the caves. Christopher suggested that both passages would lead to the mountain's heart, so they chose the left. After all, the orcs had come from there.

It was pitch black inside the mountain as they walked down the eight-foot wide passage hand in hand so not to lose anyone. They were occasionally directed by Brandon to duck or step up a step or to do some other action in order to avoid something unseen in the darkness. After what seemed an eternity of wandering, Brandon whispered for them to stop. "There's a split in the passage," he murmured to the group that had gathered as closely as possible in the cave. "The one on the left's about five feet high and barely wide enough for a man to fit. The one on the right's about the same as this one, maybe a little narrower."

"I probably couldn't fit through the smaller passage," commented Christopher. "So let's take the right."

They did as Christopher suggested and continued down the right corridor, walking slowly and learning through the hushed words of Brandon that the passage was slowly narrowing, growing smaller and smaller with each step. After a few minutes, if they held out their hands parallel to the ground, they could feel the walls on each side of them.

After a longer period, Bellus started to feel a sort of foreboding, a tingling in her stomach that warned her that something was not as it seemed. She could not figure out what it was, but the farther they went down the passage, the more powerful her trepidation grew. It finally reached a point where she could not stand it any more and had to say something. "There's something wrong here," she whispered, stopping her forward movement so that Sean was jerked to a halt in front of her and Amy ran into her back. "I can feel it. Something's not what it seems to be." She shuddered as the feeling continued to build in her stomach. Her nerves were screaming at her to turn and run, but she forced herself to stay calm.

"It's probably just claustrophobia," suggested Sean.

"Cause of who?" asked Bellus, trying to figure out what Sean had said.

"The wizard's probably playing mind games with you," said Christopher.

"Could he do that?" she asked, wondering if that could be the answer.

"Of course he could," answered Christopher. His voice had returned to its normal baritone, no longer the bass of the dark Paladin.

"You've changed back?" asked David from the rear of the party.

"Yes."

"Well, let's go a little farther. It may just be Crasen or the

closeness of the cave giving you the heebiejeebies, Bellus,"
said Sean.

"The what?"

"Making you feel strange," he answered.

"Oh." The young cleric reluctantly agreed, and they continued down the passageway, their ears straining for any
sound, hearing nothing. Then Brandon halted them. "There's
a door up ahead," he said. "Should we knock?"

"Don't be silly," said Christopher disdainfully. "We're
intruders not house-guests."

"Just thought I'd ask," mumbled the dwarf.

"Do you hear anything on the other side?" asked David in
a whisper.

Everyone strained their ears. "Nothing," answered Brandon.

"Then go ahead and open it but be ready," he said, drawing
his sword.

Bellus was feeling even worse than before. She knew that
something was wrong, but she could not determine the source
of her disquietude. She held her breath as they approached the
door, which was limned by a white light. She almost screamed
as she heard Brandon place himself against the door, heaving
mightily.

The door swung open and light flooded into the hallway
like liquid courage. They strained against the brilliant glare
and, as their eyes adjusted, viewed what lay through the
threshold. The room was about eighty feet square and was
made of pink granite. It was completely bare of furniture or
other such comfort. The light that shone so brightly in the
room had no apparent source. It did not seem to come from
anywhere; it was just there, radiating from the room itself. As
they looked across to the other wall, they saw that there was
another stone door, identical to the one they were standing
next to. It was shut fast. They then noticed, with an odd

sensation, that the floor of the room was slightly concave, lower in the center than at the walls, and had a strange shimmering carpet of light covering it. Brandon bent down and felt the floor. He raised his hand, which now had some liquid on it, and gingerly touched his tongue to his forefinger. "Water," he said thoughtfully.

"What now?" asked Sean of nobody in particular.

"I guess," answered Christopher, "one of us goes in and checks the place out."

"Yeah, but who?" asked Sean, pitying the fool who would cross the room first. That would be damned dangerous.

"You."

"Me!?" exclaimed Sean, visions of pits and spikes and arrow traps impaling him like a sacrifice while his friends watched.

"You're the thief," stated Christopher. "You're better at this than the rest of us."

Sean sighed. He knew that Christopher was right, but he did not want to enter that room; it made him uneasy. But he would never forgive himself if someone else entered and was harmed or killed by a trap he would have detected. Well if I've gotta, I've gotta. He took a deep breath and began to slowly inch his way around the side of the room, sticking closely to the left wall. He felt with each step for any type of catch, loose block, or trip wire that might set off a trap. To his relief, he found nothing, and all too quickly, he reached the door opposite his friends. He scrutinized it severely, looking at every inch of the door for a trap. His meticulous study revealed nothing except a latch with which the door could be opened and a faded symbol right above it. "There's nothing," he said to his nervously attentive audience. "It seems like a plain door."

"Are there any markings?" asked Christopher intensely.

"Just some strange, faded symbol," he answered.

"What does it look like?"

"I'm really not sure." He paused, studying it for a moment longer, trying to give meaning to the light scratches and marks that marred the otherwise smooth door. "I think it's a bolt of lightning," he said at length.

Christopher breathed a sigh of relief. "The lightning bolt's a symbol for enlightenment."

"Then should I open the door?" asked Sean.

"Yeah, go ahead."

Then it all dawned on Bellus! The water and the lightning bolt! It was all a trap! This realization struck her in the face like a sweep of the reaper's scythe! "Stop!" she screamed as Sean reached for the latch, hoping that she had not been too slow. "Get out of there! It's a trap!"

The thief did not hesitate. He turned and sprinted for the door where his startled friends were, certain that Bellus had seen something he had missed. He cursed himself as he felt the block slide under his foot and heard the quiet click of a release. He dove with all his might for the doorway as his friends recoiled from his jump and the galvanic eruption of chaos that seared the room. As soon as Sean had stepped on the catch, small holes had opened in the ceiling and several lightning bolts leapt from them into the water on the floor, turning the room into one gigantic electric oven. Sean felt an explosion of pain in his leg as he plunged into his friends, knocking Christopher sprawling.

Sean lay, sweating and shaking, more scared than he had ever been; then Bellus was there. She hugged him strongly, taking his thoughts away from the pain that seared his left leg. He had taken one of the lightning bolts directly in it. He looked down at the smoking appendage and smelt the cloyingly sweet smell of charred flesh. He fought the dizziness that tried to swallow him and remained conscious as Bellus released his body and placed her hands on the melted tissue of his convulsing leg. The touch hurt so badly that he wanted to retch, but he swallowed the bile, pure stubbornness overcoming his nausea. Where the hell's shock when you need it, he thought to himself before feeling a surge of power and coolness sweep through him. Then, as quickly as it had come, the pain left, and he sighed with relief as he turned onto his back. He then became uniquely aware that Bellus had helped him sit and was holding him tightly against her more-than-girlish bosom. He found himself fighting once more, but this time to keep his hormones under control. He finally pulled himself together and freed himself from the cleric's grasp. He stood up, feeling momentarily dizzy, and fell against the wall, his strength slowly returning.

"Enlightenment, huh?" groaned the thief.

Christopher shrugged. "I was wrong. Sue me."

"I'll fuckin' sue ya, you bastard," spat Sean, reaching for Christopher with the intent of beating some sense into him, but Bellus held him back with a gentle hand on his forearm.

"Well, I guess we know what the first line of the inscription meant," stated David flatly, changing the subject very abruptly.

"Huh?" asked Sean unintelligently as he continued trying to regain his senses.

"You know, 'Beware the simple and embrace the difficult.'" he answered.

Sean was not feeling too bright today—though he had just narrowly escaped a very intense brightness—and felt inclined to make David spit it out. "I don't understand."

David stared at Sean incredulously. "We should have taken the smaller and more difficult passage back there instead of following the easier one. It led to a trap."

"Oh," said Sean, the light finally dawning. He then felt the top of his head, wondering if his hair was standing on end from the shock he had received. He ran his fingers through the knotty mess experimentally and discovered that it was definitely sticking up a little more than usual. He matted it down and inspected his leg where the scar was rapidly disappearing like a fleeting memory of agony. His trousers were still smoking, but his leg was intact. He sighed and thanked God for clerics. Then he thought to himself what an irony that was; thanking God? Was God even in this realm? He was not sure. If so, what God? He thought about Galead and laughed to himself, wondering if this world had been created by a feminist.

"Should we continue this way or go back?" asked Brandon after a short rest.

"Well, if you don't mind wading through a pool of electrified water, we could continue forward, but I'd rather take the road less trapped," answered Sean.

David glared at the thief and harumphed. "You're definitely no poet," he said caustically.

Brandon turned and began trudging back the way they had come, the others close behind. They soon returned to the small, oddly shaped passage and began worming their way through it. There were many places where they stumbled and Jodi would have fallen once if David had not caught her. They quickly came across a place where the passageway branched off to the right. They could see a faint light at the end of that passageway while the one in front of them continued in darkness.

"Do we head toward the light?" asked Brandon pointing down the cave, "or continue the way we're going."

"Go toward the light," answered David.

"Wait," broke in Christopher. "Let's think about this first. Didn't the inscription say something about the light and the dark?"

"Yeah," answered Amy. "It said 'Stay in the dark and avoid the light. Destroy the light and enter yourself.'"

"Well, both can't apply here, can they?" asked Sean. "We can't avoid the light and destroy it at the same time."

"Maybe we have to destroy it from a distance. You know, with a bow or something," suggested Brandon.

"I don't think so," said David. "The two lines probably aren't related. They must have meaning for different parts of this mystery."

"David's right," said Christopher. "I say we just listen to the first line right now and follow the dark passage."

They continued down the dark passage, following Brandon, relying on him for their sight. After what seemed an eternity of stumbling around in pitch blackness, the passage began bearing to the right. It seemed to circle around for quite a way.

"I think this is taking us back behind that lighted place," said Bellus, "but I can't really be sure in this darkness. It's too easy to get confused."

"You're right," agreed Brandon. "We've slowly maneuvered our way around behind it."

They accepted Brandon's word because he was a dwarf, and dwarves were raised in the underground and simply knew this type of thing. Their trust was soon found to be well-placed for the passage quickly emptied them into another hallway. To the right was another stone door like the ones they had seen before and there was a faint light outlining its edges.

"I wonder what's behind door number one," thought David aloud as they stared at it in the torchlit hallway.

"I don't think I want to know," said Sean, rubbing his leg in memory, wondering if there was another trap for him to spring in the immediate vicinity.

"We're probably better off not knowing," agreed Christopher.

They heard grunts and snorts from behind the door.

"Orcs," said Jodi quietly, "or worse."

They turned their attention away from the door and looked down the hallway they had just entered. It resembled some great corridor in a castle much more than a cave under a mountain. It was smoothly carved with torches lining the walls, one every ten feet or so, casting enough light to walk comfortably down the way.

"Let me go first," Sean heard himself say before he could stop. "I'm the thief." He walked to the front and slowly began walking down the hall, searching for any strange or out-of-place object on the floor, the walls, or the ceiling. Their progress was slow but sure as they continued this way for twenty or thirty minutes. They gradually became aware of another, more intense light a short distance in front of them. They continued slowly up the passage, growing progressively nearer to the beacon that morbidly drew them like a burning town to a ship full of family members. As they grew closer, they noticed that the light was coming from a doorway that stood open at the end of the passage. They soon reached it and peered into the room it opened on to.

What they saw was definitely not what they had expected. The room was quite large, spanning one hundred feet at least on each wall, and filled to brimming with a tremendous assortment of items. There were chairs and a table on the right side of the room and a bed and two trunks on the left. There was also a bookshelf against each wall filled with books on every subject you could possibly imagine. Every wall was covered with an elaborate arras, depicting all kinds of brutal, murderous acts being committed by everything from demons to cherubs and children. Every wall that is, except the far one, which seemed to be made of one gigantic mirror that stood completely barren of anything except cruel reflection. But this was not what surprised them so much. In the very center of the room was a huge table with a single chair in front of it. There were books and maps, bowls and amulets, oculars and other mysterious things strewn carelessly about on its top, but taking up a great portion of the table was a candle as big around as a mature oak! The candle was burning but no wax melted and there did not seem to be any on the table or the floor. It seemed impossible that a candle that big could be made and even more impossible that the rickety table it sat on had not yet fallen!

It took the group a short time to take all of this in, and it was not until they had that they became aware of the solitary figure that stood in front of the table. The haggard character slowly turned and fixed them with an icy stare. The group noticed with a start that the face that leered at them now was the same face that had watched them the entire night. This old man looked precisely like Mount Apocrys itself!

As they stood there, practically frozen and knowing not what to do, a cracked and crooked grin spread across the aged face and it let a single cackle, like a parrot's squawk, escape from its mouth. That solitary outcry stated as clearly as any word that this man had been overcome by what he had seen and experienced and now grew steadily more and more insane.

The face then cleared of all expression, except those icy black eyes that continued to tell of the insanity within. He spoke and none of them could help but do as he commanded. "Enter!!!" he screamed. "Who do you think you are that you can invade my solitude in this way?! What do you want?!"

As they cautiously crept into the room, Christopher gazed at Crasen deeply, fear and wonder crowning his brow like a crown. As he gazed into the older wizard's eyes and took in the past, the present, and the future that shone in those black orbs, he felt more fear and foreboding creep up his spine into his mind. He wondered, Is this what I'll become? Is this what the future holds in store for me as a wizard? Is this what the magic will do to me?

Christopher shook himself and raised his voice to equal the magnitude with which Crasen had addressed them. "Our names are unimportant!" he shouted. "And we have come in search of an amulet!"

"You can find such trinkets in other places than my home!" raged Crasen. "Why have you come here?!"

"Because the amulet we seek is special! It has the power to teleport us out of this dimension!"

"Why do you want to leave this world?!"

"That's our business," interrupted Brandon from Christopher's side.

The old man turned his gaze on the dwarf and stared down at him, fury glowing in his eyes like a firestorm of spite. Christopher also stared at Brandon, annoyance and fear for the dwarf reflecting in his sensate eyes. Brandon looked up at him and shrugged innocently. "Sorry. It seemed appropriate."

Christopher almost chuckled, but he managed to contain himself and continued, removing Crasen's attention from Brandon. "Crasen, we don't want to bother you, but we need that amulet desperately! Will you give it to us and let us go on our way?!"

Crasen stared at Christopher in silence for a short time, noticing his youth but also seeing the determination and intelligence that was apparent in the younger man. "You can't have it!" he screamed at last. "It's mine! You can't have it!" Crasen raised his hands, his black robes falling away to uncover skeletal arms. He brought these same arms down with a strength that would not be expected of such fragility and let fly a huge fire ball. Christopher was prepared, however. He made a single gyrating gesture in front of him, and as the fire ball reached him, it exploded as if it had struck a wall, sparks flying everywhere.

"Stay behind me!" screamed Christopher to the group. Brandon raised his axe, preparing to charge the wizard, but a single, sharp word from Christopher halted him in his tracks. "He can't be hurt by any of your weapons until his magical

defenses have been destroyed! I'll have to deal with him!"
Christopher raised his arms and let fly a ball of white heat, but
Crasen raised a single hand and caught it. He hurled it back at
Christopher who waved it off with a hand gesture. Crasen then
began throwing a barrage of fire balls, lightning bolts, and
other, less easily distinguished spells at the tiny group. Christopher blocked them all but he was quickly growing weak. The
Magic Shield was a spell that took too much energy, and the
strain was showing on his face. He tried throwing some spells
of his own at Crasen, but they were all either caught and
returned or simply destroyed with a gesture.

The entire group was despaired by the merciless onslaught
that Christopher bore for them. Jodi was on the verge of tears
as she screamed to herself, We can't have come this far for
nothing! We've got to succeed! We've got to! She frantically
gazed about her for something to help them beat Crasen, and
what she was surprised to see was David, creeping along the
left wall like a cat stalking its prey. He was unprotected and
vulnerable! He had been lucky so far only because Crasen had
all his attention turned on Christopher and the rest of the
group. Then, for one long second, the words of Lady
Gahdnawen echoed in Jodi's mind like an expostulation of
distress. "Stay by his side. You'll know when the time comes.
Heed my words and do as I say." The words echoed in her head
like a scream, imploring her to help David! But how?! Then
it dawned on her. Now she knew why the Lady had mentioned
her knowledge of Jodi's secret gifts. It was a covert way of
letting her know that she would have to use them. She knew
what she had to do but dreaded doing it, fearing that it might
reveal her for what she truly was, but she owed David too
much...

The battle raged on and the party was huddled behind
Christopher: Sean and Brandon at the front, Bellus and Amy
behind them with Jodi sitting between them and a little back.

Then, all of a sudden, there was a vacancy in the tiny group. There was no longer a figure between the two clerics. There were only robes of deep blue...and a small, black spider that quickly scurried up the wall.

At that same moment, there was a roar from behind the group, in the hall they had just left. Brandon, Sean, Bellus, and Amy all whirled at the noise. They saw a group of huge figures lumbering toward them from up the hall. As one of the figures was outlined by torchlight, Brandon knew what they were. "Trolls," he breathed. These beasts were huge! Muscles rippled across their hairy torsos as they pounded down the hall, hoots and roars bellowing from their frothing, tooth-lined mouths. Brandon was ironically grateful that there were only three of them. He felt that if there had been any more, they assuredly would have been lost without Christopher's help, but as it stood, they did have a fighting chance against the fearsome, vicious beasts...a slim one.

Renewed

acquaintances

David was almost even with Crasen along the left wall. He watched the battle that ensued almost abstractly, concentrating on what he knew had to be done if he were to save the lives of his companions. He was the only one that could do it. He had almost solved the riddle that was scratched into the face of Mount Apocrys. As soon as he had seen the great candle on the table, he knew it was the light that had to be extinguished, but he did not understand the rest. "Destroy the light and enter yourself." He could destroy the light easily enough, but how was he supposed to enter himself. It made no sense. He continued to creep around Crasen, hoping that the last part of the riddle would come clear before he reached the table.

While sparks flew in the room, he continued to crawl furtively along the wall, concentrating on being unnoticeable—not too easy for such a big guy. Then he heard the clang of metal on metal and an insane chuckle from the old wizard. David chanced a glance back at his friends and saw them battling a group of trolls. He knew he could not help them and prayed that they could take care of that menace. He removed his attention from the distraction and continued to crawl around the wizard. He soon made his way to the back of the table and began worming his way across the floor toward it. He knew that if he could reach it, they would live, but if he did not... He felt the tension on him like a tangible force: an impossibly heavy weight holding him down and forcing him to move too slowly. He fought the pressure and continued crawling across the floor as quickly as he dared, a creeping, agonizing pace. He reached the back edge of the table and slowly stood, surveying the room's inhabitants, trying to ascertain what he had missed while the table and its contents had obscured his vision.

Brandon, Sean, Bellus, and even Amy were fighting the trolls. One of the beasts lay on the floor unmoving, a gash across its ugly face that could only have been made by an axe. As he watched, another fell under Bellus' blade and received a second stab in the back of its neck, severing its spine below the medulla, assuring that it would not move again. Crasen was still throwing all sorts of spells at Christopher who valiantly fought back, strain glistening on his forehead like the tears of hope. A swarm of hornets was coming toward the battling party at the moment, but Christopher threw a fire ball at them and they were incinerated, leaving ashes like fine dust in the air.

David spent no more time looking at his friends. He slowly reached around the huge candle that was now directly in front of him and locked his hands on its other side where they just barely met. He then braced himself and pulled with all his might. He channeled all his strength into one mighty heave and, with relief, felt the candle grudgingly give way as it slowly slid towards him. He continued pulling with every ounce of strength he had in his body and soon heard a crack! The table was breaking under the strain!

Crasen heard the noise and whirled. "No!" he screamed as

he raised his hands to destroy David with one mighty maleficent incantation, but the warrior continued pulling on the candle with all his might. It finally fell just as the wizard brought his arms down like an executioner's axe, symbolizing death to all that opposed him.

David braced himself for the scorching pain he knew he would feel when the wizard's unspeakable spell seared him. His only sorrow was that he would not see Jessica again, but as he gave himself into fate, he heard a growl from his right and felt something large and furry slam into his side with the force of a falling star. He fell hard to the floor with the beast on top of him. As he hit the ground, he felt a surge of heat pass over his head. He caught a glimpse of the black fur of the monster on top of him in the shattering light of the fire ball as it hit the mirrored wall, showering sparks all over him.

Then, looking under the table, he saw another light originate from where he knew his friends had been and watched the fiery conflagration fly out and slam into Crasen. He was knocked onto the already-cracked table which shattered under his meager weight, crashing to the floor in splintering shards. Crasen then jumped back up, his robes flaming brightly, and ran towards the small, huddled group in the doorway. David saw a glimmer of light on steel as an axe fell, slicing the flaming torso from skullcap to groin.

David turned his attention to the figure on top of him and heaved mightily, feeling relief as the beast flew satisfyingly off his chest into the darkness. He turned his gaze toward the mirrored wall where the fire ball had struck it, expecting to see it shattered, but to his amazement, it was whole. As he gazed into the mirror, he saw himself, a reflection of solitude, staring back. Even though it was too dark to see clearly, his reflection was as lucent as if it were daylight, maybe even clearer. In that instant, the answer to the last line of that elusive riddle dawned on him! "Enter yourself," it said, but it actually meant that you had to enter your reflection, the image of yourself. David staggered to his feet and ran towards the "other David" who, a little more slowly, as if lethargy held his feet to the floor, ran toward him. As David plunged into what should have been the mirror's glass, he did not feel it shatter. It gave way to his solidity and, like cobwebs or an extremely viscous fluid, folded around him, encasing him in a shimmering aura of pellucidness. Sparks flew from his flesh like static. As the glimmering pall of liquid mirror leaked off his flesh, he knew that he had passed through the mirror black and toward the ending of his quest. As David plunged onward, another figure, unbeknownst to him, followed silently through the fluorescent film on four padded paws.

Christopher found himself standing in total, uninhibited darkness, wondering what had just happened. He had seen David's reflection glowing in the mirror and watched as two shadows passed through it. Then the torches in the hall and even the smoldering form of Crasen and the table were engulfed by darkness, suffused with absolute nothingness, leaving them in blackness like an ocean of emptiness. Christopher shook himself into action. His first thought was to get some light and discover what had happened, so he returned to the hallway for one of the torches and lit it, calling for the others to do the same.

"What the hell happened?" asked Sean as he reappeared in the room, his face visible in the light of his and Christopher's glowing torches.

"I haven't the slightest idea," answered Christopher helpfully, "but I think I'd like to get a closer look at that mirror." He slowly walked up to the mirrored wall, the others following just as curiously. He held his torch high, out in front of him so he could see and inspect the mirror as thoroughly and completely as possible. He could not see anything at all odd about it; so he handed his torch to Brandon and gingerly placed his palms flat against the cool surface. All he felt was solidity, benign glass. "I don't get it," he said. "It must be magical." He glanced at Sean who stood next to him, peering at him disdainfully.

"No shit, Chris," he said. "I thought all mirrors swallowed people."

Christopher scowled at him. "I just can't tell in what sense it's magical or how its activated," he explained, leering at Sean as he imitated the wizard's study of the mirror.

"Well, don't look at me," said the thief. "I don't know anything about magic."

"Obviously."

"Let's clean this place up," said Amy from back at the fallen table, cutting Sean off before he could retort Christopher's remark. She was holding her torch over the broken table, looking for anything that might aid in solving the mystery of the mirror. "Maybe there's something in this mess that'll tell us what we need to know."

So they began cleaning the room, and Christopher thumbed quickly through Crasen's books of magic, canceling the protective spells placed on them one by one, hoping the answer might be in one of them. None of their attempts, however, uncovered anything helpful, only a white mouse that scurried out the door.

"I don't get it," whispered Christopher, shaking his head. As he stood, frustration and annoyance creasing his brow, a cold wind blew through the room like a presage to change, and the torches were snuffed out as if huge tears had extinguished their exuberant joy. "What the—" he began but stopped as the room erupted in effervescent light. "Hell," he finished as the blinding light faded to a comfortable level, leaving Christopher snowblind.

As their eyes adjusted to the light, they each saw, standing

in the middle of the room, right in front of the table, two figures
clothed in white satin robes. Each of them was terribly
beautiful and radiated an aura of knowledge, the older one to
such an extent that they nearly had to avert their eyes to avoid
her terrible omniscience.

With a start, Brandon realized that he knew both of the
figures, though they were dramatically changed from the last
time he had seen them. Lady Gahdnawen stood on the left,
smiling at them as they stared back, incomprehensive. Brandon finally broke the silence in the oppressive room, his voice
half unbelieving and half jubilating as he quietly breathed the
name of the other glistening form: "Jessica."

The room David now inhabited was lit by torches that
lined each wall every two feet or so. The chamber was small,
probably only twenty feet square. From the spot where David's
momentum had carried him, he stood face to face with the
statue of a robed wizard. This figure was a younger, more sane
version of Crasen, with the same build and chiseled facial
features, but its eyes held none of the insanity that marked
Crasen. With myriad emotions playing in his mind, David
noticed the golden amulet that hung about its neck, glittering
in the torchlight. It was about the size of a large man's fist and
carved in the shape of a nine-pointed star. Each tip of the star
had a different stone garnishing it—garnet, turquoise, peridot,
opal, pearl, emerald, ruby, sapphire, and diamond, clockwise
from twelve o'clock. Other than the gems, the only other
marking that marred its surface was a figure carved in the
image of a hawk at the amulet's center.

As David reached for the dangling amulet, he heard a
growl from behind him. He wheeled, remembering the beast
that had knocked him down after he destroyed the candle. He
saw a black panther standing only a few feet from him, looking
up at him with its great green, elliptical eyes that spoke clearly

of more than animal intelligence. The cat's shining, opalescent fur shimmered in the flickering lights, accenting its muscular body as its tail slowly swung from side to side. David stared incredulously at the slowly wagging tail. It was not moving with the natural swish used to shoo flies; it was actually wagging, the refined movements of a tamed or domesticated animal.

David stared at the beast's tail, mesmerized for a short time before returning his bewildered gaze to its magnificent, unflinching eyes. He stood motionless, swallowed by their deep green, oceanic depth for a moment, taking in their every facet and clean perfection. As he watched the panther, it started to walk towards him at a slow, easy gait. For some reason, David was unafraid of the great cat with its tremendous teeth and pointed claws that could gut a caribou with a single swipe. There was something about the way it wagged its tail and the way it met his gaze with an almost pleading inquiry of understanding. He watched it walk up to him until it was close enough to touch. There it sat back on its great haunches and stared up at him again with its sorrowful eyes, imploring comprehension, and as David watched, two great tears welled in them and rolled down its furry cheeks. But that's impossible, he thought. Cats can't cry. While David watched, confused and unsure, the panther closed its sad eyes, slowly bowing its head as though in acquiescence, and its body began to change. It slowly stretched out, growing longer in the limbs and stomach as the hips rounded and grew less muscular, more fleshy. And the fur slowly sank into its skin until its lengthening, bare body was covered only with pale white skin. On its head, the hair grew longer and slowly changed from black to brown, from brown to copper, and from copper to deep auburn. Its front limbs became slender arms and the forepaws slowly altered into hands with delicate fingers tipped with dainty nails instead of claws. Its rear legs stretched out into two finely shaped feminine legs ending in delicate, faintly callused feet. The hard, muscular chest softened and rounded into small, delicate breasts, and the long jaw shrunk down to a small nose and petite mouth with full, pink lips. The ears receded and reformed in the head's sides, and the eyes rounded, paling to blue with large tears welling in them. The face became more elliptical and the cheekbones raised themselves, creating round cheeks while the chin smoothed and the neck lengthened, thinning to that of a delicate young woman.

David found himself staring in fascination and not revulsion at the naked form of Jodi as she sat, hunched over at his feet. She slowly raised her head and met his gaze uncertainly with tear-filled eyes, not knowing how he would react to her metamorphosis. David paused for only a moment before offering her his hand which she gingerly accepted. She straightened slowly, rising to her feet with David's help where she stood, shivering from the damp coldness of the room. David undid the clasp at his neck and removed the cape that he had worn from the Temple, placing it around her shoulders and fastening it once more with his brooch. Jodi accepted the cape gladly and pulled it tight around her. "Thank you," she murmured almost inaudibly, uncertainty dripping from her voice like tears, begging for some ointment to assuage her fear.

"God, Jodi, what's happened?" asked David quietly, overwhelmed by what he'd seen. "That was no illusion."

"I can't tell you now," she answered in a voice that shook from strain and fear of revulsion. "But I will…soon. I promise." David started to demand the story from her, but Jodi's exhausted voice cut through him as easily as ire.

"Please," she begged, her chin shaking softly as a great tear rolled down her cheek, forming an arroyo of dismay on her face.

David stared a moment longer at her racked form, seeing that Jodi was physically drained and emotionally unstable. Something about the set of her face and the sadness in her soul sparked him to accept her, unquestioning for now, so he nodded and began to explain what he was doing. "When we were back at the Temple, Lady Gahdnawen came to me and told me something I have to do if Jessica's going to live. That's why I'm here. I have to return to our world alone. You can wait for me here…"

Jodi stopped him with an upraised hand, her strength returning because she knew that she would need it for the next couple of hours. "She came to me, too, David. She told me to stay within an arm's reach of you for the rest of our journey wherever you might go. So I'll come with you and there's nothing you can do to stop me."

"But—"

"No buts about it, David. I'll do what she told me if it kills me. I'll return with you."

David was quiet for a short time before finally sighing in resignation. "Very well, but I don't have time to tell you what I'm going to do, so just follow my lead. No matter what I say, don't act surprised and support me. If you don't, we may not be able to get back. Okay?"

Jodi was confused but David's stolid urgency was enough to convince her of his sincerity and surety. In truth, she was not really sure what "world" they were returning to, but she did know that she had to follow the Lady's orders even if David knew her secret. "All right," she agreed.

David nodded and lifted the amulet over the statue's head. He placed it around his own neck and ushered Jodi to his side. He placed one arm around her waist and started pressing some of the jewels on the amulet in the order that Lady Gahdnawen had told him. He then tapped the inscription of the hawk two times with his third finger and gripped Jodi stronger, watching the amulet intently.

For a moment nothing happened, but then, all of a sudden, the carved hawk on the amulet's face began to move, flapping its wings slowly, and sprung out of the amulet into the air. It began to grow until it reached the size of a great condor and flew up above David, gripping his shoulders in its talons and lifting him, Jodi in his arms, off the ground. Then everything started moving. The walls around them began gyrating, going faster and faster with every second that passed until it all went black and they could see nothing, hear nothing, and feel nothing. Indeed, for a moment David was not sure whether Jodi was still with him, but the resistance of a quick squeeze assured him of her presence. As thoughts of inexistence flitted through David's mind, an explosion of light erupted all around them, and they felt themselves being placed on the ground again. The talons released David and the hawk disappeared. David noticed that the signet of the bird had returned to the amulet. He released his grip on Jodi and looked around, realizing that he recognized the place in which they stood. They were in a room with a large mahogany table in its center. Around the table several chairs were placed, and seven still figures sat in them, unmoving, as if petrified. Another figure sat at the head of the table in a large black chair. It was Doctor John Richards who smiled at them broadly from that same place he had sat so many Saturdays in their seemingly distant past. His eyes took them in coldly and his strong, wiry hands gripped the arms of his ebony chair so hard that the veins bulged all the way up his forearms. He softly chuckled to himself. "Welcome back, my friends."

"Hello Brandon," said Jessica, a broad smile twisting her lips. With that infinitesimally simple illustration of happiness, joy spread like wildfire into the hearts of her previously disjointed friends. "I'm back."

They practically jumped to Jessica's side, hugging her and proclaiming their joy, while Bellus quickly joined her mother, excitedly telling her what she had experienced. Jessica returned everyone's hugs and answered their questions about her health as honestly and completely as she could. They never even noticed the gestures and arcane words that Lady Gahdnawen whispered while their attention was completely on Jessica. They only felt very forgetful for a brief moment, as if they had forgotten something they never should have been able to, but they quickly recovered.

"How'd you get here?" asked Amy, grasping Jessica's hand in a firm grip which she refused to relinquish.

"That was my doing," answered the smiling form of Lady Gahdnawen from just outside the circle of friends. "I transported us here."

"If you could teleport all the way out here, Lady, why did you only transport us as far as you did?" asked Christopher suspiciously. "Why didn't you move us here directly?"

"Because that would have shown Menovence how much power I have. He thought me as weak as most mortals, and that was his undoing. He underestimated me."

"I take it you've been completely healed of your hurt?" asked Brandon, returning their attention to Jessica.

"Yes," she answered, a shadow passing over her face. "I only hope that nothing like that ever happens to me—or any good-hearted person—again." After a short silence, she continued, a smile returning to her face like the sun coming out from behind a cloud. "But now it's time to be happy and to prepare for the future, not dwell in the past."

"Agreed," said Sean, "so will you tell us where David's disappeared to?"

"That's a story that only he can answer for you," asserted Gahdnawen, "and I'm sure he will."

The group stared at her for a long moment, wondering

whether to pursue that train of thought further, but they realized that the Priestess would tell them no more—she never did. So they accepted her answer as the best they would get.

"Then tell us about this mirror," said Christopher, gesturing at the shimmering wall that stood opposite them.

"That mystery is one that I'll happily solve for you," she answered. "It's not real."

"It certainly feels real," asserted Sean.

"Yes," she answered, smiling at the thief oddly. "But it's not material. It's a trick of light and shadow, an illusion."

"Then Jodi can just dispel it for us, can't she?" asked Brandon as they slowly returned to the glass wall. "Speaking of our illusionist, where has she got to?"

"I don't know," said Sean. "I haven't seen her since the trolls attacked us."

"Do you think something's happened to her?" asked Amy, alarm crisscrossing her face.

"She's safe," said Gahdnawen, shattering their alarm. "She's with David."

"And we won't know where that is till they tell us, right?" asked Sean, disgust lacing his voice.

The Lady nodded. "You need to pay attention to the test at hand."

"Well, if Jodi isn't here, how do we dispel this illusion?" asked Brandon, consternation creasing his brow as he stood, arms akimbo.

"I think I know," said Christopher, his face shining with the glee of someone grasping a concept that previously baffled him. "I think I've figured it out."

"Then please enlighten us," said Sean, glancing down at the charred remnants of his pant leg. "No, forget I said that. Just tell us your theory."

The wizard smiled. "The key's in what the Lady said. It's a trick of the light and seems solid enough when inspected under light, but when is a trick of the light always seen through?"

"In the dark!" exclaimed Amy.

Christopher nodded as did Lady Gahdnawen. "It's like the message at the mouth of the cave said: 'Destroy the light and enter yourself.' When the cavern's in darkness, there can't be any tricks of the light, so the illusion is destroyed, and you can walk through the mirror and metaphorically walk through yourself."

"Well, if that's the answer of how to get through the mirror," said Brandon, "then the next question is 'What's on the other side'?"

"There's only one way to find out," said Jessica, "and that's to go there." She waved her hand majestically and they found themselves in darkness once more, but oddly, they could still see their reflections in the mirror as clear as day— maybe clearer.

Christopher, Lady Gahdnawen, Jessica, and the others, all but Sean, plunged through the mirror with little hesitation, sparks and light crackling as they passed. Sean faced the clone of himself and muttered hesitantly, "To boldly go where no man has gone before." He took a deep breath and stepped through the mirror in a shower of sparks, praying the whole time that they were not being tricked.

When Sean opened his eyes, he was standing in a small, torch-lit room with the others gathered around him in silence. A statue of a robed wizard stood in the middle of the room, attracting all attention to it. The thief noticed with a sardonic smile that the statue was of Crasen as he would have appeared years earlier, before the dark powers took over his mind.

After they had studied the room thoroughly, Amy asked where David and Jodi were.

"I already told you that you won't know till they return," answered Gahdnawen.

"What I meant was that there aren't any exits out of here except the mirror. How'd they get out?"

"Where they went, doors don't lead. They had to find another way." There was a twinkle in the Lady's dark eyes that said more than her words. Something was going to happen, something that excited her.

"When will they get back?" asked Sean, annoyed once more at her ability to answer their questions without helping at all.

"Soon," she promised. "Very soon."

David smiled at Doc Richards who sat in his great black chair, regarding them curiously. "Hello, Doc. Long time no see."

"Not really," he answered, still smiling. "It's only been a couple of hours my time since you left. Let's see." He looked thoughtful for a moment. "It would have been about three weeks for you, wouldn't it?"

"Yep," answered David.

"Where're the rest of your friends?"

"Jodi and I are the only ones left," answered David, a gleam in his eyes.

"Really?!" asked Richards, genuinely surprised. "I would've thought most of you would have survived. What happened?"

"Inside Mount Apocrys, a group of trolls snuck up behind us, and in the ensuing battle, they were killed."

"What about Jessica? She wasn't with you in the mountain."

"True," said David, an eyebrow raised. "She died from a spell put on her by a malspirare, but how'd you know she wasn't with us?"

"Don't you know?" asked the Doc, amused. As they did not answer, he continued. "I'll tell you in due time, but aren't you upset by Jessica's death?"

"It hurt at first," answered David, looking pensively at his own form sitting at the table, motionless. "But then I found that Jodi was more than willing to take her place." He put an arm around the startled and confused form of Jodi, pulling her close to him. She did not resist, trying not to look surprised, but she was not really sure where they were or what the hell was going on. The place looked oddly familiar but…Then memory struck her and she nearly gasped. My God! I forgot! How could I forget about home? She was so awed that she almost jumped when the Doc spoke.

"I see." Richards nodded, noticing Jodi's lack of clothing. "I'm sure she does it very well." He paused, thoughts wandering as Jodi was fighting furiously to control her blush now as her true personality reasserted its control. He was trying to decide if he should trust David or not. He did not understand why the warrior was so calm about everything; he had expected a struggle, but then, perhaps the death of Jessica had weakened David enough to allow Graham to assert some amount of control. If that were true, then he would be desensitized to the deaths of people he knew and would bounce back more quickly. He decided to question a little further and see how Jodi would act under such scrutiny. "Let's go to my living room and talk. It's more comfortable there." He stood and led them into another room in the despondent house. This chamber was larger than the one they had been in, with a sofa and two chairs placed strategically around a television and a fireplace. Richards sat down in one of the chairs that faced the sofa and ushered them to sit. David and Jodi sat closely, turned so they could face the Doc. David placed an arm about Jodi's shoulders. "Jodi," said the Doc, "you're not too talkative today." David tensed.

"Not really," she answered, "but then again, I never have been much for chatter." She smiled at him, hoping that the answer was good enough to cover her silence. She could hardly think straight. She did not know what to say or how to act or even what was going on. She forced herself to concentrate on what was happening around her. She had to answer the questions right if they were going to make it back to their friends once more. Back to our friends, she thought. They're still in Sidan. We've got to save them. She felt David at her side and concentrated, watching how the Doc reacted to her answer.

"True," shrugged Richards, noticing her discomfort and uncertainty. The Doc decided that she had been taken over a lot too and was simply readjusting to her surroundings. So the possibility of her lying convincingly enough to deceive him was not very good.

Good, thought Jodi. He accepted it.

"Won't you tell us how you knew that Jessica wasn't with us in Mount Apocrys?" interrupted David.

"If you wish but I'll have to start at the beginning and it's a long story," he answered.

David nodded.

"Very well. It began about five years ago when I was teaching in a small, private university in southern Texas. I was approached numerous times by a strange old woman who kept mumbling some sort of prophetic mumbo-jumbo to me that I couldn't even begin to comprehend. She accosted me on my way home from work almost every day, and whenever I left my house, she was there, prophesying to me. I called the cops about her, but whenever they were around, she wasn't. So I finally got sick enough of it to ask her who she was and why the hell she was bothering me. She gave me some tremendously long sermon that I'd rather not repeat right now—I probably couldn't anyway. But the gist of it was that I apparently had some sort of magical power and that my destiny was supposed to carry me into another land, one of magic and monsters. At first I didn't believe her, thinking her some old biddy with an overactive imagination and an inactive brain, but she did unnerve me enough to start trying little things, just to see if I could do them. You know, lighting a candle or making a book levitate, that sort of thing, like you see the magicians do on television. Anyway, to my amazement, I could do it! I even succeeded in teleporting a cat! That was probably the funniest thing I've ever seen!" He laughed. "That poor cat must have jumped ten feet before running off, hissing and spitting furiously like an army of German Shepherds were after her! After this, I started doing some research in black magic and, even more fitting, alchemy.

"As I nurtured my powers and learned more about them, I began experimenting with so-called role playing games since they've been labeled with a notorious reputation for being too realistic. I soon learned that, to a person with magical abilities, these games really were much more than they seemed. I learned that any world you could possibly imagine in your mind does exist somewhere in the inter-dimensional multiverse. So I came up with the world you adventured in, Sidan, and soon mastered creating myself more personae in this other realm who grew very quickly into adults and died as precipitously. You met two of my living characters while you were in this other world: Rocnar Da'arputni and Tohzahi. I could see through their eyes as if they were my own. And that's how I knew that Jessica wasn't with you in the mountain. You see, I have another character who serves under Peccare, and he and the rest of Peccare's men watched you all disappear into Mount Apocrys. Jessica wasn't with you."

"I see," said David. "That's very interesting, but why'd you send us to this 'realm' in the first place."

"Because I also created an amulet, David—an amulet that could transport the person holding it from one world to another in his own form. As you know, if you stay in that world for an extended period in the body of one character, that persona begins to take control of your mind, and you're no longer who you were when you left."

As Jodi heard that remark, she realized why she had forgotten about home. Aurora's mind had taken over to such an extent that she just did not want to remember. She promised herself that she would not let that happen again.

Richards noticed her pensive look and smiled to himself. They really aren't angry. It's almost too good to be true.

"I did notice that," admitted David.

"Well, when I return to Sidan, I want to be in my own body and be able to carry more advanced weapons than swords with me. Imagine!" Richards was getting excited, a gleam of something near fanaticism in his eyes and a bead of sweat glistening on his high forehead. "With guns and grenades a handful of men could take over Sidan! I would be the ruler of an entire world!"

"So you sent us to get this amulet and bring it back to you," said David, unfelt surprise in his voice. "What makes you think we'd give it to you or even that we could make it back?"

"I knew you'd return because your characters are so powerful, and if you don't give me the amulet, I won't restore you to your real bodies," he answered, grinning broadly. He had expected this reaction.

"Won't people wonder when these kids who went to your house tonight end up dead?" asked David.

"No!" said the Doc, frantic with excitement. "That's the greatest part of all! If I choose not to restore you or you're killed, I can fill your bodies with changelings! These spirits'll take on your identity and will, in effect, be you! No one would ever know."

"Oh," said David, eyes downcast. "Sounds like you've had this worked out for a long time."

"I have!" said the Doc, his eyes flashing, "and it'll soon be put into action!"

"One more question, Doc," said David. "How'd you send us to Sidan in the first place?"

"That was the hardest part," answered Richards, all solemnity. "I had to use a little science and a little magic intermingled to accomplish that end. I put a little concoction in your tea. It consisted very simply of a francium crystal, which is hard as hell to get your hands on. I magically put it inside the sugar in your tea. Now francium reacts very vigorously when it gets wet—even the moisture in the air is enough to set it off. It fulminates violently, and when the sugar reached your stomach and the amino acids began breaking it down, the francium was exposed to the liquid in your stomach. Here I cast another little spell that transformed that explosion from a normal chemical reaction into a sort of metaphysical seizure. This little burst of energy threw your consciousness out of your body and into whatever realm you happened to be thinking of, in this case Sidan because I was describing it to you. Then you were herded into an awaiting form which happened to be the personae you had created for yourselves in our game."

"That's ingenious," admitted David. This guy might be crazy, but he's also damned smart, he thought.

"Thanks but now I'm afraid our little catching up session has reached its Armageddon," he said, growing deadly serious. "I'm gonna have to ask you to give me the amulet." He held out his hand meaningfully, wondering what David would do next.

David stared at the obviously soft palm for a second. "Just a moment, Doc. I have a proposition for you," he said, gripping the amulet in his right fist until the gems and the inscription had been superimposed in his flesh. "We really don't have any reason to stay in this world any longer. Our friends are dead, and we'd never be the same as we were. Jodi and I discussed it before we returned and have decided that we don't want to stay here. We want to return with you to Sidan?"

The Doc was really taken aback by this unexpected occurrence. He looked at them suspiciously for a moment and then asked, "If you wanted to stay in Sidan, why'd you return to talk with me at all?"

"Because it'd been our objective ever since we arrived in Sidan," answered David. "It seemed a shame to go through all this torture and then not return. Besides, it's human nature to be curious; we wanted to find out why and how we got there, and we didn't know what else to do." He paused for a moment. "Now that we've heard what you're planning, I think your idea of taking over Sidan has great promise. I'm sure Jodi'd agree with me if I were to say that returning to become rulers would be much more pleasing—certainly more exciting—than hanging around this dump of a world."

Jodi felt very confused but she thought she was starting to understand David's plan, and she had promised to back him up anyway. She nodded her agreement vigorously. "Sounds good to me. We don't have any real friends left here. Besides, I always wondered what it'd be like to be queen."

"Well you'll have to settle for a princess, Jodi," said Richards, "because I'll be the king, and I'll have my own queen." He decided to trust David and Jodi because he did not think them capable of deceiving him.

"Good enough," she answered, grinning. "As long as I have a title."

"Then I'll accept your proposition," said Richards, extending his hand happily. David accepted it, noticing how sweaty it was, and passed it to Jodi who also gripped it. "It'll be great to have company along, but you do realize that I'll have to put changelings in your bodies too, to make sure you don't betray me. If this is a trick, you'll have no way home except through me and that'll be my insurance. No other wizard in Sidan knows how to cast the counterspell that would return you to your bodies." They nodded their agreement.

Richards stood and returned to the gaming room, Jodi and David in tow. There he closed his eyes and began concentrating on something obscure. His lips moved as he mumbled strange words that were completely inaudible to their untrained ears. Then the seven bodies that were sitting at the table began to move. David and Jodi watched in horror as they saw themselves stand and look back at them. The others' bodies also stood and looked at David and Jodi in turn and then back at Richards.

"Thanks Doc," said the pseudo-Brandon. "Feels great to be in a real body again."

"Yeah, Doc," agreed pseudo-Jessica. "It's a big improvement over ages of timeless existence."

Richards simply nodded his head and smiled at them.

"Hi, David," said pseudo-David. "See ya 'round." He laughed mischievously and left the room, the others filing out after him.

"That's an eerie feeling," mumbled David, suppressing a shudder. "It gives new meaning to the term talking to yourself."

"Are you ready to leave?" asked Richards.

"I guess so," answered David.

"Good. I'll be back in a second. I'm going to get my gun and test it to make sure everything works fine in Sidan."

"Okay," said David as the Doc trotted from the room. He turned to Jodi. "Good job! Just keep it up and as soon as we get back to Sidan, jump as hard and as quickly as you can away from Richards," he said to her forcefully and turned back just as the Doc returned, squirming into his charcoal grey windbreaker.

"Give me the amulet," he said, holding out his hand and stuffing his snub-nosed .44 into his jacket's inside pocket.

David handed him the amulet and went to stand at his right

side as Jodi took his left. Richards began making the same sort of adjustments to the amulet as David had when they left Sidan but in a different order. Very quickly the strange bird that had transported them before rose out of the amulet and hooked its dagger-like talons around the Doc's arms and lifted him, David and Jodi holding on to his sides. The world began spinning again and they were enshrouded in the same nothingness that David and Jodi had experienced before. It was a terrible sensation and one they did not wish to ever feel again. The blackness encompassed them and they surrendered themselves to oblivion.

Christopher was sitting on the cold floor of that tiny room they had been living in for the last day and a half. They had not left the place except on routine forays for food and to use the bathroom, and they were all getting quite anxious for David and Jodi's return. For all they knew, the Lady might be lying and their friends could be dead or searching for them somewhere else, but that did not make sense. Why would Gahdnawen lie? No, it had to be the truth, but if it was, where were David and Jodi and when would they return?

Christopher was also curious as to what the Lady had been doing. Since they had entered the room, she had been making markings on the floor in some strange shape. He had decided that it must be some sort of strange, clerical magic. Christopher had no idea as to what she was doing and was really curious about it. The shape vaguely resembled a protective pentagram, but the five points were rounded, almost forming a circle. Christopher had asked her a few times about it but had only received the same cryptic answer: "You'll see." She would say no more on the subject. Christopher damned her for her obscurity and wished a plague on all persons—especially clerics—who insisted on keeping secrets from allies about anything. Well, his plaintiveness was getting him nowhere so he decided to try one more time in a different manner. He walked up to the Priestess and asked pleadingly, "Please Lady, what are you doing and when will our friends get back?"

"Very soon, Christopher," she answered, "and you'll understand what I'm doing when they return. As a matter of fact…" She trailed off, straightening and looking up into the air. Then Christopher felt it too; a strange density filled the room as if a storm were preparing to erupt and unleash a tidal wave of illness and destruction upon them. "Everyone!" shouted Gahdnawen. "Gather around me here." The group, confused but not knowing what else to do, gathered around her where she stood in front of the strange circular pattern she had sketched in chalk in front of the statue of Crasen.

"What—" began Brandon but he was cut off by a shushing motion from Lady Gahdnawen.

Then it all burst forth! The air seemed to shatter, slinging jagged pieces of light through the room like solid wisps of evanescent cloud. This light seemed to cut through them as they stood, shading their eyes, totally confused and frightened. When they were finally able to reopen their eyes, they saw Doctor John Richards materializing in the air inside the shape Lady Gahdnawen had drawn, holding an amulet in his hands. David and Jodi were with him, and as they appeared, they both leapt with all their might away from Richards. Though it was apparent that they put all their strength into the effort, they barely managed to clear the two-foot wide shape the Lady had drawn. They seemed to move so slowly, almost floating through the air, but as they reached the edge of the circle, their momentum took hold and they fell at a normal speed. Then the Lady raised her hands and made three quick cutting gestures in the air, and the symbol that held Richards raised up in the air and began gyrating around him, appearing as if a giant warped helix had formed itself around him.

The Doc looked at the spiral he was trapped in, then at the

faces around him, and finally at Lady Gahdnawen as she stood, a smug grin on her face. "You bitch!" he screamed, his voice sounding as if it came from the void, echoing off the walls of infinity. "What have you done?!"

"I'm sending you to the place where you belong, Richards," she answered calmly. "I'm sending you to a place where you can live out your life amongst other demons like yourself, and there you can't hurt anyone with your foul arts."

Richards looked like a trapped animal scratching at the surface of his cage which emanated sparks wherever his hands touched it, trying desperately to escape. "You fools!" he shouted at the party that stood around Gahdnawen. "She's just using you for her own purposes! If you help me kill her, you'll all be kings! You can rule by my side! Just kill her!"

They stared back at him with confusion on their faces and a sense of loathing in their hearts. Why they despised this man so intensely, they did not know, but they were sure that his intentions were purely selfish and evil. Jessica rose up at the front and fixed her glittering eyes on the Doc until he was forced to meet her piercing gaze. Then she summed up all of their feelings—all of their hatred—and spat it in his face. With all the contempt she could muster, which was plenty, she gazed deep into his eyes. Richards tried to turn away from her, but her power grasped him and held his eyes. She opened her mouth and spoke his sentence. "Go to hell, you despicable excuse for a human. You thought you could conquer Sidan; well you've only defeated yourself," she said quietly but with a voice that shook with rage and disgust, anger and hatred radiating from her like heat.

Lady Gahdnawen made one final gesture and murmured a few words, completing the cantrip. Doctor John Richards slowly disintegrated, screaming his torment, disgust, and frustration unto uncaring ears.

The party then seemed to collapse in upon itself, almost

imploding, and they held each other comfortingly. There were many words spoken and many tears shed, but these were suffused with joy at the reuniting of dear friends and relief at having conquered a being of obvious evil. Jessica explained to them that Richards was a being from another world who was trying to take over Sidan, and that they had just foiled his plans. She said that Lady Gahdnawen had told her shortly before she teleported them to Mount Apocrys.

Amid all this joy, however, there was also a deep sorrow centered around David as he saw the fruit of all his pains standing in front of him but knew that she could not remember the happiness they had shared. Jessica found no more comfort in the embrace David gave her than in any other friend's. She had absolutely no memory of the love within her.

It was all David could do to keep from breaking down and crying, but he knew that Jessica would not understand and would probably be repulsed by such action from the Cavalier hero. The only people who understood or even saw David's pain were Lady Gahdnawen and Sean. The thief felt as if his heart would break for his friend, but he knew that David would carry on in the hope that he would be able to make Jessica remember, return her to the surface of this puissant personality that inhabited the body of Sister Anna.

However, time wore on, and they soon found themselves sitting around a small fire in that same room where Crasen had been slain, chatting about their journey and what had happened since Jessica's unfortunate accident. During this period, it became obvious to David that Jodi had no recollection of her past life. He had been certain that she had remembered everything while they sat, talking with Richards, and just after they returned, she looked very confused when he did not embrace Jessica with any more reaction than he had. However, now her eyes were empty of such recognition. She must have gradually lost her memory just as she had gradually regained it, but David could not concentrate very long on that subject. His mind was too preoccupied with other subjects.

As David's wounds were still too new to bear the closeness of Jessica for a very extended period, he soon excused himself from the circle to take a walk. Sean watched him lope off into the passage outside the room and shook his head before standing and following his friend. The story Jodi was telling of the strange world she had visited but only vaguely recalled depressed the thief.

"You've got to be strong, my friend," said Sean, placing a comforting hand on David's shoulder as he caught up to him. "She'll remember with time. I'm sure of it."

"Do you really think so, Sean?" questioned David. "I'm not so sure we're up to the task ahead of us. The pressure's just too much. I don't think I can stand it."

"Oh, but you will, David," said Lady Gahdnawen as she crept up to join them. "You're a very strong person, even stronger than you know, and for Jessica, you'll have the strength of many. Have faith in yourself. I do."

"Me too," put in Sean. "We can do it, but only if we keep gently urging, and we can only do that if we have a clear picture of what's to come. Trust me, my friend. We will conquer."

"Thank you," said David somberly. "Both of you. I needed the support."

"Any time, buddy," asserted Sean, giving his friend a heartfelt hug.

"Are you guys coming back?" called Bellus to the three figures standing just outside the room.

"Go ahead," suggested David. "I'm gonna take a short walk. I'll be back soon."

David wandered along the lit hallway back towards the door where the trolls had come from. He turned into the dark section and traipsed off a little further. There he sat down, staring off into the darkness. The things he saw in that void were not comforting. He watched himself and Jessica back on Earth just as he had when she had been hurt and he thought she was dead. However, these memories fleeted by very quickly. What took up most of his attention were the memories of him and Jessica since they had been in Sidan. He watched as he had comforted her on the day they arrived and while Sean and Brandon were in Estrus. He saw her glorious wrath at the destruction of that homestead where the girl had been raped and her brother prematurely torn from her mother. He watched Peccare attempt to rape her, and he watched them teasing each other in bed at The Blue Dragon in Tyrol. Along with these visions, he watched himself interacting with each of his fellows: Brandon and Jodi, Christopher and Amy, and especially Sean. The thief had been a great help to him and was the only friend he had left. It was left up to them to save the others, and he was very uncertain about that. No matter what Sean and Gahdnawen said, David could not convince himself that everything would be all right. He knew with a certainty that frightened him that things would never return to normal.

With a sigh, he stood and started back towards his friends. Sean watched with concern as David crept back into Crasen's room and sat down next to the fire, warming his hands and staring deep into the small blaze. He spoke only sparingly to everyone and quickly retired for the evening. He feigned sleep while the others continued their rejoicing, and after they all finally lay down, he still could not sleep. He lay awake and forced himself to repress his emotions. He made himself a promise that he would not let his feelings show, that he would keep control, knowing that he would have to do just that until such a time as Jessica remembered their relationship, whenever that might be, tomorrow or twenty years from now—either way, he would be waiting.

Lethal tendencies

The next day, or what passed for day in that oppressive blackness, did not dawn with the rising sun and the laughter of birds fleeing the brunt of the impending winter but, instead, with a sighing yawn followed by a stretch. This extemporaneous declaration of weariness came from Jessica as she awakened by the embers of the fire. She sat up and stretched, working the stiffness out of her muscles and looked around her. Most everyone was still asleep, but David was up, repacking their supplies, garbed only in a tight pair of trousers. His immense body glistened with sweat that flickered and reflected the sparse light still emanated by the fire. She watched the muscles flexing and unflexing with his movements. In silhouette, she noticed his ruggedly handsome visage—the firm chiseled jaw, the slightly pointed nose, the high cheeks, the long brown hair that encased his face majestically. Even in such dim light, his ice blue eyes glittered, orange-red dots reflected in them. Jessica felt a very odd sensation when she noticed the sadness that was obvious in his face, the white scar multiplying its effects on his face. She had the immediate urge to go to him and comfort him, offer him some solace for the loss he had received, whatever it may be.

At her movement, he became aware of her. When he turned to face her, Jessica was shocked by the look he gave her; it was so heart-wrenchingly sad, so painfully needful. She could not resist her clerical urges any longer and stood to go to his side. David turned away.

"What's wrong, David?" asked Jessica. "I can see the pain in your face."

"I'm fine," he answered, avoiding her gaze.

She took his hand and turned him towards her. "What is it, my friend? You can tell me."

She watched an inner struggle play across his face, but very quickly, too quickly, all expression left it. His face was a tabula rasa that she could not penetrate. "I said I'm fine," he murmured, pulling himself from her grasp. He kept his face turned downward for a moment, flexing the hand she had held. He still felt a little phantom pain in the finger it was lacking, but he felt more pain when he remembered how Jessica had stroked that sore.

"Ah," said Jessica, misinterpreting the gesture. "You're bothered by the loss of your finger. That's quite natural. You'll adapt to it, and soon you won't even notice it's missing." She did not really believe that was the problem, but for some reason her body resisted the attempt to look deeper.

David faced her once more. "I'll always know it's missing, Jessica. Always."

Something in the way David spoke affected Jessica deeply. She felt herself step back from him involuntarily, her breath catching in her throat. In that moment, she noticed how handsome he was, how strikingly handsome. If only I weren't a cleric... she caught herself thinking and quickly stifled the idea. That was blasphemous, especially for such a powerful cleric. Besides, she loved being one of Galead's chosen; it was a great honor.

"Is this a private party, or can anyone join in," said Sean

from beside Jessica. Seeing David's obvious discomfort, he had come to break the tension and give his friend some relief.

"So you finally woke up," said Jessica to the thief. "I thought you were a lighter sleeper than that."

"Only when I need to be. Isn't it about time we got outta here?"

David nodded and continued packing while Sean began waking the others. Jessica watched David for a moment longer, analyzing and eliminating her feelings, before she also began packing.

Once everyone was awakened, it did not take long to assemble what little baggage they had left. As they finished, Lady Gahdnawen called for their attention. "I must return to the Temple right away," she said seriously. "They need me, so I'm going to teleport myself there and leave you to follow on foot."

"Is that where we're supposed to go now?" asked Christopher, frowning deeply at the thought of having to return to the Temple. He was very uncomfortable there.

"Where else would you go?" asked the Lady in answer.

"She's got a point, Chris," said Sean with a grin.

Christopher grunted.

"Anyway," continued Gahdnawen, "once you're there, we can talk more about what's to come. I'll offer you all the comfort of the Temple for the winter. It looks to be a long and cold one."

"That sounds like a wonderful idea," asserted Jessica. "It'll give us all a chance to rest."

Gahdnawen nodded. "Good, but I've got to go; I've delayed too long already. Things don't go well at the Temple if I'm not around, and there's always a lot for us to do. So, farewell." She began to make the motions of the spell when Jodi cut in.

"Wait! Why don't you take us back with you? Why should

we travel by foot?" she asked as Gahdnawen began to fade and the wind began to blow once more through the room.

"Because your journey hasn't ended yet. There's still something left for you to do," she answered. "Farewell, until we meet again!"

As the Lady disappeared totally, the echoes of her last words resounded in the closed quarters. "What did she mean?" asked Amy in disgust. "Haven't we done enough already?"

"I dare say we have, but we won't be able to rest until we've done everything she has in store for us," answered Christopher spitefully.

"The thing the Lady speaks of is not for her; it's simply what Galead has revealed to her as something that must come to pass," cut in Bellus, defending her mother.

"She's right," supported Jessica.

Christopher stared coldly at them both for a moment before deciding to leave the subject alone for the mean time. After a moment of silence, Brandon suggested that they get the journey underway.

As they returned to the door leading from Crasen's room to the hallway, they all joined hands, David purposefully avoiding Jessica's, and they returned up the passage hand in hand, torches lifted high for good sight. This time, however, the mood was a bit lighter, and they did not feel the pressure weighing so heavily on their shoulders.

They followed the same path they had taken on their way into the cave, noticing with relief that the oppressive air that had been so prominent in their trek down the cavern was no longer present. They soon burst forth from the cavern into the light of mid-morning like newborns screaming to be free of their mothers' wombs. They stumbled down the face of the mountain under the warm sun that shone down through the leaves of late autumn, maroon and brown splashes amid the branches.

As they returned to the valley they had stayed in before entering Apocrys, they continued in a slightly different direction from the one that had brought them into the mountains, and they began to chat idly. Christopher finally asked Jessica about her experience with the malspirare. She shuddered before answering the question. "When it happened, I suddenly felt as if somebody had reached into my stomach, grasped my liver, and ripped it out. I collapsed from the pain and from some other feeling that, even now, I can't quite identify...something like fear seasoned with sadness and anger. I felt myself falling, as if into a deep sleep, but I was awake. Instead I hovered on the border of consciousness for a little while, feeling like somebody had hold of my heart and was slowly squeezing all the blood out of it. My breath came short and in gasps as I fought for life. Then I saw a nightmare face: a dark, demonic visage, with sable skin and burning eyes. The face opened its great mouth which was lined with short sharp teeth and laughed at me, mocking me! I fainted again but not fully this time. It was as if I were lying on my back looking up into a totally dark night sky, with no stars or moon, and there was a bright ball of light hovering above me like Tantalus' apple. I knew that if I were to ever recover, I had to reach it, but no matter how hard I struggled or how far I stretched, I couldn't quite reach it. And as I watched and struggled, I saw it slowly diminishing as a thin beam of shining light spiraled out of it and disappeared, gyrating up into the sky above me. Then the flow slowed and I felt hopeful. After what seemed an eternity, I heard a deep-throated scream of rage and pain, and a new face appeared above the ball. It was Lady Gahdnawen. She smiled down at me and grasped the ball in her hands, slowly pushing it down toward me. I reached for it, and as I grasped it, it expanded to envelope me, completely encircling my body. The next thing I knew, I woke up in the Lady's room at the Temple of Galead, weak and helpless."

"How horrible!" said Bellus from where she walked in front of Sean, shuddering with sympathetic revulsion.

"It wasn't an experience I'd like to repeat," agreed Jessica, another shudder racing up her spine.

"Well, I'm just glad it's over!" exclaimed Amy. "Can we talk about something else, now?"

So they trudged on northeasterly, talking of lighter matters and not thinking much about what would happen to them in the near future. Around noon, they stopped beside a brook that wound its way down the slope of a particularly tall, snow-capped peak. Here they ate some of the rations that remained from the Temple.

After the meal, they continued, chatting in the same idle fashion, but they soon began to feel worry creeping up their spines like so many spiders, and the farther they traveled, the more intense the feeling became. After all of the times they had experienced such foreboding, they new better than to ignore their senses, so they continued slowly and in silence. Very soon they came to an area where they would have to pass between two very steep rock faces. It reminded Sean of a smaller version of the Grand Canyon. The two faces, each probably nearing two-hundred feet in height, climbed up over their heads, and they were forced to walk down a path that was barely fifty feet wide. It gave them a terribly claustrophobic feeling, as if, any minute, the walls were going to fall down on top of their heads.

"Do we have to go this way?" asked Amy meekly. "Isn't there an alternative?"

"Not unless we go back to Mount Apocrys and go on the path we used to enter the mountains," answered Brandon.

"I have a funny feeling that this is the place where we'll encounter whatever it was the Lady spoke of," said Sean pensively.

"If so," said Christopher, "wouldn't it be wise to simply

continue down this path and have whatever-it-is happen to us so we can get on with our lives."

"It would definitely get it over with a lot faster," agreed Sean.

"Then I say we follow it," put in Jodi, "and be cautious."

"Sounds good to me," said Christopher. "I vote with Jodi."

They all reluctantly agreed that they really had no choice in the matter and decided to follow the canyon to face whatever it would bring their way. So they continued down the path, paying close attention to everything around them, wondering when it—whatever it was—would happen.

After they had traveled a quarter mile or so down the path, the cliff faces began to grow less steep, signaling the start of their termination. They began to hope that they were not going to have any trouble, but their hopes were shattered very quickly when Christopher, in the middle of the group, halted suddenly. "Stop!" he said in a tight whisper. "There are beings nearby!"

"How many?" inquired David urgently.

"I'm not sure. A lot."

"Are they human?" asked Brandon.

"Yes…and no. Something else is here too. Be careful."

So they continued with as much caution as is possible, trying not to look as if they expected anything, but constantly on the peripheral lookout. Because of this, they were prepared when, from behind a large pile of rocks that stood like a cenotaph a short distance in front of them, a large number of men jumped out, swords drawn and axes raised. There was a shout from their midst and more men rounded the top of the canyon, each with bows strung and arrows knocked, preparing to let fly a rain of death into the trapped party's midst.

David looked on this, little surprised, but wondering who these men could be. Then he saw, standing at the front of the throng, a hugely built man with a pernicious grin creasing his broad face. It was Peccare! David damned himself for having forgotten the Lady's warnings and Richards' comments about this evil man and his lackeys. He jerked his sword from its scabbard, light coruscating on the razor-sharp blade like promised expedience. And for the moment his worries about Jessica were totally forgotten.

Knowing that they did not have enough time to turn and run, David, Brandon, Sean, and Bellus formed another cordon around the others.

"Well, my friends," gloated Peccare as he smirked at his trapped prey. "It looks like I've managed to snare you again."

"You weren't able to keep us last time, Peccare," returned David. "What makes you think this time'll be any different?"

"Last time I was bold and underestimated you. Now I know better. There're more than two score men around us with arrows pointed at your hearts. If you try anything now, you will die, and for later purposes, I brought something a little more sure to hold you." He dangled some chain in his left hand, grinning with malicious intent. "This time you won't live through our encounter, and your dear friends," he eyed the women eagerly, "will taste the pleasures of true men. Especially your little cleric there," he added, gesturing at Jessica who returned a haughty stare, trying to hide the confusion she felt.

Christopher stood motionless next to David. For some reason, he was completely unafraid, as if some other force had laid its hand upon his heart, holding his concentration at its peak and suppressing his fear. As he listened to David's conversation with Peccare, a strange feeling was building within him, moving him to search for its source. Once again he felt some other entities in the area—they were definitely not human; somehow, they were more, much more. Then a voice or what passed for a voice in telepathic communication whispered in his mind, ordering him to act and informing him of what was to come. At first Christopher was uncertain and reluctant to react, but as the voice continued its cajoling, his confidence welled and he suppressed a laugh. "Excuse me," he cut in, halting David in mid-sentence. "I think we've had enough banter. Peccare, you have one last chance. You and your men can turn and leave now, or you all will surely die."

Laughter rippled through Peccare's men, and the leader raised an eyebrow himself. "Wizard, you don't scare me. There's nothing you could do quick enough to halt forty arrows aimed at your heart. You don't have the power."

"What're you doing?" mumbled David to the wizard. "Don't provoke him. I've got a plan."

"Trust me, David," whispered Christopher. "We're quite safe. Follow my lead. When I attack, follow me."

"But—"

"No time for it. Just trust me." He stared hard at David before returning his attention to Peccare. "You have ten seconds to leave or you'll die. Ten, nine, eight…"

"Wizard, don't try any tricks. You don't stand a chance."

"Seven, six, five, four…"

"Don't be a fool."

"Three, two, one. Your last chance, Peccare. Will you surrender?"

"No, I won't, you pompous idiot! I'll skin you alive and feed you to the pigs!"

"Very well."

At that moment, something unimaginable happened. Simultaneously, many gaunt grey figures with featureless faces, eyeless sockets, and clawed fingers rose from the earth in front of each of the archers and grasped them by the arms. Then they slowly sank back into the earth, dragging the screaming archers with them.

"The Etolea," breathed David in amazement.

In a matter of seconds, all the archers were buried up to

their necks in pure rock. Some struggled to break free, but mostly, they were already dead, crushed by the stone.

Peccare and his remaining soldiers watched in disgusted amazement as a quarter of their force was destroyed by grey gnome-like creatures. Shock overwhelmed them but only for a moment.

However, Christopher was waiting for that moment. "Now! Attack!" he shouted, a bolt of lightning flaring from his fingertips. It blew the rocks that had hidden Peccare from their view into shards of tiny stone, showering their assailants with a rain of dust.

David, Brandon, Bellus, and Sean dove at Peccare and his men as they stood in momentary shock, hoping to drive their advantage as far as they could. However, the mercenaries were well trained and reacted quickly, bringing their weapons to bare on David and his allies. Steel sung and metal clashed! The war cries of two races echoed through the canyon as man and dwarf alike gave throat to their most heartfelt rage and slashed and chopped at their opponents, disgust and rapacious hatred flashing in their steely eyes like morbid voracity. Bloody pieces of gore flew in the air as steel met flesh and it parted beneath the razor-sharp blades! David, Brandon, Bellus, and Sean all fought ferociously, stabbing and slashing, parrying and thrusting! Their opponents' bodies littered the floor of the chasm, bloody heaps of lifeless flesh, but there were just too many of them! Though the Etolea had destroyed the archers, there were still at least thirty men with which to contend. Though the protectors fought on, Peccare's men just kept coming, making the defenders fight harder and harder beyond what they thought were their limits but were merely thresholds of numbness, relieving them of the pain in their muscles and tendons. They had slowly been pushed back to where Christopher stood with the women and then further, forcing everyone to stumble on the unsteady ground.

Sean fought on, hoping beyond hope that some aid would come to them, knowing that it would not. Where's John Wayne when you need him? Then there was a yell and a tremendous horde of soldiers erupted over the horizon and began their descent down into the combe. At first, Sean felt despair settling over him like a dark cerement, but then he noticed the surprised and worried looks that flew from his opponents' eyes as they noticed the figures. Some of them rushed to meet this new force.

Amidst the turmoil, a yell erupted from the midst of the attackers. "It's an illusion!" screamed Peccare. The startled men looked at their leader suspiciously, wondering if he had gone mad. In answer Peccare ran up to meet the new onslaught and passed directly through one of the men as they reached the bottom of the chasm. Another yell erupted as the men returned their attention to their trapped enemies, ignoring the phantom army that fell upon them like powerless spite. As the phantasm reached them and passed through, Jodi let the illusion dissipate into nothingness, and the battle continued as though nothing had happened.

They fought harder, just trying to hold their position, hoping that something would happen to give them the strength to win this overwhelming battle, but once again, they were being forced backward. Now some of Peccare's men were trying to encircle them, hoping to close a trap by pushing them in too close to fight.

Then, like a flash of caustic hatred, arrows rained down on them in a shower of death. One black-feathered arrow found its mark in Amy's stomach, staining her alabaster robes crimson, discoloring her eyes with pain. Agony twisted her features, leaving her face a visage of despair, and a scream echoed from her lips, reverberating with pain. She fell hard to the earth with the impact of the arrow, and the momentum of her own disbelief laid her flat on the ground.

Christopher ripped an arrow out of his own left leg with a blare of anger and knelt beside Amy's contorted form, searching for the source of these arrows. The Etolea had taken care of the archers, or so he thought. Then he saw; some of Peccare's men had climbed to where the archers had died and commandeered their bows. They were then preparing to fire another round. As Christopher looked into Amy's twisted face, an ague of hatred and helplessness wracking his body with destructive impulses.

Something snapped in the wizard as he heard David scream, "Help us! Do something to those archers!" and he reacted by leaping to his feet, longing to use a fireball or lightning bolt on the people who had hurt Amy, but he knew that any explosion could bring the walls of the barranco down on their heads. So with frustration echoing from his eyes, he waved his hands and uttered the words of his sleep spell. Around half of the archers dropped like flies, falling into a deep coma-like sleep and tumbling down the cliff, slight landslides following them. "That's all I can do! A more powerful spell would cause a landslide!"

He whirled back to Amy and found Jessica already bent over her. She had already torn Amy's robe and removed the arrow from her side. The wounded cleric was now unconscious, either because of some spell of Jessica's or simply from pain. Jessica placed her hands on Amy's stomach and chanted the spell, praying for healing. When she removed her hands, the wound was closed and the scar had almost entirely faded.

Christopher knelt beside Amy as Jessica placed a hand on his punctured leg, casting another healing spell. Christopher felt the surge of power as the wound closed, and comforting warmth spread through his emotionally wounded body.

Jessica then placed a hand on Amy's brow and muttered a singular word. As the echoes of eldritch power wavered in the air, Amy's eyes reopened and she looked up into Christopher's face, the remnants of pain rolling down her cheeks. Christopher found himself unable to offer Amy the comforting she obviously needed, but then something changed in her face and the pain disappeared. Christopher could not isolate the emotion playing across her brow, but he knew she was all right and some change was taking place in her.

The stalwart warriors fought bravely, but they were being worn down, their energies spread too thin. "We can't hold them much longer!" yelled David back to those he sought to protect, watching in dread as the remaining archers nocked their bows. "If we don't get help, we're dead!"

Silence reigned in the cordon's center for a moment before Jessica turned to Christopher and whispered something in his ear. The wizard's eyes lit up and he nodded ferociously, raising his hands with palms pointed outward. "To me!" he yelled with all of his might. A little startled but still responsive, the four protectors leapt backwards until they were right next to Christopher. At that same instant, the wizard made several gestures and a shimmering blue bubble encircled them, crushing the attackers on the outside between the bubble and their comrades. They struck the sphere with fists and swords to no avail; not a dent was made. Arrows bounced off the top.

"What've you done?" asked Brandon, breathless. "Now we're trapped inside this bubble! They'll simply wait us out! You can't hold this forever!"

"Be silent!" breathed Christopher with as much strength as he could muster, most of his power bent on sustaining the bubble. "We aren't done!"

Jessica closed her eyes and concentrated. She mumbled a few words as the others peered at her, confused and hopeful. Then she raised her arms until each of her hands were placed palm outward against the bubble towards each cliffside. Then she started shaking her hands violently from side to side.

There was a rumble and the earth beneath their feet began to shake as if an army of giants were approaching. The rumble increased exponentially, causing the ground to vibrate even more powerfully as Jessica shook harder, sweat beading on her frowning forehead. Then the method to this madness dawned on the confused party as rubble high up on the top of the cliffs began rolling downward, gaining in velocity and volume as rocks bowled over the few remaining archers and grew closer to Peccare and his fear-stricken force. As Jessica let her arms fall and opened her eyes, the boulders poured down onto the floor of the canyon, crushing both earth and men. The rocks slammed into the shimmering blue ball that encompassed the small party, battering them around and crushing people into bloody pulps against its sides, but the force shield held and the crease on Christopher's brow deepened. Very quickly the landslide threw enough spilth against the force shield to create a pile higher than David's waist. Then, as suddenly as it had started, the landslide stopped.

As Christopher let the shield drop, David looked around and saw almost no motion amidst the rubble. A few of Peccare's men had survived, but they were no longer interested in the fight. Instead, they concentrated on fleeing or helping wounded friends unbury themselves.

"When'd you learn that?!" asked Sean of Jessica who fell to the rubble with exhaustion and culpability as she realized the magnitude of the death she had caused. Killing one person was bad enough, but this many was simply too much.

"Lady Gahdnawen taught me the spell just before we teleported to Mount Apocrys," she answered quietly. "She said it might be of use to us."

"Well, it certainly was," commented Christopher, grinning from ear to ear with victory's morbid euphoria.

"I hate having to kill so many people," continued Jessica with a wilting look for the wizard. She passed her hand across her eyes, praying fervently that the death would be wiped away with her tears.

"Sometimes there's no way to avoid killing," commented Brandon.

"But why so much?"

They searched in the rubble for survivors to free or put out of their misery, but there were very few who lived who had not already fled. Soon, Sean called his friends over to a large pile of rocks near where Peccare and his men had hid from them. "Hey guys!" he shouted happily. "Look what I've found!"

As they all arrived, they noticed that Sean was holding an evil-looking curved dagger in his right hand. "Do you recognize this dagger?" he asked of David.

David took the dagger and turned it over and over in his rough hands. As he peered at its foot-long blade, decorated with spiraling flowers and at the curved handle that was fashioned into the head and neck of a hunting bird flanked by two smaller eagles' heads, one curving up and one down, a vision flashed in his mind. He saw his friends bound to trees around him while a large man cut deep gashes into his chest as he strained against the bonds that held him secure like Promethean chains. "It's Peccare's dagger," he said grimly.

"I thought so," smiled Sean. "Look at what else I found." He pointed down at something that lay amid the boulders at his feet. A large, muscular left arm that had been torn from somebody's shoulder lay, still twitching in the rubble, blood running out of its joint. "It still grasped the dagger when I found it."

"Where's the rest of him?" asked Christopher.

"He's probably buried somewhere under all these rocks," answered Sean. "Or, if he lived through the landslide, he would've crawled off to die. No one can live for long without an arm."

"So we're finally free of him," said Jodi, a morbid smile twisting her lips.

"I think it's safe to say so," agreed Brandon.

"Good!" exclaimed Jodi. "Maybe we can finally rest in safety for a while!"

They left Peccare's arm and walked down the length of the barranco, trying to get as far away from the carnage as they could, but as they reached its end, darkness settled about them. They built a large fire and broke out their sleeping gear, preparing for a good rest. However, not everyone could sleep. David took the first watch, still needing time to think, to contain himself. He had almost said too much that morning when confronted with being alone with Jessica, but thanks to Sean no damage was done. He was sure now that he would be able to stay under control. While his mind wandered, he drank way too much wine, trying to find a little comfort in its warmth. However, the liquid courage he found left all too soon.

And so he watched everyone else sleep. However, unbeknownst to him, Jessica could not sleep either. She lay awake chastising herself for the thoughts she had about David earlier. They were friends and that was all, but then why did she feel so close to him? Why did he look so sad? And why was he so damned attractive?

As they lay there, asleep and forgetful or awake and dreaming, they did not see the figure that peered down at them in brooding silence like a gargoyle perched atop the barranco less than a quarter mile away. Peccare weakly pulled the bloody tunic that was wrapped around his fragmented left shoulder tighter, trying to stay the loss of blood. He took another swig from a vial filled with a rank black liquid. "Graham, you'll pay for what you've done," he said to himself, his voice shaking with rage and weakness. "If it's the last thing I ever do, I'll kill you! I'll kill you all! You'll pay for murdering my men and for crippling me! Now I have the advantage! You think me dead! But I promise I will return! I will return!" He was silent for a moment before standing and laughing loudly; his laughter was so hateful and so cutting that it echoed off the walls of the barranco, reverberating with rage. The volume carried it a great distance into the night, disturbing all forms of life that heard it, chaffing their hearts with abrasive hatred. Peccare turned and stumbled off into the night, a trail of blood and evil the only remnants of his passing.

David and Jessica were startled by a sound that resounded in their ears as if Death himself had let loose his rage. "What was that?" asked Jessica, sitting up.

"I don't know," answered David. "It sounded like someone laughing."

"Maybe it was an animal," offered the cleric hopefully. "There's no telling what kind of beasts roam these mountains."

"Maybe," conceded the warrior.

Jessica sat in silence for a moment, trying to think of something to say to her friend, but nothing came. She could not think of anything; for some reason she felt terribly awkward.

"Go back to sleep," said David, releasing her from that burden. "We've got a long day of traveling ahead of us." So she lay back down and found sleep none too quickly; her mind was on other matters, and she could concentrate on nothing except her discomfort with David.

Epiphany

Amy's dreams during the first part of that evening were quite average. They consisted of the usual disjointed characters and places, nothing out of the ordinary. However, as the night wore on, they grew steadily more potent and realistic, as if they were not dreams at all but an extension of reality, a continuation of every day life. The worst of these nocturnal excursions came around three in the morning, and Amy felt that she was nearly awake, but she could not quite bring herself to open her eyes. Fight as she would, it was as if her eyes were forcibly being held closed. She had a frightening image of a coin stuck in each eye as in preparation for burial, but this she forced out of her mind and gave into the visions from beyond that coruscated before her closed eyes.

Through an inky darkness she swam. Though she felt a solid floor beneath her, the air about her was so thick, so horribly dense, that she had to pull herself forward with her arms just as she pushed with her legs—much like swimming through a liquid such as mercury. Her aim seemed to be a patch of light in the darkness a great distance ahead, and no matter how hard she struggled, she just could not seem to gain any ground on it. As she pushed harder, she became aware of another patch of coruscation behind her, but as she looked closer, she realized that what she had at first glance mistaken for light was really a darkness so intense, so deeply insentient that it seemed to shed an anti-light forward, toward her like groping tentacles. It was then that she became inexplicably aware of the fact that it was chasing her, attempting to reach her before she escaped into the real light before her. So she redoubled her efforts, both from determination and panic, in an attempt to foil the darkness' evil plan, to gain the sanctuary that offered itself.

It was purely by accident that she happened to glance to her right where she saw a most unexpected sight. What she first viewed was a scene she had observed a week or two in the past and had since viewed regularly in nightmares. There was the decapitated head of a middle-aged man stuck on a spike in front of a razed homestead. As she gazed at the visage twisted in pain and sorrow, it rotated on the spike to face her, cracking noises accompanying its turn. Its dead glazed eyes were obviously viewing only what the dead can see; however, she had the distinct impression that they were fixed on her as the mouth opened to speak. The words that issued forth were a foul impersonation of human speech, and as the words left the swollen tongue, vaporous clouds billowed out of the mouth to bring a fetid stench to Amy's nostrils, much like the charnel depths of a mausoleum. "Help me," moaned the voice. "Help me." It repeated those two words over and over, and each time the head spoke, it seemed to grow more and more repulsive until the mere sight of it sickened Amy, made her stomach try to retch. However, she swallowed the bile with her fear and forced herself to reach out to the head. She gagged as her hands came to rest on its sticky, rotten flesh, but she forced herself to cast the spell that would numb the poor man to his pain. His sigh was the only thanks Amy received, but it was more than enough to make the momentary revulsion well worth while.

Then she remembered the aggressor behind her and turned to check on its progress, sure that her momentary halt would be her downfall. To her surprise, however, she noticed that the thing had actually lost ground on her. In fact, she was a great deal closer to the light ahead of her than she naturally should have been, but the distance was still quite discouraging. She trudged onward and momentarily glanced behind her, and was greatly affected when she saw that the anti-light had already regained its advantage and was pressing forward. Amy turned and pushed harder until she became aware of another scene from her past appearing but to her left this time.

There was a young girl, thirteen maybe fourteen, lying on the ground spread eagle in a terribly obscene image of des-ecration. She was naked, bruised, battered, and covered with blood from cuts and her nefarious violation. As Amy viewed the scene of innocence's slaughter in renewed horror, she remembered the many nightmares that had plagued her about this poor young soul and her horrible plight. The young girl seemed to sense Amy's presence and sympathy and raised her battered face to meet the cleric's gaze with lifeless eyes. "Restore me," she moaned in a not-yet fully-matured voice that croaked with the strain of speech from beyond the grave. Like the disembodied head of Amy's previous experience, she repeated those two words over and over again until the cleric reached out to her. She embraced the youth and comforted her as best she could, murmuring a spell of forgetfulness and restoration.

As she felt the child's release of frustration, Amy knew that she had forfeited her own life to the impending darkness that was behind her. She turned to meet her pursuer and defend herself as best she could, but she then realized that she was once again far ahead of the darkness. The light was now a good deal closer than before, and she understood that her reward for doing the right thing was that she would be saved from the evil that chased her. So she smiled to herself and pressed forward, wondering what her next test might be, and she was soon answered in a way that she had not nearly expected.

She pushed a little farther and found herself plummeting at unreal speeds downward into darkness that she at once recognized as Absu, known by a thousand other names, Tartarus, the Abyss, Hades, Hell. At first she felt fear as of yet unparalleled in her life, but she forced that aside, knowing that her goddess would let nothing evil befall her. She had been forgiven for her sins and believed sincerely that Galead would protect her from such evil. With this thought, she felt her speed greatly diminishing until she had stopped entirely and was standing on firm ground in that unbelievably thick air once more.

She looked forward and saw that the light was only a short distance in front of her. She could easily reach it with two large steps. She smiled at her success and turned to check on the darkness that had been pursuing her, certain that it had turned back, giving up on her. She was rewarded by seeing that indeed it was a great distance behind her; however, it had not stopped following her. It was quickly speeding in her direction. At first, she did not understand its purpose for she would undoubtedly reach the light before it grew anywhere near her. But then she noticed a small object lying between the darkness and herself. Even as her gaze fell on it, she recognized the form of a terribly tiny infant. In fact, a little closer scrutiny revealed it to be a fetus, not even having developed human traits yet. She was not even sure how she had recognized it as a baby at first. When she looked at it now it looked like nothing more than a lump of flesh, but she was quickly reminded of the part of the scene at the razed homestead that had offended her even more than the vision of the decapitated head and the raped young girl. Before she had fainted that day, she had been overwhelmed by a vision of what had happened inside the cabin. She saw the rape of the pregnant mother and the removal of her unborn baby. She saw the horrified look on the father's face as he was decapitated, staring at his dead wife and what would have been his child. However, what had caused her to pass out was a vision of that little fetus as it was removed from its mother. She remembered distinctly seeing it move as if in distress before it was abandoned on the floor, and there she had seen it wiggle what would become little hands and feet given a fair chance. As she had seen that pitiful scene, she had passed out, welcoming the blackness as an escape from such abhorrence.

Now, as she looked at the fetus lying on the ground, she knew beyond any doubt that it was that same little being who had not been given the opportunity of life. In that same moment, she was forced to make the most difficult decision of her life. She had to decide whether to accept the solace offered by the light she had been racing toward or to return and try and save the little fetus from the blackness that was quickly rushing to envelope it. Though she had no reason to believe that the little being was alive, she knew that she had to make sure, had to rescue it from the anti-light that was about to destroy it. So she raced toward the baby as quickly as she possibly could. She fought harder against the resistance than she had ever fought against anything in her life, and she was rewarded. She managed to reach the baby before the darkness, and she reached down and picked it up, cradling it against her body. As she soothed it, she was rewarded by response. It squirmed against her breast and obviously looked up at her with what would soon be eyes. "Thank you, mother," spoke the fetus in an unmistakable voice that issued from no vocal chords or mouth. It was stated directly from the baby's heart, not needing any auditory transformation. Amy was not at all surprised, and she smiled down at her baby happily.

She then looked back up, feeling an instinctual maternal fear for her baby. What she saw was the anti-light mere feet from her. She did not have time to turn let alone get back to the light; she was caught, inescapably trapped. She only had time to shout as loud as she could, "Galead! Save my baby!" As she finished her plea, the anti-light collided with her, and she was knocked backward with incredible force, blacking out from the impact.

Amy had awakened everyone with her screams and writhing. At first they thought she was just having bad dreams, but when they could not wake her, they knew it was something more. No matter what they tried, her shouting and shaking never abated, and even Jessica's attempt at a calming spell had no affect on her. She was beyond all of them. They were all greatly relieved, especially Christopher, when after what seemed like hours, she calmed and completely stopped her odd behavior. However, after several minutes of relaxation, her flailing returned tenfold and it was all Christopher could do to keep her from rolling into the fire. It was then that they noticed the bloodstain on her robe. The arrow wound had reopened and was bleeding profusely. They tried in vain to hold her down so that Jessica could heal her again, but it was to no avail. Soon, however, she calmed down again, and as she stopped writhing, the wound closed, leaving not even the smallest scar. Jessica examined her thoroughly but found nothing. They finally gave up, and she slept the rest of the night through, though none of the others could bring themselves to even close their eyes. Amy could not be awakened.

Early the next morning, while everyone was repacking their belongings, Christopher still sat by Amy's side, trying to understand what had happened to her. Though he had no idea about specifics, he was certain that some change had come over Amy that night. It was this odd transformation that Lady Gahdnawen had alluded to when she talked to him of what was to come.

As he pondered, Amy slowly opened her eyes and met his midnight gaze with eyes of silver. Christopher had to force himself not to flinch at the odd change. Where her cornflower blue irises had been, reflecting so much emotion, now only silver remained and in those deep eyes, there was something very odd, something completely unique. As they stared at each other, Christopher knew that something utterly inexplicable had happened to his lover that night, and it was something that she could never share with him, never express to anyone.

As they stared at each other, Christopher placed on Amy's breast a white book bound in leather. "Lady Gahdnawen told me to give this to you when the time came," he said. "It's your spellbook."

Amy smiled at him and accepted the book, placing a hand across its cover, stroking it with long, precise fingers. She then returned her gaze to Christopher's dark visage, eerie eyes flicking across his face with tangible affect. When she spoke, her voice was the same one that the wizard had grown accustomed to and loved dearly, whether he could adequately express it or not. She smiled as she said those words that would change the lives of the inhabitants of Sidan forever. "I'm having your baby, Christopher," she murmured distinctly enough for all in the clearing to hear, and as they turned, startled by her speaking as much as by what she said, she fell into another deep slumber, leaving the camp in stunned silence.

Christopher turned and met the gazes of his friends, and the emotion that played across his dark brow was not happiness, not confusion, not even surprise. It was fear. The dark wizard was afraid, not of being a father, but of what his child would be.